NUMBER 64

Yale
French
Studies

Montaigne:
Essays in Reading

D1564747

Yale French Studies

Gérard Defaux, *Special editor for this issue*

Liliane Greene, *Managing editor*

Editorial board: Charles Porter (Chairman),
Peter Brooks, Paul de Man, Karen
Erickson, Shoshana Felman, John
Gallucci, Richard Goodkin, Fredric
Jameson, Roddey Reid

Staff: Karen Erickson, John Gallucci, Elise
Hsieh

Editorial office: 315 William L. Harkness
Hall.

Mailing address: 2504A Yale Station, New
Haven Connecticut 06520.

Sales and subscription office: Yale
University Press, 92A Yale Station, New
Haven, Connecticut 06520.

Published twice annually by Yale University
Press.

Printed in the United States of America by
The Vail-Ballou Press, Binghamton, N.Y.

ISSN 0044–0078

ISBN for this issue 0–300–02977–2

EDITOR'S PREFACE

Quand on lit trop vite ou trop doucement, on n'entend rien.
—B. Pascal

C'est l'indiligent lecteur qui pert mon subject, non pas moy.
—M. de Montaigne

This enterprise—let us acknowledge it from the start—contains nothing surprising or original in itself. It is for the most part, and like any enterprise of the same nature, the result of the mood of the time. CE N'EST DONC PAS RAISON, LECTEUR, QUE TU EMPLOYES TON LOISIR EN UN SUBJECT SI FRIVOLE ET SI VAIN: [IT WOULD THEREFORE BE UNREASONABLE, READER, TO SPEND YOUR LEISURE ON SO VAIN AND FRIVOLOUS A SUBJECT.] Indeed, what purpose would be served in pretending to master the event when it is clear, on the contrary, that the event is mastering and shaping us? Like language, fashion—intellectual fashion—subsumes both critic and writer, forming him, whether he likes it or not, for better and for worse. It has a definite structuring effect on his preoccupations and discourse. One who claims to resist or escape it is either very shrewd or very deaf. And, it must be said, very stubborn and foolish. For after all, we are already aboard, *embarqués*. This classical and very suggestive metaphor of the ship immediately brings to the mind certain ironic reflections of Brant, Erasmus, or Pascal. For man, this imperfect and powerless creature, wisdom lies in following the current. Going upstream would be proof of one's presumptuousness: *Quod si discrepet a lege chori, ridiculus habeatur.* And if such an exercise can be accused of unpardonable conformity, resignation, or compromise by Alceste, it does nevertheless have—see Philinte—its virtues.

In any case, if one thing seems today certain in the domain of literary criticism, it is the fact that this current leads directly into a problematics of reading and interpretation; the fact that it leads us straight to a character whose role—although crucial—has been rather neglected up to now: I mean the reader. Today the author is no longer in good repute, to say the least. Far from arousing interest, he engenders, on the contrary, suspicion. He seems, for excellent reasons—notably the abuse, naiveté, and weaknesses of the biographical type of criticism—and also for others that are less relevant—

one has to renew from time to time one's own discourse and perspectives—
to have been permanently expelled from our critical and conceptual
paradise, a victim, perhaps, like everyone else, of the offensive recently
launched against the Western metaphysic of the subject. Chimera, phan-
tom, mirage; a simple linguistic sign, a deconstructed and rejected simulacrum which no activity, no construct, no writing can ever bring into
existence and to which criticism wrongly attached itself in its first
wanderings, lingering over it too long in the wake of Sainte-Beuve and
Lanson. Those who, in spite of everything, still have today the temerity to
be interested in the author's intentions, in the conscious dimension of his
creation—realities which are, it is true, very problematic in themselves—
are perceived as behind the times, as witnesses of a by-gone—and
prestructuralist—era. And—a significant shift—those critics who are mad
about this new religion, psychoanalysis, and who strive to determine and
reconstitute the structures of the unconscious, no longer locate this latter
in him (the author) but in his text. Parallel to this, and in a very
consequential and logical way, the text ultimately finds its own being and
meaning, its referent, radically questioned. Whether a representation of
reality or the vehicle of an ideology, the text is no longer a strictly defined,
whole and closed object, a unit, an entity, but the exploded, empty, and, in
the end, undecidable locus of all absences, of all texts and of all possible
meanings *(sens)*. Plurality has succeeded truth; drift—Derrida's
itérabilité[1]—reflexive questioning, the play of difference and polysemy has
followed univocity and grounded certainty. And what the critic exhumes
and reconstructs henceforth is no longer, as in the past, the so-called
"objective meaning" that the author allegedly intended to enclose in his
text, but the very impossibility of assigning to this text any meaning
whatsoever, of mastering it, of fixing it, of immobilizing it once and for all in
a single, ultimate interpretation.

In return, the reader, worthy of everyone's attention and tender care,
target aimed at by all, has been himself, for several years, elevated into a
comfortable and flattering position of superiority. It is true that without
him the text would remain, literally speaking, a dead letter. It is equally true
that he has over the author, this latter being most often defunct, the
apparent advantage—but only apparent, as he is more *narrataire*, reader as
such, a concept, than anything else—of being present and living, of
speaking, of constituting a tangible reality. It is finally and perhaps

1. See, on this topic, Thomas M. Greene's inspired chapter, "Historical Solitude," in his
recent book, *The Light in Troy. Imitation and Discovery in Renaissance Poetry* (New Haven
and London: Yale University Press, 1982), especially pp. 11–16.

especially true that all the interest devoted to him today by the critic—the *hypocrite critique, son semblable, son frère*—is only, in the end, a strategic and useful detour, a stratagem of self-love *(amour-propre)* which allows him, with an innocent look on his face, to take an interest in himself under the guise of another, to make himself the subject of his own discourse— Anouilh would say to contemplate his own navel. Finally, in my opinion all the literature which has been devoted lately to what is called on this continent "Reader-Response" or "Audience-Oriented Criticism"[2] should be read as participating in the killing of the concept of author and, concurrently, in the promotion of the critic and his discourse so characteristic of our time. This literature constitutes the sign of an assertive demand, of a growing appetite for power. Indeed, how is it possible to account for this contemporary displacement—very noticeable, since Barthes—which leads us irresistibly from a *practice* to a *theory* of reading, sometimes even to a *theory of theory*, except through this project—which is, moreover, acknowledged—of mastery, by means of a deliberate will which is now driving the literary critic into a forgetfulness of the object which constitutes however his raison d'être, forcing an interpretation and reading not of the text but of his own activities as reader and interpreter? This is the reason why, today, one no longer wonders about the fact that it is after all the author who writes his text and who generally intends to give it a meaning *(sens);* and why, following in this respect the example of Barthes and Derrida, the question is rather of knowing whether in the end it is not the reader himself who fabricates, who produces, and even writes the text. The author has become a nuisance, an encumbrance, someone who prevents things from running smoothly.

Far be it from me, however, to split hairs, to approve or not approve of this displacement of the center of interest, this drift both strategic and inevitable which leads us successively from author to text and from text to reader, or to pass judgment on the legitimacy or absurdity of this clearly narcissistic project, and on the unquestionable *libido dominandi* which underlies it. I leave the trouble of swelling the flood of glosses and commentaries to the specialists of the question, to the metatheoreticians of our new scholasticism. My aim, both more modest and more practical, is rather to point out the extent to which this above mentioned displacement constitutes, for every reader of Montaigne, the golden opportunity for a

2. On this subject, I refer the reader to the two recent collections of essays: *Reader-Response Criticism: From Formalism to Post-Structuralism*. Edited by Jane P. Tompkins (Baltimore and London: The Johns Hopkins University Press, 1980); and *The Reader in the Text: Essays on Audience and Interpretation*. Edited by Susan R. Suleiman and Inge Crosman (Princeton: Princeton University Press, 1980).

critical renewal, radical and necessary in every respect; the extent to which it would be futile—whatever critical party one belongs to—not to think of making use of the undeniable affinities, of the surprising community of preoccupations which exist between Montaigne and our own time; the extent to which, finally, our strategies, our presuppositions, our current speculations, insofar as they overlap his own, constitute the most adequate and pertinent means imaginable for approaching the text of the *Essais* in a perspective and spirit proper to him.

Accordingly, my main purpose here has been, from the start—the reader has by now understood this—of taking maximum advantage of an eminently favorable critical configuration by placing, if I may say so, the text of the *Essais* on the program of our "modernity." This modernity, in its somewhat exacerbated intellectualism, its epistemological skepticism, its questioning of language, its circular and reflexive approach, its denunciation of—and at the same time its obsession with—the impossible presence, sometimes (unfortunately not always) its annihilating irony, its taste for paradox and play, was already, strangely, that of Montaigne. The moment seemed all the more propitious to me in that certain individual initiatives were already proceeding in this direction. In fact, all about us in an uneven haphazard way—in England with Terence Cave, in France with Claude Blum, Michel Charles, Antoine Compagnon and André Tournon, on this continent with C. Bauschatz, Michel Beaujour, Lawrence D. Kritzman, Richard L. Regosin, S. Rendall, François Rigolot and A. Wilden[3]— Montaigne's *Essais* are beginning to be read from the perspective of our

3. T. Cave, *The Cornucopian Text: Problems of Writing in the French Renaissance* (Oxford: at the Clarendon Press, 1979), pp. 271–321; Claude Blum, "Les *Essais* de Montaigne: les signes, la politique, la religion," in *Columbia Montaigne Conference Papers*, D. M. Frame and M. B. McKinley, eds. (Lexington: French Forum Publishers, 1980), p. 9–39; M. Charles, *Rhétorique de la lecture* (Paris: Editions du Seuil, 1977); A. Compagnon, *Nous, Michel de Montaigne* (Paris: Seuil, 1980); A. Tournon, *Montaigne: la glose et l'essai*, Sorbonne thesis (1980); C. Bauschatz, "Montaigne's Conception of Reading in the Context of Renaissance Poetics and Modern Criticism," in *The Reader in the Text*, op. cit., p. 264–91; M. Beaujour, *Miroirs d'encre* (Paris: Seuil, 1980); L. Kritzman, *Destruction/Découverte: Le fonctionnement de la rhétorique dans les Essais de Montaigne* (Lexington: French Forum Publishers, 1980); R. Regosin, *The Matter of My Book: Montaigne's Essays as the Book of the Self* (Berkeley: Berkeley University Press, 1977); S. Rendall, "Dialectical Structure and Tactics in Montaigne's 'Of Cannibals,' " *Pacific Coast Philology*, XII (Oct. 1977), pp. 56–63; and: "The Rhetoric of Montaigne's Self-Portrait: Speaker and Subject," *Studies in Philology*, 73, no. 3, p. 285–301; F. Rigolot, "La Pente du 'repentir': un exemple de remotivation du signifiant dans les *Essais* de Montaigne," in *Columbia Montaigne Conference Papers*, op. cit., p. 119–34; A. Wilden, *"Par divers movens on arrive à pareille fin:* a Reading of Montaigne," *MLN*, 83 (1968), p. 577–97. This list is by no means exhaustive. One could, for example, add to it J. Brody, *Lectures de Montaigne*, the publication of which is slated for September 1982.

preoccupations and our concepts. In order to accelerate this movement, nothing then was more natural than to conceive not only of regrouping these scattered enterprises but also of widening this new hermeneutic circle by soliciting the cooperation of several critics whose attention Montaigne had not yet retained.

But this project—I would like to make this clear—was not only dictated to me for reasons of mere opportunity, or indeed of opportunism. I also saw in it a possibility of expressing an entirely personal opinion on the different critical efforts brought to bear since Villey on the text of Montaigne, on the naïvetés, the unanswerable questions, the inadequate perspectives, the dead end streets, the false problems which chronically lead these efforts astray, throw them off center, divert—and even entertain—them. I also saw in this project an opportunity heretofore only dreamed of, for *trying out (essayer)* my judgment, for exercising it against a *rude jouteur,* for settling the score with several frustrations of a pedagogical nature—frustrations which any so-called specialist of the Renaissance must experience when, having exhausted the usual historical, biographical, and thematic presentations, he is finally compelled, facing the students in his seminar, to confront the text of the *Essais* directly in the actual reality of its "variations," of its "lusty sallies," and of its "embroilment." All of this was envisaged in the hope, often disappointed, of arriving at something other than the handy exclamation of the commentator—more prudent than really "subtle"— mentioned by Montaigne in his chapter "Of the art of discussion" (III:8): "Voylà qui est beau" (937) ["This is beautiful" (715)]. For after all, the workman is judged on the quality of his work, not on his ability to produce theoretical considerations or to hide behind worn-out generalities; he is judged on his talent for interpreting the texts which he reads in a way that is at once pertinent, intelligent, and ordered. This observation is perhaps more true for this occasion than for any other, since the author himself constantly enjoys defying his "indiligent lecteur," reminding him on every page that his book is not made for "principiants" ["beginners"].

In order to take up this challenge in the most efficient way, I naturally thought not only of mobilizing all the critical arsenal which is at our disposal today, but also of devoting one section to each of the essential questions under consideration. I must acknowledge that only the first part of the project has been reasonably fulfilled. It seems to me indeed that the different readings attempted in the following pages, philological (i.e. stylistic and Spitzerian) with Jules Brody, philosophical with Catherine Demure, psychoanalytic with François Rigolot, intertextual with Starobinski, anthropological with Tzvetan Todorov, etc., represent the main present critical trends adequately.[4] On the other hand, I was able to keep only two of the three sections originally conceived: "Theoretical Prolegomenon," and "Readings of Montaigne." The third, "Montaigne as Reader," reader of other texts, reader of his own text, is not, strictly speaking, represented here. It is far too central and pervasive to constitute a section in itself. Given the reflexive nature of his text, to speak of Montaigne is necessarily to speak of Montaigne as Reader. This particularity is alluded to and analysed in almost every essay.

I sincerely hope that this collection of essays will be of interest not only to the teacher, or to the sixteenth-century specialist, but also to the general reader—to that reader Montaigne himself might have called the *honnête homme.*

Out of concern for a uniform presentation, it has been agreed that all references to Montaigne's text would be made 1) for the original French, according to the edition of P. Villey, reedited by V. L. Saulnier, *Les Essais de Montaigne. Edition conforme au texte de l'exemplaire de Bordeaux* (Paris: PUF, 1978); 2) for the English version, according to the edition of D. Frame. *The Complete Works of Montaigne* (Stanford: Stanford University Press, 1957). Any reference made according to other editions will therefore be indicated in a note.

It goes without saying that I warmly thank all those who have participated in this modest but exciting adventure. Their generosity and talent have made everything possible. Special thanks are due to those who unstintingly worked against time to get translations ready, including those whose translations did not finally find a place in this issue: John Gallucci, Robert Roza, Alain Toumayan, Michel Haas, Pierre Saint-Amand, Christiane La Marca, Kristine Rodriguez, and Karen Erickson.

As for Liliane Greene, her competence, her critical sense, her kindness and devotion, are beyond all praise.

GÉRARD DEFAUX

Translated by John Gallucci

---

4. For my own essay in reading, I refer the reader to my "Un cannibale en haut de chausses: Montaigne, la différence et la logique de l'identité," *MLN,* 97 (1982), p. 919–57. It constitutes the practical application, the *mise en pratique,* of the theoretical considerations which I develop in this issue.

Theoretical Prolegomenon

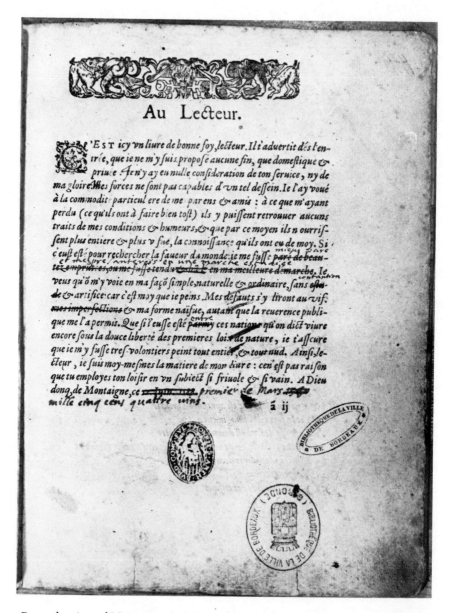

Reproduction of Montaigne's *Avis au Lecteur,* from the famous so-called *Exemplaire de Bordeaux,* the 1588 edition of the *Essais* which includes Montaigne's handwritten corrections. With the kind permission of the Bibliothèque Municipale de Bordeaux.

THOMAS M. GREENE

Dangerous Parleys—*Essais* I:5 and 6

"Tout ce qu'on peut dire de la plupart de ces chapitres-la,
c'est qu'il n'y a rien à en dire."
—Pierre Villey

The opening page of the *Essais* introduces the reader to terror—the massacre of a city's inhabitants by the Black Prince, who has taken it by force and who is finally deterred only by the exemplary heroism of three defenders. This first essay continues with anecdotes instancing other examples of cruelty and compassion, most of them involving a military siege: Conrad III at Guelph, Dionysius at Rhegium, Pompey at the city of the Mamertines, Sylla at Perusia, Alexander at Gaza, Alexander at Thebes. The concluding paragraph records the slaughter of six thousand Thebans and the enslavement of the remaining thirty thousand. This terror at the opening of the book is anything but rare. The elements of horror and cruelty in the earlier essays of Montaigne have been insufficiently noted and insufficiently explained. Their presence is all the more remarkable in view of their comparative infrequence in the mature essays. It is equally remarkable that the ubiquitous military anecdotes in the very earliest essays (most of them preceding I: 1 in the chronology of composition) tend to involve the siege of a city or fortress. The siege is the locale of peculiar menace, the contest which exacerbates cruelty and, when successful, conventionally authorizes the harshest carnage.

Specific anecdotes add substance to these impressions. For the defender, even the limited choice of military options can be perilous. Essay 1: 15 ("On est puny pour s'opiniastrer à une place sans raison") [One is punished for defending a place obstinately without reason] cites a number of recorded massacres victimizing those foolhardy enough to resist too long. Yet the succeeding essay ("De la punition de la couardise") [Of the punishment of cowardice] cites examples of those commanders who exposed themselves to the charge of cowardice by yielding too easily and who were justly punished by degradation. The defender, it appears, must walk a fine line, if indeed one exists. The next essay but one ("De la peur")

3

[Of fear] opens with examples of self-destructive madness which overwhelms terrified men under siege. I: 34 offers a series of miracles: walls of invested cities which fall by divine will without attack, or the more recent case, truly wonderful, of a wall blown up which settled down neatly into place again. I: 47 cites the case of the Roman commander Vitellius whose siege of a city was repelled because his troops taunted the defenders too caustically. II: 3 ("Coustume de l'isle de Cea") [A custom of the island of Cea] in its long catalogue of recorded suicides, individual and communal, returns again and again to the city reduced to despair by an encircling army. I: 24 narrates an incident clearly analogous to these others which Montaigne witnessed as a child: the governor of a city walks out from a secure building to address a frenzied mob and is killed. Miracles aside, all of these stories evoke an intensity of violence whose narrow spectrum runs from peril to nightmare. As a set, they outdo in brutality the other military anecdotes which accompany them.

I have not yet mentioned one more early essay, or rather two twin essays, whose organizing situation is the siege. These are I: 5 ("Si le chef d'une place assiégée doit sortir pour parlementer") [Whether the governor of a besieged place should go out to parley] and I: 6 ("L'heure des parlemens dangereuse") [Parley time is dangerous]. These are apparently among the earliest of all (1571–72), and in the 1580 edition they are among the very simplest in structure: a bare series of brief stories scarcely mortised by minimal commentary. Although they mute to a degree the explicit brutality of their companion essays, they offer a useful focus for the study of the motif or the obsession which unifies them. They also introduce a distinctive element missing elsewhere, a third tactical option—the possibility of a parley, a verbal negotiation, between the opposing forces. This element complicates the primitive oppositions of the other anecdotes and confers a special interest on these crude and laconic texts.

For all their ostensible simplicity, however, they do not lack their puzzles and reversals. First reversal: I: 5 opens not with the decision of the defending commander posed by the title but with the corresponding decision of the investing commander (should he win an advantage by faking a truce to negotiate?)

(a) Lucius Marcius legat des Romains en la guerre contre Perseus roy de Macedoine voulant gaigner le temps qu'il lui falloit encore a metre en point son armée, sema des entregets d'accord, desquels le roy endormi accorda trefve pour quelques jours, fournissant par ce moyen son ennemy d'opportunité & loisir pour s'armer: d'ou le roy encourut sa dernier[e] ruine. Si est ce que le Senat Romain, a qui le seul advantaige de la vertu

THOMAS M. GREENE   5

sembloit moyen juste pour acquerir la victoire trouva ceste praticque laide & des-honneste, n'ayant encores ouy sonner a ses oreilles ceste belle sentence, *dolus an virtus quis in hoste requirat?* [*Aeneid*, II, 390] Quand a nous moings superstitieux, qui tenons celuy avoir l'honneur de la guerre, qui en a le profit, & qui apres Lysander, disons que ou la peau du lyon ne peut suffire, qu'il y faut coudre ung lopin de celle du renard, les plus ordinaires occasions de surprinse se tirent de ceste praticque: & n'est heure, disons nous, ou un chef doive avoir plus l'oeil au guet, que celle des parlemens & traites d'accord. Et pour ceste cause c'est une reigle en la bouche de tous les hommes de guerre de nostre temps, qu'il ne faut jamais que le gouverneur en une place assiegée sorte luy mesmes pour parlementer.[1]

Lucius Marcius, legate of the Romans in the war against Perseus, king of Macedonia, wishing to gain the time he still needed to get his army fully ready, made some propositions pointing to an agreement, which lulled the king into granting a truce for a few days and thereby furnished his enemy with opportunity and leisure to arm. As a result, the king incurred his final ruin. Yet the Roman Senate, judging that valor alone was the just means for winning a victory, deemed this stratagem ugly and dishonest, not yet having heard this fine saying ringing in their ears: "Courage or ruse— against an enemy, who cares?" As for us, who, less superstitious, hold that the man who has the profit of war has the honor of it, and who say, after Lysander, that where the lion's skin will not suffice we must sew on a bit of the fox's, the most usual chances for surprise are derived from this practice of trickery. And there is no time, we say, when a leader must be more on the watch than that of parleys and peace treaties. And for that reason there is a rule in the mouth of all military men of our time, that the governor of a besieged place must never go out to parley. [16–17]

There are really two questions at issue: the *ethical* choice of a Lucius Martius, chastised by the senate for his unscrupulous strategem, and the *tactical* choice of the captain who must weigh the advantages of the profferred armistice. In the incident cited, both commanders appear to have selected the wrong alternative; Lucian commits an error of morality and Perseus of prudence. Both errors seem to stem from the ambiguity of a truce which fails to conclude hostilities for good and creates a grey area of ethics and judgment suspending all conventional rules. The polarity attacker/ defender then yields to a second polarity ancient/modern, since the contemporaneous world is represented as heedless of all promises, ironically "moings superstitieux," less scrupulous regarding good faith than the

1. French text from *Essais. Reproduction photographique de l'édition originale de 1580*, ed. Daniel Martin, 2 vols. (Geneva: Slatkine and Paris: Champion, 1976), I, pp. 20–22.

Roman senate. Yet in another reversal, the integrity of antiquity is blurred by the Virgilian quotation (Courage or ruse—against an enemy, who cares?), which subdivides the ancient member of the polarity by distinguishing republican honesty from imperial deceit. Aeneas's aphorism might be the motto of faithless modernity. He seems to share a grey area of history with the Spartan general Lysander.

Up to this point, the evidence presented would dictate a negative answer to the question of the essay's title; under the given circumstances, negotiation is suicidal. This will also be the conclusion of the sequel essay; the hour of parleying *is* dangerous. But here in I: 5, in another reversal, this implication receives a qualification.

> Du temps de nos peres cela fut reproché aus seigneurs de Montmord & de l'Assigni deffandans Mouson contre le Conte de Nansaut, mais aussi à ce conte celuy la seroit excusable, qui sortiroit en telle facon, que la surté & l'advantaige demeurat de son costé, comme fit on la ville de Regge, le Conte Guy de Rangon (s'il en faut croire Monsieur du Bellay: car Guichardin dit que ce fut luy mesmes) lors que le seigneur de l'Escut s'en approcha, pour parlementer: car il abandonna de si peu son fort, que un trouble s'estant esmeu pendant ce parlement, non seulement monsieur de l'Escut & sa trouppe, qui estoit approchée avec luy se trouva la plus foible, de façon que Alexandre Trivulce y fut tué, mais luy mesmes fust contrainct, pour le plus seur, de suivre le Conte, & se getter sur sa foy a l'abri des coups, dans la ville.[2]

> In our fathers' day the seigneurs de Montmord and de Lassigny, defending Mouzon against the count of Nassau, were blamed for this. But also, by this reckoning, a man would be excusable who went out in such a way that the security and advantage remained on his side; as Count Guido Rangone did at the city of Reggio (if we are to believe Du Bellay, for Guicciardini says it was he himself) when the seigneur de l'Escut approached to parley. For he stayed so close to his fort that when trouble broke out during this parley, Monsieur de l'Escut not only found himself and his accompanying troop the weaker, so that Alessandro Trivulzio was killed there, but was constrained, for greater security, to follow the count and trust himself to his good faith, taking shelter from the shots inside the town. [17]

Properly managed, a sortie to parley *can* be profitable. The tortuous syntactic convolution of this long sentence and the factual uncertainty (does the credit go to Rangone or Guicciardini?) introduce new types of blurring, but through the distractions one can isolate the crucial tactical factor on the victor's side: he left behind his bastion *only a little*. This

2. Martin edition, pp. 22–23.

crucial calculation not only leads to the death of a prestigious enemy leader but forces a humiliating reverse upon the besieging leader, who ends within the walls dependent upon the defender's good will. We assume, without learning from Montaigne, that the supplicant is accorded grace. The text leads us to question only the word of the outsider, not the insider. The defender tends to appear as a moral virgin; only the attacker is a potential rapist or seducer.

The incident at Reggio throws into doubt the negative answer to the title-question which the Macedonian incident had appeared to imply. It remains for a final incident to obscure the question definitively by providing the one remaining outcome which is theoretically possible.

> Si est ce que encores en y a il, qui se sont tres bien trouvés de sortir sur la parolle de l'assaillant: tesmoing Henry de Vaux, Chevalier Champenois, lequel estant assiegé dans le chasteau de Commercy par les Anglois, & Berthelemy de Bonnes, qui commandoit au siege ayant par dehors faict sapper la plus part du chasteau, si qu'il ne restoit que le feu pour acabler les assiegés soubs les ruines, somma ledict Henry de sortir a parlementer pour son profict, comme il fit luy quatriesme, & son evidante ruyne luy ayant esté monstrée a l'oeil il s'en sentit singulierement obligé a l'ennemy, a la discretion duquel apres qu'il se fut rendu & sa trouppe, le feu estant mis a la mine les estansons de bois venant a faillir le chasteau fut emporté de fons en comble.[3]

> Yet it is true that there are some who have done very well by coming out on the attacker's word. Witness Henri de Vaux, a knight of Champagne, who was besieged in the castle of Commercy by the English. Barthélemy de Bonnes, who commanded the siege, after having the greater part of the castle sapped from outside, so that nothing remained but setting fire in order to overwhelm the besieged beneath the ruins, asked the aforesaid Henri to come out and parley for his own good; this Henri did, preceded by three other men. And, convinced by what he was shown that he would have been ruined without fail, he felt remarkably obliged to his enemy, to whose discretion he surrendered himself and his forces. After this, the fire was set to the mine, the wooden props gave way, and the castle was demolished from top to bottom. [17]

This final reversal ends the original published version of the essay, which I have now quoted in its entirety. It leaves the hostile parties pacifically together outside the castle as the previous story left them inside the city, and here, one gathers, the "discretion" of the attacker is to be trusted as it could not be earlier. The essay might be said to leave the question whether

3. Ibid., pp. 23–24.

to go out to parley permanently up in the air, so to speak, since the text is void of authorial intervention beyond the sarcasm of the two phrases: "belle sentence," [fine saying] applied to Virgil, "moings superstitieux" [less superstitious] applied to modern tacticians. Yet even this conclusive inconclusiveness will be reversed as we turn to the opening of the sequel essay. "Toute-fois" [However] it begins, and after a longer catalogue of disastrous sorties by gullible defenders, it in turn ends with a timid authorial leap onto the shoulders of a Stoic philosopher. The writer's position on the *tactical* question, the options of the besieged, can only be inferred from the ambiguous evidence of the twin but divergent essays. On the *ethical* question he edges into the second essay through the opposition of two other voices. We just catch sight of Montaigne as thinker in the final antithesis of Ariosto and Chrysippus.

> Fu il vincer sempremai laudabil cosa
> Vincasi o per fortuna o per ingegno, [*Orlando furioso*, 14, 1]
> disent-ils mais le philosophe Chrisippus n'eust pas esté de c'est advis: car il disoit que ceux, qui courrent a lenvy doivent bien employer toutes leurs forces a la vistesse, mais il ne leur est pourtant aucunement loisible de mettre la main sur leur adversaire pour l'arrester, ny de luy tendre la jambe, pour le faire cheoir.[4]

> To conquer always was a glorious thing,
> Whether achieved by fortune or by skill, *(Ariosto)*
> so they say. But the philosopher Chrysippus would not have been of that opinion. For he used to say that those who run a race should indeed employ their whole strength for speed but that, nevertheless, it was not in the least permissible for them to lay a hand on their adversary to stop him, or to stick out a leg to make him fall. [19]

This seems to align the essayist with the philosopher, but the alignment is tacit, merely implicit. And even this tiny, almost imperceptible gesture of approval is made after the terrible problem of the siege has been elided into a metaphorical footrace. Later published versions would render the approval slightly more visible ("le philosophe Chrisippus n'eust pas esté de cet advis, *et moy aussi peu . . .*" [29]) [The philosopher Chrysippus would not have been of that opinion, *and I just as little*]; they would also introduce further incidents, complications, quotations, citations of authority, together with a fuller though somewhat straddling comment on the ethical issue in I: 6, and in I: 5 a new auto-referential ending affirming the writer's quickness to accept the word of others. This credulity, which cuts against those

4. Ibid., pp. 26–27.

prudential concerns present earlier, represents one more reversal in the form of an afterthought.

Considered as an integral text, this fifth essay might be said to possess unity only in the persistence of its portentous theme and in the consistency of its failure to resolve its own questions. Together with its companion, it stands as a chaos of diverging or conflicting events, quotations, opinions perspectives, shifts of the issue at hand. All we can ascertain with certainty as we stand back from the two conflicted texts as from Book One as a whole is that the dilemma of the man surrounded and the question whether speech is of use to him are indeed of pressing concern to the writer.

What remains obscure is the basis of this concern, and given the reticence of these little sketches, especially taciturn in their original form, the interpreter is obliged to turn to the appropriate larger context, which can only be the entire work in which they take their modest place. But this step, though necessary, is problematic, since the *Essais* repeatedly throw out versions of inside/outside antitheses.[5] Many of the antitheses can be read back into the siege motif so as to render it in varying degrees metaphoric. One could then consider the work as a series of explications or unpackings of a dramatic situation tranformed into a trope. This becomes problematic only because the potential "explications" are so numerous and entangled that the original obsession will emerge as overdetermined to the point of meaninglessness. If in other words we scrutinize the *Essais* for all the ways in which the siege motif might be understood to "symbolize," we may be left with a blur as inconclusive as the uninterpreted point of departure. To avoid this impasse, the most promising procedure would be to follow those directions which the texts themselves offer most insistently, to privilege those hints whose networks of reinforcement prove densest, without denying the potential relevance of other networks and other metaphoric displacements.

The most obvious extrapolation is biographical. Montaigne is a landowner whose property is walled during a period of civil conflict and routine pillage. He marvels in fact that it has remained intact, (b) "encore vierge de sang et de sac, soubs un si long orage, tant de changemens et agitations voisines" (966). ["still virgin of blood and pillage, under so long a storm, with so many changes and disturbances in the neighborhood" (737).] The

---

5. For useful discussions of the inside/outside polarity in Montaigne, see Richard L. Regosin, *The Matter of my Book. Montaigne's "Essais" as the Book of the Self* (Berkeley: University of California Press, 1977), especially pp. 82–90, and Jules Brody, *"De mesnager sa volonté* (III:10): lecture philologique d'un essai," in *O un Amy! Essays on Montaigne in Honor of Donald M. Frame,* ed. R. C. La Charité (Lexington, Ky.: French Forum, 1977), pp. 34–71.

sexual metaphor is not to be disregarded; for the proprietor, the invasion of his house would be experienced as the breaking of a hymen. Domestic anxiety, remarks Montaigne, is the peculiar product of civil war alone. (b) "Les guerres civiles ont cela de pire que les autres guerres, de nous mettre chacun en eschaugette en sa propre maison. . . . C'est grande extremité d'estre pressé jusques dans son mesnage et repos domestique" (971). ["Civil wars are worse in this respect than other wars, that they make us all sentinels in our own houses. . . . It is a great extremity to be beset even in our household and domestic repose" (741–42).] A passage toward the end of "De la phisionomie" [Of physiognomy] narrates the attempt by a neighbor to capture Montaigne's house by a ruse, a ruse which fails through the intended victim's trusting manner. This threat of violence is not however altogether distinct from the threat of daily affairs to the man of letters. The significant interior may not be the property as such but the tower library. (c) "C'est là mon siege. J'essaie . . . à soustraire ce seul coin à la communauté. . . . Miserable à mon gré, qui n'a chez soy où estre à soy" (828). "There is my throne. I try . . . to withdraw this one corner from all society. . . . Sorry the man, to my mind, who has not in his own home a place to be all by himself" (629).] It is impossible to distinguish firmly the military press which threatens the landowner from the press of affairs which threatens the meditative solitary. But the physical withdrawal to a quiet place is impossible to distinguish in turn from the mental withdrawal to an inner quietude. The *coin*, the corner where one can reign alone, already contains in germ a metaphor of psychological space which other contexts will make explicit. (b) "Si je ne suis chez moy, j'en suis tousjours bien pres" (811). ["If I am not at home, I am always very near it" (615).] This metaphoric dimension of the "chez moy" in the *Essais* emerges so commonly and spontaneously that the reader almost overlooks its figurative force.

In a passage justifying his failure to fortify his house against marauders, Montaigne writes that "any defense bears the aspect of war" and invites attack, then remarks of his house: (c) "C'est la retraite à me reposer des guerres. J'essaye de soubstraire ce coing à la tempeste publique, comme je fay un autre coing en mon ame" (617). ["It is my retreat to rest myself from the wars. I try to withdraw this corner from the public tempest, as I do another corner in my soul" (467).] This internal corner clearly corresponds to the "arriereboutique" [back shop] of the essay on solitude (I:39) (a) ". . . en laquelle nous establissons nostre vraye liberté et principale retraicte et solitude" (241). ["in which to establish our real liberty and our principal retreat and solitude" (177).] The evocation of this internal withdrawal does not lack military imagery. (a) "Nous avons une ame contournable en soy mesme; elle se peut faire compagnie; elle a dequoy assaillir et dequoy defendre, dequoy recevoir et dequoy donner" (241). ["We have a soul that can be turned upon itself; it can keep itself company; it has the means to attack and the means to defend, the means to receive and the means to give" (177).] But the most powerful image at the close of the essay suggests a defensive cunning and contracted force still more absolute: (a) "Il faut faire comme les animaux qui effacent la trace, à la porte de leur taniere" (247). ["We must do like the animals that rub out their tracks at the entrance to their lairs" (182).] It was this profound impulse to lie still in a spiritual center, beleaguered, alert, solicited but cautious, which brought Montaigne home from the Bordeaux *parlement,* and it is this impulse, more than any other, which seems to underlie the obsession with the siege.[6]

The experience of the *parlement* may not be irrelevant to the twin essays that concern us, since the title of I: 6 ("L'heure des parlemens dangereuse") contains the word and the title of I, 5 a cognate form ("parlementer"). A useful gloss on these essays can be found in the opening pages of "De l'experience" [On experience] (III:13), where legal abuses bring into focus the capacity of language for obliquity, ambiguity, treachery, and self-subversion. (b) "Cette justice qui nous regit . . . est un vray temoignage de l'humaine imbecillité, tant il y a de contradiction et d'erreur" (1070). ["This justice that governs us . . . is a true testimony of human imbecility, so full it is of contradiction and error" (819).] Jurisprudence is (b) "generatrice d'altercation et division" (1066) ["generating altercation and division" (816).] Law does not offer (b) "aucune maniere de se declarer qui ne tombe en doubte et contradiction" (1066) ["a way of speaking (one's) mind that does not fall into doubt and contradiction" (816).] The wish for an absolute intercourse beyond ambiguity and contradiction is already present in I: 5, which begins by positing a Roman purity betrayed both by event (Lucius Marcius' stratagem) and by quotation ("Dolus an virtus . . . "). The military *parlement,* like the judicial, places the heaviest pressure on direct language since, as we have seen, there is no time when a commander must be more wary. The quotation from Virgil that closes I: 6 (added in 1588) can be read as an expression of Montaigne's fantasized escape from the verbal and the equivocal.

(b) Atque idem fugientem haud est dignatus Orodem
Sternere, nec jacta caecum dare cuspide vulnus:

6. The image of the wild beast withdrawn to its den sends us back to the aphorism of Lysander in I, 5, where the crafty commander is told to supplement the lion's skin with the fox's. Trickery with language is foxy; presumably reliance on pure valor requires no speech, involves no engagement, places no strain on individual integrity, remains leonine.

Obvius, adversosque occurrit, seque viro vir
Contulit, haud furto melior, sed fortibus armis. [*Aeneid* X, 732–35 (291)]

Nor did he deign to knock down from the rear
Fleeing Orodes with an unseen spear:
He passes, veers, and man to man, in fight,
He proves the better, not by stealth but might. [19]

To attack from behind would savor of linguistic obliquity, would be analogous to the tricky indirections of negotiations; the ideal struggle is silent, face to face, on a plain outside a city, as here in the *Aeneid*. It matters little if even this fantasy, having descended to language, is faintly undermined by our remembrance that it depicts the brutal tyrant Mezentius. The only alternative would be mutual confidence, *fiance*, which the opening of I: 6 has ruled out in modern times. (a) "Ne se doit attendre fiance des uns aux autres, que le dernier seau d'obligation n'y soit passé: encore y a il lors assés affaire" (28). ["parties should not trust one another until the last binding seal has been set. Even then there is plenty of room for wariness" (18).] The final seal of commitment (real or metaphorical?) points back again to a judicial parallel; the effect of the analogy is to imply a nostalgia for a finality which is supradiplomatic, suprajudicial, supralinguistic. Even after the ostensibly final seal, one must be on one's guard. In effect there is no conclusion to a conflict; that might only be produced by the frontal, mute assault of a Mezentius, slugging it out hand to hand—a kind of salvation. The Mezentius quotation is immediately preceded by an anecdote wherein Alexander refuses a lieutenant's advice to (b) "se servir de l'avantage que l'obscurité de la nuit luy donnoit pour assaillir Darius" (29). ["to take advantage of the darkness of night to attack Darius" (19).] It is tempting to extend this obscurity metaphorically to evoke that dimness of indirect, verbal engagement which the writer wants to evade.

   Thus these apprentice essays seem to condone indirectly their author's choice to withdraw from a parliament into his tower bastion. Here one might suppose that there would be fewer *heures des parlemens dangereuses*. Yet if we look to the early essays as products of pure interiority, we will of course be disappointed. The first versions of I: 5 and 6 appear to be almost entirely the contrary, a collection of actions by other men reported in other writers' books, bearing as we have noted only the barest traces of authorial commentary. What is besieging the mind on these pages are the words, experiences, and opinions of cultural memory, to the degree that the writer's own voice seems scarcely audible. Montaigne has opened his text as Montmord and Assigni opened their gates, and seems to have suffered

   7. I have altered slightly Frame's translation.

something of their fate, a fate he fails to specify though we gather it to have been unpleasant. Even in this essay's later versions, where the authorial voice can intermittently be made out, it merely makes one in a somewhat cacophonous chorus. The self is hedged about by all those who solicit entrance to the allegedly self-defining text; the self is exposed to the wounds, the subversions, the variances of opinion, the linguistic and moral codes pressing about it. In the final versions of I: 5 and 6 the writer's own outlook, to the degree that it is felt at all, is jostled by that of the Roman senate, the Achaians, the ancient Florentines, contemporaneous Frenchmen, of Virgil (or Aeneas), Cleomenes, Xenophon, Ariosto, Alexander. There is no "arriereboutique," no untraceable lair, although the yearning for one might well be a reasonable consequence of the crowded page. Montaigne, one might say, has taken a step which is called in "L'heure des parlemens dangereuse" a "pas de clerc."

> A Yvoile seigneur Iullian Rommero *aiant fait ce pas de clerc* de sortir pour parlementer avec monsieur le Conestable, trouva au retour sa place saisie. [29]

> At Yvoy, Signor Giuliano Romero, having made the novice's blunder of going out to parley with the Constable, on his return found his place seized. [19]

Modern French has lost this idiom, which associates the clerkly with the naive, but we understand it here with more clarity than its author may have intended. A cleric may, in certain situations, be reasonably associated with the unworldly; the question hovers whether this handicap extends to all who have taken it upon themselves to write.

Thus if we consider the essays themselves, we have no difficulty in making out a textual equivalent to the military drama. Wherever else in Montaigne's experience the threat of invasion lies, it can be found unmistakably upon the pages he is beginning to produce. In a later essay he would confront clairvoyantly the aggressive dimension, the *murderous* dimension of this solicitation from outside.

> (b) Or j'ay une condition singeresse et imitatrice: quand je me melois de faire des vers ... ils accusoient evidemment le poete que je venois dernierement de lire; et, de mes premiers essays, aucuns puent un peu à l'estranger. . . . Qui que je regarde avec attention m'imprime facilement quelque chose du sien. Ce que je considere, je l'usurpe: une sotte contenance, une desplaisante grimace, une forme de parler ridicule. . . .
> (c) Imitation meurtriere comme celle des singes horribles en grandeur

et en force que le Roy Alexandre rencontra en certaine contrée des Indes. [875]

> Now I have an aping and imitative nature. When I used to dabble in composing verse . . . it clearly revealed the poet I had last been reading. And of my first essays, some smell a bit foreign. . . . Anyone I regard with attention easily imprints on me something of himself. What I consider, I usurp: a foolish countenance, an unpleasant grimace, a ridiculous way of speaking. . . .
> A murderous imitation, like that of the horribly big and strong apes that King Alexander encountered in a certain region of the Indies. [667]

The anecdote that follows tells how these apes were led to hobble or strangle themselves by men who exploited their imitative bent. The murderous capacity of compulsive imitation can apparently be directed either at one's models or at oneself. Montaigne finds it both in his nature ("condition") and his book, malodorous and destructive. The early essays which stink of others are those precisely haunted by the terror of the siege. Perhaps the younger Montaigne fears the fate of those captains in I: 16 who surrendered their bastions too quickly and suffered for it. Perhaps he fears (or envies?) the fate of Henri de Vaux; he might, through the act of writing, pass outside himself altogether, yield to his besiegers, turn around and see his self explode forever.

To write at any rate is to face the risk of invasion, capture, destruction, murder. Perhaps the struggle between inside and outside is the struggle imposed by the composition of the *Essais*. We can follow this struggle *metaphorically* through the various implications of Montaigne's intersecting images and anecdotes, or we can follow it *intrinsically*, through the unevenly developing power of assimilation, the absorption of anecdote, allusion, and quotation by a unique, recognizable voice, a distinctive moral style. One allows oneself to be conquered, one surrenders one's tower, one's city, if one reads and writes credulously, obsequiously, without independent judgment. One has to learn how to speak without leaving the gate behind.

In view of the felt risk, one may wonder how the first essays ever came into being. Two or three answers can be made. One can point first of all to the freedom of reception as a mark of underlying assurance. The apparently humble and gullible hospitality may mask a secret pride, a reserve which is not hospitable, a confidence on the writer's part that he can be strengthened by his chosen and willed vulnerability. From this miniscule egoism, almost invisible in the first version of I: 5, would grow the bulk of the *Essais*. The caution, the wariness, the ambivalent receptiveness of these early sketches would remain in their denser and more poised successors; we can watch the interplay in simpler form at the outset, where we are given a radical metaphor with which to trace the intertextual drama.

But aside from this nascent confidence, Montaigne seems sometimes to perceive the act of writing not as exposure but protection, not as centrifugal but centripetal. This at least is the basis of the apology in the brief but fascinating "De l'oisiveté" [Of idleness] (I:8), where writing involves the exorcism of wild and disorderly fantasies, just as the cultivation of a field removes weeds and just as the fertilization of a woman by an alien seed ("une autre semence") produces normal offspring rather than shapeless lumps. Here it is the mind abandoned to reverie, undisciplined by writing, which runs off like an escaped horse ("faisant le cheval eschappé"). Writing centers and fortifies the mind, even if it admits a little of the alien. In this formulation the writer maneuvers like Guy de Rangon, emerging just a little to make his capture and then retire. We remember that in I: 15 those who defend their cities *too* stubbornly are exposed to terrible vengeance.

In still other formulations of the apprenticeship phase, we find repeated images of tremendous pressures unhealthily bottled up. Too much sexual desire can make a man impotent.

(a) De là s'engendre par fois la défaillance fortuite, qui surprent les amoureux si hors de saison, et cette glace qui les saisit par la force d'une ardeur extreme, au giron mesme de la joüyssance. [13]

From that is sometimes engendered the accidental failing that surprises lovers so unseasonably, and that frigidity that seizes them by the force of extreme ardor in the very lap of enjoyment. [7]

The news of bad fortune can paralyze response, until relief comes in an outpouring of tears and speech (I:2). Too much eagerness to write well hampers composition, just as water in a full bottle is hampered by its own pressure from issuing through the neck (I:10). Images like these bespeak a terrific expansive energy acutely in need of release. But there is also a recognition that the release must be guided by an authentic external resistance.

(a) L'ame esbranlé et esmeuë se perde en soymesme, si on ne luy donne prinse: et faut tousjours luy fournir d'object où elle s'abutte et agisse. [22]

The soul, once stirred and set in motion, is lost in itself unless we give it something to grasp; and we must always give it an object to aim at and act on. [14]

The essay from which this is quoted (I: 4—"Comme l'ame descharge ses passions sur des objects faux, quand les vrais luy defaillent") [How the soul discharges its passions on false objects when the true are wanting] fails to specify what the *object vrai* would be; one might presume it to be the thought and writing of another man. Here the *prinse*, the clutch of otherness, is not dangerous but necessary, a tonic encounter which saves the soul from its unbridled solitude.

The conflict of the siege then is both life-threatening and life-preserving. We cannot miss in any case the debate just below the surface of the apprentice essays over the prudence, the ethics, and the hygiene of their composition. The question whether or not to parley contains the question whether or not to write. To use language is to be invaded and to invade. To parley is to assume the vulnerability of a writer, to enter the grey area of language, of interchange, of the *prinse* of oppositions. Montaigne was by no means insensitive to this contingent, dialogic, oppositional character of discourse.

> (c) Nous raisonnons hazardeusement et inconsidereement, dict Timaeus en Platon, par ce que, comme nous, nos discours ont grande participation au hazard. [286]

> "We reason rashly and inconsiderately," says Timaeus in Plato, "because, like ourselves, our reason has in it a large element of chance." [209]

We hear in this remark the appeal and the safety of silence, which is opposed to speech and perhaps more authentic.

> (a) Le nom, ce n'est pas une partie de la chose ny de la substance, c'est une piece estrangere joincte à la chose, et *hors d'elle.* (my italics) [618]

> The name is not a part of the thing or of the substance, it is an extraneous piece attached to the thing, and outside of it. [468]

This exteriority of the name is the exteriority, and thus the inferiority, of all words, artifically and arbitrarily connected to the thing, the true, valid, inner, voiceless substance, the silent *res.* Between this authenticity and hazardous expression lie the crucial thresholds of the lips and the page. Any utterance or act of writing is a *sortie,* a leaving behind the bastion of the private self. A *parlement* is an *essai,* a hazardous initiative, a lowering of defenses. Speech will betray the beleaguerment of those forces which only silence can hold at bay. Speech is already an acceptance of infiltration and contamination, because language to have meaning has always already been used, because Montaigne's language in particular is composed of external

examples, opinions, tropes, sentences. One defines one's position in relation to others (Chrisippus, the Roman senate) and against others
(Xenophon, Cleomenes, Ariosto). The alternative is that refusal of contact
which is seen intermittently as sterile, as producing shapeless lumps, and as
sustaining: (a) "Ce n'est pas pour la montre que nostre ame doit jouer son
rolle, c'est chez nous, au dedans, où nuls yeux ne donnent que les nostres"
(623). ["It is not for show that our soul must play its part, it is at home,
within us, where no eyes penetrate but our own" (472).] In writing this
tribute to the *chez nous*, Montaigne is of course exposing it to others; he is
violating that pure interiority which he entrusts to paper (and thus violates)
so often. The muteness of pure interiority, of the beast in its den, is often
praised but in the very praising subverted. Elsewhere he resigns himself to
the dialogue within all discourse.

> (c) Je propose les fantasies humaines et miennes, simplement comme
> humaines fantasies, et separement considerées, non comme arrestées et
> reglées par l'ordonnance celeste, incapables de doubte et d'altercation:
> matiere d'opinion, non matiere de foy; ce que je discours selon moy, non ce
> que je croy selon Dieu. [323]

> I set forth notions that are human and my own, simply as human notions
> considered in themselves, not as determined and decreed by heavenly
> ordinance and permitting neither doubt nor dispute; matter of opinion, not
> matter of faith; what I reason out according to me, not what I believe
> according to God. [234]

Here an implication emerges which anticipates Bakhtin, that human
discourse necessarily contains "altercation."

We have noted the oddity of an essay whose titular concern is with the
prudence of a defender but whose opening paragraph, among others, deals
with the ethics of the besieger. These two pairs of options, ostensibly so
different in military terms, begin to approach each other in discursive
terms. Once one has made a verbal foray from one's bastion, one is already
on the road to becoming an invader, if not a seducer. Montaigne is alert to
the risk.

> (b) Il y a tant de mauvais pas que, pour le plus seur, il faut un peu
> legierement et superficiellement couler ce monde. (c) Il le faut glisser, non
> pas s'y enfoncer. (b) La Volupté mesme est douloureuse en sa profondeur.
> [1005]

> There are so many bad spots that, for greatest safety, we must slide over
> this world a bit lightly and on the surface. We must glide over it, not break
> through into it. Even sensual pleasure is painful in its depth. [768]

(b) J'essaie à tenir mon ame et mes pensées en repos. . . . Et si elles se desbauchent à quelque impression rude et penetrante, c'est à la verité sans mon conseil. [1020]

I try to keep my soul and my thoughts in repose. . . . And if they sometimes veer under some rough and penetrating attack, it is in truth without my consent. [781]

Both passages betray a certain ambiguity which blurs the image of penetration. Is the writer's sensibility male or female? Perhaps it partakes of both. The element of aggression is present in any case, and it is subject to considerations of both prudence and ethics. There is the risk of penetrating too far; there is also the risk of attacking too much. (b) "Nous empeschons . . . la prise et la serre de l'ame à luy donner tant de choses à saisir" [1009] ["We impede the mind's grasp and grip by giving it so many things to seize" (771).] The last of the essays seems to attribute a certain "animosité" [animosity] and "aspreté" [bitterness] to all writing. [1066] And the "Institution des enfans" will discuss the risk of assaulting the classics too directly. (c) "Je ne luitte point en gros ces vieux champions là, et corps à corps: c'est par reprinses, menues et legieres attaintes" (147–48). ["I do not wrestle with those old champions wholesale and body against body; I do so by snatches, by little light attacks" (108).] Even for the post-Humanist that Montaigne became, engagement with antiquity involved a circumspect struggle. Thus beneath the concern for the threatened center, one distinguishes an interest in the policy of attack. To go out to parley is already to begin to take the offensive.

Revisions of the first paragraph of I: 5 will suggest subtly that speech and action lie upon a single spectrum. The Roman senate, disapproving the stratagem of Lucius Marcius,

(a) "accuserent cette pratique de leur *stile* (c) antien. . . . C'estoient les *formes* vrayment Romaines. . . . (a) Il appert bien par le *langage* de ces bonnes gens qu'il n'avoient encore receu cette belle sentence: 'dolus an virtus quis in hoste requirat?' " [25]

["condemned this practice as hostile to their old style. . . . These were truly Roman forms. . . . It clearly appears from the language of these good men that they had not yet accepted this fine saying: 'Courage or ruse—against an enemy, who cares?' " (16)]

Here the word *stile* adumbrates a moral code. Today we may feel the word as a metaphor, since a rhetorical term seems to have replaced a normative one. But for Montaigne there may have been no sense of transferal; for him ethics and language interpenetrate each other, as they do for most Renaissance writers. Each utterance and each act of writing possess a moral character, so that soldier, legislator, and writer can be judged by a single criterion. Each is governed by a moral style. In the gradual emergence of a moral style lies the interest of the earlier essays, and also their achievement. In the apprentice essays, one feels the resistance the composed self has to overcome in order to declare itself. One cannot really speak of subtexts, since the appropriations lie on the surface; one can only speak of a subself which gradually reveals itself through its power to absorb, which is to say rewrite, Seneca, Plutarch, Lucretius, Diogenes Laertius. We come progressively to respect this composed self precisely because it has accepted its vulnerability, its engagement in discourse, and has struggled with the resistance of alterities.

The siege may fade from the mature essays because Montaigne acquires confidence in his own moral style and its capacity for assimilation without risk. The self-destructive reception without assimilation is what Montaigne calls *pedantisme.*

> (a) Nous prenons en garde les opinions et le sçavoir d'autruy, et puis c'est tout. Il les faut faire nostres. . . . (b) Nous nous laissons si fort aller sur les bras d'autruy, que nous aneantissons nos forces. [137]

> We take the opinions and the knowledge of others into our keeping, and that is all. We must make them our own. . . . We let ourselves lean so heavily on the arms of others that we annihilate our own powers. [101]

As Montaigne matures, the danger of this annihilation, this pillage or rape, tends to diminish without altogether disappearing. A posthumous addition to "L'heure des parlemens dangereuse" signals a new willingness to enter the equivocal play of diplomacy.

> (c) Il n'est pas dict, que, en temps et lieu, il ne soit permis de nous prevaloir de la sottise de nos ennemis, comme nous faisons de leur lascheté. Et certes le guerre a naturellement beaucoup de privileges raisonnables au prejudice de la raison. [28–29]

> It is not said that, at a given time and place, it is not permissible for us to take advantage of the stupidity of our enemies, as we do of their cowardice. And indeed war has by nature many privileges that are reasonable even at the expense of reason. [18]

With the passing of years, parleying became less dangerous and less reprehensible, the siege motif less relevant, because the self could allow itself to be permeable. A passage in the essay I: 50 ("De Democritus et

Heraclitus") constitutes a kind of manifesto of the soul's transformative energy.

> (c) Les choses à part elles ont peut estre leurs poids et mesures et conditions; mais au dedans, en nous, elle [l'ame] les leur taille comme elle l'entend. . . . La santé, la conscience, l'authorité, la science, la richesse, la beauté et leurs contraires se despouillent à l'entrée, et recoivent de l'ame nouvelle vesture, et de la teinture qu'il lui plaist: brune, verte, claire, obscure, aigre, douce, profonde, superficielle, et ce qu'il plaist à chacune d'elles: car elles n'ont pas verifié en commun leurs stiles, regles et formes: chacune est Royne en son estat. [302]

> Things in themselves may have their own weights and measures and qualities; but once inside, within us, she [the soul] allots them their qualities as she sees fit. . . . Health, conscience, authority, knowledge, riches, beauty, and their opposites—all are stripped on entry and receive from the soul new clothing, and the coloring that she chooses—brown, green, bright, dark, bitter, sweet, deep, superficial—and which each individual soul chooses; for they have not agreed together on their styles, rules and forms; each one is queen in her realm. [220]

Each soul has its *stile, regle,* and *forme,* which not only render matter profound or superficial, but also brown or green; the style tinctures matter with its own indissoluble shading. This is the victory of the soul and preeminently of the writer, since it liberates him from beleaguering hostilities. It is not too much to say that the ultimate subject of the *Essais* is this transformative *stile* of their author's soul. "(a) Qu'on ne s'attende pas aux matieres, mais à la façon que j'y donne." [408] ["Let attention be paid not to the matter, but to the shape I give it" (296).] This indeed is what essentially he seeks in other writers. "(c) Tous les jours m'amuse à lire en des autheurs, sans soin de leur science, y cherchant leur façon, non leur subject." [928] ["Every day I amuse myself reading authors without any care for their learning, looking for their style, not their subject" (708).] If one neglects this progressive discovery of the *façon* as his own final accomplishment as well as others', one is likely to misunderstand Montaigne's book. If one reduces this *stile* to a purely linguistic or rhetorical comportment, then one misses anachronistically its energy and breadth. As Montaigne writes, his trust grows in the integrity of his own *façon* and its power to negotiate with his classics.

There remains to be sure a certain wariness.

> (b) Quand j'escris, je me passe bien de la compaignie et souvenance des livres, de peur qu'ils n'interrompent ma forme. Aussi que, à la verité, les bons autheurs m'abattent par trop et rompent le courage. [874]

When I write, I prefer to do without the company and remembrance of books, for fear they may interfere with my style. Also because, in truth, the good authors humble me and dishearten me too much. [666]

The impulse to withdraw remains a temptation, but each page belies this alleged surrender of the literary memory; the *souvenance* is not so easily or perhaps so willingly abandoned. The strongest defence against marauders, we learn from the careful householder of "De la vanité," [Of vanity] is not to lock one's gates. The third book bears witness to a less private conception of solitude.

(c) Qui ne vit aucunement à autruy, ne vit guere à soy. [1007]

He who lives not at all unto others, hardly lives unto himself. [769]

(c) Ma forme essentielle est propre à la communication et à la production: je suis tout au dehors et en evidence, nay à la société et à l'amitié. [823]

My essential pattern is suited to communication and revelation. I am all in the open and in full view, born for company and friendship. [625]

It is true that a yearning emerges in "De l'experience" [Of experience] for a purely uninterpreted experience, for pure and absolute knowledge without commentary and without a secondary voice. But this desire, which remains active, can be balanced against the willing acceptance of linguistic duality in the same essay: each word belongs equally and rightfully to its speaker and its auditor. (b) "La parole est moitié à celuy qui parle, moitié à celuy qui l'escoute." [1088] ["Speech belongs half to the speaker, half to the listener" (834).]

Terence Cave discerns a vacuum at the center of the *Essais*, which constitute a failed attempt to compensate for the loss of La Boétie.

As they proliferate around the space left by the absence of La Boétie—like decorative motifs around a missing painting—they can only designate with greater and greater intricacy their own condition of exile and *écoulement*, so that finally the focal absence reveals itself to be that of Montaigne himself.[8]

Each reader of Montaigne will find the metaphor that suits best his own impressions. But Cave's focal absence at the center fails to account for that tincturing of the external as, in Montaigne's own metaphor, it enters and crosses the threshold of the soul. This stylization or coloring of things by a central sensibility is the dominant activity of the *Essais*; it defines that

8. Terence Cave. *The Cornucopian Text: Problems of Writing in the French Renaissance* (Oxford: Clarendon Press, 1979), p. 299.

human *façon* which brings us to them as it brought Montaigne to his preferred masters. If in place of the Renaissance vocabulary one substitutes the terms of post-Saussurian linguistics, one skirts anachronism. Cave writes:

> Discourse can never be a transparent vehicle for a given content. Asserting its own presence, it contaminates, obscures, and renders invisible its reference; the resolution of meaning is deferred to some future articulation which will never occur.[9]

This contamination and postponement constitute the text's "diseased nature." But if Renaissance rhetoric approves the technique of *contaminatio*, if discourse pretends neither to transparence nor to reference but to a tincturing *stile*, then there is no pathology of obscurity or deferral; the creation of a transformative moral style is everywhere achieved. Cave cites effectively the myth of the Danaids, whose leaking buckets forestall plenitude, but Montaigne's predilections lead more frequently to images of solid centers and surroundings which encroach upon each other as the center expands or contracts, negotiates or withdraws, stiffens or softens. Each alternative might be regarded as "a movement toward death" (Cave, p. 298), but only if it is understood always to stop short. Death would lie in the collapse of centric resistance, in the suicidal *imitation meurtriere*, or it would lie antithetically in the absolute resistance of silence, the permanent closing of the gate, the refusal of speech. We know that there is a living self when there is a locus of dialogic "altercation." Speech contaminates Montaigne as it contaminates everyone, but for the cunning negotiator, speech saves as well as threatens; it preserves the fortress-self from the two mortal tactical extremes.

The neighbor who invades Montaigne's estate by a ruse of murderous intent is disarmed finally by his host's trustfulness, an apparent simplicity which is spontaneous but not naive. "(b) Je suis peu deffiant et soubçonneux de ma nature," he remarks, [1060] ["I am by nature little given to distrust and suspicion" (812)], and it is this clear-eyed credulity that preserves his life. The essay with which we began (I:5) ends on the same note, in an addition of 1588.

> (b) Je me fie ayseement à la foy d'autruy. Mais mal-aiseement le fairoy je lors que je donnerois à juger l'avoir plustost faict par desespoir et faute de coeur que par franchise et fiance de sa loyauté. [27]

9. Cave, *Cornucopian Text*, p. 318.

> I put my trust easily in another man's word. But I should do so reluctantly whenever I would give the impression of acting from despair and want of courage rather than freely and through trust in his honesty. [17]

Trust seems both spontaneous and tactical; it may coexist with fear, but not so as to reveal fear. This partial and qualified trust is Montaigne's response to the problem of these twin essays, "l'heure des parlemens dangereuse." His book reveals his cautious, gradual extension of faith to the voices who encircle him on its pages, as he gained faith that his own quirky, placid voice could be heard through theirs and above theirs and *in* theirs. The *Essais* might be said to adumbrate a textual theology like one their author hated: Lutheranism. A man accepts both the estrangement of the word and its promise of engagement; in a grey area without rules, he is saved by his *fiance*. But here this perennial interchange is embraced with a secular temperance: (b) "Celuy qui se porte plus moderéement envers le gain et la perte, il est tousjours chez soy." [1009]]"He who bears himself more moderately toward winning and losing is always at home" (771).][10]

10. I have again altered slightly Frame's translation.

ANTOINE COMPAGNON

A Long Short Story: Montaigne's Brevity

How are we to read the *Essais?* Simply put, what is their unity? The book, the chapter, the sentence? All these answers have been suggested, yet none has proved satisfactory. They circle about an enigma or else they repress a contradiction, for the *Essais* are at once copious and brief. That they are abundant goes without saying. But what can it mean to speak of brevity in an author known for prolixity, famous for the abundance or indefinite extensibility of his material, as analysed in Terence Cave's recent work on the Renaissance text?[1]

"Qui ne voit que j'ay pris une route par laquelle, sans cesse et sans travail, j'iray autant qu'il y aura d'ancre et de papier au monde?" ["Who does not see that I have taken a road along which I shall go, without stopping and without effort, as long as there is ink and paper in the world?"] Montaigne asks this at the very beginning of "Of Vanity," a rhetorical question accompanied by surreptitious pleasure. (b) "Et quand seray-je à bout de representer une continuelle agitation et mutation de mes pensées, en quelque matiere qu'elles tombent, puisque Diomedes remplit six mille livres du seul subject de la grammaire? Que doit produire le babil, puisque le begaiement et desnouement de la langue estouffa le monde d'une si horrible charge de volumes?" (III:9, 946). ["And when shall I make an end of describing the continual agitation and changes of my thoughts, whatever subject they light on, since Didymus filled six thousand books with the sole subject of grammar? What must prattle produce, when the stammering and loosening of the tongue smothered the world with such a horrible load of volumes?" (721).] Montaigne everywhere condemns human babble. The impossibility of closure, the fatal indefiniteness of the book is associated with the reflexive character of his writing, even if Montaigne sees a sign of the times in this grotesque proliferation of babble: "L'escrivaillerie semble

1. Terence Cave, *The Cornucopian Text: problems of writing in the French Renaissance* (Oxford: at the Clarendon Press, 1979).

24

estre quelque simptome d'un siècle desbordé (946)." ["Scribbling seems to be a sort of symptom of an unruly age" (721).] But what distinguishes Montaigne's book as his own is his special faculty of glossing and commenting upon himself.

"Nous ne faisons que nous entregloser" (1069). ["We do nothing but write glosses about each other"(818)] he says in "Of Experience" stating, as he does so, a general principle of writing and of its overflowing fecundity. Then he resumes, and an addition, inserted here into the "exemplaire de Bordeaux," enters in to unite gesture to word: (b) "Combien souvent et sottement à l'avanture ay-je estandu mon livre à parler de soy?" (III:13, 1069) ["How often and perhaps how stupidly have I extended my book to make it speak for itself!" (818)] A new addition follows glossing "sottement". Reflexivity or self-commentary is the means of an interminable extension, an *amplificatio* proper to the *Essais*, this indefinite and potentially infinite book.

However, it was not always so. True, the *Essais* of Book III are long, the 1588 additions to Books I and II extensive, while those of the "exemplaire de Bordeaux" continue indefinitely. In the "Apology" which, it is true, is a very long chapter even by the standards of Book III, Montaigne said, calling upon the reader or perhaps Marguerite de France to whom it was dedicated: (a) "Vous, pour qui j'ay pris la peine d'estendre un si long corps contre ma coustume" (II:12, 557) [You, for whom I have taken the pains to extend so long a work contrary to my custom(418).] I will return to the metaphor of the chapter or essay as body, but it is at the moment Montaigne's "custom" of 1580 which interests me and which, with the exception of the "Apology," is that of relatively short chapters.

One has only to imagine the appearance of the 1580 edition, which is not often done because modern editions include the later additions.[2] However, out of the ninety-four chapters that comprised the 1580 *Essais*, sixteen had less than two pages. The 1580 essay was brief. Chapter 52 of Book I, aptly titled "Of the Parsimony of the Ancients," contains two terse paragraphs, lengthened simply, in 1588, by the addition of a small clause.

This is why critics had, for a long time, the tendency to scorn the oldest chapters of the *Essais*. Pierre Villey considered them "very thin", while the chapters of Book II were "very slight" being, like "Of riding post" or "Of thumbs," "the mere juxtaposition of a few facts, a few remarks which struck Montaigne in the course of his readings."[3] The complaint against

2. See the photographic reproduction of the original 1580 edition of the *Essais*, published by Daniel Martin (Geneva: Slatkine and Paris: Champion 1976).

3. P. Villey, *Les sources et l'évolution des "Essais" de Montaigne*, 2nd edition (Paris, Hachette, 1933), vol. 2, p. 227.

these chapters is that, being simply collections of anecdotes, they lack development and commentary.

This has led to the tendency for recent criticism to revalorize these chapters, demonstrating that they are not as short as Villey would like to think. I will cite a few such attempts, for they offer insights into the definition of Montaigne's brief form, at once a unity, a whole and an element, a part. This is the essential ambivalence of the fragment, at once a whole and a part, unity and element, which one finds from the beginning in the first short essays of Book I. Criticized as unities—for Villey they are merely collections or gatherings in the tradition of miscellanies—they are now reconsidered as parts of the whole, parts of the greater unity which is the book. It, in turn, provides the coherence and firmness that the chapter or the essay lacks.

Michel Butor, in his *Essais sur les "Essais,"* is among those recent critics who have gone in search of the properties of the whole, of a unity transcending the disarray of the *Essais.* He insists on the centrality of La Boétie in Book I and looks for a way to organize all the chapters around a median, the twenty-ninth, which indeed introduces the "Twenty-nine sonnets of Etienne de La Boétie."[4] This enterprise remains entirely faithful to Montaigne—who reveals in chapter XXVIII, "Of friendship," that:

> (a) Considérant la conduite de la besongne d'un peintre que j'ay, il m'a pris envie de l'ensuivre. Il choisit le plus bel endroit et milieu de chaque paroy, pour y loger un tableau élabouré de toute sa suffisance; et, le vuide tout au tour, il le remplit de crotesques, qui sont peintures fantasques, n'ayant grace qu'en la varieté et estrangeté. Que sont-ce icy aussi, à la verité, que crotesques et corps monstrueux, rappiecez de divers membres, sans certaine figure, n'ayants ordre, suite ny proportion que fortuité? [I:28, 183]

> (a) As I was considering the way a painter I employ went about his work, I had a mind to imitate him. He chooses the best spot, the middle of each wall, to put a picture labored over with all his skill, and the empty space all around it he fills with grotesques, which are fantastic paintings whose only charm lies in their variety and strangeness. And what are these things of mine, in truth, but grotesques and monstrous bodies, pieced together of divers members, without definite shape, having no order, sequence, or proportion other than accidental? [135]

Except for the center, which was supposed to have been La Boétie's *Discours de la servitude volontaire,* published separately in 1576, and which became the twenty-nine sonnets included from 1580 to 1588, the other chapters

4. Michel Butor, *Essais sur les "Essais"* (Paris, Gallimard 1968).

have no organizing principle or structure. Nevertheless, the book forms a triptych, following the usual Renaissance custom of associating books and paintings, with twenty-eight chapters before the twenty-nine sonnets and twenty-eight after.

The chapters around this center remain, according to this scheme without order. Daniel Martin, going farther than Butor, invents a global architecture for the *Essais*. He borrows his model from the arts of memory, much in vogue in the sixteenth century. These "artificial memories" were borrowed from the *Rhetoric to Herennius* and the dialogue *Of the Orator [De oratore]*, where Cicero recommends imitating painters by keeping in mind an architectural painting as a mnemonic device.[5] In this case, Montaigne would have preconceived a detailed structure for his cathedral. Thus: "One must enter into the *Essais*, with the blueprint of their architecture in hand."[6]

There is something fanciful in the mystical search for exhaustive systems of mnemonic reading in the *Essais*, as for images and passages which harmonize together in some underlying mathematical construction or monumental Palladian theater. Should the unity ascribed to the *Essais*, triptych, altarpiece, or cathedral, be compared to that which Proust claims for the *Recherche*, a unity the invention of which is considered to have made possible the transition from the poorly fitted pieces of the puzzle of *Jean Santeuil* to a work that is both completely coherent and a succession (itself indefinite and expansive, interrupted only by death) of individual fragments, multiple visions, dislocated and discontinuous facets and perspectives? But this merely intensifies the enigma: is construction, in spite of Proust's insistence, really what constitutes the unity of the *Recherche?*

The architectural models of Butor, Martin, and others confer upon the book a symmetry, a premeditated completion, the global and closed character of a system of predisposed spaces where each chapter occupies its necessary place. Yet, without a doubt, one might envision a different model of unity, more open and supple, that organic unity of plenitude and proliferation closer to the descriptions in Book III.

For the moment, let us distinguish only between external schemas, formal models imposed upon the *Essais* which deny the chapters a part of their autonomy and individuality, and the more modest proposals of Richard Sayce, who seeks to surmount the *Essais'* apparent disorder,

5. See Frances Yates, *The Art of Memory* (London: 1966. French translation: Paris, 1975).

6. D. Martin, Introduction to the photographic reproduction of the 1580 edition of the *Essais*, op. cit., p. 25. See also "Pour une lecture mnémonique des 'Essais': une image et un lieu," *Bulletin de la société des amis de Montaigne*, 5, 31–32, (1979).

contradiction, and absence of form without, however, merely making generalizations. Where Butor and Pierre Barrière before him furnish global interpretations of each book,[7] Sayce contents himself with finding connections between successive chapters and essentially thematic sequences and variations. He speaks of "antechamber" and "appendix" chapters framing a main chapter.[8] However, to do this is to sacrifice the originality of a chapter and its "short form" for a weak and banal thematic unity in a small group of chapters, which moreover Sayce supposes "ought to be taken as parts of a whole and not as separate entities."[9]

Recently, Marianne Meijer has reintroduced the idea of thematic sequences in Books I and II, considering the chapter as a variation on a theme to be discerned through relationships of contiguity. This is not, however, the primary concern of the chapter's development, and the themes orchestrating the sequence turn out to be so general, so self-evident, that they cannot account for the specificity of the chapters and the particular sequences in which they are inscribed. This reading tends to assimilate—and Marianne Meijer does it explicitly—the short form of the *Essais* up to 1580 and the discontinuous writing which occurs as of that date.[10] The same writing procedure could be seen at work both in the additions and digressions that form the different layers of the text after 1580, and in the succession or chain of short and abrupt chapters before 1580.

Discontinuity in Book III and *brevity* in Books I and II become, then, two sides of an identical writing procedure, one which reads, rereads, adds and incessantly comments, in a perpetual *ruminatio* according to the medieval definition of *lectio*. Marianne Maijer uses this identification to read the first two books as though their structure were the same as that of the third. She discovers in the former a few large virtual chapters of which the actual small chapters form successive elongations. In short, it would be merely a difference of presentation—in the typographic sense—of what had always been (before as well as after 1580) a writing of digression.

Without going this far, it seems important, given the evident spatial discontinuity of the *Essais* (if only that of the printed page which sets off

7.   *Pierre Barrière, Montaigne, gentilhomme français* (Bordeaux: 1948). The themes of the three books would be, respectively, retirement, suicide, and diversion.

8.   Richard A. Sayce, "L'ordre des Essais de Montaigne," *BHR*, 18, 1956. and *The Essays of Montaigne*, (London, 1972).

9.   R.A. Sayce, *The Essays of Montaigne*, op. cit., p. 264.

10.   Marianne Meijer, " 'Des postes' et 'Des pouces'; plaisanteries ou points de repère?" *Columbia Montaigne Conference Papers, French Forum Monographs*, 27, Lexington, Kentucky, 1981. On the first chapters of the *Essais*, see also Raymond C. La Charité, "The Coherence of Montaigne's First Book," *L'Esprit créateur*, 20, (1980).

quotations), to insist upon the temporality engaged in discontinuity and in brevity. Montaigne himself explains "ce fagotage de tant de diverses pieces" [(a) "This bundle of so many disparate pieces" (574)] that are the *Essais* in one of his relatively rare remarks on the form of the book before 1580 by the fact that the book (a) "s'est basty à diverses poses et intervalles" (II:37, 758) ["has built itself up with diverse interruptions and intervals" (574).] The diversity of the *Essais* therefore results from the intermittence of their writing, whether before or after 1580. Paradoxically, that is, contrary to those who deny such unity to the *Essais*, this proposition grants a greater, or at least a temporal, unity to the short initial chapters, and this persistent question of unity therefore arises only with Book III.

Montaigne also associates brevity with time. It is through a consideration of time, the time of reading, that he justifies the passage from the short chapter of Book I to the long chapter of Book III, from the "short form" to discontinuous writing. This occurs on that famous page of the chapter "Of vanity," "Cette farcisseure est un peu hors de mon theme" (994). ["This stuffing is a little out of my subject" (761),] which gives way to a long digression on the *Essais* themselves: (b) "Je m'esgare, mais plustost par licence que par mesgarde. Mes fantasies se suyvent, mais par fois c'est de loing, et se regardent, mais d'une veuë oblique" (III:9, 994). ["I go out of my way, but rather by license than carelessness. My ideas follow one another, but sometimes it is from a distance, and look at each other, but with a sidelong glance" (761).] The two pages of digression, marked in the "exemplaire de Bordeaux" by several additions, culminate, after a condemnation of obscurity, in this addition:

> (c) Par ce que la coupure si frequente des chapitres, de quoy j'usoy au commencement, m'a semblé rompre l'attention avant qu'elle soit née, et la dissoudre, dedeignant s'y coucher pour si peu et se recueillir, je me suis mis à les faire plus longs, qui requierent de la proposition et du loisir assigné. En telle occupation, à qui on ne veut donner une seule heure on ne veut rien donner. Et ne faict on rien pour celuy pour qui on ne faict qu'autre chose faisant. Joint qu'à l'adventure ay-je quelque obligation à ne dire qu'à demy, à dire confusément, à dire discordamment. [III:9,995–96]

> Because such frequent breaks into chapters as I used at the beginning seemed to me to disrupt and dissolve attention before it was aroused, making it disdain to settle and collect for so little, I have begun making them longer, requiring fixed purpose and assigned leisure. In such an occupation, if you will not give a man a single hour, you will not give him anything. And you do nothing for a man for whom you do nothing except

while doing something else. Besides, perhaps I have some personal obligation to speak only by halves, to speak confusedly, to speak discordantly. [762]

Montaigne moved from the short form, in his early work, to the looser style of Book III (he says) in order to retain the reader's attention, to require of him a sustained effort. Brevity suspends attention, all the more so in that Montaigne admits in the conclusion to the addition, to not speaking altogether clearly. Certainly this allusion to the final obscurity of his plan calls forth the addition: (b) "l'obscurité, laquelle, à parler en bon escient, je hay (c) bien fort, (b) et l'eviterois si je me sçavois eviter" (III:9, 995). ["obscurity, which, to speak in all earnest, I hate very strongly, and I would avoid it if I could avoid myself" (763).]

Thus, the chapter of Book III is such that is requires more than an hour of reading, as a gage that subtlety will not escape application: the criterion is quantitative, and here he immediately encounters an obstacle. If no serious reading can be done for less than an hour at a stretch how, on the other hand, is it then possible to retain the reader's attention for that amount of time? This obstacle seems all the more serious in that Montaigne returns again and again to the theme of the fateful threshold of an hour's reading to speak of the difficulty he has in crossing it. In the chapter "Of books," during one of his most severe attacks on Cicero in the *Essais*, Montaigne writes:

> (a) Mais, à confesser hardiment la verité . . . sa façon d'escrire me semble ennyeuse, et toute autre pareille façon. Car ses prefaces, definitions, partitions, etymologies, consument la plus part de son ouvrage; ce qu'il y a de vif et de mouelle, est estouffé par ses longueries d'apprets. Si j'ay employé une heure à le lire, qui est beaucoup pour moy, et que je r'amentoive ce que j'en ay tiré de suc et de substance, la plus part du temps je n'y treuve que du vent. [II:10, 413–14]

> But to confess the truth boldly . . . his way of writing, and every other similar way, seems to me boring. For his prefaces, definitions, partitions, etymologies, consume the greater part of his work; what life and marrow there is, is smothered by his long-winded preparations. If I have spent an hour in reading him, which is a lot for me, and I remember what juice and substance I have derived, most of the time I find nothing but wind; [301]

The emptiness of the word is opposed to the truth of the thing as empty wind to life and marrow, essence and substance. This is the babbling of rhetoric. And Cicero's verbosity offends Montaigne.

On the other hand, he also mentions the threshold of an hour's reading in the chapter "Of the art of discussion," this time in order to praise Tacitus:

(b) "Je viens de courre d'un fil l'histoire de Tacitus (ce qui ne m'advient guere: il y a vint ans que je ne mis en livre une heure de suite) "(III:8, 940). ["I have just run through Tacitus' *History* at one reading (which rarely happens to me; it has been twenty years since I put one whole hour at a time on a book)" (718).] Montaigne then asks himself what are the qualities of "writing" with which Tacitus has held him breathless: "Il ne retire pas mal à l'escrire de Seneque: il me semble plus charnu, Seneque plus aigu" (941). ["He rather takes after Seneca's writing; he seems to me more meaty, Seneca more pointed" (719).] Nevertheless: (b) "Il plaide tousjours par raisons solides et vigoreuses, d'une façon pointue et subtile, suyvant le stile affecté du siecle: ils aymoyent tant à s'enfler qu'où ils ne trouvoyent de la pointe et subtilité aux choses, ils l'empruntoyent des parolles" (III:8, 941). ["He always pleads with solid and vigorous arguments, in a pointed and subtle fashion, following the affected style of his time. They were so fond of an inflated manner that when they did not find any point and subtlety in the things, they borrowed it from the words" (719).] The praise is qualified. Although Tacitus is taxed for his inflated style and suspected of caring more for words than for things (according to that ancient opposition ever at work in the *Essais*), what makes him readable for an hour, as opposed to Cicero— even if Montaigne will later revise his judgment and read Cicero at length— is his "pointed and subtle" style. In this Tacitus resembles Seneca, and in the 1588 edition Montaigne compares him to Plutarch as well, to both Seneca and Plutarch, who had already and similarly been opposed, in the chapter "Of books," to Cicero and to the boredom Montaigne then felt in reading him.

Curiously enough, Plutarch and Seneca had been especially praised in that essay for the small doses in which they could be taken:

(a) Ils ont tous deux cette notable commodité pour mon humeur, que la science que j'y cherche, y est traictée à pieces décousues, qui ne demandent pas l'obligation d'un long travail, dequoy je suis incapable. . . . Il ne faut pas grande entreprinse pour m'y mettre; et les quitte où il me plait. Car elles n'ont point de suite des unes aux autres. [II:10, 413]

They both have this notable advantage for my humor, that the knowledge I seek is there treated in detached pieces that do not demand the obligation of long labor, of which I am incapable. . . . I need no great enterprise to get at them, and I leave them whenever I like. For they have no continuity from one to the other. [300]

Montaigne goes on to compare at length the *Moral Essays* and the *Epistles*, before concluding in these words: "Seneque est plein de pointes et saillies;

Plutarque, de choses" (413). ["Seneca is full of witty points and sallies, Plutarch of things" (301).] Montaigne always makes the same distinction, and Plutarch wins the competition, he who so judiciously noted of Homer: (a) "le seul autheur du monde qui n'a jamais soulé ne degousté les hommes, se montrant au lecteur tousjours tout autre, et fleurissant tousjours en nouvelle grace" (II:36, 753). ["He is the only author in the world who has never sated or palled on men, appearing ever entirely different to his readers, and ever blooming in new grace" (p. 570).]

The paradox is remarkable: Tacitus, Seneca, and Plutarch can be read for an hour at a stretch, unlike Cicero, because they can be read at intervals. Their writings are detached, without sequence, and their style is pointed and subtle. One can devote time to them because they do not demand it. Montaigne, wishing to be read for longer than an hour (as he says in Book III) must attain this equilibrium: to be readable for an hour because readable in a moment.

Here we must move from one meaning of brevity to another, perhaps from *brevitas* as a genre to a *brevitas* which is actually a form.

The short chapters of Books I and II—short rather than brief—militate against rhetoric which, as Montaigne notes in broaching the subject "Of the vanity of words," has as its goal (a) "de choses petites les faire paroistre et trouver grandes" (I:51, 305). ["to make little things appear and be thought great" (221).] According to a 1588 addition: (b) "C'est un cordonnier qui sait faire de grands souliers à un petit pied." ["That's a shoemaker who can make big shoes for a small foot."] He uses this image, a commonplace since Quintilian, of words as clothes which should properly fit the body. Toward the end of the chapter, Montaigne airs his complaints against Aretino for the latter's grandiloquence and audacity, his (a) "façon de parler bouffie et bouillonnée de pointes, ingenieuses à la verité, mais recherchées de loing et fantasques, et outre l'eloquence" (I:51, 307). ["turgid style, bubbling over with conceits, ingenious indeed but farfetched and fantastic" (223).]

Rhetoric, according to Montaigne (and this is why he reproaches Cicero), serves to inflate, aggrandize, swell and finally to weary with its continuity and concatenation. He admits of himself: (b) "je grossis et enfle mon subject . . . et encore par extension et amplification" (III:11, 1028). ["I magnify and inflate my subject . . . and further by extension and amplification" (786).] A motif completely opposed to rhetoric appears in an addition to the "exemplaire de Bordeaux": (c) "La parole vive et bruyante, comme est la mienne ordinaire, s'emporte volontiers à l'hyperbole" (1028). ["A lively and noisy way of speaking, such as mine ordinarily is, is apt to be carried away into hyperbole" (786).] The original text already defended itself against such accusations by returning constantly to the "verité nue et crüe" ["naked and unvarnished truth,"] "sans exaggeration, sans emphase et remplissage" ["without overemphasis or padding."] The rhetoric which Montaigne condemns is that of *amplificatio*.

Montaigne sides with *brevitas* against the notion of abundance as a kind of *ubertas*. However, it is something of a choice between Scylla and Charybdis for, if *ubertas* describes a *modus oratorius* pertaining to the pulpit or the barrister's bench, then dense *brevitas* belongs to the *modus scholasticus* of Scholastic philosophy. Both are equally undesirable. Montaigne, like Erasmus, goes in quest of a third solution besides rhetoric and scholasticism. Of Cicero's discourses, which "languissent autour du pot" ["languish around the pot"] Montaigne clearly declares: (a) "ils sont bons pour l'escole, pour le barreau et pour le sermon, où nous avons loisir de sommeiller. . . . Ce sont autant de parolles perdues pour moy" (II:10, 414). ["They are good for the school, for the bar, and for the sermon, where we have the leisure to nap . . . these are so many words lost on me" (301).] However, the dilemma of the *modus oratorius* and the *modus scholasticus* can be transcended by a *brevitas* reconcilable with the indefinite extensibility of writing, its *copia* rather than its *ubertas*.

THE ABRUPT STYLE

"C'est un langage coupé/qu'il n'y espargne les points et lettres maiuscules" ["It is an abrupt style/may he not be sparing of periods and capital letters"]: Montaigne recommends to the printer in a note from the "exemplaire de Bordeaux."[11] In accordance with the senecanism and anticiceronianism of the sixteenth century, Montaigne opposes the "abrupt," pointed style to Cicero's periodic eloquence which he criticizes, along with Tacitus' *Dialogue of the Orators*. (a) "Les orateurs voisins de son siecle reprenoyent aussi en luy ce curieux soing de certaine longue cadance au bout de ses clauses, et notoient ces mots: 'esse videatur,' qu'il y employe si souvent. Pour moy, j'ayme mieux une cadance qui tombe plus court, coupée en yambes" (II:10, 415–16). ["The orators who lived near his time also reprehended in him his sedulous care for a certain long cadence at the end of his periods, and noted the words *esse videatur* which he uses so often. As for me, I prefer a cadence that falls shorter, cut into iambics" (303).] He praises the swinging or hopping rhythm of the living word, (b) "les devis pointus et coupez que l'alegresse et la privauté introduict entre les amis" (III:8, 938)

---

11. *Essais*, municipal edition, Bordeaux, 1906, vol. 1, p. 428.

["the sharp, abrupt repartee which good spirits and familiarity introduce among friends" (717)] as against ciceronian atticism.

Thus Montaigne formulates that famous definition of the ideal style in the chapter "Of the education of children": (a) "Le parler que j'ayme, c'est un parler simple et naif, tel sur le papier qu'à la bouche; un parler succulent et nerveux, court et serré, (c) non tant delicat et peigné comme vehement et brusque ... (a) plustost difficile qu'ennuieux, esloingné d'affectation, desreglé, descousu et hardy: chaque lopin y face son corps; non pedantesque, non fratesque, non pleideresque, mais plustost soldatesque, comme Suetone appelle celuy de Julius Caesar; (c) et si ne sens pas bien pour quoy il l'en appelle" (I:26, 171–72). ["The speech I love is a simple, natural speech, the same on paper as in the mouth; a speech succulent and sinewy, brief and compressed, (c) not so much dainty and well-combed as vehement and brusque ... (a) rather difficult than boring, remote from affectation, irregular, disconnected and bold; each bit making a body in itself; not pedantic, not monkish, not lawyer-like, but rather soldierly, as Suetonius calls Julius Caesar's speech; (c) and yet I do not quite see why he calls it so" (127).]

Every term counts in this long enumeration, and Friedrich has noted that the passage closely follows Erasmus' letter criticizing the "monkeys of Cicero," written in 1527 and published in 1529: *"malim aliquod dicendi genus solidius, adstrictius, nervosius, minus comptum magisque masculum."*[12] All these qualities can be found in Montaigne: *solidius* = solid; *adstrictius* = brief and compressed; *nervosius* = sinewy; *minus comptum* = irregular, unkempt; *magisque masculum* = soldierly. The similarities, according to Friedrich, may derive from a common source, Quintilian's critique of effeminate asianism. More recently however, Margaret Mann Philips has found in the neo-Latin poet Jean Dampierre a link between the anti-ciceronianism of Erasmus and that of Montaigne.[13]

Dampierre, in a very long didactic poem, praises Erasmus' style and repeats all the adjectives that Montaigne will later use, including *minus comptum*, or unkempt. But these comparisons do not suffice, for Montaigne's adjectives are more precise and more complete than those of Erasmus or Dampierre.

On the subject of "simple and natural," Montaigne comments: (b) "J'ay naturellement un stile comique et privé" (I:40, 252) ["I have naturally a humorous and familiar style" (186)] in a chapter appropriately entitled "A

12. Hugo Friedrich, *Montaigne*, French translation: (Paris: Gallimard 1968), p. 421.
13. Margaret Mann Philips, "From the *Ciceronianus* to Montaigne," in *Classical Influences On European Culture, A. D. 1500-1700*, ed. R. R. Bolgar, (Cambridge: Cambridge U. Press 1976.)

consideration upon Cicero." Most importantly, these comments identify the style Montaigne idealized in "Of the education of children" with his own natural style. Simple and natural, humorous and familiar, these constitute the low style, *humile atque cotidianum sermonis genus*, according to Quintilian, one which is inferior to the *genus sublime* and the *genus mediocre* in the canonical trinity of *tripertita varietas*.[14]

"Tel sur le papier qu'en la bouche" ["The same on paper as in the mouth"] is the second characteristic he describes, which thus refuses to separate the written from the oral. It is remarkable that Montaigne does not assert this distinction, since he is certainly one of the first artisans of a French written style. In fact, he rallies against such a distinction, perhaps because he had first been a jurist and had been obliged to speak "the same in the mouth as on paper." The paradigm for the *genus humile* is, in his view, private conversation, to which he will devote one of the chapters of Book III, and fidelity to the force of the living word is what confers value upon writing. Book II of the *Essais* ends with a dedication to Mme. de Duras, where it is promised that she will find in the book the author whom she has known: (a) "Vous y reconnoistrez ce mesme port et ce mesme air que vous avez veu en sa conversation" (II:37, 783). ["You will recognize in them the same bearing and the same air that you have seen in his conversation" (595).] It is the last phrase of the first edition of the *Essais* that constitutes the first lines of Book III: (b) "Je parle au papier comme je parle au premier que je rencontre" (III:1, 790). ["I speak to my paper as I speak to the first man I meet" (599).]

The qualities that follow define senecanism and stoic atticism. These are common to Erasmus and Dampierre, and they are the stylistic qualities that Gelli gives his character in *The Fantastic Discourses of Justin Tonnelier*, published in 1566, "in a low and badly woven style, not continuing along a straight line, but often interrupted."[15] Finally, they are qualities common to all anti-Ciceronianism in the Renaissance.

First and foremost, the style is abrupt, here called "vehement and brusque," "irregular, disconnected." Montaigne notes, even more pointedly, in the chapter "A consideration upon Cicero": (b) "Mon langage [est] trop serré, desordonné, couppé, particulier," (252) ["as my language is in every way . . . too compact, disorderly, abrupt, individual;" (186)] which he opposes to the periodic style, (b) "une belle enfileure de paroles courtoises" (252) ["a fine string of courteous words" (186),] for which he claims to be

14. Quintilian, *Institution oratoire*, XI:1, 6.
15. J.B. Gelli, *Les discours fantastiques de Justin Tonnelier* (Lyon: 1556), p. 10. Cited by Margaret McGowan in *Montaigne's Deceits: the art of persuasion in the "Essais"* (Philadelphia: Temple U. Press, 1974), p. 174.

little gifted (I:40, 252). Elsewhere: (a) "Il n'est rien si contraire à mon stile qu'une narration estendue: je me recouppe si souvent à faute d'haleine" (I:21, 106). ["There is nothing so contrary to my style as an extended narration. I cut myself off so often for lack of breath" (76).]

The second trait of senecanism, *subtilitas*, Montaigne recognizes in his own style, or at least in the ideal style, as "plustost difficile qu'ennuieux" ["rather difficult than boring".] While Cicero was judged boring and criticized for it, "difficulty" reveals itself to be a stylistic quality. Montaigne occasionally uses the word to describe an addition, a (c) "chose brève" or "quelque embleme supernumeraire": "une petite subtilité ambitieuse" (III:9, 964) ["a brief thing," "a certain supernumerary emblem," "a small, ambitious subtlety" (736).] But *subtilitas* must not be too difficult, it must not become *obscuritas*, a word which appears frequently in Montaigne as a term of reproof.

Finally, the most important characteristic of the senecan style is *brevitas:* speech that is "court et serré" ["brief and compressed,"] "trop serré" ["too compressed,"] on which Montaigne here and there prides himself. *Brevitas* approaches *acumen*, or pointedness, profound thought couched in few words.

In spite of his insistence on the spontaneous and natural, Montaigne's *sermo humilis* is studied, or at the very least reflected upon in the terms of a contemporary debate. "Si mon inclination me porte plus à l'imitation du parler de Seneque, je ne laisse pas d'estimer davantage celuy de Plutarque," (638) ["And if my inclination leads me more to imitate Seneca's style, I nonetheless esteem Plutarch's more" (484)], evokes a very stylistically conscious Montaigne, who is also conscious of the limits of *brevitas* and *subtilitas*, of the risks involved in concision and difficulty, especially when clarity is renounced and the style approaches the *obscura brevitas* of Tacitus, who forges from *acumina* his *abruptae sententiae et suspiciosae* (II:17, 638). (a) "Mon langage n'a rien de facile et poly: il est aspre (c) et desdaigneux, (a) ayant ses dispositions libres et desreglées." Etc. (a) "Mais je sens bien que par fois je m'y laisse trop aller, et qu'à force de vouloir eviter l'art et l'affectation, j'y retombe d'une autre part:

> brevis esse laboro,
> Obscurus fio.   [II:17, 638]

["As for the rest, my language has no ease or polish; it is harsh (c) and disdainful, (a) with a free and unruly disposition." "But I am quite conscious

16. On Senecanism and anti-Ciceronianism in the sixteenth century, see Morris W. Croll, *Style, Rhetoric, and Rhythm*, (Princeton: Princeton Univ. Press, 1966); G. Williamson, *The Senecan Amble* (London, 1948 and Chicago, 1966); Marc Fumaroli, *L'Age de l'éloquence* (Geneva, 1980): the first part of the work concerns the quarrel of Ciceronianism.

that sometimes I let myself go too far, and that in the effort to avoid art and affectation, I fall back into them in another direction:

> I strive to be concise,
> And grow obscure.   [483–84]

As Horace says in the *Ars poetica:* "I labor to be brief and I become obscure."

The danger of brevity is Tacitan obscurity, terseness, and Montaigne does not fall prey to them. He does not cultivate *subtilitas, brevitas* for its own sake. An addition in the "exemplaire de Bordeaux" which, after the quotation of Horace, puts things in their proper place, testifies to this problem: (c) "Platon dict que le long ou le court ne sont proprietez qui ostent ny donnent prix au langage" (II:17, 638). [(c) "Plato says that length and brevity are properties which neither decrease nor increase the worth of style" (484).] Rather, the function of the abrupt style, of the "cours rompu" ["intermittent flow"], as Montaigne says of the poet who (c) "verse de furie tout ce qui luy vient en la bouche" (III:9, 995) [". . . pours out in a frenzy whatever comes into his mouth" (761)] the advantage of abrupt or disjointed writing, of ellipsis, asyndeton and anacoluthon is to eliminate the apparent logic of periodic discourse, which deceives and wearies the reader:

> (b) J'entends que la matiere se distingue soy-mesmes. Elle montre assez où elle se change, où elle conclud, où elle commence, où elle se reprend, sans l'entrelasser de paroles, de liaison et de cousture introduictes pour le service des oreilles foibles et nonchallantes, et sans me gloser moymesme. [III:9,995]

> I want the matter to make its own divisions. It shows well enough where it changes, where it concludes, where it begins, where it resumes, without my interlacing it with words, with links and seams introduced for the benefit of weak or heedless ears, and without writing glosses on myself. [761]

The abrupt therefore matters less than the absence of a syntax that disengages the reader: "Qui est celuy qui n'ayme pas mieux n'estre pas leu que de l'estre en dormant ou en fuyant?" (995) ["Who is there that would not rather not be read than be read sleepily or in passing?" [761] Montaigne reconciles his brief and uneven style, opposed to (a) "cet autre stile aequable, uny et ordonné" (II:17, 638) ["that other style that is even, smooth, and orderly" (484)] with the long chapter, with which he concerns himself in an addition on the same page of the chapter "Of vanity"—both exhort the reader to apply himself.[17]

17. One must compare the opposition of the periodic style and of that other, lacking in logical articulation, to the distinction made by Aristotle, in the *Rhetoric*, between the so-called

The abrupt style, subtle and brief, defeats rhetoric as well as scholasticism: it is "non pedantesque, non fratesque, non pleideresque" ["not pedantic, not monkish, not lawyer-like"] and eliminates the *modus oratorius* versus *modus scholasticus* dilemma because it no more lends itself to the "School" than to the podium or the barrister's bench. Montaigne terms the style "soldierly" to emphasize its vehemence. (a) "Je veuz des discours qui donnent la premiere charge dans le plus fort du doubte," ["I want reasonings that drive their first attack into the stronghold of the doubt" (301),] he objected to the lengthy and languorous Cicero (II:10, 414). It is Caesar's style, one which Montaigne privileges over Sallust (a) (II:17, 638). But does "soldierly" provide a satisfactory definition? Moreover, Montaigne merely says, "plustost soldatesque, comme Suetone appelle celuy de Julius Caesar," ["rather soldierly, as Suetonius calls Julius Caesar's speech,"] and an addition in the "exemplaire de Bordeaux" casts doubt on the term: (c) "et si ne sens pas bien pour quoy il l'en appelle" (I:26, 172a) [(c) "and yet I do not quite see why he calls it so" (127).]

It may be that the hesitation of layer (c) applies less to "soldierly" as a description of Caesar's style than to the qualifier "soldierly" itself, even in its adequation with the *sermo humilis*. In fact, it contradicts another addition, (b), here inserted, which describes a quality of *brevitas* altogether opposed to martial imagery:

(b) J'ay volontiers imité cette desbauche qui se voit en nostre jeunesse, au port de leurs vestemens: un manteau en escharpe, la cape sur une espaule, un bas mal tendu, qui represente une fierté desdaigneuse de ces paremens estrangers, et nonchallante de l'art. Mais je la trouve encore mieus employée en la forme du parler. [I: 26, 172]

I have been prone to imitate that disorder in dress which we see in our young men—a cloak worn like a scarf, the hood over one shoulder, a neglected stocking—which shows a pride disdainful of these foreign adornments and careless of art. But I think it is even better employed in our form of speech. [127]

What lies behind this metaphor of the clothing of words, this apology for loose and bombastic garments, altogether unmilitary, that in fact contra-

---

"implex" style, that of the periodic and subordinated clauses, and the so-called "coordinated" or sewn-together, enthreaded style, "which has no end in and of itself," and which simply allows ideas to follow one another. This *eiromené lexis* has Herodotus as its model. (Aristotle, *Rhetoric*, III:9, 1409–24). See A. Wartelle's remarks, translated by M. Dufour and A. Wartelle (Paris, 1973). The coordinated style is not necessarily brief, resembling rather Montaigne's long sentence cut into bits, but it defies, similarly and complementarily, the logic of the periodic style.

dicts the way in which the text initially pursued and commented upon the
"soldierly" in strict Quintilian tradition? (a) "Je n'ayme point de tissure où
les liaisons et les coutures paroissent, tout ainsi qu'en un beau corps, il ne
faut qu'on y puisse compter les os et les veines" (I:26, 172). [(a) "I do not like
a fabric in which the seams and stitches show, just as in a handsome body
we must not be able to count the bones and veins" (127).] This is a well-
known complaint against overly researched words and turns of phrase,
against eloquence that travesties and against "les atours et le manteau"
["the attire and the cloak"] that are borrowed ornaments. But what, then, is
this rakish, disorderly clothing which Montaigne praises in 1588 and which
cannot be mistaken for Asian affectation? It is studied negligence, *negligentia diligens*, the natural within the elegance already belonging to Ciceronian atticism, translated into Italian by Castiglione as *sprezzatura*, an art so
accomplished that it seems natural, disdainful, nonchalant. The cloak worn
like a scarf displays itself more, betrays itself as an added element and
reveals rather than masks the *integritas* of the body. The addition in the
"exemplaire de Bordeaux" which follows: (c) "Toute affectation, nommee-
ment en la gayeté et liberté françoise, est mesadvenante au cortisan. Et, en
une monarchie, tout Gentil'homme doit estre dressé à la façon d'un
cortisan. Parquoy nous faisons bien de gauchir un peu sur le naïf et
mesprisant" (I:26, 172). [(c) "Any affectation, especially in the gaiety and
freedom of French, is unbecoming to a courtier. And in a monarchy every
gentleman should be trained in the manner of a courtier. Wherefore we do
well to lean a little in the direction of naturalness and negligence" (127).]
seems to confirm the idea that the 1588 addition, softening the rigor of the
qualifier "soldierly," refers in fact to *negligentia diligens* or *sprezzatura*.
Careful negligence in dress and in the courtier's behavior, as in the word and
in writing, form a single notion, which finally renews its ties with a Cicero
liberated from the yoke of rhetoric. The page, with all of its additions,
renders precisely the meaning of "disdainful" with which Montaigne
willingly qualifies his style; "aspre (c) et desdaigneux, (a) ayant ses dispositions libres et desreglées" (II:17, 638(a)–(c) ["harsh (c) and disdainful, (a) with
a free and unruly disposition." (483)] Disdainful of art, that is, surpassing
it—this is the *sprezzatura* of the *Cortegiano* and the *negligentia diligens*
Jean Dampierre attributes to the abrupt style of Erasmus. Montaigne evokes
it again in an addition to the "exemplaire de Bordeaux," thus giving a more
complete sense to "disarray" and "disorder" which in 1580 lacked positive
content.

The last stylistic quality Montaigne praises in "Of the education of children" appears in the phrase "chaque lopin y face son corps" ["each bit making a body in itself."] Both the metaphor of "bit" and that of the body require attention. Both terms argue for a fragmented reading of the *Essais*, whereby not only every chapter but also every sentence would be closed and complete, individual and autonomous, a body and a bit.[18] The result is a demand for a "parler sec, rond et cru" ["dry, plain, and blunt"], a speaking "maigrement" ("meagerly") for which Villey faults Montaigne. (b) "Et m'offre maigrement et fierement à ceux à qui je suis" (I:40, 253). [(b) "I offer myself meagerly and proudly to those to whom I belong" (186).]

Montaigne speaks of his familiar correspondents, concerning whom it seems to him "qu'ils le doivent lire en [son] coeur, et que l'expression de [ses] paroles fait tort à [sa] conception." ["that they should read (his) feelings in (his) heart, and see that what (his) words express does an injustice to (his) thought" (186).] There is another link in the notion of the letter between Seneca's *brevitas* and that of Montaigne. It is, in fact, a propos of letters, in the chapter "A consideration upon Cicero," that Montaigne adds those several pages of digression on his (b) "stile comique et privé," his "parler sec, rond et cru qui tire, à qui ne me cognoit d'ailleurs, un peu vers le dedaigneux" (I:40, 252–53). ["a humorous and familiar style," "a dry, plain, blunt way of speaking, which, to anyone who does not know me otherwise, verges a little on the disdainful" (186).] that is, on his *sermo humilis*, his *brevitas* and *subtilitas* in the practice of *negligentia diligens*. Justius Lipsius, who was head of the anti-Ciceronian movement and whose style owed allegiance to Seneca and Tacitus, maintained a correspondence with Montaigne after 1580.[19] His letters are full of praise, and Montaigne admired him as well, calling him, after Turnebus' death, (b) "le plus sçavant homme qui nous reste" (II:12, 578). ["the most learned man we have left" (436).] Lipsius' *De constantia*, published in 1584, also foreshadows the chapter "Of vanity" in Book III of the *Essais*: Lipsius, even more than Montaigne, abandons himself to the patchwork of quotation.

Justius Lipsius, in the preface to his *Lettres*, published in 1576, then again in his 1591 *Epistolica Institutio*, defines a new style manifestly indebted to Erasmus and bearing affinities to Montaigne's definition, formulated in 1588 and later, of the ideal essay.[20] The letter, according to Lipsius, is a spontaneous genre, involving no rewriting and only the briefest

18. See A. Thibaudet, "Le quadricentenaire d'un philosophe," *Revue de Paris*, Feb. 1933.

19. On Lipsius and Montaigne, see Camilla Hill Hay, *Montaigne lecteur et imitateur de Sénèque*, (Poitiers, 1938). Above all, see M.W. Croll, "Juste Lipse et le mouvement anticicéronien à la fin du XVIe siècle et au début du XVIIe siècle," *Revue du Seizième siècle*, 1914, vol. 2, and "Attic Prose: Lipsius, Montaigne, Bacon," in *Schelling Anniversary Papers* (New York, 1923). These articles are reprinted in *Style, Rhetoric, Rhythm*, op cit.

20. See Marc Fumaroli, op cit., p. 152 and following.

rereading—*bis non scribo, bis vix eas lego.* It belongs to the low style, *sermo humilis* or *exilis,* intermittent and brief, appropriate for private communication rather than public address, the *actio forensis.* It is characterized by *exilitas* or *tenuitas:* dry, meager, and slender, subtle, brief and dense, it rejects the periodic style. Montaigne's analysis, in the long appendix to "A consideration upon Cicero," is similar: (b) "J'escris mes lettres tousjours en poste . . . et ne les transcris jamais. . . . Je commence volontiers sans project; le premier traict produit le second" (I:40, 253). ["I always write my letters posthaste. . . . and I never have them copied. . . . I am prone to begin without a plan; the first remark brings on the second" (186).] Montaigne convinces himself that his style would have been better suited to letter-writing, to the point where he remarks nostalgically, in the "exemplaire de Bordeaux," recalling the death of La Boétie: (c) "Et eusse prins plus volontiers ceste forme à publier mes verves, si j'eusse eu à qui parler" (I:40, 252). ["And I would have preferred to adopt this form to publish my sallies, if I had had someone to talk to" (185–86).]

Lipsius makes concision and clarity the two great values of the new style. The analogy with Montaigne is not at all artificial; indeed a description of Lipsius' style could well be applied to Montaigne:

> Son style ne laisse pas d'être fort coulant, éloquent, facile, et plein d'agrémens, quoiqu'il soit concis, serré et tout rempli de pointes. Et c'est ce qui paroît avoir été presque sans exemple jusqu'à présent. Cette brièveté singulière de style n'a ni ténèbres ni obscurités. Son ordinaire est de dire beaucoup de choses en peu de mots, et le sens de ses pensées s'étend avec d'autant plus d'effusion et d'abondance, qu'il paroît d'abord serré dans un petit nombre de paroles.[21]

> His style does not relinquish smoothness, eloquence, ease, and adornment although it is concise, compressed, and full of points. And this is what seemed to have been without example until the present. That singular brevity of style has neither shadows nor obscurities. It is his wont to say many things in few words, and the meaning of his thoughts extends with even greater effusion and abundance for having seemed at first compressed into a small number of words.

"CHAQUE LOPIN Y FACE SON CORPS"

The choice of the *sermo humilis,* characterized by concision and clarity, by *brevitas, perspecuitas*—Montaigne evokes Epicurus' "linguistic perspicuity," or the simplicity of his words—and finally by *subtilitas,*

21. Adrien Baillet, *Jugemens des savans sur les principaux ouvrages des auteurs* (Amsterdam, 1725), vol. II, p. 193. Cited by G. Williamson, op. cit., p. 124.

which avoids *obscuritas* but which nevertheless economizes in order to keep the reader alert, renounces both the lengthy *modus oratorius* and the learned, dense *modus scholasticus*. Montaigne is fully aware of this dilemma and of the means to transcend it: (a) "Les Atheniens (dict Platon) ont pour leur part le soing de l'abondance et elegance du parler; les Lacedemoniens de la briefveté, et ceux de Crete, de la fecundité des conceptions plus que du langage: ceux-cy sont les meilleurs" (I:26, 172–73). ["The Athenians, says Plato, give their attention to fullness and elegance in speech, the Lacedaemonians to brevity, and the Cretans to fertility of thought rather than of language; the last are the best" (128).] Of the three concepts proferred Athenian *ubertas* and Lacedaemonian *brevitas*, rhetorical abundance and laconic concision, remain imperfect and are revoked in favor of Cretan fecundity. This plenitude, of things rather than words, is *copia*, which differs from *ubertas* by conforming to *brevitas*. In the *De copia* Erasmus was not advocating abundance or prolixity, but rather *breviter et copiose dicere*, that is, a concision which results from *varietas*, a capacity for variation permitting one to be brief or to have at hand the one fitting turn of phrase. *Varietas*, a plenitude or fecundity which is contained in abundance and restrained in subject matter, combines *brevitas* and *copia*. And that fecundity which Montaigne attributes to the Cretans is the capacity to say the most with the fewest words.

This theme recurs in the *Essais*. Again, in the chapter "Of the education of children," he writes: (a) "Le monde n'est que babil, et ne vis jamais homme qui ne die plustost plus que moins qu'il ne doit; toutesfois la moictié de nostre aage s'en va là" (I:26, 168). ["The world is nothing but babble, and I never saw a man who did not say rather more than less than he should. And yet half of our life is wasted on that" (124).] Babble pertains to *amplificatio*, and Montaigne's remedy in matters of education conforms to the notion of *varietas* or Erasmian *copia*: (a) "Mais que nostre disciple soit bien pourveu de choses, les parolles ne suivront que trop" (I:26, 169). ["Provided our pupil is well equipped with substance, words will follow only too readily" (125).]

In the appendix to the chapter "A consideration upon Cicero," Montaigne plays with this relation: (c) "J'honnore le plus ceux que j'honnore le moins . . . Et me presente moins à ceux à qui je me suis le plus donné" (I:40, 253). ["I honor most those to whom I show least honor; . . . And I tender myself least to those to whom I have given myself most" (186).]

It is in the chapter "On some verses of Virgil," when comparing the vigorous language of the ancients, particularly Virgil and Lucretius, to the weakness and affectation of their successors, that Montaigne best describes that litotes which, according to Gide, comes to define classical art. He accomplishes this through a series of short, antithetical sentences reminiscent of Seneca. (b) "J'ay desdain de ces menues pointes et allusions verballes qui nasquirent depuis. A ces bonnes gens, il ne falloit pas d'aigue et subtile rencontre: leur langage est tout plein et gros d'une vigueur naturelle et constante; ils sont tout epigramme, non la queuë seulement, mais la teste, l'estomac et les pieds" (III:5, 873). Etc. ["I despise those petty conceits and verbal tricks that have sprung up since. These good people needed no sharp and subtle play on words; their language is all full and copious with a natural and constant vigor. They are all epigram, not only the tail but the head, stomach, and feet" (664–65).] Montaigne continues by discussing that equation of words that forms the litotes, over which Cicero's *Brutus* attributed to Demosthenes the supreme mastery[22]: (c) "Elles signifient plus qu'elles ne disent" (III:5, 873). ["The words mean more than they say" (665).] he says in an addition to the "exemplaire de Bordeaux."

Understandably, the theme of Lucretian and Virgilian verse, which is sexual, calls out for these considerations on litotes, and Montaigne goes on to say, of Virgil's successors, (b) "Que Martial retrousse Venus à sa poste, il n'arrive pas à la faire paroistre si entiere. Celuy qui dict tout, il nous saoule et nous degouste; celuy qui craint à s'exprimer nous achemine à en penser plus qu'il n'en y a." (III:5, 880). ["Let Martial turn up Venus' skirts as high as he pleases, he will not succeed in revealing her so completely. He who says everything satiates and disgusts us; he who is afraid to express himself leads us on to think more than there is" (671).]

Montaigne applies the necessity for an art of litotes—always conceived of in terms of more and less—to his own writing as well, notably in an addition to the chapter "A consideration upon Cicero" in the "exemplaire de Bordeaux." The passage begins with his usual censure of words: (c) "Je sçay bien, quand j'oy quelqu'un qui s'arreste au langage des Essais, que j'aimeroye mieux qu'il s'en teust" (I:40, 251). ["I know well that when I hear someone dwell on the language of these essays, I would rather he said nothing" (p. 184).] Montaigne defends himself by claiming that the book could have been much longer, more prolix and abundant. "Pour en ranger davantage, je n'en entasse que les testes. Que j'y attache leur suitte, je multiplieray plusieurs fois ce volume" (251). ["In order to get more in, I pile up only the headings of subjects. Were I to add on their consequences, I would multiply this volume many times over" (185).] Whence come stories and allegations with little or no commentary, which depend upon the work of the reader. "Elles portent souvent, hors de mon propos, la semence d'une matiere plus riche et plus hardie, et sonnent à gauche un ton plus delicat, et pour moy qui n'en veux exprimer d'avantage, et pour ceux qui rencontreront mon air" (251). ["They often bear, outside of my subject, the seeds of a richer and bolder material, and sound obliquely a subtler note, both for myself, who do not wish to express anything more, and for those who get my drift" (185).] As "semence d'une matiere plus riche" ["seeds of a richer material"] the text has the value of a *semen dicendi*, a discourse at its moment of birth, which is that of *acumen*, of the pointedness in Lipsius.

On the horizon lies the risk of obscurity, "laquelle," says Montaigne, "à parler à bon escient, je hay (c) bien fort, (b) et l'eviterois si je me sçavois eviter" (III:9, 995). ["(obscurity), which, to speak in all earnest, I hate very strongly, and I would avoid it if I could avoid myself" (762).] Litotes, like subtlety, is ambivalent if it can be understood to refer to the oracular form condemned in "Of prognostications": (c) "sur tout leur [aux superstitieux] preste beau jeu le parler obscur, ambigu et fantastique du jargon prophetique, auquel leurs autheurs ne donnent aucun sens clair, afin que la posterité y en puisse appliquer de tel qu'il luy plaira." (I:11, 44). ["But what gives them an especially good chance to play is the obscure, ambiguous, and fantastic language of the prophetic jargon, to which their authors give no clear meaning, so that posterity can apply to it whatever meanings it pleases" (29).] More decidedly, the "petite subtilité ambitieuse" ["small, ambitious subtlety"], as Montaigne calls his addition to the chapter "Of vanity," is a double-edged sword: (b) "Ces exquises subtilitez ne sont propres qu'au presche. ... A quoy faire ces poinctes eslevées de la philosophie sur lesquelles aucun estre humain ne se peut rassoir ... ?" (III:9, 988–89) ["These exquisite subtleties are only fit for preaching. ... What is the use of these lofty points of philosophy on which no human being can settle ... ?" (756)] Pointedness, or subtlety, is here likened to eloquence and philosophy, becoming invalid when used for its own sake rather than as the seed for thought.

The problem posed by the too-subtle subtlety (its ambitiousness) and the too-elliptical seed (its ambiguity) is that of an excessive autonomy relative to the main body of the text. "Chaque lopin y face son corps" ["Each bit making a body in itself"] was the wish Montaigne expressed for the *sermo humilis* he loved. Pascal judged it remarkable that, in Montaigne's style, each element was detachable and could be taken as a whole, "la manière d'écrire qui se fait le plus citer" ["A manner of writing which makes itself most quotable."][23] The praise is as equivocal as that which

23. Pascal, *Pensées*, edited by L. Lafuma, 745.

elicits it: the presence, in the *Essais*, as tendencies or consequences of brevity, of detachable formulae which occasionally take the shape of the subtleties *acumina* and *semina dicendi*.

There are isolated apophthegms in Montaigne which announce the French aphorism of the seventeenth century and which, in effect, give rise to a certain misunderstanding, as evinced by the number of books which, over the centuries, have sought to reduce the *Essais* to a list of maxims. The most recent work of this kind, E. Lablénie's *Montaigne, auteur de maximes*, posits the following: "Ces maximes sont même une des caractéristiques, et sans doute la caractéristique essentielle du style de Montaigne." ["These maxims are even one of the characteristics, and, doubtless, the essential characteristic of Montaigne's style."][24] This premise authorizes him to collect seven or eight hundred maxims, representing, according to him, "sous une forme dense and frappante . . . l'essentiel de la pensée de Montaigne" ["in dense and striking form . . . the essence of Montaigne's thought."][25]

No, the maxim is certainly not the essential characteristic of Montaigne's style, but it does belong to the category of *brevitas*, which includes brevity of form. Lapidary sentences and aphoristic formulae are found in clusters from the very earliest chapters on. He employs a whole succession of them in "That to philosophize is to learn to die," a title which is itself a lapidary assertion: (a) "Il est incertain où la mort nous attende, attendons la par tout. La premeditation de la mort est premeditation de la liberté. Qui a apris à mourir, il a desapris à servir" (I:20, 87). ["It is uncertain where death awaits us; let us await it everywhere. Premeditation of death is premeditation of freedom. He who has learned how to die has unlearned how to be a slave" (60).] The desire for a balance of form manifests itself in these aphorisms which translate Seneca, going one better than him in those symmetrical formulations which recall the "pointes et saillies" ["points and sallies"] of the *Letters to Lucilius*. For example, again from the beginning of Book I, on death: (a) "Si la douleur est violente, ellse est courte; si elle est longue, elle est legiere . . . Tu ne la sentiras guiere long temps, si tu la sens trop; elle mettra fin à soy, ou à toy. . . . (c) Si tu ne la portes, elle t'emportera" (I:14, 57.) ["If the pain is violent, it is short; if it is long, it is light. . . ." (a) You will not feel it very long, if you feel it too much; it will put an end to itself, or to you. . . . (c) If you cannot bear it, it will bear you off" (p. 38).] Montaigne's playfulness approaches paranomasia: (b) "Je m'esgare, mais plustost par licence que par mesgarde" (III:9, 994) ["I go out of my way,

24. E. Lablénie, *Montaigne, auteur de maximes* (Paris: 1968), p. 13.
25. Ibid., p. 17.

but rather by license than carelessness" (761),] which can certainly be reproached in the name of an ethic of things versus words, which Montaigne elsewhere advocates. More doubtful yet is the following statement: (b) "Si j'estois du mestier, je (c) naturaliserois l'art autant comme ils artialisent la nature" (III:5, 874) ["If I were of the trade, I (c) would naturalize art as much as they artify nature" (666),] an aphorism notable not only because of its explicit formulation of *negligentia diligens* or *sprezzatura,* but also because it illustrates the degree to which Montaigne improves his maxims in the process of rereading them. The 1588 edition read: "Si j'estois du mestier, je traiteroy l'art le plus naturellement que je pourrois." ["If I were of the trade, I would treat art as naturally as I could.").] The formulation lacked vigor; symmetry, subtletly, and *sprezzatura* were missing.

Perhaps the ancient Platonic opposition between words and things is transcended, the cult of *res* being reconciled with the stoic concern for *sententia,* for the sentence. In "Of the education of children" Montaigne protests against the memorization of Ciceronian maxims: (a) "On nous les placque en la memoire toutes empennées, comme des oracles où les lettres et les syllables sont de la substance de la chose" (I:26, 152). ["They slap them into our memory with all their feathers on, like oracles in which the letters and syllables are the substance of the matter" (112).] But a little further on he concedes the value of the same Ciceronian sentences, praising their closure and autonomy: (a) "Aille devant ou apres, un'utile sentence, un beau traict est tousjours de saison" (I:26, 170). ["Before or after, a useful maxim or a fine touch is always in season" (p 126).] In the "exemplaire de Bordeaux" he goes farther: (c) "S'il n'est pas bien à ce qui va devant, ny à ce qui vient apres, il est bien en soy" (I:26, 170). ["If it does not suit what precedes or what follows, it is good in itself" (126).] It is difficult to say whether Montaigne shares this opinion or whether he simply publishes it. However, the ambiguity itself denounces the paradox which emerges in the aphorism.

The additions to the "exemplaire de Bordeaux" are clearly aphoristic. E. Lablénie writes: "leur nombre ne fait que s'accroître d'un livre à l'autre et d'une édition à l'autre des *Essais.*" ["Their number increases from one book to another and from one edition to another of the *Essais.*"][26] He finds in the maxims confirmation of Montaigne's reading method. In "Of the education of children," Montaigne suspends the moderate discussion concerning the inculcation of a distrust of authority to conclude with aphorisms that radicalize his point: (c) "Qui suit un autre, il ne suit rien. Il ne trouve rien, voire il ne cerche rien. *Non sumus sub rege; sibi quisque se vindicet.* Qu'il sache qu'il sçait, au moins" (I:26, 151). [He who follows another follows

26. Ibid.

nothing. He finds nothing; indeed he seeks nothing. *We are not under a king; let each one claim his own freedom.* Let him know that he knows, at least" (111)]. These are all borrowings from Seneca. Yet Montaigne condemned the practice of accumulation in Tacitus whom, because of this tendency, he esteemed a lesser writer than Seneca: (b) "C'est plustost un jugement que (c) deduction (b) d'Histoire; il y a plus de preceptes que de contes. Ce n'est pas un livre à lire, c'est un livre à estudier et apprendre; il est si plain de sentences qu'il y en a à tort et à droict" (III:8, 941). ["This is rather a judgment of history than a recital of it; there are more precepts than stories. It is not a book to read, it is a book to study and learn; it is so full of maxims that you find every sort, both right and wrong" (719).]

Paradoxically, aphorisms, "pointes," and witticisms affirm or assert, whereas Montaigne warns above all against this tendency of language to decree, which he denounces in the "Apology," thus providing a justification for the interrogative form of his device, (b) "Que sçay-je?" (II:12, 508) ["What do I know?"] Aphorisms, especially from the moment they are judged "bien en soy," have nothing in common with *semina dicendi*, the small subtleties of discourse in its nascent stages. They are, rather, decrees or precepts, as Montaigne points out in the case of Tacitus. In vain, he insists on the stop-and-start quality of his style: (a) "Mes conceptions et mon jugement ne marche qu'à tastons, chancelant, bronchant et chopant" (I:26, 146). [My conceptions and my judgment move only by groping, staggering, stumbling, and blundering (107).] Nonetheless, like Seneca and Lipsius, Montaigne ends up with detachable sentences which have to do with that same memory he denied implementing in his rhetorical usage. The paradox of the sentence in Montaigne is at once its appearance of moral truth and its mnemonic function.

How can one prevent such a practice? There is, doubtless, only one remedy for the immediate universality of the aphorism, and that is the particularity of the anecdote. There are two kinds of writing in the *Essais*, a short, pointed elliptical style and a long, balanced, and prolix style for personal and historical anecdotes. Can one therefore say, from one book to another, from one edition to another of the *Essais*, that the anecdotes are effaced in favor of maxims? This is not really convincing, since maxims alone do not comprise the additions to the "exemplaire de Bordeaux." In the *Essais*, the anecdotal style holds its own: there are ample narrative and parenthetical sentences, complex and rigorously structured which, as in a fable, contain as much information as possible within a single period and create suspense by concluding with a cascade of present participles.[27]

27. See Floyd Gray, *Le Style de Montaigne*, op. cit., pp. 25 and ff. for an analysis of the undulating sentence by compartments.

Must one infer, then, that Montaigne's ideal style is one which he does not employ? Does he renounce the *sermo humilis* for the *sententia* on the one hand, both as adornment and as maxim, according to Quintilian's definition, and for the anecdote on the other? Rather, writing as *semen dicendi*, a small segment awaiting its *amplificatio*, balances, with precarious equilibrium, the lapidary and the sentence which proceeds piecemeal. Hovering between maxim and anecdote, it privileges neither. For this reason the *Essais*, at once concise and sprawling, must be read "on the run."

The problematic unity of the *Essais*, that is of their long and short chapters, can in no way be resolved by referring to the *brevitas* of the style. On the contrary, *brevitas* itself remains equivocal. Nevertheless, brevity of style and the unity of the book are inseparable questions, if only because, in the end, they abut in the unity of the sentence, aphorism, or anecdote.

The totality and unity of the book or the project is a recurrent theme in the *Essais*. However, it appears late, in Book III, where Montaigne takes up the question of style, which manifests his consciousness as writer. It also appears after the fact, in the margins of the "exemplaire de Bordeaux": "Mon livre est tousjours un" ["My book is always one."][28] This imagined unity, sought after by a few contemporary critics in the fragmented 1580 edition, assumes, in their view, an architectural form. Montaigne ridicules the rhetoric of architecture:

> (a) Je ne sçay s'il en advient aux autres comme à moy; mais je ne me puis garder, quand j'oy nos architectes s'enfler de ces gros mots de pilastres, architraves, corniches, d'ouvrage Corinthien et Dorique, et semblables de leur jargon, que mon imagination ne se saisisse incontinent du palais d'Apolidon; et, par effect, je trouve que ce sont les chetives pieces de la porte de ma cuisine. [I: 51,307]

> I don't know whether it happens with others as with me; but when I hear our architects puffing themselves out with those big words like pilasters, architraves, cornices, Corinthian and Doric work, and suchlike jargon, I cannot keep my imagination from immediately seizing on the palace of Apollidon; and in reality I find these are the paltry parts of my kitchen door. [223]

The architectural model cannot provide unity for the *Essais* because it sacrifices the unity of the chapters and, more importantly, that of the sentences, for their part in the larger construction and their integration into the whole.

Montaigne, in praising *brevitas*, always links it to health, which

28. See especially III:2, 805; III:9, 964.

conforms to the notions of *sanitas* and *integritas* that Cicero attributed to Lysias in the Brutus.[29] Thus, Montaigne opposes the natural and the healthy to that which is scholastic and artistic, or artificial (III:8, 926). It goes without saying that it is in Socrates that he discovers a patron of healthy discourse: (b) "Voylà pas un plaidoyer (c) sec et sain, mais quand et quand naïf et bas" (III:12, 1054). ["Is that not a (c) sober, sane (b) plea, (c) but at the same time natural and lowly" (806).] Further on he describes Socratic discourse as composed of a (c) "hardiesse inartificielle et niaise" (III:12, 1054)[". . . unstudied and artless boldness and a childlike assurance" (807).] A number of terms reappear which previously defined the *sermo humilis* in opposition to (b) "graces . . . pointues, bouffies et enflées d'artifice" (II:12, 1037) ["charms . . sharpened, puffed out and inflated by artifice" (793).] He understands Socratic irony in its proper sense, defined as *brevitas*, litotes, or reticence, the quality of one who says less rather than more, he who is discreet when confronted with braggarts. On the one hand, therefore, there is the sickly, inflated or puffed out, and on the other Socrates, the healthy, dry and lean, in a word, the ironic, which lacks the ruse of dissimulation. Socrates is, for Montaigne, above all a model of style.

The metaphor for good style, rather than being one of architecture or construction, takes an "organic" or "living" form. The originating analogy, a *topos* since the time of Quintilian, states that words should cling to things like clothes to the body. But Montaigne invigorates this commomplace when he applies Seneca's phrase, (c) *Contextus totus virilis est,* "leur discours est un mâle tissu" (III:5, 873) ["Their whole contexture is manly" (p. 665)], to the verses of Lucretius and Virgil whose themes are sexual.

On the whole, the anatomical metaphor applies just as well to the entire book as to the sentence. Monstrous and grotesque, with additions grafted into it in all directions, this body nevertheless gathers together the *membra disjecta* into a future wholeness, like the non-preestablished structure of printing-plate. (c) "Je m'estalle entier," Montaigne exclaims, after the fact, "c'est un SKELETOS où, d'une veuë, les veines, les muscles, les tendons paroissent, chaque piece en son siege" (II:6, 379). ["I expose myself entire: my portrait is a cadaver on which the veins, the muscles, and the tendons appear at a glance, each part in its place" (274).] Each sentence has a place, not in any *a priori* construction, but in a model which itself carries the form of its future realization.

During his adolescence, Proust read a great deal of Emerson, that preacher of transcendental naturalism and promoter of the "organic principle" in literature. It is this principle, rather than any premeditated struc-

29. See Alain Michel, op. cit., p. 436.

ture, that permits the passage from the exploded fragments of *Jean Santeuil* to the disjointed style of the *Recherche*. The *Recherche*, infinitely expansive between beginning and end, centrifugal and decentered, extending, in effect, over the period from 1914 to 1918, lacked even that central panel which Montaigne once borrowed from his friend La Boétie. Is this not the message conveyed by the image of the cathedral, at once organic and architectural, forever finished and yet never completed? What is the organic principle of the *Recherche* if not the "natural artifice" of a narrator, the ingenious first person perfected in the *Contre Sainte-Beuve*, that nominal, or rather pronominal, convention, *je?*

(b)"Comme quelqu'un pourrait dire de moy que j'ay seulement faict icy un amas de fleurs estrangeres, n'y ayant fourni du mien que le filet à les lier." (III:12, 1055). ['Even so someone might say of me that I have here only made a bunch of other peoples' flowers, having furnished nothing of my own but the thread to tie them" (808).] The thread is the syntax: that first person master key that suffices to bring unity to the *Essais* and which provides the balance between *brevitas* and *amplificatio*, between the word and the book.

Translated by Carla Freccero

ANDRÉ TOURNON

Self-Interpretation in Montaigne's *Essais*

1. THE AUTHOR'S REMARKS "TO THE READER" AND THE SINGULARITIES OF THE *ESSAIS*

Let us be naive enough to take the author's dissuasive preface at its word, illogical enough to then read what follows, and obstinate enough to try to justify the attention given to such a "vain and frivolous subject." Let us not minimize the implications of the preface[1] or invoke such pretexts as the author's ironic modesty. We are left then with only one method for evaluating the author's remarks "To the reader" without neglecting the objective meaning of a work which takes up all of the problems posed by the crisis of humanism[2]: we must always remember that these writings are the expression of personal *"fantasies"* (fancies) and as such refuse the guarantee of values which usually mask the caprices of writing—"doctrine," authority, inspiration, or simply work. An immediate consequence derives from this principle, and it will affect the mode of analysis and structuralization of the text: in this book all incidental interventions, remarks and comments should not be considered accessory, treated as if they were in parenthesis or outside the dialectic of the text, as if they showed the hesitations or confirmation of Michel Eyquem. These interventions are a part of the text, and they play an essential role in its organisation. This is a truism, but its application presents several difficulties. It is customary to impose spontaneously sharp demarcations, to distinguish the separate voices in counterpoint with each assuming a part of the message in such a manner that its homogeneity is preserved in each segment. On the other hand, if the preface and its many echoes throughout the text are taken seriously we must suppose that the textual fabric is designed to organize and link together

---

1. This last position is adopted by Villey, who, dating the text from 1580, considers that it only expresses "the conception which Montaigne had at that time of his *essais*" (notice, p. 3). But see I:8 analysed further on; the beginning of III:2, written much later; and the (c) additions which repeat the idea, for example in II:6 and II:18.

2. See on this point Géralde Nakam, *Montaigne témoin de son temps*. Thesis, Paris-Sorbonne, 1980.

51

these disparate elements, or better yet that these occasional reflections are only actualizing an inherent virtuality of discourse. They reveal within the "énoncés" the contingent act of enunciation which produced them as well as the tentative judgment which is being tried out.[3]

Montaigne continually insists on this perspective. Since the time when he first started to write down his thoughts he was careful to distinguish his project from those of philosophers, moralists, and compilers whose field of work could be related to his. In the chapter "Of idleness"[4] he insistently affirms that since he has not preoccupied himself with "certain subjects" which "bridle and control" him his mind can only give birth to "chimera and fantastic monsters"—unfruitful for himself and for others. His only reason for saving such reputedly useless products is to grasp the aberrant activity of which they are evidence: "pour en contempler à mon aise l'ineptie et l'estrangeté, j'ay commencé de les mettre en rolle." ["in order to contemplate their ineptitude and strangeness at my pleasure, I have begun to put them in writing."]. Subjected to a reflective critique, the text becomes a document enabling the writer to surprise his own thought at work. Its traditional function of gathering and transmitting knowledge is reduced to a secondary role, as if it were neutralized by a sort of ἐποχή. Later, when the imminence of publication confronts him with potential readers, the same intention manifests itself in the self-portrait theme with the same reservations about the value of the ideas expressed, these "inept remarks."[5] The clearest expression of this formula comes at the beginning of the chapter "Of Books":

> Qui sera en cerche de science, si la pesche où elle se loge: il n'est rien dequoy je face moins de profession, Ce sont icy mes fantasies, par lesquelles je ne tasche point à donner à connoistre les choses, mais moy. [II:10, 407]

> Whoever is in search of knowledge, let him fish for it where it dwells; there is nothing I profess less. These are my fancies, by which I try to give knowledge not of things, but of myself. [296]

3. This aspect of the *Essais* has been perfectly defined by J. Y. Pouilloux: "All discourse in the *Essais* is presented at the same time as an element of critical discourse, a critical discourse itself of its own elements." *Lire les Essais de Montaigne* (Paris: Maspero, 1969), p. 85. See also H. H. Ehrlich, *Montaigne, La critique et le langage.* (Paris: Klincksieck, 1972). We are here concerned with applying this principle to the analysis of the text.

4. A. Eckhardt recognizes in this chapter a "primitive preface to the *Essais*" (*B.H.R.* 9 (1947), 160–63); Montaigne seems to date it from the beginning of his retirement (Since I have recently retired to my home . . .) which is confirmed by a reference to P. de Messie, read around 1572.

5. The word appears in an address "To Mme de Duras" (II:37, 783), a kind of afterword to the edition of 1580. Cf. I:26, 148. and II:8, 385.

This could be an excuse or an admission of nonchalance if, in spite of such remarks, the *Essais* conformed to didactic genre models, discourses, treatises, or "lessons." But another characteristic distinguishes the *Essais* from these forms: the peculiarities of their composition which have puzzled sixteenth-century readers as well as modern critics. Montaigne also insists upon this aspect of his work; he demands the right to proceed haphazardly. He juxtaposes this declaration with a reference to the reflective nature of his project, the faculty he employs, and the uselessness of the resulting ideas. The source is again the well known passage "Of books:"

> La science et la vérité peuvent loger chez nous sans jugement, et le jugement y peut aussi estre sans elles: voire la reconnoissance de l'ignorance est l'un des plus beaux et plus seurs tesmoignage de jugement que je trouve. Je n'ay point d'autre sergent de bande à ranger mes pieces que la fortune. A mesme que mes resveries se presentent, je les entasse; tantost elles se pressent en foule tantost elles se trainent à la file. Je veux qu'on voie mon pas naturel et ordinaire, ainsin detraqué qu'il est. Je me laisse aller comme je me trouve: aussi ne sont ce pas icy matieres qu'il ne soit pas permis d'ignorer, et d'en parler casuellement et temerairement. [409]

> Knowledge and truth can lodge in us without judgment, and judgment also without them, indeed the recognition of ignorance is one of the fairest and surest testimonies of judgment that I find. I have no other marshal but fortune to arrange my bits. As my fancies present themselves, I pile them up, now they come pressing in a crowd, now dragging single file. I want people to see my natural and ordinary pace, however off the track it is. I let myself go as I am. Besides, these are not matters of which we are forbidden to be ignorant and to speak casually and at random. [297]

These are so many challenges to scholarly rigor, to the truths it invokes, and to the rules of the *dispositio* which organize these truths into an autonomous discourse with a self-effacing scriptor who remains a simple agent in the transmission of knowledge. These observations, which are too obvious to merit further development, show us what course to take: relate the two principal singularities of the book—its reflective aim and its deliberate incoherence—so that each factor illuminates the other, and define on this basis a sort of logic of the *essai*. In short, a stratified text in which assertions and arguments are combined with comments on the text itself causing a necessary break in the organization of the discourse. The resulting irregularity is not simply a fortuitous "disorder," it is the consequence of a system in which expression and a critique of thought take precedence over the rules of rhetoric. Thus the anomalies of composition, the incoherences, and the gaps are significant and must be addressed without attenuation or reduction.

2. "J'ESCRIS DE MOY ET DE MES ESCRIS . . ."

A preliminary objection: such a mode of reading runs the risk of attributing excessive importance to these anomalies which are unevenly distributed throughout the work and often innocuous enough not to have compromised its success. Besides, we know that sixteenth-century authors more discreetly allow themselves such digressions, even in didactic treatises.[6] Let us consider those chapters of the *Essais* which reputedly conform to the usages of humanist prose writers and are not likely to disturb the reader. We will see that interferences between discourse and commentary, however discreet, alter the logical structure of these passages and denature ideas which are seemingly the most faithful to the traditions of paranetic literature. Let us take for example Chapter 14 of Book I. To show *"Que le goust des biens et des maux depend en bonne partie de l'opinion que nous en avons."*(51) [*That the taste of good and evil depends in large part on the opinion we have of them* (33)] Montaigne accumulates maxims, arguments and examples of moral resolution, but his intention, announced at the beginning, is to consider them at a distance to see if "que ce que nous appellons mal ne le soit pas de soy . . . *voyons s'il se peut maintenir*" (51) [that what we call evil is not evil in itself . . . let us see whether this can be maintained]. The conclusion suddenly reveals the hidden intention secretely at work in this passage which P. Villey calls a "philosophical essay" (50).

> Or sus, pourquoy de tant de discours, qui persuadent diversement les hommes de mespriser la mort, et de porter la douleur, n'en trouvons nous quelcun qui face pour nous? Et de tant d'especes d'imaginations, qui l'ont persuadé à autruy, que chacun n'en applique il à soy une le plus selon humeur? S'il ne peut digerer la drogue forte et abstersive, pour desraciner le mal, au moins qu'il la preigne lenitive, pour le soulager."[67]

> Well then, why, out of so many arguments which in various ways persuade men to despise death and endure pain, do we not find one that will do for us? And of all the many kinds of fancies which have persuaded others, why doesn't each man apply to himself the one that best suits his

---

6. Cf. M.M. Payne de la Garanderie, L'harmonie secrète du De asse de G. Budé. (*Bulletin de l'Ass. G. Budé,* 1968), p. 473–76., and L'architecture textuelle à la Renaissance (*Etudes seizièmistes offertes au Pr. V.L. Saulnier,* Droz, 1980), pp. 65–73.

humor? If he cannot digest the strong purgative drug to root out the trouble, at least let him take a palliative one to relieve it. [47]

We seemed to be following a demonstration but we end up with a list of calming or fortifying potions which each will choose and take according to his temperament. The final commentary accuses the most serious maxims of arbitrariness. It does not however nullify them: it is certainly Montaigne who formulated or invoked them. They are temporarily assumed and then reduced to their real function of *placebos*, and even after this final operation they subsist: "on n'eschappe pas à la philosophie," (ibid). [We do not escape philosophy (ibid).] In other words, the discourse remains intact and its status is modified only by the effect of a secondary voice. But this voice is incorporated into the text and tends to inform it surreptitiously.[7] This is sufficient to create a doubling of the entire text, as if a tracery of potential quotation marks appeared around each maxim and example and between which this imperious philosophy which "one doesn't escape" was itself caught and turned into a tool in the service of a higher lucidity. In the same vein, much further in the text, Montaigne is amused at the ingenuity his mind displays in finding advantages in his bladder ailment: "s'il persuadoit comme il presche, it me secourroit heureusement" (III,13, 1090). [If it could persuade as well as it preaches, it would help me out very happily (836).]

Elsewhere the same principle generates more unstable configurations. For example the chapter "Of moderation": the main part of this passage is composed of exhortations to conjugal temperance which, except for a few "boutades," would meet with the approval of any confessor, however intolerant of weaknesses of the flesh. But at the end of the sermon, after the expected conclusion: "Il n'est en somme aucune si juste volupté, en laquelle l'excez et l'intemperance ne nous soit reprochable" (I:30, 200). ["In short there is no sensual pleasure so just that excess and intemperence in it are not a matter of reproach" (148)], an entirely different conviction is expressed:

> Mais, *à parler en bon escient*, est-ce pas un miserable animal que l'homme? A peine est-il en son pouvoir, par sa condition naturelle, de gouter un seul plaisir entier et pur, encore se met-il en peine de le retrancher par discours: il n'est pas assez chetif, si par art et par estude il n'augmente sa misere. [Ibid]

> But to speak in good earnest, isn't man a miserable animal? Hardly is it

7. In addition to the introduction and conclusion, see p. 55: "L'intelligence qui nous a été donnée . . ." and 57: "D'avantage, cela doit nous consoler . . ." The variants mark the chapter with analogous ideas (b) 61; (c) 57, 62, 67).

in his power, by his natural condition, to taste a single pleasure pure and entire, and still he is at pains to curtail that pleasure by his reason: he is not wretched enough unless by art and study he augments his misery. [Ibid]

The full force of these opening remarks then becomes apparent: "Nous pouvons saisir la vertu de façon qu'elle en deviendra vicieuse si nous l'embrassons d'un desir trop aspre et violent . . ." (197). ["We can grasp virtue in such a way that it will become vicious if we embrace it with too sharp and violent a desire" (146).] What must then be "bridled" and "restrained"? The licit pleasures of marriage, or the abusive restrictions imposed by theologians and philosophers whose lesson Montaigne has repeated? Both without a doubt, but then it is clear that the text contains its own critique—an idea reduced to a logical paradox by the precept: "Soyez sobrement sage" ["Be soberly wise"], a "subtile consideration de la philosophie" (Ibid). ["subtle consideration of Philosophy" (Ibid).] This is not, strictly speaking, a contradiction or a dialectical progression: the antithetical assertions refer to different levels of the text. The opening and closing remarks of the discourse are aimed at the text itself. As if to alert the reader to this doubling of his language, Montaigne is careful, for once, to indicate that the central arguments are not his or not entirely his: "Les sciences qui reglent les meurs des hommes, comme la théologie et la philosophie, elles se meslent de tout. . . . Je veux donc *de leur part,* apprendre ceci aux maris." ["The branches of knowledge that regulate men's morals, like theology and philosophy, enter in everywhere. . . . So, *on behalf of theology and philosophy,* I want to teach husbands this."] Is this irony as would suggest this parenthesis from the (a) version: "car il y a grand danger qu'ils ne se perdent en ce desbordement"—which is only slightly attenuated by the (c) variant? A bit further, on the subject of conjugal relations not aimed at procreation, he peremptorily affirms: "Cela tiens je pour certain qu'il est beaucoup plus sainct de s'en abstenir" (199, n.2). We must renounce any attempt to divide the ironic from the serious and face up to the anomaly; these precepts are given as true and at the same time considered from the outside as opinions to be examined.

The gap between text and commentary, while not always forcing such continual reassessment, can confer an unusual structure to a whole chapter. This affirmation for example: "je hay entre autre vices, cruellement la cruauté, et par nature et par jugement, comme l'extreme de tous les vices" (II:11, 429). ["Among other vices, I cruelly hate cruelty, both by nature and judgment, as the extreme of all vices" (313).] Two indications can be readily drawn from this, one concerning the subject who announced this sentence (he has manifested a character trait and a conviction) and the other

concerning the object at hand (cruelty is "the most extreme of all vices.")
Montaigne constructed Chapter 11 of Book II by associating the two
interpretations: the opening remarks on the relation between natural
goodness and the different degrees of virtue proceed from one interpretation, and from the other comes a condemnation of cruel practices which is
prolonged into a meditation on the "general devoir d'humanité," which
demands respect for all living creatures. There is no logical relation between
these two discourses. The first could pass for a "long preamble" according to
P. Villey (421). We cannot conclude from this that the text is eclectic, but its
meanings are arranged on two levels and are in response to two radically
different questions: what does a condemnation of cruelty imply, and is it
because of virtue that I feel such horror for this vice?

The system becomes more complicated when Montaigne reflects on a
third party's thought. For example in the section *Of anger* he cites an
anecdote of Aulu-Gelle according to which Plutarch knew how to chastise
without becoming angry. This serves as a pretext to change the subject by
moving from a maxim on equanimity to the character of the author—"Les
escrits de Plutarque, à les bien savourer, nous le descouvrent assez" (II:31, p.
716), ["Plutarch's writings, if we savor them aright, reveal him to us well
enough"(541).] This observation he cites justifies the move from text to
author. This is also an occasion to examine rapidly the importance which
should be given to the personality of an author in evaluating his doctrine, in
other words the legitimacy of the operation being undertaken in this
context. This last point is presented as a "discours à quartier" [digression]
and rightly so because the theme of the chapter is not treated. But it is no
less pertinent because it is a factor in the organization of these pages and
unveils their complex underpining. The subject under consideration really
is anger, but also Plutarch who condemns it, as well as Montaigne and his
reading of the moral treatises of the philosopher, and the anecdote found in
Aulu-Gelle, as for him . . .

This play of mirrors breaks apart the functioning of humanist thought.
To what purpose? A final text, and a simpler one, gives us an idea. In the
chapter entitled "On the uncertainty of our judgment" Montaigne enumerates pro and con arguments on several questions of strategy and tactics.
Actually, the last lines emphasized by the title indicate what is really at
stake and quite different from the traditional conclusions about the
element of chance in battles:

> Ainsi nous avons bien accoustumé de dire avec raison que les evenemens
> et issuës despendent, notamment en la guerre, pour la pluspart, de la
> fortune, laquelle ne se veut pas renger et assujectir à nostre discours et

> prudence ... Mais, à le bien prendre, it semble que nos conseils et
> deliberations en dependent bien autant, et que la fortune engage en son
> trouble et incertitude aussi nos discours." [I:47, 286]

> Thus we are quite wont to say, with reason, that events and outcomes
> depend for the most part, especially in war, on Fortune, who will not fall
> into line and subject herself to our reason and foresight ... But if you take it
> rightly, it seems that our counsels and deliberations depend just as much
> on Fortune and that She involves our reason also in her confusion and
> uncertainty. [209]

This idea, discernable throughout the chapter in the author's insistence in
presenting only "possible discourses," engulfs the subject in the disorder
and opacity of events he seeks to understand. Thought becomes suspicious
of its own activity and suspects that its movements are as capricious as
nature's fluctuations. The philosophical enterprise of the *Essais* seems to
proceed from this idea: capture thought as it disperses into "fantasies,"
arrest its movement without disguising the contingency of its judgments,
"regulate" it without limiting its investigations, while simultaneously
exercising the functions of deliberation, decision and self-criticism of a
judge who doesn't rely on the law and knows that his competence can be
challenged. To remain faithful to this intention, the word must become
double, and deliberation must know and control its own wanderings. The
writing which records these acts must itself be articulated in such a manner
as to include in its discourse the bifurcations which alter its illusory unity
and the interstices which leave room for reflection as well as the recurring
ironic reminders about subjectivity and the "uncertainty of our judgment."

The full significance of this project does not become apparent until the
"Apology for Raymond Sebond" definitively ruins the ambitions of all
dogmatisms, undermines the dialectical apparatus which gives them a
semblance of consistency, and even disqualifies the critic's pretention to be
the final judge. It would thus be dangerous to attribute to this work the
determining cause of Montaigne's "manner." The order is probably just the
opposite; the unusual arrangements which disrupt discourse appear in his
first writings and it is at least probable that the philosophy of the *essai* grew
out of these writings by a progressive development of their meaning and an
ever more conscious exploitation of the possibilities they offered. Their
origin? The caprices of Seneca and Plutarch's *ordo neglectus*, the "discours
bigarré" [multicolored discourse] found in the "devis" [dialogues] which
sixteenth-century authors added to their stories.[8] Another more restrictive

8. On the *ordo neglectus* (or *fortuitus*), see H. Friedrich, *Montaigne* (Paris: Gallimard,
1968), pp. 364–67. On the "discours bigarré" G. Pérouse, "De Montaigne à Boccace et de Boccace
à Montaigne, contribution à l'étude de la naissance de l'essai" in *La Nouvelle française à la
Renaissance* (a collection by L. Sozzi; Slatkine, 1981), pp. 13–40.

influence were the procedures of juridical commentary known to Montaigne from his thirteen years of practice in the law courts of Bordeaux. In the writings of jurists like Alciat, who dealt with the legal tradition of the Bologna school, one finds certain charateristics of the *Essais:* commentary on several levels, returns to the author's point of view, and the affirmation, reiterated in the very form of the propositions, of the uncertainty inherent in all commentary—both that proposed by the innovator and those he refutes. This same attitude of a critic aware of the precariousness of his opinions is analogous to what the *Style de la Chambre des Enquêtes* prescribes for the jurists whose responsibility it was to review a case. He was supposed to analyse them and add commentary from the points of view of custom, Roman Law and its commentators, royal ordinance, and case histories, and at each step he was to question the legitimacy of his own conclusions[9]. In such work, complicated by the endless possibility of judging "equitably" and by the crisis which humanism caused in legal theory, Montaigne, could have found reasons, long before the *Essais*, to be wary of all doctrine. He could also have learned to suspect his own judgment and develop the techniques of commentary which allowed him to show his own hesitations in the organisation of his writings. We should not be surprised then to see him arrange into paradoxical commentaries his first chapters composed at the beginning of his writing career, long before the formulation of a theory of the *essai*[10] and before the reader had been presented with the autoportrait motif which is an imperfect representation of this theory.

3. THE PARADOX OF THE REFLECTIVE TEXT

These last indications do not simplify our task: it is easier to explain the structure of a text in terms of a preconceived plan than to proceed from the opposite direction by directly examining its fabric before inquiring about the meaning of the operations which constitute it. The case of the *Essais* is particularly thorny because its special feature—internal commentary—excludes traditional rhetorical models or distorts them. Not that Montaigne was ignorant of such models or refused to employ them, but although they inform the material of the text they do not control its arrangement. For the combination of propositions and commentary breaks

9. *Le Style* . . . was edited and commented by P. Guilhiermoz, *Enquêtes et procès* (Paris: A. Picard, 1892). The influence of juridical commentary and practices on the conception of the essai is analysed in our thesis, *Montaigne: la glose et l'essai*, Paris-Sorbonne, 1981, Ch. IV.

10. See B. Bowen, *The Age of Bluff*, (University of Illinois Press, 1972). All the structures of paradoxical commentary appear starting with the oldest dated passages *(La glose et l'essai*, Ch. II).

a rule of logic even more imperious than the prescriptions of rhetoricians. The paradox of the Liar illustrates this principle *a contrario:* Si vous dictes: "Je ments, et que vous dissiez vray, vous mentez donc" (II:12, 527). ["If you say 'I lie' and if you are speaking the truth, then you lie" (392).] This aporia, as B. Russell has shown[11], is caused by a confusion in the declaration "I lie" between two assertions of different orders, one taking the other as its object. The impasse remains in the attenuated form of a pseudocontradiction, when the proposition is split up and addressed to several locations of a supposedly coherent discourse; this kind of teaching discredits itself and "nous voyla embourbez." ["There we are stuck in the mud."] Pyrrhonians are troubled by an analogous difficulty: "quand ils disent: Je doubte, on les tient incontinent à la gorge pour leur faire avouër qu'au moins assurent et sçavent ils cela, qu'ils doubtent" (ibid). ["When they say 'I doubt,' immediately you have them by the throat to make them admit that at least they know and are sure of this fact, that they doubt."] This problem, which can only be eluded by the expedient "Que sçay-je?," is found in the paradoxical structure of the "Apology for Raymond Sebond" defense-accusation of the object designated by its title as is stated in the incorporated commentary in the form of a challenge to the reader. ("Ce dernier tour d'escrime icy. . . . c'est un coup desesperé, auquel il faut abandonner vos armes pour faire perdre à vostre adversaire les siennes." 558) ["This final fencer's trick. . . . It is a desperate stroke, in which you must abandon your weapons to make your adversary lose his." (418–19)] A similar role is played by all incidental and liminary formulas qualifying the subject under consideration as futile. "Personne n'est exempt de dire des fadaises . . . Les miennes m'eschappent aussi nonchalamment qu'elles le valent" (III:1, 790). ["No one is exempt from saying silly things . . . Mine escape me as nonchalently as they deserve" (599).] This is how the most vehement chapter of Book III is presented. The same goes for commentary used as an argument. The principle of "moderation" (all abuse is illegitimate) generates, as we have seen, two propositions which can be resumed as follows: 1) the abuse of what is authorized is illegitimate and 2) the abuse of the maxim I have just formulated is illegitimate. It is impossible to associate these two propositions in a properly constructed logical expression: they are not of the same order. However, the text deduces them from the same premises and is a continuous progression, not a series of pro and con arguments as in the case

11. Bertrand Russell, *An enquiry into meaning and truth* (London, Allen & Unwin, Ch. IV.) "I lie" is analysed thus: "there is a proposition *p* of order *n* which I announce, and *p* has falsehood of order *n*." The expression with quotation marks around it, ("I lie"), which has as its object *p*, itself constitutes a proposition *q*. of the order n + 1 and the latter is unequivocally false since I make no assertion of order *n* in pronouncing it.

of the text "A custom of the island of Cea." A synthesis is called for but cannot be arrived at, as in Escher's engravings of aberrant geometrical figures. Sometimes Montaigne openly exploits ironic possibilities in this type of proposition. Thus on the subject *Of vanity* "Il n'en est à l'aventure aucune plus expresse que d'en escrire si vainement" ["There is perhaps no more obvious vanity than to write of it so vainly."]—an apparent tautology: in fact an epistomological paradox based on the model *Encomium Moriae.*[12] As an image of its object the sentence is acceptable, but considered as a proposition it distorts the truth tables. "Je parle vainement" ["I speak vainly"] is similar in form to "I lie." The explicative structures announced by this preamble appear openly and give the chapter its singular coherence by organizing it into a series of reflections grafted on to each other. In his taste for wandering, the theme of the *essai*, Montaigne discovers a style of life removed from the norms, and in this same operation and in the text it produces he discovers in a few dispersed pages the meaning and the modes of his work as a writer.

The layered construction of the text, further complicated by the effects of additional variants, renders the *Essais* incompatible with the "ordon-nances logiciennes et Aristoteliques (II:10, 414) [("logical and Aristotelian arrangements)" (301)] which underlie humanist rhetoric. The frequent acknowledgements of disorder in the text are thus justified. But these must be interpreted as disclaimers opposed to an artificial order—"ingenieuse contexture de parolles et d'argumentations" (ibid), ["ingenious contexture of words and argumentations" (ibid)]—which serve to mask the fundamen-tal inconsistency of any discourse which conceals its own origins, presup-positions, criteria, and the precariousness of the opinions it expresses. Montaigne has the right to claim, in his "Of the art of discussion" that the mode of metalogical expression he adopts is orderly and pertinent to his subject in spite of the inevitable gaps and displacements; for "On ne faict point tort au sujet quand on le quitte pour voir du moyen de le traiter" (III:8, 926). ["We do no wrong to the subject when we leave it in order to see about the way to treat it." (706.)] More generally, thought can abandon its theme at any time to examine its own workings, question its acquired knowledge or exploit its incidental potentialities. So many disruptions of the discursive order are necessary if the mind is to "regulate itself, in other words if it is to control its operations and keep on its course. Far from being the mark of fortuitous digressions, these textual irregularities are the effect of a perhaps

---

12. The notion of epistemological paradox has been applied to Erasmus and Montaigne, notably by R. L. Colie, *Paradoxia epidemica* (Princeton University Press, 1966), with excellent results; since then the path has been followed by many critics.

unprecedented intellectual integrity. It is the integrity of a philosopher suspicious of the external trappings—dogmas and ideological postulates—provided by his own culture, and who tries to free himself from these limitations by controlling the operations of his thought from within in order to arrive at sound judgments on the world and on himself.

The reader, however, is confronted with an uneven textual surface, broken in places and wound around itself like a Moebius strip—"Nous voyla embourbez" . . . ["There we are stuck in the mud"]

4. INDICATIONS FOR READING

Rhetorical models determine the reception of messages as much if not more than their production: it is in accordance with them that the inflections, the coherence, and the aim of a discourse is perceived. In the present case, even if such models remain valid in identifying separately the phases of the argument, they always risk being inadequate for the whole text and on this account inoperable or even misleading. This danger of misunderstanding is not just related to the articulation of propositions but to their object as well. What is the subject of the chapter "Of Cato the Younger"? The man himself? The calumnies he suffered, or Montaigne's aptitude to appreciate his greatness? Or an anthology of poetic praise? We are tempted to emphasize the initial examination of conscience, corroborated by the satire against contemporaries who cannot "concevoir la splendeur de la vertu en sa pureté naifve" (I:37, 231). ["to conceive of the splendor of virtue in its native purity." (170).]

Cato seems to be introduced only to serve as an example ("comme Plutarque dict que . . ." ["as Plutarch says" (ibid).] and then disappear in a preterition. ("Mais je ne suis pas icy à mesmes pour traicter ce riche argument" ibid). ["But I am not equipped to treat this rich subject" (ibid)]. Such an interpretation would attribute to the text an introspective purpose; the evocation announced by the title would be subordinated to this aim. This is a plausible reading but incomplete, for it is not insignificant that Montaigne has chosen as an example the suicide of Cato. He is taking a stance against St. Augustine who is among those who attribute it to ambition. The idea is to see in the stoic hero "un patron que nature choisit pour montrer jusques où l'humaine vertu et fermeté pouvoit atteindre" (ibid). ["a model chosen by nature to see how far human virtue and constancy could go."] The whole chapter is organized in the manner of a phenomenological description simultaneously revealing what Montaigne discovers about himself, what Cato represents for an "ordered judgment," and the appropriate language to celebrate his "virtue and resolve."

We are given some indication of this mirror arrangement characteristic of the *essai*: the disjunction between the title, which designates the objective theme, and the unexpected preterition which explicitly abandons the theme. To paraphrase: these pages are devoted to Cato although I only mention him. Features of this type seem to allow us to outline a solution to the methodological problems posed by the *Essais*. The clearest distinction between propositions coordinated in an unusual or paradoxical fashion and those that are simply incoherent is to be found in their mode of presentation. An anomaly presented as such by the author cannot be considered initially as purely fortuitous. Even reduced to an excuse, the remark which alerts the reader indicates that the anomaly has been taken into consideration, admitted, if not expressly intended, and that it can have a meaning. For example this is the effect of the remarks addressed to the reader of the *Apology* or the comments about the disconcerting presentation of the chapter *Of vanity*.[13] In other words, if two assertions are logically incompatible and cannot be related, a third voice has only to intervene, indicating the difficulty, and coherence is restored, and meaning, explicit or implicit, becomes possible. A system constructed in such a fashion requires exegesis, makes it legitimate and guides it; the risk is always to propose an erroneous interpretation, but not to invent at the same time the problem and its solution by postulating continuity in a disparate series and ingeniously imagining secret relations between its terms.

This interpretive principle allows us to exploit what is precisely the difficulty of Montaigne's work. Since "(s)on theme se renverse en soy" (III:13, 1069) ["(his) theme turns in upon itself" (818)] and commentary and text constantly converge, the organization of chapters, for the most part, cannot be discursive. But there are numerous indications capable of orienting our reading in places where normal relations have no need to be emphasized since the author disdains such interventions when "la matière se distingue soy mesme" ["the matter makes its own divisions"] and there is no need for "parolles de liaison ou de coustume introduites pour le service des oreilles foibles et nonchalantes (III:9, 995). ["interlacing it with words, with links and seams introduced for the benefit of weak and heedless ears" (761).] The whole problem is then to locate such indications, determine exactly their meaning and implications, and to define the types of relations and disjunctions our method has identified in order to be able to recognize them in the absence of an explicit indication. In short, to derive from the

13. See on these pages "Montaigne et l'alleure poetique" *B.H.R.* 1971 pp. 155–62.

Essais rules of reading which are applicable to them and outline a system capable of integrating normal rhetorical devices, whose presence is confirmed by the arrangement of details, with nondiscursive structures of commentary, paradox, and connotative expression.

The situation is relatively clear when Montaigne points out his disgressions by explicit remarks in the original version or in the variants, (particularly revealing in this area). The major difficulty is then to distinguish pertinent indications from simple appraisals: the latter, almost always pejorative, are determined by the criteria of common rhetoric which is incompatible with the *Essais*. We learn nothing precise from these indications, unless indirectly, about the text they refer to. On the other hand, positive indications are pertinent—announcements, transitions, formulas of presentation and criticism, references to prior texts—all of these show the inflections and attitudes of the author, his presuppositions, the status and function of his arguments, and the degree of probability he accords them. These are the "énoncés séparables" defined by J. Y. Pouilloux,[14] but they can be effectively exploited only if they are related in each instance to the context in which they were written: otherwise only formal aspects will be analysed and the other features of the text will be constantly neglected—What does Montaigne *say*? What does such a chapter mean?—on the pretext that in the critical enterprise of the philosopher "the subject itself is of little importance."

Other more numerous indications for reading are less easy to discern and interpret. Simple designations, they do not elucidate their object; they simply note its importance and assign it a function in the textual framework without further clarifications. Thus at the beginning of a (b) addition to the chapter "Fortune is often met in the path of reason" Montaigne briefly notes: "Pour la fin" (I:34, 222). ["A final example" (165).] The place of the anecdote introduced by these words—two outlaws commit mutual suicide and die together in each others arms—is thus expressly chosen and set apart from the context which is a collection of examples juxtaposed in a series, but for what reason? We could conjecture that this last story, especially dramatic and edifying, confers a providential aspect to "Fortune" whose effects recorded up to this point had been attributed to caprice and chance as well as to "reason." The addition would then have the role of diverting the meaning of the collection composed in 1580 which parodied somewhat the overly pious considerations of chroniclers on these kinds of coincidences. We are not certain of this interpretation, but some interpretation, no matter how reckless, this one or another, is indispensable. An intention of Montaigne, which remains to be found, is indicated in the text.

14. *Lire les Essais de Montaigne*, op. cit., pp. 38–40 (following citation, p. 86).,

These enigmatic signs should be tabulated and analysed, but this is not the place. By way of compensation, a few remarks about one of these indications whose briefness is perplexing: a title.

5. "ET, POUR VENIR AU PROPOS DE MON THEME . . ."

Les noms de mes chapitre n'en embrassent pas tousjours la matière, souvent ils la denotent seulement par quelque marque . . . [III:9, 994]

The title of my chapters do not always embrace their matter; often they only denote it by some signs . . . [761]

By this formula, found among some other remarks about the irregularity of his writings, Montaigne seems to give his titles a double function: name the corresponding text by a simple reference point, and emphasize in these texts an aspect or a point which the "careless reader" might overlook. This second effect operates only when there is a perceptible shift between the text and the "name" it bears: instead of a resumé, a note—in other words an indication which is itself placed in a privileged position. We can appreciate the effectiveness of such a procedure by examining a chapter relatively free of the anomalies which identify the characteristic structures of the *Essais*. We will also consider the incorporated commentary which simultaneously provokes and illuminates such anomalies. *Of freedom of conscience:* a short treatise in which the author's only role is to present the facts or testimony and to evaluate them briefly; of well-known rhetorical forms: praise followed by a debate, some thoughts about Julian the Apostate sufficiently audacious to merit straightforward presentation without the detours deemed indispensable elsewhere to "bolster a vain and empty subject" or renew a "noble and well-worn" one such as the tears of Heraclitus or Democritus' laugh (I:50, 301). In short, no apparent difficulty in the form of the text. But why not have entitled it: "On the Emperor Julian, known as the Apostate"?

It would be tempting to consider the given title as misleading, and to dismiss it; its purpose would be to disguise a dangerous endorsement, the major part of the text, and Montaigne's sympathetic presentation of the virtues of philosophical paganism.[15] But such a reading is based on two indefensible postulates: 1) a simple trick with the title would succeed in covering up an explicit endorsement covering two and a half out of four

15. Without examining the problem of the title, M. Butor, in his treatment of these pages, makes them into a simple "Apology for Julian the Apostate," *Essais sur les Essais* (Paris: Gallimard, 1968), pp. 131–39).

pages, 2) a chapter entitled "Of the liberty of conscience" would not arouse suspicions. Let us imagine Montaigne naive enough to think that the censors of the Holy Office or the Sorbonne would content themselves with a perusal of the book's table of contents and would only verify passages whose titles had caught their attention. He then would have chosen as the title for an heterodox exposé the terms of the problem with which civil and religious authorities were the most preoccupied in the religious crisis of his era! If one insists on misrepresenting Montaigne as a timid author how could he be accused of such a blunder? Furthermore, in the body of the text, and thus addressed to a reader who knows its contents, we find this transitional phrase: "Et, pour venir au propos de mon theme . . ." (671). ["and to come to the subject of my discussion . . ." (569)] which introduces the question announced by the title and underlines its importance as if to reduce the preceding considerations to the level of preliminary remarks. This is enough to prevent us from neglecting the "name" which "designates by a certain mark" the subject matter of the chapter; we must now determine its exact functions.

The title hides nothing; of the two questions treated it designates the one related to current religious conflicts. Following this orientation, the opening sentences of the chapter seem to announce something entirely different than the following reprobation of the zealots of the first centuries who mutilated the writings of Tacitus and defamed Julian the Apostate. The allusion to "unjust, violent, and even foolhardy judgements" which the Catholic faction is given to "in this debate which presently divides France in a civil war," refers instead to the recent memory of the Saint Bartholemew's Day Massacre and to the intrigues of the Ligueurs who reject the edicts of 1576 and 1577, considered too favorable to the Protestants, and call for new massacres. Because of this fact, the long development on Julian the Apostate appears to be a substitute for another discourse, closer to contemporary preoccupations which remain latent. As remarkable as it is, the rehabilitation of the pagan Emperor is not what the first sentences seemed to announce and, as we will see, the meaning of the essay is discreetly oriented by this other question left in suspense.

In addition, this deviation makes clear the disjunction between the exordium and the conclusion of the chapter. This considerations on the effect of freedom of conscience, (do they attenuate or exacerbate "civil strife?"), are not in agreement with the initial maxim nor with the proposed verifications. The freedom of conscience theme proceeds from a remark on the anti-Christian policies of Julian the Apostate which is simultaneously included in the portrait of the Emperor and set apart as an "exergue" by the

above mentioned transition. Thus the whole chapter seems to be constituted by the combination of two logically independent discourses which
partially overlap: the tribute to Julian which completes the first part weighs
the "unjust and hasty" partiality of church historians and introduces the
second part which presents the different measures taken in response to the
warring sects. If we resume the two sections we obtain the following
outline with the common elements underlined:

> (a) Good intentions often lead to wrongdoing: the Christians mutilated the
> writings of Tacitus and vilified *Julian the Apostate, an exemplary prince,*
> *although hostile to Christianity*—. . . (b). . .*Julian the Apostate, exem-*
> *plary prince, but hostile to Christianity,* advocated freedom of conscience
> in order to aggravate dissention in the Church; our kings hope to attenuate
> it by the same means; what really is the case?

The unity is artificial. To assure mediation the central portion of the text is
given a double fonction of argument and then introduction. The accent
shifts from the merits of Julian to his hostility towards the Christians
which functions as a concessive proposition in the first part and an
adversative one in the second. This does not produce a sharp cleavage
between the parts but rather an optical effect, "of several reflections" in
which the meaning of the whole passage varies.

   This unstable arrangement brings out a problem. The opening remarks
about Julian (a), which are perfectly clear, project an oblique light on the
second section (b) capable of obscuring its contours. Taken by itself, section
(b) would constitute an argument acceptable to any Ligueur: the edicts of
Beaulieu and Poitiers would have as a precedent the "recipe" used by the
Apostate to "fan the flames of civil dissention" and destroy Christianity!
But taking (a) into consideration, the message is not so simple; the tribute to
Julian does not coincide with the ulterior motives discovered in his
recommendations of mutual tolerance. For the list of his favorable
qualities—chastity, justice, sobriety, vigilance, military valor, serenity in
the face of death—is not just the sum of his personal attributes but also an
outline of the ideal monarch or leader which moral and political treatises of
the era opposed to the stereotype of the "Machiavellian tyrant." This is
confirmed by the references to Scipio, Alexander and above all Epaminondas (cf II:36 and III:1). However, the motive attributed to Julian at the end of
the text bears the specific mark of the "tyrant's" politics as defined in these
same treatises: secretly encourage dissention among one's subjects to
divide their strength and dominate them more easily. In his *Discours sur les*
moyens de bien gouverner, Innocent Gentillet mentions this ruse three

times (III:15, 30 and 31) and ruefully accords it such effectiveness that he can only oppose it by the threat of divine vengeance. Because of this fact, and on account of its double function, the portrait of the great man becomes disparate. That Julian was "wicked in everything pertaining to religion" can be overlooked; this does not compromise his specifically human virtues, or less still his qualities as a prince. Besides, without approving of his pagan convictions, Montaigne does attenuate his criticism; there really was no apostasy on the part of this man who had adhered to Christianity only "in obedience to the laws." Superstitions admittedly, but at the moment of death they inspire him with a serene acceptance of his destiny for which he renders thanks to the ancestral gods.[16] On the other hand, when Julian seeks "to fan the flames of civil dissention" by laying the trap of freedom of conscience for the Christians his image changes; the irreprochable Emperor is transformed into an enemy of the common good, concerned above all with maintaining power and disguising an agitator's tactics as peaceful arbitration. Unusual behavior for *"celuy qui avoit son ame vivement tainte des discours de la philosophie, auquels il faisoit profession de regler toutes ses actions"* ["one whose soul was deeply dyed with the arguments of philosophy, by which he professed to regulate all his actions"] and an unusual apologist who records this fact without pointing out the contradiction.

We could think this was an oversight if a discreet remark did not once again bring the anomaly to our attention and allow us to interpret it. The fifteen lines which describe Julian's stratagem are explicitly given as a translation: "Il couvait, *dit Marcellinus . . .*" ["he incubated, *says Marcellinus . . .*"] and at the end "Voylà ses mots à peu pres." ["Those are very nearly his words."] It is exceptional for Montaigne to delimit his sources so clearly. When he feels the need to cite his sources he contents himself with a single formula at the beginning or the end. This case is all the more remarkable here since there are so many unrevealed "larcenies" in the surrounding text; almost the entire portrait of the Emperor is based on Ammianus Marcellinus' epilogue (*History;* 25, 4) which supplies the facts and commentary. Although he appropriates the historian's material he does make an allusion to him to confront him with others in those passages (665,

16. The addition from the (c) text p. 671 following these words is significant; the phrase "Thou hast conquered, Nazarene," whose authenticity is denied by Montaigne, would have been an admission of failure, unworthy of the hero. An almost identical version can be found in the 1580 version (p. 670, n. 1); it was supressed in 1588, undoubtedly because of Church censorship; and then reestablished and above all displaced so as to complete the evocation of Julian's death. This is evidence of a refusal to allow a falsification to persist which touched upon the decisive moment.

671) which deal with Julian's attitude towards the Christians. Concern for accuracy on a crucial point where he must substantiate his claims? Not entirely. The facts recorded by Ammianus Marcellinus and Zonaras are analysed and it is by deduction, as though we were reading *through* the text, that Julian's gentle spirit is revealed. To justify this circumspect reading Montaigne even advances that Ammianus was "well disposed towards our position" (which is very doubtful) and thus suspected of some partiality. The allegations are thus situated as though at a distance, to be deciphered and examined: the words of Ammianus, Zonaras and Eutropius not of Montaigne who quotes them in his inquiry and adds to them his own commentary. The last references on the freedom of conscience are a part of this series: the accusations they make, appearing under the signature of the historian, must be critically examined. This time the reporter refrains from any direct commentary, for the reader can judge; the surrounding context encourages him to partially impugn this deposition, just as earlier the remarks about Julian's equity were presented alongside the charge of persecution and prepared a favorable verdict. "The Emperor Julian, known as the Apostate was not a tyrant"; "our kings" in adopting a policy of tolerance were certainly not trying to aggravate conflicts; as for the effects of freedom of conscience, this is very difficult to foresee: "One could say, on the one hand . . . but on the other, one could also say . . ." this is the formula of "the uncertainty of our judgement." Everything leads us to suspect that the witness was predisposed against the accused and sought to attribute ulterior motives to him. Acquittal by virtue of a reasonable doubt.

But is it just a question of Ammianus Marcellinus' impartiality and the true intentions of the pagan Emperor? Under this problem we see another, the "theme" of the chapter, and the point where its disparate elements converge. Who decides, in the final instance, the meaning of "freedom of conscience" if not those to whom it is accorded? If "passion compels them outside the limits of reason" towards "violent, unjust, and even foolhardy judgments" they will be ready to massacre each other as soon as the "limits and constraints of the law" are lifted. It remained for the sectarians of the fourth century to confirm or belie Julian's opinion—"having surmised from the cruelty of certain Christians that there is no more fearful beast for man, than man himself." It remained for the Protestants and Catholics of the sixteenth century to determine the meaning of the measures taken by the kings of France and Navarre reduced to the role of agents of a History which dominates them—"n'ayant peu ce qu'ils vouloient, ils ont fait semblant de vouloir ce qu'ils pouvoient." ["having been unable to do what they would, they have pretended to will what they could."] Montaigne had several reasons to foresee the worst. "Il n'est point d'hostilité excellente comme la chrestienne" (II:12, 444). ["There is no hostility that excels Christian hostility" (324).] This remark will only appear later, as a footnote to the *Apology for Raymond Sebond* but here, in the first lines, he has just observed that "unjust councils" are adopted even by "good people" who follow "le meilleur et le plus sain party . . . celuy qui maintient et la religion et la police ancienne du pays." ["the best and most healthy position . . . that which maintains both the old religion and the old government of the country."] A long time before he was able to find similarly pessimistic observations and predictions in the *Mémoire touchant l'Edit de Janvier 1563* whose author is presumed to be La Boétie, according to P. Bonnefon.[17]

> Il y a tantost huit mois qu'il y a interim par toute la France et que . . . chacun suit son eglise, ses chefs et sa police ecclésiastique. Quel fruit avons-nous reconnu de cette tolerance? Tousjours les choses sont allées en empirant et le desordre a augmenté à vue d'oeil . . . Car tousjours la mesme cause des troubles qui ont été demeure et, à mon avis, augmente. C'est la diversité des religions et l'establissement de diverses eglises et contraires polices." [20–21; cf. the whole context, 16–27]

> For almost eight months there has been a truce throughout France and each follows his own church, its leaders, and governing bodies. What have been the fruits of this tolerance? Things have continued to get worse and disorder has increased before our eyes. . . . For the same cause of the troubles remains and, in my opinion, increases. It is the diversity of religions and the establishment of diverse churches and oposing hierarchies. [Translation by Matthew Senior]

In citing this observation that the edicts of tolerance might have had and still could have the opposite effect, Montaigne does not refute these

17. P. Bonnefon, "Une oeuvre inconnue de La Boétie: les mémoires sur l'édit de Janvier 1562", R.H.L.F., 1917, pp. 1–33 and 307–19. We know from Montaigne himself that La Boétie wrote the "Mémoires de nos troubles sur l'Edit de Janvier 1562." Is he talking about the same text? P. Bonnefon's arguments (pp. 1–3) just establish presumptions; G. Nakam was consulted on this question (I wish to thank her here for her contribution) and considers this hypothesis to be quite plausible. If we admit it, we can see why Montaigne did not publish the work of his friend. The entire second part, which proposes a reform in the organisation of the Church and the Catholic cult which would be acceptable to the Hugenots (?) and initiated by the King of France, was outdated since the pontifical bull of January 26, 1564 confirming the Council of Trent promulgations. As for the first part, it presented the edict of 1562 as harmful and demanded the interdiction of Protestantism in France; it could have been used by intransigent Catholics just as the Hugenots had used the *Discours de la Servitude Volontaire* in 1574. It was undoubtedly better to keep these writings unknown in "such an unpleasant season." But this was a matter which raised questions about the "freedom of conscience."

propositions, he simply considers another possibility. It remains to be seen what will happen and to judge the Christians according to their acts.

Thus the entire chapter acquires the force of a summons: this "freedom of conscience," what will each of you do with it? Here the hommage to Julian the Apostate, which was substituted for the expected consideration of the civil war, finds its raison d'être. Let us return to the beginning of the "Apology for Raymond Sebond" in the original version this time:

> Nous devrions avoir honte qu'és sectes humaines il ne fust jamais partisan, quelque difficulté et estrangeté que maintint sa doctrine, qui n'y conformast aucunement ses deportemens et sa vie: et une si divine et celeste institution ne marque les Chrestiens que par la langue. [II:12, 442]

> We ought to be ashamed that in human sects there never was a partisan, whatever difficult and strange thing his doctrine maintained, who did not to some extent conform his conduct and his life to it; and so divine and celestial a teaching as ours marks Christians only by their words. [322]

The Apostate "professed to base all of his actions" on pagan "philosophical discourses," and "in truth there is no sort of virtue of which he has not left remarkable examples." His apologia contains an example and a challenge analogous to the test he had implicitly proposed to the Christians of his times. In allowing that "each without constraint or fear follow his own religion" he left them the choice and the responsibility to act towards each other as men or wolves. The problem in the sixteenth century had not changed. And the reader is summoned to reply, in the manner of Montaigne, following the example which is presented to him; he must make an *"essai"* by which he will find out if he himself is not "unjust, violent, and foolhardy." For to recognize the obvious merits of an apostate is to admit the right to error in its extreme form—not just an heretical interpretation of a few articles of faith, but the deliberate rejection of the whole Christian creed; this is what it means to guide one's thought and judgment by the philosophical principle of freedom of conscience: to each his truth. It is all a matter of consenting to be lucid, and one is tempted to designate as an emblem for the book the dialogue between Julian and the bishop of Chalcedonia who: "osa bien l'appeller meschant traistre à Christ." ["actually dared to call him a wicked traitor to Christ."] Julian replies: "Va, miserable, pleure la perte de tes yeux. A quoy l'Evesque encore repliqua: Je rens graces à Jesus Christ de m'avoir osté la veue, pour ne voir ton visage impudent" (669). ["Go, wretched man, and weep for the loss of your eyes. To which the bishop further replied: 'I give thanks to Jesus Christ for having taken away my sight, so that I may not see your impudent face.'"] As proud as it is, the holy man's rejoinder defines rather well the perspective of those who, in the sixteenth century, quarrelled about faith from under the visors of their helmets. And to "Frater François" who later in Rome reproached him "d'avoir excusé Julien ["For having excused Julian"] (*Journal de Voyages*, Belles Lettres, p. 232) and to "avoir logé entre les meilleurs poetes de ce siecle un hérétique (ibid, and III:10, 1013) ["For having placed an heretic among the best poets of this century."] Montaigne could also have replied: "Va, misérable, pleure la perte de tes yeux." ["Go, wretched man, and weep for the loss of your eyes."]

"POUR LA FIN"

These last remarks perhaps dispel the mirage or the cybernetic nightmare which was vaguely visible on the horizon of this present study: a text which reads and comments upon itself, a meditating machine operating by itself with interlocking, superimposed circuits, connected by interferences and closed upon an ultimate loop; and a reader whose only role would be to operate the control panel and inspect its networks, a labyrinth whose road signs refer one to another, infinitely, showing no exit . . . The auto-exegesis of the *Essais* does not thus close upon itself, and neither Montaigne's reflections, nor the text with incorporated commentary which it produces are reduced to a soliloquy. For everything in this book is arranged to pose ironic or serious questions and to solicit the reader's replies and his choices, as we have just seen, "quelquefois luy ouvrant chemin, quelquefois le luy laissant ouvrir" (I:26, 150). ["Sometimes clearing the way for him, sometimes letting him clear his own way" (110).] This is also the source of difficulties and the necessity for a critical apparatus which doesn't allow one to stop on some commonplace maxim while ignoring the complex and unstable system which brings it into play. On the part of a Pyrrhonian who knows no other form of intellectual communication than that of the "conference," this is not a trap nor a gratuitous divertissement; it is a matter of provoking thought.

Translated by Matthew Senior

GÉRARD DEFAUX

Readings of Montaigne

Il n'y a pas de hors-texte.

—J. Derrida

Qu'on ne s'attende point aux choses dequoy je parle, mais à ma façon d'en parler. . . . Car nous sommes sur la maniere, non sur la matiere du dire.

—M. de Montaigne

Let us begin with what might appear as the silliest question of all, but which is in fact the most basic and unavoidable one in the field of literary criticism: are we still capable of reading Montaigne? Can we still—that is four centuries after the text of the *Essais* was written—"le suivre par espaulettes" ["follow him step by step,"] carefully noting "par où il se surmonte" et "se rehausse," "poisant les mots, les phrases, les inventions une apres l'autre" ["where he surpasses himself"] and "where he rises high,"]["weighing the words, the phrases, the inventions, one after the other"?] Or on the contrary, must we, as with Virgil, "nous oster de là" ["get away from there" (715)], lower our arms and acknowledge that the only mastery which we might claim is, in reality, that of knowing that we will never know anything for certain—including knowing that we know nothing?

I feel it is proper that the answer to that question be given in some detail. I am convinced, perhaps wrongly, that Montaigne's writing had a triple purpose: to understand others and the world around him, to understand himself, and—last, but not least—to be understood. And I am equally convinced that he strove all the more to do everything necessary to reach his goal as he was, in other respects, perfectly aware of the worrisome autonomy of language and of the inumerable traps it sets for anyone who intends to represent and transmit anything at all by means of it. I therefore believe, in principle, that a reading of Montaigne does not essentially depend on the domain—which is today privileged—of aporia, of the impossible or the undecidable.[1] But I also believe that, in order to be

1. Those who today, moreover, define reading as both a necessary yet undecidable act do nothing more than to substitute one reading—their own—for their colleagues'; they are too, generally speaking, excellent readers. Montaigne would have said: "tant de paroles pour les paroles seules" ["so many words for the sake of words alone."]

productive and to illuminate the text without repeating it, distorting it or going out of it, a reading of Montaigne must respect a certain protocol and be carried out from a precise outlook and in accordance with precise conditions; and that if this protocol of reading, these conditions and outlooks are not adopted, we will never develop anything but an apparent interpretation of Montaigne's text which will ultimately be unfaithful and fatal to its object. Hence the question which now arises, a question concerning the "operating instructions": if I declare that Montaigne's text is, in my opinion, a readable text, a text written in order to be read, but underline at the same time the fact that this "readibility" depends on certain particular rules and conditions, what do these latter consist of? What must be avoided or followed, *quid sit in lectione utile, quid contra evitandum,* in order to approach the text of the *Essais* in a truly *critical* way, i.e. in a way which can be considered both effective and pertinent to its object?

Since instruction—as Montaigne himself remarks—is much better done by opposition *contrariété* than by example, and since it is, moreover, much easier to attack the errors of others than one's own, my answer to this question will first assume a totally negative form. This answer will consist in the assertion that any reading of the *Essais,* in order to be at least *possible* if not productive, must at all cost avoid three dangers which are the cause of much straying and foundering and which are even less excusable today in our explorations not only because their existence has been manifest for some time now, but also because the experience—on the whole rather infelicitous—of certain of our predecessors might have served as a warning to us as imprudent "Cosmographers" (152). I am speaking of 1) the obsession with the referent, 2) the temptation to anthologize, 3) the confusion of the voices and levels of discourse.

I call "obsession with the referent" this preoccupation—if not exclusive, at least dangerously dominant—that Montaignian criticism, from its very beginnings, has exhibited in general, not for the text of the *Essais* as such, but for the author, the flesh and blood person who expresses himself in the text and who declares that he is portrayed there. Yet this is an author whose only reality today is quite obviously that which the text gives him, a reality which could not exist except in and through the text and which, however—with infinite patience, ingenuity, and talent—one stubbornly wishes to reconstruct as an independent entity existing not only *outside* the text but also, and in the most unexpected way, sometimes *against* it. One wishes to do this, forgetful of the obvious, given facts that the text itself provides. It is true that nearly all our "classics," from Villon to Proust, have suffered and still suffer from this so-called reconstruction. Such an exercise is tempting and even, in a sense inevitable. But no one, I feel, with the exception, perhaps, of J. J. Rousseau, has been more subjected to this approach than Montaigne, whose text, "consubstantial" (665, 509) with its author, perpetually invites the reader to extrapolate in this direction. Indeed, seldom has a text authorized to such a degree a displacement—natural, as it were—toward its author, or so clearly stated its mimetic vocation, its referential and descriptive aims. Furthermore, it even seems that Montaigne's writing, after the irreparable loss of Etienne de La Boétie, arose out an irrepressible—and eternally reborn—desire for representation, that it was in its entirety supported, structured, and finally consumed by this desire.[2] Montaigne himself forewarns us from the start, in his famous notice "To the Reader" of 1580, saying that he is himself the "matter" of his book; that he wrote it in order to reveal himself, to make himself known to his relatives and friends; that he has kept nothing hidden about himself, his "defects" or the imperfections of his "natural form" "forme naïve"; that he is only sorry that respect for social conventions, for what he calls "reverence publique" ["respect for the public"], has prevented him from depicting himself "tout entier, et tout nu" ["entire, and wholly naked."] This notice is taken up again, expanded, and commented upon page after page. Everywhere, each time he has the opportunity to do so, Montaigne expresses his intention, his desire, his obsession to "se pourtraire au vif" ["portray himself to the life"] (386, 278), to represent "les choses pures" ["things as they are"] (205,152), without "corrupting" or "debasing" their essence. Throughout the *Essais*, this desire to make language into the locus par excellence of transparence and authenticity, a locus too of some miraculously "recaptured" *recouvrée* (810, 622) presence, is cast into the same syntactic mold, enabling the same formulae, the same imperious and marked turn of phrase, to be rediscovered. We encounter in fact an astonishing permanence of desire and its expression:

(c) Je me descris sans cesse. [II:6, 378]

I am constantly describing myself. [273]

2. See on this subject the excellent remarks of T. Cave, *The Cornucopian Text: Problems of Writing in the French Renaissance* (Oxford: at the Clarendon Press, 1979), p. 302: "The *Essays* propose a series of *referents* without which writing would appear as vacuous and false; they are grounded in a desire to represent nature, reality, the self, experience. But they also repeatedly call in question the status of those referents, and thus make evident their own *vanité*."

(a) Je veux qu'on voye mon pas naturel et ordinaire, aussi detraqué qu'il est. [II:10, 409]

I want people to see my ordinary and natural pace, however off the track it is. [292]

(a) Je veux representer le progrez de mes humeurs, et qu'on voye chaque piece en sa naissance. [II:37, 758]

I want to represent the course of my humors, and I want people to see each part of its birth. [574]

(b) Je me haste de me produire et de me presenter, car je ne veux pas qu'on s'y mesconte. [II:8, 396]

I hasten to bring myself out and put myself forth: I do not want people to be mistaken about me . . . [288]

(a) Je ne veux tirer de ces escrits, sinon qu'ils me representent à vostre memoire au naturel. [II:37, 783]

I want to derive nothing from these writings, except that they represent me to your memory as I naturally am. [595]

(b) Je suis affamé de me faire connoistre. [III:5, 847]

I am hungry to make myself known. [643]

(a) Quel que je me face connoistre, pourveu que je me face connoistre tel que je suis, je fay mon effect. [II:17, 753]

Whatever I make myself known to be, provided I make myself known such as I am, I am carrying out my plan. [495]

Therefore, standing as a résumé of the whole, the famous declaration of Montaigne in his chapter "Du repentir" (III:2, 806): "Icy, nous allons conformément et tout d'un trein, mon livre et moy. Ailleurs, on peut recommender et accuser l'ouvrage à part de l'ouvrier; icy, non: qui touche l'un, touche l'autre. *Celuy qui en jugera sans le connoistre, se fera plus de tort qu'a moy* . . ." ["In this case, we go hand in hand and at the same pace, my book and I. In other cases, one may commend or blame the work apart from the workman; not so here; he who touches the one, touches the other. *He who judges it without knowing it will injure himself more than me* . . ." (611–12).] One could quite reasonably gloss this declaration, without betraying it too much, with the well-known formula: *le style, c'est l'homme*, or by this other one: *Tolle, lege, ecce homo.*

It is therefore understandable that great scholars like Donald Frame, Alexandre Micha or, even more recently, Roger Trinquet, could write the kind of books they wrote. It is also understandable that François Rigolot, who on this continent has done more than anyone else to bring our interpretation of Renaissance texts to the pure level of the signifier, devotes in this very collection of essays a study of distinctly Lacanian inspiration to an event which he feels was of major importance in Montaigne's life—i.e. the tragic loss of Etienne de La Boétie—and to the traces, the profound marks that this event has, according to him, left on the text of the *Essais*, on the very particular type of relationship which is then established between Montaigne and his activity as writer. Indeed, who could defend the view that it is possible, whenever one reads the *Essais*, to study the work "à part l'ouvrier" ["apart from the worker,"] to touch one without automatically and necessarily touching the other, after all the converging and repeated declarations that Montaigne does not cease to make on this subject? But, at the same time—a crucial distinction, indeed—who does not see that what interests F. Rigolot in his Lacanian study, contrary to his predecessors, is no longer the referent per se, i.e. Montaigne's consciousness or unconscious such as they can be reconstructed from the text and outside of it, but rather the *letter itself,* their signifier: that is, no longer Montaigne's consciousness or unconscious as they may have existed—and such as literary critics have tried to reconstitute them, more or less successfully—but Montaigne's already textualized consciousness or unconscious, mediated through writing, forever inscribed in the very tissue of the text? This is a distinction that has nothing to do with the specious *distinguos* of modern scholasticism, since it merely means that the work finally reacquires a supremacy over the man that it should never have lost; that consequently, and properly speaking, this work becomes an end for the critic—an end, and no longer a means only—and that where once prevailed the ultimately sterile obsession with the referent, there now reigns henceforth the unique, clear-sighted, and unambiguous concern for the letter.

For in the last analysis, combining as effectively as one might both ingenuity and erudition, traditional biographical criticism offers us an ever more "humanized" portrait of Montaigne, a portrait that becomes more and more "ondoyant et divers" (9) ["undulating and diverse" (5).]: the fact remains nevertheless that the leap which this form of criticism makes outside of the text leads it, methodologically speaking, into a cul-de-sac. It leads to questions which must necessarily remain unanswered, to a stubborn desire to resolve problems which are obviously not open to any solution. What kind of results indeed, can a literary criticism hope to achieve which labors questions over the precision with which Montaigne approaches reality, "grasps" and "renders" it? Its entire activity ultimately consists in wondering if, as the painter claims, the portrait truly resembles the original, if the "peinture" ["painting"] does not betray the person, if, in a word, "the Self of the *Essays*" and that of "the man who wrote them" are the same or not.[3] Postulating what is impossible and from the start locking itself in aporia, a strategy of this kind necessarily condemns its authors to the most radical impotence, to the endless repetition of the same groundless discourse. This point of view presupposes a given which, decidedly, does not allow for any verification—since it no longer exists—and which, forever gone with the wind, consequently no longer depends on the realm of being, but on the hypothetical realm—at best *vraisemblable* and *possible*—of narration and fiction. Montaigne, however, had warned us of this: he is writing his book "à peu d'hommes et à peu d'années" (982) ["for few men and for few years" (751).] He is especially writing it for those neighbors, relatives, or friends, who already know him and will be perfectly capable of judging the veracity of the testimony he leaves them, who will take pleasure "à [le] racointer [et] repratiquer en cett' image" (669) ["(in) associating and conversing with him again" (503)], who will be able, finally, to "y retrouver aucuns traits de [ses] conditions et humeurs" ["recover here some feature of (his) habits and temperament"] and thus "nourrir," by means of this book, "plus entiere et plus vifve, la connoissance qu'ils ont eu de [lui]" ("Au Lecteur"). ["keep the knowledge they have had of (him) more complete and alive" ("To the Reader").] Since the self (the referent) is no longer here today to guarantee the truth of its representation we have no choice but to give up a practice which, in any case—Montaigne reminds us of it himself in his chapter "De la vanité" ["Of vanity" (III:9)]—supposes on the reader's part "[une] particuliere science" ["things particularly known,"] a direct, intimate knowledge of the subject described. We are forced to abandon any inclination to compare the original with its copy and to fall back on the text alone, approaching it with points of view and concerns which differ from those of Montaigne's contemporaries. Since his death, there has not been, there is no longer, there will never be anything exterior to the text, any *hors-texte* a propos of the *Essais*.

In denouncing what I have called the obsession with the referent, my

3. Questions which are those, for example, of R. Sayce, *The Essays of Montaigne. A Critical Exploration* (London: Weidenfeld and Nicolson, 1972), p. 68.

aim was not to refuse thereby all legitimacy to a type of scholarly research that is based—partially or not—on biographical facts. This cannot be helped; there is no way out. Montaigne said it: *"Celuy qui jugera de mon livre sans connoistre que nous allons conformément et tout d'un trein, luy et moy, sans connoistre que qui touche l'un touche l'autre, celuy-là se fera plus de tort qu'a moy"* ["He who will judge my book without knowing that we go hand in hand and at the same pace, my book and I, without knowing that he who touches the one, touches the other, he will injure himself more than me . . ."] This warning duly taken into account, my only concern in this matter was to distinguish carefully between two modes of conceiving of and guiding this type of research: one that is traditional and seemingly doomed to failure, for it is bound, in Jacques Derrida's words, "à transgresser le texte vers autre chose que lui"[4] ["in transgressing the text, moving toward something other than it,"] in reconstructing on the outside of the textual space, and by using this space as a *means*, a purely fictional being— or, if one prefers, a being whose fictional or historical status will always be, whatever one may do, whatever precautions one may take, impossible to determine. The other mode of research, more in touch with linguistic and structuralist speculations, with recent psychoanalytical theories and with the possible application of these theories to literature, shifts its ground from the referent to the signifier, thus leading the reader back to the only "reality" which is available and analyzable today: that is, the text. The first mode, which was of course useful in its time, but which today seems to have taught us all it could, is naturally to be shunned. The second one, on the contrary, fertile in promises and in still unexplored possibilities, is naturally to be followed.

Named for lack of a better term as the "temptation to anthologize" *tentation du florilège*, an expression (as one will notice) rather limited in scope, our second danger creates what is perhaps for the interpreter an even more pernicious risk, one which is less easily skirted than the former, for the following reasons. First, because it necessarily participates in any hermeneutical enterprise, being located in the text, at its very level, at the very intersection of the page and the critic's gaze. Second, because the very specificity of the text here in question, its peculiar structure—what Montaigne himself calls its "embrouilleure" ["embroilment,"] its "alongeails" ["extensions,"] and other spirited "variations," its appearance as a ["marquetterie mal jointe" (969)] ["Ill-fitted patchwork" (736)], as a formless amalgam, as an "amas" of "pieces" and "paremens empruntez" (1055) ["a heap" of "pieces" and "borrowed ornaments" (855)], all these "mouvemens

4. J. Derrida, *De la grammatologie* (Paris: Les Editions de Minuit, 1967), p. 227.

impremeditez et fortuites" (963) ["Unstudied and unpremeditated gestures" (735)] which, being the product of ["chance" (219)] and of that
"moment's whim," dictate, according to him, the elaboration of the text. In
a word, all these well known characteristics which make of the *Essais* a text
forever in the making, a fragmented, unfinished, reflexive and open text,
bear this risk, this temptation, to its peak. Nothing is in fact more
legitimate and tempting for the literary critic confronted with a text of this
nature than to act on the authority of the disorder, negligence and
fragmentation which he believes he finds there in order to indulge in an
undue tinkering *bricolage* with the text. After all, does not our own raison
d'être—for us who are professional critics—lie precisely in explicating
texts, i.e. in rendering them more accessible and transparent, more *readable*
than they are? in accounting for the difficulties raised in their interpretation
by substituting everywhere causality for chance, clarity for obscurity, and
order for disorder; by bringing to the surface systems and structures,
intentions and reasons concealed in the profundity of the text? And, in order
to carry out successfully this project of mastery, this twofold task of
uncovering and penetration, what then is more expedient and obvious than
to devote oneself at first, impelled by Montaigne's own example—i.e.
within the limits of the most demanding critical orthodoxy—to a "pillo-
tage" ["plundering"] of the text's finest flowers, to a pious and sanctifying
gathering of the most memorable and best written maxims, with the
obvious, moral aim of compiling from these an annotated catalogue and of
thus presenting the reader (always in search of instruction) with not only
the text's "substantificque moëlle," but also the pith, essence and even
quintessence of all wisdom and happiness? And, since a first step generally
calls forth a second one, since, as it is said, the more one takes the more one
wants, what then is more necessary and logical—widening our horizons—
than to devote oneself to a thematic reading of Montaigne's *Essais*, to the
fabrication of one of those syntheses whose titles—as predictable and
repetitive as the characters in Marivaux or Balzac—are only too familiar to
us: "Montaigne and Death," "Montaigne and Religion," "Montaigne and
the Portrayal of the Self," or even—such subtle variations!—"The Conservatism," "The Stoicism," or "The Scepticism" of Montaigne? All of these
synthetic products, except for a few nuances, always inevitably end up with
the same conclusions and condemn their authors to a sterile repetition of
the same discourse. Yet, since Villey, they embody much of our critical
activity, an activity whose model (enthroned, as it were, by the considerable
success of Hugo Friedrich) mobilizes the energy of literary critics to such an

extent that the newcomers who would consider questioning it today are rare.

Aside from the reenactement of the same with the same and the rehashing *ad nauseam* of the same quotations, the same analyses and the same motifs, this method has nevertheless exhibited many other weaknesses—weaknesses which are even less excusable today for having been, for a long time now, pointed out with a critical verve, felicity and pertinence that leave very little to be desired. I am alluding here, as is undoubtedly clear, to the remarkable work of Jean Yves Pouilloux, *Lire les Essais de Montaigne* (Paris: Maspero, 1967). But a *new* discourse, a discourse which upsets and questions the idols and practice of the moment is always a discourse which is poorly received. It is obvious that Pouilloux has not been truly understood. It is clear however that those who stubbornly read the *Essais* as "un vray seminaire de belles et notables sentences" ["a true flower-bed of beautiful and notable maxims"] can only commit the errors that he denounces.[5] Thus we have a new *Odyssea malorum*, which would be worthy of Homeric heroes if it were not due, this time, to a kind of inexplicable deafness, to a refusal to listen to the voices of the text, to an unwillingness to be sensitive to its nuances and its modes of enunciation. Thinking, thanks to their method, that they are gathering up Montaigne's essential thought, such critics are most often merely collecting maxims translated and transplanted from Seneca, Cicero, Ecclesiastes or Plutarch. Proclaiming loud and clear their intention to produce a truly *critical* work, they deny themselves, from the start, the very possibility of a productive reading, whether by "ordonnant le désordre avant de l'avoir interrogé" ["bringing order to the disorder before having investigated it,"] or by searching for the "ordre profond" which is necessarily hidden under the "désordre apparent," or finally by concluding that this disorder is not disorder, but the height of art, an *artistic* disorder due to the mimetic intention of the portraitist, to this desire to be completely faithful to the object he portrays.[6] Worse yet: by privileging as they do (for reasons both esthetic and ethical, the *plaire* and *instruire* of French Classicism) certain sections of the text to the detriment of others, they actually destroy the text, carrying out a reductive operation, a denaturing—Montaigne would say a *pelotage* (433)—which is in fact unjustifiable. They throw the door open to all the manipulations of those who think, consciously or not, that

5. Pouilloux, op. cit., p. 20. The phrase is Etienne Pasquier's.
6. Ibid., p. 26 ff.

literary analysis consists in isolating fragments of the text in order to make them say, if not everything, then at least something entirely different from what they would say if they were interpreted *in vivo*, in their original context. They forget, to use François Roustang's striking expression, that "toute citation faite sans analyse conjugue immédiatement la dérision et l'obscurantisme"[7] ["any quotation made without analysis immediately involves derision and obscurantism."] Furthermore, in this atomization and rewriting, they are forgetful of the respect which they owe the text and, in particular, of the manifold difficulties enclosed within it—difficulties which it is precisely their task to try to explain and which, consequently, they have no authority to sidestep.

If a first conclusion can be drawn from these summary observations, it is certainly this paradox of a literary criticism which, on the one hand, willingly chooses as its task the "explication" of a literary text but which, on the other, seems to do everything to postpone both the time and place of this explication. In order to explain this paradox in its turn, is it not necessary to mention the fear of a *fiasco*, of a more decisive trial? These sexual connotations are in no way gratuitous, since these practices whose existence I have just recalled betray in the end the same desire to flee, the same deafness and unwillingness to encounter the text directly: since they do not approach the center of the text, i.e. the level of the signifier, but its outside, at a distance, as it were, with less of a risk to themselves. And in doing so, they totally disregard the two points—density, temporality—from which the text unfolds itself. In all, and with few exceptions, the attitude of the literary critic toward Montaigne's text strangely reminds us of the attitude of the Racinian hero. There is in him, for example, the same contradiction between doing and saying as in Titus. He seems to suffer from the same love and the same impotence. He says that he loves, he says that he wants to love, but he does not do what he says. And, ineluctably, there follows the same consequence: *invitus invitum demisit*. He gets out of it, as we have seen, either by dedicating himself body and soul to the hypothetical and always fictional reconstruction of the referent, or, as is suggested by the incontestably apodictic dimension of any "plundering" of the *Essais*, by clinging exclusively to the signified which the text carries. And in both cases the critic naturally makes the text—the mauled and mishandled text—assume the risks that he himself is unwilling to take.

In this respect, there is perhaps nothing more revealing than the monumental work by Hugo Friedrich.[8] Both its archetypal value and the

7. François Roustang, *Un Destin si funeste* (Paris: Les Editions de Minuit, 1976), p. 36–37.
8. H. Friedrich, *Montaigne*. Traduit de l'allemand par R. Rovini (Paris: Gallimard, 1968).

admiration it inspires lead me to use it here as an example. And if my present remarks do not go so far as to sound a note of discord in posterity's ringing praise, they are nonetheless intended to point out that—a fact whose evidence is rather disquieting—Friedrich's stated ambition is not in any way, *stricto sensu*, specifically literary. His critical enterprise—as he reveals it to us clearly in his foreword—essentially derives from the history of ideas. What he seeks to isolate and describe above all in Montaigne is, firstly, *a thought* in its entirety and its continuum; secondly, the importance and significance of this thought in our historical becoming. This explains the vast thematic groupings that he abstracts from the individual essays, which he never considers as the end of his analysis but as its basic material, from which he constructs his own text. This also explains the methodological bias which is an entirely natural result of his procedure: that is, to deal with individual essays in themselves—I mean in their totality—in "exceptional cases" only. The author justifies this *parti pris* in a few brief remarks, as if it needed no justification, alleging not only the inherent necessities of his project but also the unfortunate lack of an orderly and synthetic mind that Montaigne regrettably reveals in his text. Since there are only "very few" essays which constitute a "whole," since—alas!— in other respects Montaigne "ne prend jamais une vue d'ensemble de ce qu'il a déjà dit sur un sujet" ["never adopts a comprehensive view of what he has already said on a subject,"] and finally, since "aucun passage n'exprime à lui seul toute l'étendue de sa pensée sur tel ou tel" ["no passage expresses itself the full range of his thought on this or that subject,"] a critic who, like himself, essentially proposes to "distribuer la matière de Montaigne par sujets" ["divide Montaigne's themes according to subject matter,"] is, as a consequence, "*autorisé* (I underline) à regrouper les textes dispersés pour les accorder ensemble" ["*authorized* to regroup the scattered texts in order to reconcile them with each other".][9]

If this reasoning itself needs no commentary, this is not true of the principles on which it is based. It is generally a waste of time to try to put to the test the soundness of an argument: it flows naturally, as they say; it never lacks good and convincing reasons. On the contrary, time is fruitfully spent if one closely examines the validity of its premises—the chinks in the armor. For in the end nothing, except of course the requirements of his historian-of-ideas project—except too, perhaps, an inappetence, a lack of real interest in all that depends on a problematic of writing in Montaigne— *authorizes* Friedrich to say that the *Essais*, taken in themselves, form only rarely "a whole." The very arrangement of the subject in "chapters," the

9. Friedrich, op. cit., p. 9.

relative self-sufficiency *autonomie* of these chapters in the book (What Montaigne calls the lack of "continuity"), the often repeated affirmation that each of them constitutes, properly speaking, an *essay*, a testing of his judgment—all of this persuades us that, on the contrary, the essay—the "chapter"—is the only significant textual unit in Montaigne's work. And if Friedrich had had a clearer notion of the literary object, he certainly would not have attempted, to quote again J. Y. Pouilloux,[10] to "organiser le désordre des *Essais*" ["to organize the disorder of the *Essays*"]: that is, to sum up, to "regroup" reflections which are scattered in different places, to "prendre une vue d'ensemble" ["adopt a comprehensive view"] of such and such a subject, to impose, finally, on the work a treatment which its author, an avowed enemy of all systems, would never himself have conceived. Instead, he ought to have used his talent to "poser la question de ce désordre même" ["to pose the question of this very disorder."]

This is an extremely pertinent and fertile question, which will not only allow us to define a protocol of reading better suited to the nature of the text, but also to avoid without harm the third and last risk in our exploration, that danger to which I referred as the confusion of the voices and levels of discourse. By this I mean the insensitivity on the part of the critics, the lack of discernment which obscures the nuances, differences and contradictions in Montaigne's work, which transforms a subtle exercise in writing—an analysis of the self by the self through the process of *écriture*—into a treatise of practical ethics, which pushes us into a simplification and reduction of the whole, into taking each word in the text literally, forgetful of the spirit which quickens the letter. It is not enough, for example, to act on the "authority" (both word and thing should be avoided) of Montaigne's authorship, to say subsequently that all the discourses which we find in the *Essais* belong to him absolutely *(proprement)* and to the same degree, that they have the same direct and immediate relationship to him, that they are all of the same nature and perform the same function. Of course, they all are in a sense incontestably his, but certain ones are more so than others. In this respect, the capital distinction that Montaigne himself establishes at the beginning of "Of repentance" (III:2) should receive more attention from us than it has heretofore. The passage is well-known: but has it ever really been understood? To be sure, says Montaigne to us, my soul is always, as in the past, "en apprentissage et en espreuve" (805) ["in apprenticeship and on trial" (611).] If it could finally "prendre pied" ["gain a firm footing,"] "je ne m'essaierois pas, je me resoudrois" ["I would not make essays, I would make

10. Pouilloux, op. cit., p. 40–41.

decisions."] I therefore continue, as before, to write "essays." But I no longer am writing them in exactly the same way, nor for the same reasons: I am now giving them a different function. Before, if writing already constituted for me the means of portraying myself and of making myself known, it also was used by me to *form* myself. My project was therefore twofold: on the one hand, descriptive and directed toward others: on the other, normative and reflexive, turned in upon itself. Today, however, I no longer have the ambition of making myself other (better) than I am, of (as he will likewise say in II:18, in a late addition—layer (c)—to his chapter "Du démentir"[11]) "[me] dresser et composer pour m'extraire" (665) ["to fashion and compose myself to bring myself out" (504).] I am now content with *telling*, with *representing* myself, with *narrating* myself such as I momentarily am, with offering the reader "un contrerolle de divers et muables accidens et d'imaginations irresoluës et, quant il y eschet, contraires" (805) ["a record of various and changeable occurrences and of irresolute and, when it so befalls, contradictory ideas" (611).] This project of representation, of portraying the "passing," motivates me entirely from now on. It is no longer my concern to form man—to form *myself*—but to represent myself as already (and rather poorly) formed. For this reason I define my book not only in relation to others but also, and especially, in relation to itself, to this other that it has been:

(b)   Les autres forment l'homme; je le recite et en represente un particulier bien mal formé, et lequel, si j'avoy à façonner de nouveau, je ferois vrayement bien autre qu'il n'est. Meshuy c'est fait. [III:2, 804]

Others form man: I tell of him, and portray a particular one, very ill-formed, whom I should really make very different from what he is, if I had to fashion him over again. But now it is done. [610]

From this, it seems to me, there follows first of all the obligation for us readers, not to encompass in a single glance, not to place on the same level the 1580 text of the *Essais* and the text added by Montaigne after this date, whether this latter be in the form of his third book or in the form of those famous additions, "alongeails" and commentaries with which he will fill in

11. "Et quand personne ne me lira, ay-je perdu mon temps de m'estre entretenu tant d'heures oisifves à pensements si utiles et agreables? Moulant sur moy cette figure, il m'a fallu si souvent dresser et composer pour m'extraire, que le patron s'en est fermy et aucunement formé soy mesmes . . . " (665) ["And if no one reads me, have I wasted my time, entertaining myself for so many idle hours with such useful and agreeable thoughts? In modeling this figure upon myself, I have had to fashion and compose myself so often to bring myself out, that the model itself has to some extent grown firm and taken shape" (504).]

the margins of the equally famous Bordeaux edition. Secondly, there follows the necessity of our asking ourselves the signification of this intended difference, its implication and consequences.

I think that a first answer to this question consists in saying that Montaigne's voice is much more *directly* perceived by us after the publication of the *Essais* of 1580. Before this date, indeed, Montaigne's writing generally remains submissive to its models. What we call the play of intertextuality is there fully exercised. Like the good humanist he is, Montaigne cheerfully plunders his sources. And the result very often seems, at least superficially, to be a "pastissage de lieux communs" (1056) ["concoction of commonplaces" (808).] At times, to be sure, borrowing is acknowledged as such. It is the single thing on the page which introduces a rupture in the otherwise perfect continuity of the discourse. But in the majority of cases, simply dressed à la Montaigne, translated into the "vulgaire" ["vulgar tongue"] and directly "transplanté" ["transplanted,"] it confounds itself in its new "solage" ["soil"] with the few "raisons et inventions" (408) ["reasonings and inventions" (296)] of the author. This is the period when Montaigne "desrobe ses larrecins, et les desguise" (1056) ["hides (his) little thefts and disguises them" (809)], when he uses more "de l'autruy" than "du sien," when he makes "dire aux autres" ["others say"] what he himself, left to his own resources of language and sense, could not "si bien dire" (408) ["say so well' (296).] It is finally the time of apprenticeship when, by his own admission, certain of the essays that he composes "puent un peu a l'estranger" (875) ["smell a bit foreign" (667).] And it is, at that time, others—Seneca, Plutarch, Virgil, Lucretius, or Cicero—who speak to us through Montaigne: "Me veus-je armer contre la crainte de la mort? c'est aux despens de Seneca. Veus-je tirer de la consolation pour moy, ou pour un autre? Je l'emprunte de Cicero" (137–38). ["Do I want to arm myself against the fear of death? I do so at Seneca's expense. Do I want to draw consolation for myself or for another? I borrow it from Cicero" (101).]

After 1580 on the other hand—and I say this without wishing in any way to overemphasize the opposition, to make it sharper than it is—this "bookish and borrowed" self-complacency gradually yields to a greater independence of thought and writing. We are thus no longer dealing with essays which, as with the majority of those in the first two books, directly acknowledge their glosses or their parasitic and derived status.[12] Here

12. Indeed, the essays in the first two books which begin with a quotation borrowed either from poetry (Virgil, Lucretius, Homer, Ovid), or from philosophical tradition (Seneca, Epictetus, Cicero, etc.) are numerous; and their avowed ambition is to act as a modest commentary of these illustrious fragments.

Montaigne is no longer commenting on the classical authors but narrating himself. He tells us what he thinks of virtue and expediency, of glory and repentance. He describes for us, on the whole, the essentials of his existence, his tastes, his habits and pleasures, his intellectual and political convictions, his travels and his book, his time as mayor of Bordeaux, the ways in which he welcomes the ineluctable end and in which he fights within himself the advances of old age and sickness. The henceforth exclusive project of self-representation frees him to a great extent from his models and sources. This is the period—the grand period—when Montaigne makes "un miel tout sien" (152) ["a honey which is all (his)" (111)], when what he borrows from others is used by him less for initiating and sustaining his remarks than for "enhancing" (296) them; when he felt himself, whatever he might want to say, sufficiently *exercised* and *formed* not only in order to speak alone and in his own name, but also to question openly the authority of the Ancients, his illustrious predecessors, to subvert and properly deconstruct their discourse, to unveil the precarious- ness of the foundations on which they rest, the inconsistencies, manipula- tions and contradictions—and even, bluntly, the stupidities—which they propound. Hence, of course, the ringing recantation with which, to use Montaigne's own vocabulary, he "bedecks" his "traicté de la phisionomie" ["treatise on physiognomy" (III:12)]: "Fussé je mort moins allegrement avant qu'avoir veu les *Tusculanes*? J'estime que non . . . Ils s'en venteront tant qu'il leur plaira. *Tota philosoforum vita commentatio mortis est.* Mais il m'est advis que c'est bien le bout, non pourtant le but de la vie . . ." (1039, 1051) ["Should I have died less cheerfully before having read the *Tuscu- lanes*? I think not . . . They may boast about all they please. *The whole life of a philosopher is a meditation on death* [Cicero]. But it seems to me that death is indeed the end, but not therefore the goal, of life" (794, 805).] Singular Montaigne!

However necessary and fundamental it be, this distinction that we have just established between the two types of Montaigne's relationship to his discourse—distance and involvement *(engagement)*—remain too vague and general to allow for, in itself, the elaboration of a protocol of reading. It helps us, to be sure, to understand how, when one sometimes believes he is quoting Montaigne and expressing this thought, one is, in fact, only quoting Montaigne quoting the thought of Seneca or Cicero; how too Montaigne's text is, especially before 1580, a text in which Montaigne makes others speak as often as he does. But this distinction does not in my opinion become properly effective, operational, until it is doubled with consider- ations which are synchronic, i.e. considerations centered no longer on the history of the text, on its becoming, but on its depth and the perennity of its structures, on everything which, in the text—although dependent on this supremely temporal process called writing—nevertheless eludes time's mastery, originating as it does outside of time. I am speaking of this "système de commentaire" ["system of commentary,"] of this "double statut" ["two-fold status"] of Montaigne's text, of this undeniable reflexivity which constitutes it and by means of which, constantly detaching itself from its subject—from its "theme"—straying from it, leaving it "pour voir du moyen de le traicter" (III:8, 926) ["in order to see about the way to treat it" (706)], it finally takes itself for subject and theme. This mirror strategy which defines a double registre of writing is expressed by Montaigne himself in essay III:13 with these two admirable phrases: "J'escry de moy et de mes escrits comme de mes autres actions . . . mon theme se renverse en soy" (1069). ["I write of myself and my writings as of my other actions . . . my theme turns in upon itself" (818).] Jean Yves Pouilloux, definitely valuable for anything that has to do with a problematic of writing in Montaigne, possesses the special merit of having been the first to have pointed out these particularities and the proper inferences to be drawn. His conclusions have been again recently taken up most convincingly by André Tournon.[13] We no longer have the right to ignore them.

What Pouilloux and Tournon have thus essentially reminded us of is that the text of Montaigne is the locus of both an *enunciation* and a *judgment*. The enunciation is apodictic: its function and its unique raison d'être, so to speak, is the transmission of a truth. The argumentation to which it has recourse is either of a dialectical (syllogism) or rhetorical (enthymeme) nature; it naturally uses, as a starting point, a preexisting discourse, a discourse which is already constituted, canonized, viewed as an authority in its field. This discourse can be, for example, that of the philosophical tradition issuing from Antiquity (Stoicism, Epicurism, Skepticism); that of Medieval scholasticism (Aristotle, Cicero); even that of official (so to speak) humanistic knowledge of the time (History or "Cosmography," Law, Medicine, Theology). It constitutes of course Montaigne's basic material, the starting point from which his own writing will unfold. For a while, but only for a while, Montaigne adopts this discourse of the other and makes it his: he makes it his or, more precisely, he *tests* it (*il l'essaye*). This practice explains why, in Montaigne's writing, several voices make themselves heard. It allows one to understand that this plurality of voices is due less to the supposed poverty of Montaigne's invention than to his deliberate intention to put to the test the prevailing codes and the

13. In his yet unpublished Sorbonne thesis, *Montaigne: la glose et l'essai.* An important work, indeed.

knowledge they carry. This practice also allows us to uncover a first meaning in the word *essai*, a meaning of which one finds a perfect illustration in the chapter "Que philosopher c'est apprendre à mourir" ["That to philosophize is to learn to die" (I:20)] In his *Essais*, Montaigne tests the discourse of others.

Judgment defines the second level of Montaigne's writing. It naturally has the enunciation as its object. It confronts this latter, defies it, draws it into a duel, into a subtle and tense intellectual jousting, submits it to a critique in which judgment itself not only tests and strengthens itself but also reveals itself to the reader, takes shape in writing, records its activity, leaving on the page the traces of its efforts, of its failures or advances. Judgment has therefore, as Pouilloux says, an analytical function. It is through judgment, through its intervention, that these considerations, many times quoted and which Montaigne enjoys marshaling in his first two books, are to be explained: "Le jugement est un util à tous subjects, et se mesle partout. A cette cause, aux essais que j'en fay ici, j'y employe toute sorte d'occasion" (I:50, 301). ["Judgment is a tool to use on all subjects, and comes in everywhere. Therefore in the essays that I make of it here, I use every sort of occasion" (219).] Or yet again: "C'est icy purement l'essay de mes facultés naturelles, et nullement des acquises" (II:10, 407). ["This is purely the essay of my natural faculties, and not at all of the acquired ones" (296).] And: "C'est prou que mon jugement ne se defferre poinct, duquel ce sont icy les essais" (II: 17, 653). ["It is enough that my judgment is not unshod, of which these are the essays" (495).] It is through judgment too that one can explain what Pouilloux very aptly calls "le double jeu du discours des *Essais*" ["the double play of the discourse of the *Essays*,"] the transition from that first instance of writing when "les affirmations étaient accumulées en fonction d'une vérité qu'elles disaient" ["when affirmations were piled up in relation to a truth affirmed,"] to this second when "elles sont *démontées* (we would perhaps say today *déconstruites*, [deconstructed]) pour que soit découvert le mensonge qu'elles se cachent"[14] ["they are taken to pieces in order to reveal the lie which they hide to themselves."] Such is the exercise conducted with order and rigor which will become, in the third book, the "art de conferer" ["art of discussion,"] and which allows us to uncover here a second meaning in the word *essai* as used by Montaigne and as illustrated in, for example, chapter I:14 ("Que le goust des biens et des maux depend en bonne partie de l'opinion que nous en avons" ["That the taste of good and evil depends in large part on the opinion we have of them."]] or in chapter II:10 ("Des livres" ["Of books"]]: by testing (*essayant*),

14. Pouilloux, op. cit., p. 101. One should also note this other phrase, p. 105: "L'essai analyse les illusions et les impostures de toute posture."

in his *Essais,* the discourse of others, by seeing whether, as he himself says, these discourses "se peuvent maintenir" ["can be maintained,"] Montaigne tests his own judgment.

This second meaning, rather banal in itself because so direct, acquires major importance by its implications. It suddenly becomes the locus where everything is drawn and resolved, the very principle by means of which our reading will define and justify itself. In its turn, it allows us to account for two singularly modern, and complementary, characteristics of Montaigne's writing: namely, on the one hand, a studied devalorization of all that has to do, within this writing, with the "message," with the "ideological content," i.e. with the *signified;* parallel to this, on the other hand, the indubitable valorization, the promotion of all that has to do, within writing, not with the subject itself, the argument, the theme that is treated, but with the *act* of judgment, with the *intellectual performance* for which this subject, transformed into an object, becomes the pretext: and this performance, which is transcribed by its author and thus made readable, visible on the page, ineluctably brings us to the level of the *signifier.* Montaigne expresses this double characteristic in his text in different ways. First, by the statement, taken up again and again, that he always lets chance offer him his subjects, that he would willingly accept them "sur une mouche" ["on a fly,"] that all are equally productive and suitable to him. Secondly, by the repeated warnings that he cares little about the subject matter, that the possession of the truth does not prevent one from being a fool,[15] and that what counts above all for him is not so much the *substance* of the debate as its *form,* not so much the cause in itself as the *advocate* who defends it. Hence these phrases that one cannot meditate enough, and which all make clear the same disenchantment in regard to content, the same interest in form *(contenant),* in the "orderly," "wise," and "competent" way in which he expresses and uses the latter: (a) "Qu'on ne s'attende point aux choses dequoy je parle, mais à ma facon d'en parler" (II:10, 408). ["Let attention be paid not to the things of which I speak, but to the way I speak of them" (296).][16] "Ce que j'en opine, c'est aussi pour declarer la mesure de ma veuë,

15. Essay III:8, p. 928; (b) "Ce n'est pas à qui mettra dedans, mais à qui faira les plus belles courses. Autant peut faire le sot celuy qui dict vray, que celuy qui dit faux . . . Tout homme peut dire veritablement; mais dire ordonnéement, prudemment et suffisamment, peu d'hommes le peuvent." ["The question is not who will hit the ring, but who will make the best runs at it. He who speaks true can speak as foolishly as he who speaks false . . . Any man can speak truly, but to speak with order, wisely, and competently, of that few men are capable" (708).]

16. Montaigne later proposes a different version: "Qu'on ne s'attende pas aux matieres, mais à la façon que j'y donne" ["Let attention be paid not to the matter, but to the shape I give it."]

non la mesure des choses" (ibid, 410). ["And so the opinion I give is to declare the measure of my sight, not the measure of things" (298)] and especially this one, which says it all: (b) "nous sommes sur la maniere, non sur la matiere du dire" (III:8, 928). ["We are concerned with the manner, not the matter, of speaking" (708).] This "matiere du dire" matters little, indeed, since it is, at the most, only an opportunity to exercise his judgment, to put this latter to work in and by means of writing; since too, for Montaigne, it is ultimately this work and its written trace which alone are truly essential; since, finally, as Tournon very aptly points out, Montaigne's discourse never principally aims to illustrate—or render illustrious—the remarks chosen by chance, but "de manifester et de mettre à l'épreuve l'attitude de celui qui le tient".[17] ["but to show forth and put to the test the attitude of the speaker."]

Hence our question, and our conclusion: why not listen to Montaigne? Why not read him, why not define our protocol of reading on the basis of the coherent indices which his text gives us? Let us first be careful, taking advantage of the experience accumulated by our predecessors, not to yield unthinkingly to the call of the referent. We are not here studying a text in order to go outside of it, but in order to remain within. As Jules Brody says elsewhere, in one of his philological readings: "The man is dead, only his words endure." Let us accept this obvious fact, that the text is the only reality which we possess and that it is the text, and not the author, which must marshal our energies. Let us then understand, once this first step is taken, that Montaigne's text is a reflexive text, a text ruled and structured by a system of commentary, a text of many voices and levels; that Montaigne is making use of a subject matter which is common; that he makes this matter into a means for an end; that this proposed end is both this subject matter and his judgment; and that it is within this twofold test (essai), within this confrontation between an intelligence and an object-text, within the way in which this intelligence assimilates, masters and speaks the text, that Montaigne's interest in the Essais resides. Let us not therefore ascribe to him a "message" which, more often than not, does not belong to him, a message that he keeps at a distance, that he assumes only for the length of an essay in order to see "whether it can be maintained." Montaigne affirms absolutely nothing: except, of course, that any affirmation conceals its portion of inconsistencies and illusions; except that it is in the end impossible to affirm anything. Like ours, his project is essentially *critical*. It consists of examining, of representing, and of criticizing himself in this very activity: a double victory for judgment, over the text and over the self. And

17. A. Tournon, op. cit., p. 8.

whatever has been said, his text is in no way the locus of any ideological coherence; it is, on the contrary, the locus of the liquidation of all ideologies. What makes itself heard, its "message," is not the successive adoption of a group of philosophical systems—the grand and inevitable trilogy of Stoicism, Skepticism, and Naturalism—but the mind's resistance to any form of indoctrination, its ability to question legitimately the authority of any discourse, including its own.

The referent and signified now being assigned to their secondary role there remains of course the signifier, and not because the current fashion says so, but because such is in fact the mood of the text. This latter will be studied in its natural context, that is, the *essai*. Because, truly, it is the *essai*, not the book, or the paragraph—this recent invention—which constitutes the only textual unit worthy of the name. In my opinion, therefore, only a reading which begins by taking each of the essays individually for its object and adheres to a synthesis, a regrouping and a classification of its observations only afterwards will be legitimate, pertinent, and possible. Finally, we are convinced that, in our profession, we can never read too often the texts that we propose to analyze. Not because we too worship exclusively the signifier, but because experience has taught us that, in a text—and especially in the one which is of concern to us here—the signified results from the play of the signifier, and that he who wishes to attain the first, and not simply a construct of his own, must first closely examine the second. We believe, in accordance with W. Iser, that "the text only takes on life when it is realized," that only "the convergence of text and reader brings the literary work into existence."[18] This is why it seemed useful to us to bring together, in relation to Montaigne's text, several studies whose common concern would be reading, that elementary and refreshing act about which one theorizes so much today that we have come to forget that it too can be practiced.

Translated by John A. Gallucci

18. W. Iser, "The Reading Process: A Phenomenological Approach," in *The Implied Reader: Patterns of Communication in Prose Fiction from Bunyan to Beckett* (Baltimore: The Johns Hopkins University Press, 1974).

Readings in Montaigne

ler si doucement & d'vne façon si molle & si aisée,que ie ne
sens guiere autre action si plaisante, que celle-la estoit. Quãd
ie vins à reuiure & à reprendre mes forces,

Vt tandem sensus conualuere mei,

qui fut deux ou trois heures apres,ie me sêty tout d'vn train
r'engager aux douleurs, ayant les membres tous moulus &
froissez de ma cheute, & en fus si mal deux ou trois nuits a-
pres,que i'en cuiday remourir encore vn coup, mais d'vne
mort plus visue,& me sẽs encore de la secousse de cette frois-
sure. Ie ne veux pas oublier cecy, que la derniere chose en
quoy ie me peus remettre, ce fut la souuenance de cet accident,& me fis redire plusieurs fois, ou i'aloy, d'où ie venoy,
à quelle heure cela m'estoit aduenu,auãt que de le pouuoir
conceuoir. Quant à la façon de ma cheute on me la cachoit,
en faueur de celuy, qui en auoit esté cause, & m'en forgeoit
on d'autres.Mais long temps apres & le lendemain, quãd ma
memoire vint à s'entr'ouurir, & me representer l'estat, où ie
m'estoy trouué en l'instant, que i'auoy aperçeu ce cheual
fondant sur moy (car ie l'auoy veu à mes talons,& me tins
pour mort;mais ce pensement auoit esté si soudain, que la
peur n'eut pas loisir des'y engẽdrer) il me sembla que c'estoit
vn esclair qui me frapoit l'ame de secousse, & que ie reuenoy
de l'autre monde.Ce conte d'vn euenement si legier,est assez
vain,n'estoit l'instruction que i'en ay tirée pour moy:car à la
verité pour s'apriuoiser à la mort, ie trouue qu'il n'y à que de
s'en auoisiner. Or,comme dict Pline, chacũ est à soy-mesmes
vne tres bonne discipline,pourueu qu'il ait la suffisance de
s'espier de pres.Ce n'est pas icy ma doctrine, c'est mon estude,& n'est pas la leçon d'autruy,c'est la mienne.

EDWIN M. DUVAL

Lessons of the New World: Design and Meaning in Montaigne's "Des Cannibales" (I:31) and "Des coches" (III:6)

> Ce grand monde, que les uns multiplient encore comme especes soubs un genre, c'est le miroüer où il nous faut regarder pour nous connoistre de bon biais. Somme, je veux que ce soit le livre de mon escholier. Tant d'humeurs, de sectes, de jugemens, d'opinions, de loix et de coustumes nous apprennent à juger sainement des nostres, et apprennent nostre jugement à reconnoistre son imperfection et sa naturelle foiblesse: qui n'est pas un legier apprentissage.
> [I:26, 157–58]*

In his two famous chapters on the New World, Montaigne has quite properly been shown to be a pioneer of "cultural relativism" who was able to break out of a monolithic, self-centered view of the world to consider a foreign culture on its own terms, and to judge his own culture from the point of view of another. In "Des coches" he has been shown to be a great innovator in literary form as well, who was able to rebel against all the accepted norms of logical composition and yet to inform his essay with an almost mysterious sense of coherence and unity. But between these two approaches to the New World chapters something rather crucial is generally overlooked. Conceptual content and formal structure conspire in these chapters to create an over-all *design*—an almost architectural ordering of corresponding, complementary, or contradictory statements and passages—that transcends both form and content to produce a whole far greater than the sum of its parts, and a meaning far more probing than the one spelled out by the words on the printed page.[1]

---

*This great world, which some multiply further as being only a species under one genus, is the mirror in which we must look at ourselves to recognize ourselves from the proper angle. In short, I want it to be the book of my student. So many humors, sects, judgments, opinions, laws, and customs teach us to judge sanely of our own, and teach our judgment to recognize its own imperfection and natural weakness, which is no small lesson. [116]

1. Among recent attempts to deal directly with the relation between structure and meaning in these chapters, the most successful are the following: for "Des Cannibales"—Guy Mermier, "L'Essai *Des Cannibales* de Montaigne," *Bulletin de la Société des Amis de Montaigne*, V, 7–8 (1973), 27–38; and Lawrence D. Kritzman, *Destruction/Découverte: Le fonctionnement de la rhétorique dans les Essais de Montaigne*, French Forum Monographs, 21

"Des Cannibales" appears on the level of its explicit statements to be a paradoxical apology of the most savage inhabitants of the New World, and a corresponding condemnation of the supposedly enlightened Christians of the Old World. But in attempting to present the Cannibals of Brazil in a more sympathetic light than contemporary Europeans are wont to view them, Montaigne successively adopts five very different perspectives on the "barbarism" of this strange new culture. The first, prepared by the introductory example of Pyrrhus and the Roman army, strips from the words "barbare" and "barbarie" all of their usual negative connotations, defining them narrowly to mean nothing more than that to which we are unaccustomed: "Or, je trouve . . . qu'il n'y a rien de *barbare* et de *sauvage* en cette nation . . . sinon que chacun appelle *barbarie* ce qui n'est pas de son usage" (205). ["Now . . . I think there is nothing barbarous and savage in that nation . . . except that each man calls barbarism whatever is not his own practice" (152.]² The Cannibals are thus "barbarians" only in the literal sense that they are different from us; not in the sense that they are actually barbarous or savage.

A second perspective contradicts the first somewhat by restoring to the word "barbare" the previously excluded meaning of "sauvage," but it remains faithful to the spirit of the first by redefining this kindred word in a similarly positive way to mean nothing worse than "living in a state of nature:" "Ils sont *sauvages*, de mesmes que nous appellons sauvages les fruicts que nature, de soy et de son progrez ordinaire, a produicts" (205). ["Those people are wild *(sauvages)*, just as we call wild the fruits that Nature has produced by herself and in her normal course" (152.] Here the Cannibals are no longer seen simply to be different from Europeans, but actually to be superior to Europeans in that they have remained true to an original state of purity, while we have corrupted nature—and our own sensibilities—by our artifice and ingenuity: "Ces nations me semblent

---

(Lexington, Kentucky: French Forum, 1980), pp. 79–87; for "Des coches"—René Etiemble, "Sens et structure dans un essai de Montaigne," *Cahiers de l'Association Internationale des Etudes Françaises*, 14 (1962), 263–74; and Marcel Gutwirth, *"Des Coches*, ou la structuration d'une absence," *L'Esprit Créateur*, 15 (1975), 8–20.

2. Italics in all quotations are added for emphasis.

Since my remarks here deal strictly with the *original* versions of the two essays as they were first conceived and published, I have restored all quotations to their primitive form, indicating all modifications in the Villey and Frame texts by means of asterisks. Texts of the original editions have been verified in the following modern facsimiles; for "Des Cannibales," *Essais. Reproduction photographique de l'édition originale de 1580*, ed. Daniel Martin, 2 vols. (Geneva: Slatkine and Paris: Champion, 1976); for "Des coches," *Reproduction en phototypie de l'exemplaire avec notes manuscrites marginales des Essais de Montaigne appartenant à la ville de Bordeaux*, ed. Fortunat Strowski, 3 vols. (Paris: Hachette, 1912).

donq ainsi *barbares*, pour avoir receu fort peu de façon de l'esprit humain, et estre encore fort voisines de leur naifveté (*naïf* < *natif* = "innate," "natural") originelle. Les loix naturelles leur commandent encores, fort peu abastardies par les nostres" (206). ["These nations, then, seem to me barbarous in this sense, that they have been fashioned very little by the human mind, and are still very close to their original naturalness. The laws of nature still rule them, very little corrupted by ours" (153).]

A third perspective goes even further in restoring to the word *"barbare"* the negative associations that usually accompany it. Moreover, it concedes that those negative connotations may indeed be applied to the Brazilians after all, inasmuch as they are eaters of human flesh. Montaigne nevertheless mitigates this negative aspect of his subject by adducing classical wisdom and precedent for cannibalism, and boldly defends their anthropophagy as being less abominable by far than the more barbarous cruelty of both the Portuguese conquerors in the New World and the warring French Christians at home. Even if the Brazilians are barbarous in absolute terms, then, they cannot be considered to be barbarous by comparison with us: "Je ne suis pas marry que nous remerquons l'horreur *barbaresque* qu'il y a en une telle action, mais ouy bien dequoy, jugeans bien de leurs fautes, nous soyons si aveuglez aux nostres. . . . Nous les pouvons donq bien appeller *barbares*, eu esgard aux regles de la raison, mais non pas eu esgard à nous, qui les surpassons en toute sorte de *barbarie*" (209–10). ["I am not sorry that we notice the barbarous horror of such acts, but I am heartily sorry that, judging their faults rightly, we should be so blind to our own. . . . So we may well call these people barbarians, in respect to the rules of reason, but not in respect to ourselves, who surpass them in every kind of barbarity" (155–56).]

A fourth perspective goes one step further to extend the newly restored negative connotations of "barbare" back to the related word "sauvage," but contradicts an earlier statement by arguing that the Cannibals cannot accurately be described as "sauvages" after all. This is in fact the point of the long discussion of the Brazilians' "vaillance contre les ennemis" (208) ["valor against the enemy" (154)], in which their stoic virtue is shown to be superior to ours, and which concludes wryly: "Sans mentir, au pris de nous, voilà des hommes bien *sauvages*; car, ou il faut qu'ils le soyent bien à bon escient, ou que nous le soyons: *car* il y a une merveilleuse distance entre leur *constance* et la nostre" (212). ["Truly here are real savages by our standards; for either they must be thoroughly so, or we must be; *for* there is an amazing distance between their *constancy* and ours" (158).]

From the fifth and final perspective the Cannibals are said not to be "barbares" any more than they are "sauvages" because their songs of love and war are as refined as any of our own. In his commentary on an example of an American war song Montaigne says that it is an "invention qui ne sent *nullement* la *barbarie*" (212) ["an idea (= conceit) that certainly does not smack of barbarity" (158)]; and of a love song he declares: "Or j'ay assez de commerce avec la poësie pour juger cecy, que non seulement il n'y a rien de *barbarie* en cette imagination, mais qu'elle est tout à fait Anacreontique" (213). ["Now I am familiar enough with poetry to be a judge of this: not only is there nothing barbarous in this fancy, but it is altogether Anacreontic" (158).]

The five perspectives from which Montaigne views and attempts to judge the Cannibals of America may be summarized in the following way:

1. The Cannibals are indeed *"barbares,"* but only in so far as *"barbare"* refers to customs which are *different* from our own.

2. The Cannibals are indeed *"sauvages,"* but only in so far as *"sauvage"* means *natural,* in contrast to our artificiality.

3. The Cannibals are indeed *"barbares"* in as much as their anthropophagy is truly *barbarous,* but they are less cruel than civilized Europeans.

4. The Cannibals are *not "sauvages,"* because they are so much more *valiant* in war than we are.

5. The Cannibals are *not "barbares,"* because their poetry is every bit as *artistic* as ours is.

What this reduction allows us to see is not only that Montaigne's perspective on the Cannibals shifts markedly over the course of the chapter, but that corresponding perspectives in the first and second halves of the apology seem to negate each other according to a deliberate pattern of contradictions: perspective 1 concedes that the Cannibals are "barbares," while perspective 5 denies that they are "barbares;" perspective 2 concedes that the Cannibals are "sauvages" while perspective 4 denies that they are "sauvages." At the center of this pattern is lodged the famous comparison between New World virtue and Old World cruelty, in which the latter is roundly condemned for its greater barbarity. A peculiar symmetry in Montaigne's ostensibly meandering argument thus serves to highlight a crucial and literally central polemic against the cruelty of warring Christians at home.[3]

3. I do not wish to suggest of course that "Des Cannibales" is at all symmetrical in the usual sense that corresponding parts of the chapter deal with corresponding topics, themes or images. The "symmetry" of the chapter resides solely in the shifting *definitions* on which the argument is based, and consequently in the *line of reasoning* itself.

More important than the static symmetry that can be observed retrospectively from the end of the chapter, however, is the dynamic process of its unfolding—the gradual but radical shift in perspective over the course of the essay that in turn produces strange contortions and inconsistencies in its argument. The chapter begins with an attempt to valorize the words "barbare" and "sauvage" *positively*, in order to defend the Cannibals through the very epithets by which they are customarily condemned. As the argument proceeds, however, the more common *negative* meanings are gradually restored to these words until at the conclusion of the chapter they mean precisely what a breech-wearing European might have assumed before Montaigne undertook to convince him otherwise. Having first argued that the Cannibals are good because they are "barbares" and "sauvages" (these being positive qualities), then, Montaigne must conclude that the Cannibals are good because they are *not* "sauvages" and "barbares" (these being negative qualities)!

Montaigne's argument will appear more curious still when we realize that the gradual transvalorization of the terms "barbare" and "sauvage" is paralleled by a corollary and no less astonishing shift in the traditional opposition between Art and Nature. In the important "fruicts sauvages" analogy developed from within perspective 2, Montaigne explicitly alludes to the Art/Nature dichotomy in order to proclaim the categorical superiority of Nature over Art, and of "les loix naturelles" over "les nostres:" "Ce n'est pas raison que l'art gaigne le point d'honneur sur nostre grande et puissante mere nature" (205–6). ["It is not reasonable that art should win the place of honor over our great and powerful mother Nature" (152).] In this part of the essay the Cannibals are situated squarely in the domain of *Nature*, and their "naifveté" is pointedly contrasted with the *Art* of European civilization which is condemned as "nostre *artifice*" and "nos *inventions*" (205–6 [152]). At the end of the chapter, however, Montaigne seems to contradict himself by arguing from the opposite point of view: he now praises the very nonbarbaric *"invention"* of the prisoner's defiant war song, and the admirable *"suffisance"* of the love song (212–13 [158]).[4] Lest

4. "Invention" is used here in a modified rhetorical sense to mean a felicitous product of *inventio*—that is, a "conceit," or *"trouvaille."* The word "suffisance" (= "ability," "skill") is frequently associated with "art" and the "arts" in sixteenth-century writing. See Edmond Huguet, *Dictionnaire de la langue française du XVIe siècle*, 7 vols. (Paris: Champion and Didier, 1925–67), VII, 111; and Pierre Villey, *Lexique de la langue des Essais de Montaigne et index des noms propres* (1933; rpt. New York: Burt Franklin, 1973), pp. 637–38. This association is best illustrated by Montaigne himself at the beginning of "De l'amitié:" "un peintre que j'ay . . . choisit le plus *•noble•* endroit et milieu de chaque paroy, pour y loger un tableau élaboré de toute sa *suffisance*. . . . Ma *suffisance* ne va pas si avant que d'oser entreprendre un tableau riche, poly et formé selon l'*art*." (I:28, 183) ["a painter I employ . . . chooses the most noble spot, the

we miss the hint, he compares the latter to the work of the most manneristic Greek poet known to the late sixteenth century, Anacreon. It is clearly *Art*, not Nature, that now serves as the basis for Montaigne's apology. As if to sanction this shift the words of the love song itself contradict Montaigne's earlier assertion that human art is powerless to imitate Nature, or even to "representer le nid du moindre oyselet, sa contexture, sa beauté" (206). ["reproduc(e) the nest of the tiniest little bird, its contexture, its beauty" (152).] The song not only assumes for Art the very powers that had been denied to it before, but describes even Nature's works in terms of artifice as well: "Couleuvre, arreste toy . . . afin que ma soeur tire sur le patron de ta peinture la façon et l'ouvrage d'un riche cordon" (213). ["Adder, stay . . . that from the pattern of your coloring my sister may draw the fashion and the workmanship of a rich girdle" (158).] Over the course of the essay the Cannibals appear to have migrated from one pole to the other of the Art/Nature dichotomy.[5]

Yet another indication of the shift from Nature to Art in "Des Cannibales" is to be found in two similar digressions that immediately precede and follow the main body of the chapter. Before launching into his description of Cannibal society Montaigne introduces his informant as an "homme simple et grossier, qui est une condition propre à rendre veritable tesmoignage: car les fines gens remarquent bien plus curieusement et plus de choses, mais ils les glosent" (205). ["simple, crude fellow—a character fit to bear true witness; for clever people observe more things and more

---

middle of each wall, to put a picture labored over with all his skill. . . . My ability does not go far enough for me to dare to undertake a rich, polished picture, formed according to art." (I:28, 135)]

5. It has been shown that Art and Nature are not always completely antithetical in the *Essais*. See Alexandre Micha, *Le singulier Montaigne* (Paris: Nizet, 1964), pp. 121–33; and Yvonne Bellenger, " 'Nature' et 'Naturel' dans quatre chapitres des *Essais*," *Bulletin de la Société des Amis de Montaigne*, V, 25–26 (1978), 37–49. A much later addition to "Du pedantisme" is an especially relevant case in point: "Nature, pour montrer qu'il n'y a rien de sauvage en ce qui est conduit par elle, faict naistre és nations moins cultivées par art, des productions d'esprit souvent, qui luittent les plus artistes productions." (I:25, 137) ["Nature, to show that there is nothing barbarous in what is under her guidance, often brings forth, in the nations least cultivated by art, productions of the mind that vie with the most artistic productions" (I:25, 100).] The Cannibals' songs might indeed be considered to be examples of perfectly "natural" art, just as Anacreon himself was often considered in the sixteenth century to be "natural" by comparison with the more elevated Pindar. There is in fact a good deal of word play (art/artifice) involved in the shift discussed above. It would therefore be incorrect to perceive an *absolute* incongruity in a society which "se peut maintenir avec si peu d'artifice et de soudeure humaine" (206) ["could be maintained with so little artifice and human solder" (153)] and at the same time produces Anacreontic art. Nevertheless, the essay is clearly composed in such a way as to *suggest* a contradiction here, and what we might know from other contexts about Montaigne's "ideas" concerning art and nature not only is irrelevant, but actually interferes with a proper perception of Montaigne's design *in this essay*.

curiously, but they interpret them" (151–52).] Now the "simple" eyewitness of course resembles in his unassuming naturalness the "naifveté" of the Brazilian "sauvage" who freely obeys the uncorrupted laws of Nature. And conversely, the "fines gens" of this passage clearly resemble the corrupted Europeans who have abandoned Nature for Art.[6] An unmistakable analogy thus places Montaigne's witness along with the Cannibals themselves in the domain of the natural:

simple/fin = Nature/Art

At the end of the chapter, however, we meet a second intermediary who is judged in a very different manner. During a first-hand interview with an American "Capitaine" at Rouen, Montaigne is unable to learn as much as he would like because of the obtuseness of his interpreter: "je parlay à l'un d'eux fort long temps; mais j'avois un truchement qui me suyvoit si mal, et qui estoit si empesché à recevoir mes imaginations par sa bestise, que je n'en peus tirer guiere de plaisir" (214). ["I had a very long talk with one of them; but I had an interpreter who followed my meaning so badly, and who was so hindered by his stupidity in taking in my ideas, that I could get hardly any satisfaction from the man" (159).] What makes the interpreter inadequate is precisely what made the eyewitness so reliable. But the natural quality that had previously been given a positive value in the word "simple" is now condemned as "bestise" ["stupidity"], and the mental activity that had previously been condemned in "fines gens" as "inventions fauces" (205 [152]) is now presented in a more favorable light as "mes imaginations." "Invention" and "imagination" are of course the very words used in perspective 5 to praise the Art of the Brazilian song: the war song was an "invention qui ne sent *nullement* la barbarie" (212 [158]), and it was said of the love song that "il n'y a rien de barbarie en cette imagination" (213 [158]).

Along with the terms "barbare" and "sauvage" then, the ideas of Art and Nature undergo a radical transvalorization in "Des Cannibales." At the outset, where "barbare" and "sauvage" are positive terms, Nature is the

6. Many of the verbs used to describe what "fines gens" do to the things they witness are in fact echoed very closely in the later description of what Europeans do to the virtues and properties of Nature. The former group is said to "gloser," "alterer," "incliner" et masquer selon le visage qu'ils *les ont goustées,*" "prester á la matiere, l'alonger et l'amplifier" (205) ["interpret," "alter," "bend and disguise according to the *taste they have of them,*" "add to the matter, stretch it out and amplify it" (152)], while the latter is said to "alterer par nostre artifice," "detourner de l'ordre commun," "abastardir," "accommoder au plaisir de nostre goust corrompu," "recharger par nos inventions," "estouffer." (205–106) ["change artificially," "lead astray from the common order," "debase," "adapt them to gratify our corrupted taste," "overload by our inventions," "smother" (152).]

criterion for favorable judgment, both of Montaigne's informant and of the Cannibals of Brazil; at the conclusion, where "barbare" and "sauvage" are negative qualities, *Art* has become the criterion for favorable judgment, both of the Cannibals and of interpreters. And yet, despite this disconcerting flux in value and point of view, no reader of the essay has ever failed to notice that Montaigne's judgment of the Brazilian natives themselves remains steadfastly favorable from beginning to end. The most arresting and significant aspect of the design of "Des Cannibales," then, is this: while the absolute *judgment* it defends remains *constant* throughout, the *criteria* and the most fundamental *values* on which that judgment is founded *shift*, and are in fact completely reversed over the course of the essay.

Before we may understand what this paradoxical design actually means we must turn our attention to yet another pair of concepts that recurs throughout the chapter—*reason* and *custom*. It will be recalled that Montaigne's point of departure was the lesson drawn from the example of Pyrrhus and the Roman army, that "il se faut garder de s'atacher aux *opinions* vulgaires, et *faut juger les choses* par la voye de la *raison*, non *de* la *voix commune*" (202). ["we should beware of clinging to vulgar opinions, and judge things by reason's way, not by popular say" (150).] This axiom in fact governs the argument of the entire essay. Perspective 1 merely applies it to the particular case of the Cannibals—"il n'y rien de barbare et de sauvage en cette nation . . . sinon que chacun appelle barbarie ce qui n'est pas de son *usage*; comme de vray il semble que nous n'avons autre *touche* de la verité et de la *raison* que l'exemple et idée des *opinions et usances* du païs où nous sommes" (205). ["there is nothing barbarous and savage in that nation . . . except that each man calls barbarism whatever is not his own practice; for indeed it seems we have no other test of truth and reason than the example and pattern of the opinions and customs of the country we live in" (152).] Perspective 2 helps to define the double difficulty of judging the Cannibals properly by arguing that our own "customs" (and therefore our "opinions") are corrupt (i.e. "artificial") while theirs are pure (i.e. "natural"). The anthropological and polemical centerpiece of the chapter is then an attempt on Montaigne's part to transcend the artificial *"opinions et usances"* of his own culture in order to judge a foreign culture—and his own—by *reason* alone. This purpose is in fact explicitly stated in the concluding sentence of this long exposition: "Nous les pouvons donq bien appeller barbares, eu esgard aux regles de la *raison*, mais non pas eu esgard à *nous*" (210). ["So we may well call these people barbarians, in respect to the rules of reason, but not in respect to ourselves" (156).] Having accomplished what he set out to do, Montaigne returns once again to the underlying dichotomy of his essay in order to crown his apology with the statement that the Americans, in direct contrast to Europeans, act not according to *custom*, but to *reason:* "et, afin qu'on ne pense point que tout cecy se face par une simple et servile obligation à leur *usance* et par l'impression de l'authorité de leur ancienne *coustume*, sans *discours* et sans *jugement*, et pour avoir l'ame si stupide que de ne pouvoir prendre autre party, il faut alleguer quelques traits de leur *suffisance*" (213). ["And lest it be thought that all this is done through a simple and servile bondage to usage and through the pressure of the authority of their ancient customs, without reasoning or judgment, and because their minds are so stupid that they cannot take any other course, I must cite some examples of their capacity" (158).]

Now the hidden paradox of this long demonstration is that the "reason" of the Americans and the "custom" of the Europeans appear to be virtually indistinguishable: they are both characterized by "Art" as opposed to "Nature." Or to put the same point another way, "reason" seems to play an antithetical role in Europe and in America: since European culture is corrupted by *artifice*, the role of reason in Europe must be to transcend the distortions of "fines gens" and "art" in order to return to a natural judgment; and since American culture is *natural*, the role of reason for the Cannibals must be to transcend a "stupide" and "simple" obedience to their natural ways in order to arrive at "suffisance" and Anacreontic art. Reason, it would appear, is a far less uniform and universal faculty than Descartes would later maintain. It is defined not in absolute terms but in its opposition to custom, and since custom varies by definition from culture to culture, reason must also vary from culture to culture, both in its nature and in its function. Thus it is that while reason for the civilized European consists of a return to Nature, reason for the "sauvage" is manifested in his Art, and that "Art" and "Nature" can be as slippery and mutable as "barbare" and "sauvage" as criteria for judging the Old World, the New World, or any world at all.

Above and beyond the explicit "cultural relativism" that appeals so directly to the sensibilities (and customs) of modern readers, then, Montaigne's chapter on Cannibals is concerned with an even more profound and radical kind of relativism involving the faculties of *reason* and *judgment* themselves. In ironic counterpoint to the apparent constancy of Montaigne's judgment of the Cannibals (based itself on the Cannibals' "constancy" in war!), the essay shows that (1) his own faculty of judgment as it is applied to the Cannibals, and (2) man's very faculty of reason itself, are altogether as "vain, divers, et ondoyant" (I:1, 9) ["vain, diverse, and undulating" [I:1, 5]] as any of the attributes that characterize mankind. The formal design of "Des Cannibales" thus constitutes an immediate and compelling demonstration of a lesson that is nowhere stated but everywhere present: its shifting perspective and transvalorizations illustrate, in the text of the essay itself, the Pyrrhonian premise that "et nous, et nostre jugement, et toutes choses mortelles, vont coulant et roulant sans cesse" [II 12, 601]. ["we, and our judgment, and all mortal things go on flowing and rolling unceasingly" [II 12, 455].]

"Des coches," which appears in so many respects to be a reworking of "Des Cannibales," is composed according to a curiously similar design as well. Underlying the apparent randomness of the chapter's linear progression is a lop-sided but explicit symmetrical framework whose corresponding parts deal with comparable aspects of the Old World and the New. Following a round-about exordium on etiology in general and the causes of nausea in particular, the first half of the chapter is entirely devoted to a sequence of observations on various aspects of the theme *invention and novelty*. The processional chariots of Mark Antony, Heliogabalus and Firmus are first considered for the *"estrangeté de ces inventions"* (902). ["strangeness of these inventions" (687).] This leads to a more general discussion of the "pompes" and "magnificence" of spectacles in imperial Rome: they may be blameworthy for their excessive cost (liberality being a misplaced virtue in rulers), but they are certainly admirable for the ingenuity they reveal: "S'il y a quelque chose qui soit excusable en tels excez, c'est où l'invention et la nouveauté fournit d'admiration, non pas la despence" (907). ["If there is anything excusable in such extravagances, it is when the inventiveness and the novelty of them, not the expense, provide amazement" (692).] And finally, the spectacular ingenuity of the ancients is contrasted with the apparent poverty of the modern spirit in order to consider—and reject—a linear representation of human history according to which the world is in an irreversible decline and is inexorably approaching its end: "Comme vainement nous concluons aujourd'hui l'inclination et la decrepitude du monde par les arguments que nous tirons de nostre propre foiblesse et decadence . . . ainsi vainement concluoit *cet autre,* sa naissance et jeunesse, par la vigueur qu'il voyoit aux espris de son temps, abondans en *nouvelletez et inventions* de divers arts" (908). ["As vainly as we today infer the decline and decreptiude of the world from the arguments we draw from our own weakness and decay . . . so vainly did this poet infer the world's birth and youth from the vigor he saw in the minds of his time, abounding in novelties and inventions in various arts" (693).]

Now in the last few pages of the chapter each of the three unrelated subjects treated in the first half as a particular aspect of the theme of "l'invention et la nouveauté"—coaches, magnificence, short-sighted history—is taken up again, in reverse order, to be considered briefly in the context of the newly discovered lands of America: first, the Mexican sense of history, according to which the world is old and approaching its end; second, the magnificence of the great highway connecting Quito and Cusco; and finally, the golden litter of the king of Peru. What is particularly remarkable about this symmetrical arrangement of topics is that Montaigne has betrayed his own ideal of literary style in order to draw attention to it, adding uncharacteristically explicit indications of an intended relation between corresponding parts of his chapter:[7] "Ceux du Royaume de Mexico . . . jugeoient . . . *ainsi que nous*, que l'univers fut proche de sa fin" (913); "*Quant à la pompe et magnificence, par où je suis entré en ce propos*, ny Graece, ny Romme, ny Aegypte ne peut . . . comparer aucun de ses ouvrages au chemin qui se voit au Peru" (914); "*Retombons à* nos coches" (915). ["The people of the kingdom of Mexico . . . judged, as we do, that the universe was near its end" (697–98); "As for pomp and magnificence, whereby I entered upon this subject, neither Greece nor Rome nor Egypt can compare any of its works . . . with the road which is seen in Peru" (698); "Let us fall back to our coaches" (698).] What Montaigne would not have us miss, it would seem, is the following design:[8]

7. "Je n'ayme point de tissure où les liaisons et les coutures paroissent, tout ainsi qu'en un **corps, il ne faut qu'on y puisse compter les os et les veines." (I 26, 172) "J'entends que la matiere se distingue soy-mesmes. Elle montre assez où elle se change, où elle conclud, où elle commence, où elle se reprend, sans l'entrelasser de paroles, de liaison et de cousture introduictes pour le service des oreilles foibles ou nonchallantes, et sans me gloser moymesme" (III 9, 995.)

["I do not like a fabric in which the seams and stitches show, just as in a **body we must not be able to count the bones and veins." (I 26, 127) "I want the matter to make its own divisions. It shows well enough where it changes, where it concludes, where it begins, where it resumes, without my interlacing it with words, with links and seems introduced for the benefit of weak or heedless ears, and without writing glosses on myself" (III 9, 761).]

8. It must be emphasized that the symmetry of this design is strictly a *topical* one, and that it is not balanced in terms of actual length. The disproportionate number of pages devoted to topic 1 in the first half led René Etiemble to divide the chapter in a way entirely incompatible with its real articulation, and to base his interpretation largely on a passage concerning "our kings" that he wrongly perceived to appear at the center ("Sens et structure," p. 268). Not only is that passage not central (belonging to frame 2 of the over-all design of the chapter), but it is clearly designated by the words of the text as a mere digression within the subject of Roman pomp and magnificence: "*L'estrangeté de ces inventions* me met en teste *cett'autre fantasie:*

1. Roman coaches: Mark Antony, Heliogabalus, Firmus and their strange chariots
2. Roman pomp and magnificence: spectacles in the amphitheaters
3. Misconceptions concerning the age of the world: historical views of Lucretius and modern Europeans

> "*Nostre monde* vient d'en trouver *un autre*"
> *Old World* vice and cruelty / *New World* virtue

3. Misconceptions concerning the age of the world: religious views of the Mexicans
2. New World pomp and magnificence: the Peruvian highway
1. New World coaches: the king of Peru and his golden litter

Although it appears to interrupt a perfectly coherent discussion of history and the putative age of the world, the central section undoubtedly contains the essential point of the chapter—an encomium of American fortitude and corresponding condemnation of European vice very similar to the one we have found at the center of "Des Cannibales." Nor can it be an accident that at the very center of this central passage is lodged that masterpiece of cultural relativism, the imagined dialogue in which eight claims and demands by the Spanish are systematically and masterfully confuted from a foreign perspective in eight replies by the natives (910–11 [695]). Montaigne's composition clearly serves to highlight this crucial encounter between the Old World and the New by setting it apart at the center by means of a series of concentric frames.

As in the case of "Des Cannibales," however, an important part of the chapter's meaning resides in the actual arrangement of topics around the polemical centerpiece they frame. A crucial point about history made in frame 3 is that "nous n'allons *ny en avant ny à reculons, mais roulant* plustost, *tournoyant et changeant*" (907). ["We go *neither forward nor backward,* but rather by *wheeling, turning and changing direction*" (692).] Montaigne of course illustrates this idea in his introduction to the inhabitants of the New World by pointing out certain similarities between

---

que c'est une espece de pusillanimité aux monarques . . . de travailler à se faire valloir et paroistre par *despences excessives*. . . . C'estoit pourtant une belle chose. . . . C'estoit aussi belle chose à voir. . . . S'il y a quelque chose qui soit excusable en tels *excez*, c'est où *l'invention et la nouveauté* fournit d'admiration, non pas la *despence*." ["The strangeness of these inventions puts into my head this other notion: that it is a sort of pusillanimity in monarchs . . . to labor at showing off and making a display by excessive expense. . . . It was, however, a fine thing. . . . It was also a fine thing to see. . . . If there is anything excusable in such extravagances, it is when the inventiveness and the novelty of them, not the expense, provide amazement."]

Rome of the first and second centuries and America of the sixteenth, comparing the stoic virtue of the Indians with that of the Ancients— "Quant à la hardiesse et courage, quant à la fermeté, constance, resolution contre les douleurs et la faim et la mort, je ne craindrois pas d'opposer les exemples que je trouverois parmy eux aux plus *nobles* exemples anciens que nous ayons aus memoires de nostre monde par deçà" (909) ["As for boldness and courage, as for firmness, constancy, resoluteness against pains and hunger and death, I would not fear to oppose the examples I could find among them to the most *noble* ancient examples that we have in the memories of our world on this side of the ocean" (694)]—and regretting that it fell to the vicious modern world, rather than to the virtuous ancient world, to enter into contact with the pristine New World (910 [694]).⁹ But it is the composition of the chapter, not its explicit statements, that illustrates most strikingly the similarities between the Ancient World and the New: the three aspects of "nouvelletez et inventions" in ancient Rome considered in the first half are matched, if not bettered, by New World counterparts in the second. It would appear that the chapter is deliberately designed to suggest, through an artful arrangement of *formal* correspondences, *substantial* correspondences and similarities between Rome and America far more compelling than any that discursive argument or an examination of known facts could possibly reveal. This is truly a remarkable case of form in the service of meaning, or rather of the indissoluble welding of form and sense into a suggestive and vital piece of writing.

9. Unlike "Des Cannibales," "Des coches" represents the Americans as simultaneously possessing the best of Nature, Art and Virtue: "(1) La plus part de leurs responces et des negotiations faictes avec eux tesmoignent qu'ils ne nous devoyent rien en clarté d'esprit naturelle et en pertinence *[Nature]*. (2) L'espouvantable magnificence des villes de Cusco et de Mexico . . . et la beauté de leurs ouvrages en pierrerie, en plume, en cotton, en la peinture, montrent qu'ils ne nous *devoyent* non plus en l'industrie *[Art]*. (3) Mais, quant à la devotion, observance des loix, bonté, liberalité, loyauté, franchise, il nous a bien servy de n'en avoir pas tant qu'eux *[Virtue]*." (909) ["(1) Most of the responses of these people and most of our dealings with them show that they were not at all behind us in natural brightness of mind and pertinence *[Nature]*. (2) The awesome magnificence of the cities of Cuzco and Mexico . . . and the beauty of their workmanship in jewelry, feathers, cotton, and painting, show that they were not behind us in industry either *[Art]*. (3) But as for devoutness, observance of the laws, goodness, liberality, loyalty, and frankness, it served us well not to have as much as they *[Virtue]*." (693–94)]

The Ancients are consequently shown to be suitable counterparts in all three of these separate realms: "ces anciens Grecs et Romains . . . (1) eussent conforté et promeu les bonnes semences que *nature* y avoit produit, (2) meslant non seulement à la culture des terres et ornement des villes les *arts* de deçà, en tant qu'elles y eussent esté necessaires, mais aussi (3) meslant les *vertus* Grecques et Romaines aux originelles du pays!" (910) ["those ancient Greeks and Romans . . . (1) would have strengthened and fostered the good seeds that *nature* had produced in them, (2) not only adding to the cultivation of the earth and the adornment of cities the *arts* of our side of the ocean, in so far as they would have been necessary, but also (3) adding the Greek and Roman *virtues* to those originally in that region." (694–95)]

But there is more to Montaigne's design than this. Behind the idea that human history is nonlinear, nonteleological and repetitive, lies an episte- mological preoccupation similar once again to the one we have found to govern the composition of "Des Cannibales." More than the complexity of history, it is our false perception of a simple pattern in history that seems to interest Montaigne. Linear schemes like those of Lucretius and the Chris- tian West, the author claims, are entirely founded on ignorance—ignorance of most of the past, as well as ignorance of the state of the world in our own time (907–08 [692–93]). The conclusion to which these pages on knowledge and perception lead is the following:

> Si nous voyons autant du monde comme nous n'en voyons pas, nous apercevrions, comme il est à croire, une perpetuele** vicissitude de formes. Il n'y a rien de seul et de rare eu esgard à nature, ouy bien eu esgard à nostre cognoissance, qui est un miserable fondement de nos regles et qui nous represente volontiers une tres-fauce image des choses. [908]

> If we saw as much of the world as we do not see, we would perceive, it is likely, a perpetual **vicissitude of forms. There is nothing unique and rare as regards nature, but there certainly is as regards our knowledge, which is a miserable foundation for our rules and which is apt to represent to us a very false picture of things. [693]

Now it is precisely this statement, in which we hear such clear echoes of "Des Cannibales," that the composition of "Des coches" appears to illustrate in several different ways. First of all, the correspondences between Ancient Rome and America already mentioned show that neither civiliza- tion is "seul et rare," though each might think so in its ignorance of the other. Secondly, our own European conception of the world as old and dying is proof in itself of our overwhelming ignorance, which has hidden so long from our ken an entire continent that appears, on the contrary, to be still young and vigorous. Thirdly, our conception of the Old World as "old" and the New World as "new" is itself drawn into question by the fact that the inhabitants of this "New" World conceive of their own world, "ainsi que nous," as *old*. And finally, the Mexicans' sense that their world is old is in turn drawn into question by the fact that a very similar civilization in Rome perceived itself, some fifteen centuries earlier, to be *young*.

A fundamental epistemological lesson now begins to emerge from the text of "Des coches." The arrangement of parts within the whole suggests a multitude of mutually exclusive perceptions that various civilizations have had of themselves and of each other—all "tres-fauces images des choses"

["very false pictures of things"] that are bewildering proof of the universality of human ignorance and error. In this way the formal design of the
chapter broadens the general theme of "l'invention et la nouveauté" in such
a way as to suggest with striking force the notion that *nothing*, strictly
speaking, is ever *new*.[10] Thus is Montaigne's essay suffused with an aloof
philosophical attitude curiously at odds with its polemical passages but
entirely consonant with the illustration of cultural relativism at its
center—an attitude remarkably reminiscent of the melancholy wisdom of
Solomon:

> Quid est quod fuit? Ipsum quod futurum est. Quid est quod factum est?
> Ipsum quod faciendum est. *Nihil sub sole novum*, Nec valet quisquam
> dicere: *Ecce, hoc recens est;* Iam enim praecessit in saeculis quae fuerunt
> ante nos. [*Ecclesiastes* 1:9–10]

> The thing that hath been, it is that which shall be; and that which is done is
> that which shall be done: and there is no new thing under the sun. Is there
> any thing whereof it may be said, See, this is new? it hath been already of
> old time, which was before us. [*Ecclesiastes* 1:9–10]

As for that noble human faculty of judgment that everywhere *perceives* a
nonexistent and impossible "newness," it is clearly *vanitas vanitatum*.

Considered simply as ingenuous expositions of a particular point of
view, "Des Cannibales" and "Des coches" appear to be more or less
desultory essays whose rich and variegated digressions serve to embroider a
statement of cultural relativism, or perhaps to veil a daring polemic which
condemns the excesses of the Old World while eulogizing the natural virtue
of the New. But beneath the explicit messages and luxuriant digressions of
these chapters lies a deeper and more general meaning which is woven into
the very fabric of the chapters' composition. This "design," as we have been
calling it here, is anything but a dogmatic moral lesson. In "Des Cannibales" the apparent fixity of Montaigne's judgment is merely an optical
illusion resulting from a constantly shifting perspective and from criteria
which are entirely transvalorized over the course of the essay. More than a
simple juxtaposition of our false impressions of another culture with the
reality of that culture, or even of our view of the Brazilians with their view

10. This idea is of course corroborated by a second formal device—the well-known
circularity of the chapter which ends precisely where it began, with the subject of "coches," in
imitation of the circular (or at least rambling and repetitive) movement of history as it is
described near the center of the essay.

of us, this chapter is in fact an astonishing "peinture du passage" ["portrayal of passing"] in which the author's own judgment is shown to be completely caught up in the universal "branloire perenne" ["perennial movement."] "Des coches" is somewhat different in that its design is a more static one. But here too, the chapter's composition projects a kaleidoscopic whirl of the contradictory and erroneous perspectives from which various different worlds—the Ancient, the Modern, and the New—perceive and judge themselves and each other. Once again, the chapter's lesson concerns the variety and infirmity of human judgment. Behind the explicit moral judgments and implied cultural relativism of these chapters, then, lies not dogmatism but an even more profound kind of relativism involving the very faculty that the *Essais* themselves are an attempt to put to the test.[11]

What is perhaps most astonishing and significant in the design of these two chapters, however, is not so much the lesson itself as the oblique manner of its transmission. The text of these essays functions not as the purveyor of an extractable conceptual content but as a kind of immediate and dramatic *representation* of judgment in action, or of judgments in conflict. Rather than stating or even implying any firm conclusions, these chapters actually draw the responsive reader into an active process of discovery, allowing him to participate directly in the epistemological lesson to be learned, and even leading him on in such a way that his own judgment will serve to illustrate the vanity and inconstancy of human judgment!

Now it will be evident even to the most casual reader of Montaigne that this nondiscursive, nondidactic technique of *instruction through process* corresponds exactly to the kind of pedagogy recommended in the *Essais* themselves. The author of "De l'institution des enfans" ["Of the Education of Children"] had stated that the best textbook for a useful liberal education was the great Book of the World (I:26, 157–58 [116]). "Des Cannibales" and "Des coches" are the two chapters in all the *Essais* that deal most

11. "Quant aux facultez naturelles qui sont en moy, dequoy c'est icy l'*essay*, je les sens flechir sous la charge. Mes conceptions et mon jugement ne marche qu'à tastons, chancelant, bronchant et chopant" (I:26, 146). ["As for the natural faculties that are in me, of which this book is the essay, I feel them bending under the load. My conceptions and my judgment move only by groping, staggering, stumbling, and blundering" (I:26, 107).] "Le jugement est un util à tous subjects, et se mesle par tout. A cette cause, aux *essais* que j'en fay ici, j'y employe toute sorte d'occasion" (I:50, 301). ["Judgment is a tool to use on all subjects, and comes in everywhere. Therefore in the tests that I make of it here, I use every sort of occasion" (I:50, 219).] "C'est icy purement l'*essay* de mes facultez naturelles, et nullement des acquises" (II:10, 407). ["This is purely the essay of my natural faculties, and not at all of the acquired ones" (II:10, 296).] "C'est †assezt que mon jugement ne se defferre poinct, duquel ce sont icy les *essais*" (II:17, 653). ["It is enough that my judgment is not unshod, of which these are the essays" (II:17, 495).]

exclusively and most extensively with the strange diversity of the wide world around us. In attempting to transcribe the ideal textbook into his own book, then, Montaigne appears to have assumed for himself the role of ideal pedagogue.[12] If he were to tell us straight out that judgment is affected by the external circumstances in which it operates, or that human perception is myopic and astigmatic, he would indeed abandon his most fundamental principle of education, filling our memory with *"science"* while leaving our understanding and conscience empty (I:25, 136ff [100ff]). In order to avoid this error Montaigne, like his ideal pedagogue, "se condui(it) en sa charge d'une nouvelle maniere" (I:26, 150) ["go(es) about his job in a novel way" (I:26, 110)], communicating his revolutionary lesson by means of a no less revolutionary method. Instead of adopting the practice of those who "veulent instruire notre entendement, sans l'esbranler *et mettre en besogne*" (152) ["want to train our understanding without setting it in motion *and putting it to work*" (112)], he puts the "soul" of his reader "sur *le trottoer,* luy faisant gouster les choses, les choisir et discerner d'elle mesme: quelquefois luy *monstrant* chemin, quelquefois *luy laissant prendre le devant* . . . et ne loge rien en sa teste par **authorité et à credit" (150–51). ["through its paces, making it taste things, choose them, and discern them by itself; sometimes *showing him the way,* sometimes letting him *go on before* and lodges nothing in his head on **authority and trust" (110–11).] In short, rather than dictating to us certain insights into the nature of reason and judgment which we would then be required to learn more or less by rote along with the precepts of Aristotle, Cicero and so many other authorities, Montaigne has devised a way to make us discover those insights for ourselves, and actually to *experience* them through the very process of reading. He has composed these chapters not as dissertations, but quite literally as *exercises* designed to increase our understanding and sharpen our judgment by putting both of these faculties to the test.

But if "Des Cannibales" and "Des coches" are indeed ideal lessons devised by an ideal pedagogue, then the reader too must play his part by rising to the role of ideal apprentice. The critic who would seek to separate form from content either to extract a paraphrasable message from the vagaries of a baroque piece of writing or to analyze Montaigne's style and

12. One of the implicit lessons of "Des Cannibales" is in fact *stated* in "De l'institution des enfans," in a particularly ironic passage alluding to Montaigne's vicar and the *Cannibals* (I:26, 157 [116]). One cannot help but suspect that "Des Cannibales" is essentially nothing more that an elaboration of this passage, reworked in such a way as to present its "lesson" in a manner more compatible with its pedagogical theory, and further, that "Des coches" is yet a third version of the same essay. However this may be, the two New World chapters do appear to be deliberately designed to *do* what the two chapters on education merely *recommend.*

composition independently from their meaning, would quite obviously succeed only in imitating the foolishness of Montaigne's pedants who "vont pillotant la science dans les livres, et ne la logent qu'au bout de leurs levres, pour la dégorger seulement et mettre au vent" (I:25, 136). ["go pillaging knowledge in books and lodge it only on the end of their lips, in order merely to disgorge it and scatter it to the winds" (I:25, 100).] As working exercises, as kinetic tests of the reader's judgment, as *lessons consubstantial with their vehicle,* the New World chapters must necessarily remain inscrutable to hermeneutic and stylistic readings alike. The kind of reading they require—the only reading to which they are designed to reveal their wisdom—is a willing and active participation of the reader's judgment in the labyrinths that this master of the maieutic monologue has so painstakingly constructed for it.

This kind of reading is not without precedent, of course. It is none other than the kind practiced by Montaigne himself, and that he has described for us in the margins of his own book:

> (c) La lecture me sert specialement à esveiller par divers objects mon discours, à *embesongner mon jugement,* non ma memoyre. [III:3,819]
> (c) Les livres m'ont servi non tant d'instruction que d'*exercitation.* [III:12, 1039]

> Reading serves me particularly to arouse my reason by offering it various subjects to *set my judgment to work,* not my memory. [III:3,622]
> Books have served me not so much for instruction as for *exercise.* [III:12, 795]

Prevented by the very nature of wisdom from revealing true wisdom directly to his readers, the great assayer has designed these extraordinary New World chapters in such a way as to help us find our own way to wisdom through the peculiar kind of apprenticeship that he himself had found to be most fruitful.

TZVETAN TODOROV

L'Etre et l'Autre: Montaigne

The following pages are part of a work in progress, dealing with the transformations of the relations between the self and the other *(l'être et l'autre)* in the history of ideologies in France. By saying this, I am not trying to protect my territory, but to give information which is necessary to the understanding of the present essay. Consequently, I am not presenting an immanent reading of Montaigne's text, nor do I intend to reconstruct his intentions. Not that I consider them irrelevant; on the contrary. Still, my goal is not to reconstitute what Montaigne's text means, but to observe what it does, from a particular point of view, which is historical (in the sense of "duration"). In short, I do not read Montaigne, thinking only of Montaigne, but also, for example, of Montesquieu.

It is possible to analyse the relationship between the self and the other on three levels (which correspond to the three sections of this study): 1) the relation between *us* and others: the manner in which a community perceives those who do not belong to it; 2) the relation between *I* and the other *(autrui):* the very existence of beings other than myself, or of a social dimension of man; 3) the other *in* the self: multiplicity and heterogeneity internal to the subject. Other writers may render null some of these distinctions, or impose others; however these three levels appeared to me necessary and sufficient to examine this problematic in Montaigne.[1]

I

CUSTOM

Montaigne encounters some difficulties in deciding the power of custom: is everything custom, including the foundations of ethics, the rules

1. I would like to thank G. Defaux and F. Rigolot for communicating to me in advance the manuscripts of their essays, which are published in the present volume.

113

of reason, the principles of human behavior? Or is there a universal essence, a nature of man that is eventually hidden (but not altered) by customs? A sentence of the essay "Of custom, and not easily changing an accepted law" (I:23) illustrates this uncertainty:

> (a) Qui voudra se desfaire de ce violent prejudice de la coustume, il trouvera plusieurs choses receues d'une resolution indubitable, qui n'ont appuy qu'en la barbe chenue et rides de l'usage qui les accompaigne; mais, ce masque arraché, rapportant les choses à la verité et à la raison, il sentira son jugement comme tout bouleversé, et remis pourtant en bien plus seur estat. [117]

> Whoever want to get rid of this violent prejudice of custom will find many things accepted with undoubting resolution, which have no support but in the hoary beard and the wrinkles of the usage that goes with them; but when this mask is torn off, and he refers things to truth and reason, he will feel his judgment as it were all upset, and nevertheless restored to a much surer status. [84–85]

The first part of the sentence describes the way of the world in an apparently neutral manner: many things that appear to us unquestionable are only founded on habit; they are mere prejudices, however violent, masks that we are free to tear off. But there is a "but": when one refers to universal values, truth and reason, one is shaken instead of being reassured. Can reason sink its roots so profoundly into usage that it can no longer extricate itself without peril? In fact no, for an opposition emerges in the opposition itself, and the "but" is followed by a "nevertheless": the final state (the reference to unique truth) will still be preferable to the preceding reassuring habits.

Thus in spite of its reserve, the sentence seems to indicate that Montaigne would lean towards a more universalist position. Such however is not the reading of the majority of his texts, nor is it the reading of what is presented as his explicit platform on the question. The same essay shows in fact a significant gradation. The ideal starting point would be expressed by the sentence cited above and others of the same kind, such as: (a) "l'usage nous desrobbe le vray visage des choses" (116). ["Usage robs us of the true appearance of things" (84).] Custom is only a mask, and things do have a true aspect; but this mask is omnipresent, and shedding it is not easy. Like a shrewd tyrant, custom has imprisoned our senses and our judgment, which should in fact help us to free ourselves from it. (c) "L'accoustumance hebete nos sens" (109). ["Habit stupefies our senses" (78)], (c) "l'assuefaction [donc encore l'accoutumance] endort la veuë de nostre jugement" (112). ["habitu-ation puts to sleep the eye of our judgment" (80).] Custom is only a guest, but it is a tyrannical guest whom one cannot get rid of. Or according to Montaigne's own metaphor:

(a) c'est à la verité une violente et traistresse maistresse d'escole, que la coustume. Elle establit en nous, peu à peu, à la desrobée, le pied de son authorité: mais par ce doux et humble commencement, l'ayant rassis et planté avec l'ayde du temps, elle nous descouvre tantost un furieux et tyrannique visage, contre lequel nous n'avons plus la liberté de hausser seulement les yeux. [I:23, 109]

For in truth habit is a violent and treacherous schoolmistress. She establishes in us, little by little, stealthily, the foothold of her authority; but having by this mild and humble beginning settled and planted it with the help of time, she soon uncovers to us a furious and tyrannical face against which we no longer have the liberty of even raising our eyes. [77]

Now the return "to truth and reason" appears more problematic than we would imagine. Where then is one to find the solid ground permitting us to throw off the yoke, if our eyes report as truth what is merely prejudice, if our mind does not succeed in isolating custom as an object of its reflection since the very rules of its procedure are dictated by this very custom?

The next step in the renunciation of universal reason consists in noticing that judgments pronounced here and there, and believed to be founded on reason alone, in fact diverge from each other absolutely, and can therefore only derive from custom. No longer does this fact provoke indignation:

(a) J'excuserois volontiers en nostre peuple de n'avoir autre patron et regle de perfection que ses propres meurs et usances: car c'est un commun vice, non du vulgaire seulement, mais quasi de tous hommes, d'avoir leur visée et leur arrest sur le train auquel ils sont nais. [I:49, 296]

I should be prone to excuse our people for having no other pattern and rule of perfection than their own manners and customs; for it is a common vice, not of the vulgar only but of almost all men, to fix their aim and limit by the ways to which they were born. [215]

Ethics and aesthetics topple over on the side of relativism. (c) "Les peuples nourris à la liberté et à se commander eux mesmes, estiment toute autre forme de police monstrueuse et contre nature. Ceux qui sont duits à la monarchie en font de mesme" (I:23, 116). ["Nations brought up to liberty and to ruling themselves consider any other form of government monstrous and contrary to nature. Those accustomed to monarchy do the same" (83).]

Montaigne relates the fact without passing judgment on it: his long experience has taught him that all judgment is but the expression of habit; consequently, nothing permits him to affirm that liberty is a good, and its absence an evil; to value liberty would be proof of ethnocentrism, and to disguise habit as universal reason. This would be even more evident when it comes to judgments about beauty: who could not cite several examples illustrating the instability of the human ideal? (a) "Il est vray semblable que nous ne sçavons guiere que c'est que beauté en nature et en general, puisque à l'humaine et nostre beauté nous donnons tant de formes diverses" (II:12, 482). ["It is likely that we know little about what beauty is in nature and in general, since to our own human beauty we give so many different forms" (355).]

In these conditions, reason is only the servant of the violent mistress we have seen; instead of encompassing all customs in order to distinguish the good from the bad, its function is to find plausible justifications for the most varied customs. (b) "J'estime qu'il ne tombe en l'imagination humaine aucune fantasie si forcenée, qui ne rencontre l'exemple de quelque usage public, et par consequent que nostre discours n'estaie et ne fonde" (I:23, 111). ["I think that there falls into man's imagination no fantasy so wild that it does not match the example of some public practice, and for which, consequently, our reason does not find a stay and a foundation" (79).] (c) "Par où il advient que ce qui est hors de gonds de coustume, on le croid hors des gonds de raison: Dieu sçait combien desraisonnablement, le plus souvent" (I:23, 116). ["Whence it comes to pass that what is off the hinges of custom, people believe to be off the hinges of reason: God knows how unreasonably, most of the time" (83).] In this last phrase, reason attempts a timid reappearance: it is no longer "camouflage" reason but universal reason, for which certain things are, and whatever the custom is, intrinsically unreasonable. But all hope of victory is abandonned. It is abandonned, in any case, for Montaigne, who thus surrenders his last reservations: (c) "Les loix de la conscience, que nous disons naistre de nature, naissent de la coustume: chacun ayant en veneration interne les opinions et moeurs approuvées et receuës autour de luy, ne s'en peut desprendre sans remors, ny s'y appliquer sans applaudissement" (115). ["The laws of conscience, which we say are born of nature, are born of custom. Each man, holding in inward veneration the opinions and the behavior approved and accepted around him, cannot break loose from them without remorse, or apply himself to them without self-satisfaction" (83).] Natural reason cannot emerge from customary reason, for nature, in this matter, does not exist; what does not exist cannot be emancipated.

Elsewhere, Montaigne directly attacks the tenants of natural law: if we are to believe him, the latter is nonexistent. It seems to be founded on the following syllogism, which Montaigne draws from the skeptic tradition. *Major premise:* (a) "La verité doit avoir un visage pareil et universel" (II:12, 578–9). ["Truth must have one face, the same and universal" (436).] (a) "Ce que nature nous auroit veritablement ordonné, nous l'ensuivrions sans doubte d'un commun consentement" (580). ["What nature had truly ordered for us we would without doubt follow by common consent" (437).] *Minor premise:* (a) "Il n'est rien subject à plus continuelle agitation que les loix" (579). ["There is nothing subject to more continual agitation than the laws" (436).] (a) "I'l n'est chose en quoy le monde soit si divers qu'en coustumes et loix" (580). ["There is nothing in which the world is so varied as in customs and laws" (437).] *Conclusion:* laws are founded not on nature and truth but on tradition and on the arbitrary. (a) "Nostre devoir n'a autre regle que fortuite" (578). ["Our duty has no rule but an accidental one" (436).] (a) "Les loix de nostre pays? c'est à dire cette mer flotante des opinions d'un peuple ou d'un Prince . . ." (579). ["The laws of our country, that is to say, the undulating sea of the opinions of a people or a prince . . ." (437).] Natural law may have existed in the past, but nothing of it is left today: (b) "Il est croyable qu'il y a des loix naturelles, comme il se voit és autres creatures; mais en nous elles sont perdues" (580). ["It is credible that there are natural laws, as may be seen in other creatures; but in us they are lost" (438).]

Such a deduction may be less rigorous than it appears. First Montaigne seems not to be willing to recognize the two meanings of the word "law": the law as regularity and the law as command. "Thou shalt not kill" is obviously not a law in the first sense of the term, because murders abound; but it could be a law in the second case, and allow a judgment of an act at any place at any time (natural law). On the other hand, the skeptic argument according to which if a thing is not universally present, it cannot be true (right), is not convincing: injustice also exists; what would be universal is not the presence of just acts (or laws), but our very ability to distinguish between justice and injustice. In the same pages, Montaigne says: the proof that religions are arbitrary (and in this sense untrue) is that they are numerous. But this proof is not convincing: not only because different rituals can hide an identical religious feeling, but above all because this plurality does not prove that these religions are all equally valid.

Montaigne writes: (a) "La droiture et la justice, si l'homme en connoissoit qui eust corps et veritable essence, il ne l'atacheroit pas à la condition des coustumes de cette contrée ou de celle là; ce ne seroit pas de la fantasie des Perses ou des Indes que la vertu prendroit sa forme" (579). ["If a man knew any rectitude and justice that had body and real existence, he would not tie it down to the condition of the customs of this country or that. It would not be from the fancy of the Persians or the Indians that virtue would take its form" (436).] One has the impression that he is imprisoned by a radicalism that he himself contributed to erect, a radicalism that confines him in a kind of all-or-nothing alternative: because, to all appearances, the traditions of a country influence its laws, they no longer have any relation with universal and essential justice! But why must these two factors, natural law and the spirit of a nation, be mutually exclusive? No; since for Montaigne not everything is "natural," nothing is.

It is upon this radical relativism that the two great politico-ethical options of Montaigne are founded: conservatism at home, toleration for others. One could have imagined that the absence of any "natural" foundation in laws would have led Montaigne to accept changes easily. But the absence of a "natural" legitimacy is compensated for by an historical justification: any already existing law is *ipso facto* superior to any future law.

> (a) Selon mon humeur, és affaires publiques, il n'est aucun si mauvais train, pourveu qu'il aye de l'aage et de la constance, qui ne vaille mieux que le changement et le remuement. . . . Le pis que je trouve en nostre estat, c'est l'instabilité, et que nos loix, non plus que nos vestemens, ne peuvent prendre aucune forme arrestée. [II:17, 655–56]

> To my mind, in public affairs there is no course so bad, provided it is old and stable, that it is not better than change and commotion. . . . The worst thing I find in our state is instability, and the fact that our laws cannot any more than our clothes, take any settled form. [497–99]

On the one hand, change implies violence (for example, the religious wars in France), whereas its benefits are uncertain. On the other hand, change necessarily violates the consensus, and therefore privileges individual reason over that of the community, a fact which Montaigne considers undesirable (in this he is not modern): (c) "Me semblant tres-inique de vouloir sousmettre les constitutions et observances publiques et immo-biles à l'instabilité d'une privée fantasie (la raison privée n'a qu'une jurisdiction privée)" (I:23, 121). ["It seems to me very iniquitous to want to subject public and immutable institutions and observances to the instabil-ity of a private fancy (private reason has only a private jurisdiction)" (88).]

The other external aspect of this conservatism is toleration towards others; since there is no reason to prefer a law or custom over another, there is no reason either to despise them. Montaigne even goes out of his way to cherish diversity in all things: (a) "comme c'est la plus generale façon que nature aye suivy que la varieté", "je ne hay point les fantasies contraires aux miennes" (II:37, 786, 785), ["since variety is the most general fashion that nature has followed," "I do not at all hate opinions contrary to mine" (597).] But what is true for the relations between individuals should obtain even more for the relations between nations. (b) "La diversité des façons d'une nation à autre ne me touche que par le plaisir de la varieté. Chaque usage a sa raison" (III:9, 985). ["The diversity in fashions from one nation to another affects me only with the pleasure of variety. Each custom has its reason" (753).] Now reason is always at the service of custom. This will allow Montaigne to renounce easily the pleasures of ethnocentrism: (b) "il me semble que je n'ay rencontré guere de manieres qui ne vaillent les nostres" (III:9, 986), ["it seems to me that I have encountered hardly any customs that are not as good as ours" (754).] He never misses an occasion for mocking those who in their parochialism can only appreciate what is familiar to them: (a) "tout ce qui n'est pas comme nous sommes, n'est rien qui vaille" (II:12, 486). ["Whatever is not as we are is worth nothing" (358). This would even be the best form of education: (a) "Il se tire une merveilleuse clarté, pour le jugement humain, de la frequentation du monde" (I:26, 157). ["Wonderful brilliance may be gained for human judgment by getting to know men" (116).]

> (b) L'ame y a [dans le voyage] une continuelle exercitation à remarquer les choses incogneuës et nouvelles; et je ne sçache point meilleure escolle, comme j'ay dict souvent, à former la vie que de luy proposer incessamment la diversité de tant d'autres vies, (c) fantasies et usances, (b) et luy faire gouster une si perpetuelle varieté de formes de nostre nature [III:9, 973–74]

> The mind [by traveling] is continually exercised in observing new and unknown things; and I know no better school, as I have often said, for forming one's life, than to set before it constantly the diversity of so many other lives, (c) ideas, and customs, (b) and to make it taste such a perpetual variety of forms of our nature. [744]

Thus untrammelled by any negative judgment, he can aspire to a sort of new universalism: not because men are alike everywhere (they are not), but because their very differences are, as it were, indifferent. Montaigne sees himself becoming a citizen of the world precisely because of his toleration of others.

> (b) Non parce que Socrate l'a dict, mais parce qu'en verité c'est mon humeur, et à l'avanture non sans quelque excez, j'estime tous les hommes

mes compatriotes, et embrasse un Polonois comme un François, postposant cette lyaison nationale à l'universelle et commune. Je ne suis guere feru de la douceur d'un air naturel. [III:9, 973]

Not because Socrates said it, but because it is really my feeling, and perhaps excessively so, I consider all men my compatriots, and embrace a Pole as I do a Frenchman, setting this national bond after the universal and common one. I am scarcely infatuated with the sweetness of my native air. [743]

He would even go further than Socrates on this matter: (c) "Ce que Socrate feit sur sa fin, d'estimer une sentence d'exil pire qu'une sentence de mort contre soy, je ne seray, à mon advis, jamais ny si cassé ni si estroitement habitué en mon païs que je le feisse" (973) ["What Socrates did near the end of his life, in considering a sentence of exile against him worse than a sentence of death, I shall never, I think be so broken or so strictly attached to my own country as to do" (743).] This is not the modern praise of exile, where exteriority and willed detachment *(non-appartenance)* are chosen for their own sake; rather, Montaigne believes that he is indifferent to the values of his own country—as he is to those of other nations.

Therefore, he can only condemn those who do not share his attitude (but does not all condemnation imply some absolute?) and who still are bound to the customs and habits of their native country.

(b) J'ay honte de voir noz hommes enyvrez de cette sotte humeur de s'effaroucher des formes contraires aux leurs: il leur semble estre hors de leur element quand ils sont hors de leur village. Où qu'ils aillent, ils se tiennent à leurs façons et abominent les estrangeres. Retrouvent ils un compatriote en Hongrie, ils festoyent cette avanture: les voylà à se ralier et à se recoudre ensemble, à condamner tant de meurs barbares qu'ils voient. Pourquoy non barbares, puis qu'elles ne sont françoises? [III:9, 985]

I am ashamed to see my countrymen besotted with that stupid disposition to shy away from ways contrary to their own; they think they are out of their element when they are out of their village. Wherever they go, they stick to their ways and abominate foreign ones. Do they find a conpatriot in Hungary, they celebrate this adventure: see them rally round and join forces, and condemn all the barbarous customs that they see. Why not barbarous, since they are not French? [754]

The word "barbarous" seems to have here only a relative meaning: since all customs are equal in value, differences can only stem from more or less different points of view. The barbarian is the other, since we ourselves are civilized, and since he does not resemble us. The same idea is expressed in a famous sentence from "Of cannibals" (I:31):

> (a) Il n'y a rien de barbare et de sauvage en cette nation, à ce qu'on m'en a rapporté, sinon que chacun appelle barbarie ce qui n'est pas de son usage; comme de vray il semble que nous n'avons d'autre mire de la verité et de la raison que l'exemple et idée des opinions et usances du païs où nous sommes. [205]

> I think there is nothing barbarous and savage in that nation, from what I have been told, except that each man calls barbarism whatever is not his own practice; for indeed it seems we have no other test of truth and reason than the example and pattern of the opinions and customs of the country we live in. [152]

THE BARBARIAN

This essay, "Of Cannibals," is in fact devoted to people whose customs are very different from ours, and it could illustrate the way in which Montaigne practices his toleration towards others. Let us then verify the extent to which Montaigne's practice confirms his theories.

One striking aspect of the portrait of the "cannibal" society immediately emerges: they are described through negative and privative sentences:

> (a) C'est une nation, diroy je à Platon, en laquelle il n'y a aucune espece de trafique; nulle cognoissance de lettres; nulle science de nombres; nul nom de magistrat, ny de superiorité politique; nul usage de service, de richesse ou de pauvreté; nuls contrats; nulles successions; nuls partages; nulles occupations qu'oysives; nul respect de parenté que commun; nuls vestemens; nulle agriculture; nul metal; nul usage de vin ou de bled. Les paroles mesmes qui signifient le mensonge, la trahison, la dissimulation, l'avarice, l'envie, la detraction, le pardon, inouies. [I:31, 206–07]

> This is a nation, I should say to Plato, in which there is no sort of traffic, no knowledge of letters, no science of numbers, no name for a magistrate or for political superiority, no custom of servitude, no riches or poverty, no contracts, no successions, no partitions, no occupations but leisure ones, no care for any but common kinship, no clothes, no agriculture, no metal, no use of wine or wheat. The very words that signify lying, treachery, dissimulation, avarice, envy, belittling, pardon, unheard of. [153]

Elsewhere, Montaigne will call them people (c) "sans lettres, sans loy, sans roy, sans relligion quelconque" (II:12, 491), ["without letters, without law, without king, without religion of any kind" (362).] We become quite aware of what these cannibals are not, of what they lack; but what is their nature positively? And where does this enumeration of negative traits come from, since it obviously cannot have been provided by observation? Could it come from the analysis of our own society? Here Montaigne follows in fact a rhetorical topos: the golden age is traditionally evoked in negative terms, precisely because it is only the reverse description of our reality.

Sometimes Montaigne is more positive. The cannibals value only two things: (a) "la vaillance contre les ennemis et l'amitié à leurs femmes" (I, 31, 208) ["valor against the enemy and love for their wives" (154).] According to him, these two virtues are well represented. For this reason, the "Cannibals" are to be admired. But then, can there be universal virtues which escape a radical relativism? (a) "C'est chose esmerveillable que de la fermeté de leurs combats" (209) ["It is astonishing what firmness they show in their combats" (155).] Could bravery, under all skies, in all circumstances, be considered a virtue? For something has to allow Montaigne to pass a positive judgement on their very system of values. As far as their (c) "vertu proprement matrimoniale" (213), ["properly matrimonial value" (158)] is concerned, he has difficulty in establishing it, confronted as he is with the polygamy of the "cannibals"; but he regains ground by reminding the reader of biblical and ancient examples. Polygamy is not an evil, as proven by the fact that some of the great figures of our tradition have praised it. But is this a way of envisaging the relativity of all values? Or is it not rather a way of judging the quality of their society according to criteria derived from our own?

He encounters the same problem with cannibalism, which gives its title to the essay. This practice is merely the outcome of their warlike spirit, which is itself an undeniable virtue. To eat one's fellow-creature is not, to be sure, a meritorious action, but neither is it without excuse; as proof: (a) "Chrysippus et Zenon, chefs de la secte Stoicque, ont bien pensé qu'il n'y avoit aucun mal de se servir de nostre charoigne à quoy que ce fut pour notre besoin, et d'en tirer de la nourriture" (209). ["Chrysippus and Zeno, heads of the Stoic sect, thought there was nothing wrong in using our carcasses for any purpose in case of need, and getting nourishment from them" (155).] Here again, our own sages are called upon to justify the "cannibals" ' practices. If the great Stoics had not excused cannibalism, would it still be excusable?

The entire essay is in fact a praise of the "cannibals" and a condemnation of our society: if there are savages somewhere, they may not be where we expect them to be.

(a) Il me semble que ce que nous voyons par experience en ces nations là, surpasse, non seulement toutes les peinturs dequoy la poësie a embelly l'age doré, et toutes ses inventions à feindre une heureuse condition d'hommes, mais encore la conception et le desir mesme de la philosophie. [206]

It seems to me that what we actually see in these nations surpasses not only all the pictures in which poets have idealized the golden age and all their inventions in imagining a happy state of man, but also the conceptions and the very desire of philosophy. [153]

In that sense, these "cannibals" would in fact be an incarnation of our ideal. But how can one speak of "surpassing" without referring to a unique or universal system of values, or in any case to a system common to all the nations invoked?

In fact, Montaigne does not hide the fact that he has a unique scheme at his disposal which would permit him to understand the evolution of mankind, and at the same time, to appreciate its various stages. Originally, man was natural; during his history, he has become more and more artificial. Now, (a) "Ce n'est pas raison que l'art gaigne le point d'honneur sur nostre grande et puissante mere nature" (205–06) ["It is not reasonable that art should win the place of honor over our great and powerful mother Nature" (152)]; reason exists, then; therefore, the first centuries were (a) "les meilleurs et les plus heureux" (II:37, 766) ["the best and happiest" (581).] But the contemporary savages are like the men of the early ages, and thus are closer to nature than we are. (a) "ils jouyssent encore de cette uberté naturelle . . . Ils sont encore en cet heureux point, de ne desirer qu'au tant que leurs necessitez naturelles leur ordonnent" (I:31, 210). ["They still enjoy that natural abundance . . . They are still in that happy state of desiring only as much as their natural needs demand" (156).] They are thus superior to us: this is how the myth of the noble savage is created.

Superior or not, one thing is clear in any case: for Montaigne, superiority and inferiority do exist, and consequently also the means of judging several different societies at the same time. But then, in that case, would the barbarian not exist other than in his neighbor's prejudice? If one looks more closely, one realizes that this is in fact the case. Montaigne uses the word "barbarous" in a nonrelative sense, and even in two senses—both absolute, but conveying contrary valuations.

The first meaning is historical and positive: barbarous is that which is close to origins; however, the origins are superior to that which has succeeded them. (a) "Ces nations me semblent donq ainsi barbares, pour avoir receu fort peu de façon de l'esprit humain, et estre encore fort voisines de leur naifveté originelle. Les loix naturelles leur commandent encores, fort peu abastardies par les nostres" (206). ["These nations, then, seem to me barbarous in this sense, that they have been fashioned very little by the human mind, and are still very close to their original naturalness. The laws of nature still rule them, very little corrupted by ours" (153).] The second meaning is ethical and negative: barbarous is that which is cruel and degrading, that which in this case permits the classification of our society as more barbarous than the other. (a) "Je pense qu'il y a plus de barbarie à manger un homme vivant qu'à le manger mort" (209). ["I think there is more barbarity in eating a man alive than in eating him dead" (155).] (a) "Nous les pouvons donq bien appeller barbares, eu esgard aux regles de la raison, mais non pas eu esgard à nous, qui les surpassons en toute sorte de barbarie" (210). ["So we may call these people barbarians, in respect to the rules of reason, but not in respect to ourselves, who surpass them in every kind of barbarity" (156).] It happens that Montaigne plays on these two meanings, historical and ethical, positive and negative, within a single sentence; thus also for the word "wild" (*sauvages*):

> (a) Ils sont sauvages, de mesmes que nous appellons sauvages les fruicts que nature, de soy et de son progrez ordinaire, a produicts: là où, à la verité, ce sont ceux que nous avons alterez par nostre artifice et detournez de l'ordre commun, que nous devrions appeller plutost sauvages. [205]

> Those people are wild, just as we call wild the fruits that Nature has produced by herself and in the normal course [first meaning]; whereas really it is those that we have changed artificially and led astray from the common order, that we should rather call wild. [second meaning] [152]

It is in this last meaning, ethical and negative, that the word "barbarous" is found again in the judgment that Montaigne passes on their poetry.

> (a) Or j'ay assez de commerce avec la poësie pour juger cecy, que non seulement il n'y a rien de barbarie en cette imagination, mais qu'elle est tout à fait Anacreontique. Leur language, au demeurant, c'est un doux langage et qui a le son agreeable, retirant aux terminaisons Grecques. [213]

> I am familiar enough with poetry to be a judge of this: not only is there nothing barbarous in this fancy, but it is altogether Anacreontic. Their language, moreover, is a soft language, with an agreeable sound, somewhat like Greek in its endings. [158]

This poetry is not barbarous for it resembles Greek poetry, and the same holds for their language; the criterion of barbarism is no longer relative here, but neither is it universal: it is in fact simply ethnocentric. If this popular poetry had not by a felicitous chance resembled the Anacreontic style, it would have been—barbarous.

Confronted with the other, Montaigne is undeniably moved by a generous impulse: rather than despise him, he admires him, and he never tires of criticizing his own society. But does the other receive his due from this little game? It is doubtful. The positive value judgment is founded on a misunderstanding and on the projection upon the other of an image of the self—or more precisely—of an Ideal Ego (idéal du moi), incarnated for Montaigne by Greek civilization. The other is in fact never apprehended, never known. What Montaigne praises is not the "cannibals" but his own values. As he says himself on another occasion: (c) "Je ne dis les autres, sinon pour d'autant plus me dire" (I:26, 148). ["I do not speak the minds of others except to speak my own mind better" (108).] Now for the praise to have any value, the subject to whom it is directed should first be recognized in himself. If tomorrow Montaigne discovered that the "cannibals" did not resemble the Greeks, he should logically condemn them. Montaigne would like to be a relativist as he undoubtedly thinks he is; in reality he has never ceased to be a universalist.

He is a universalist but without knowing it—a decisive difference. The conscious universalist has to formulate the criteria that he thinks universal and try to justify them. He cannot afford to declare just his own values universal; at least he ought to anticipate any objection. But his does not hold for the unconscious universalist: his explicit attention is directed to the defense of his relativist principles; there is then every reason to believe that only his prejudices, his habits, his customs, will occupy the place (not claimed) by a universal ethic. The war-like bravery and polygamy, cannibalism, and poetry will be excused or given as examples, not on the basis of a clearly assumed universal ethic, even less on the basis of the ethic of others, but simply because these traits can be found in the Greeks, who incarnate Montaigne's own personal ideal.

The relativist does not judge others. The conscious universalist can condemn them, but he does so in the name of an explicit ethic, which can then be automatically questioned. The unconscious universalist cannot be attacked, since he pretends to be a relativist; but this does not prevent him from judging others and imposing his own ideal on them. He exhibits the aggressivity of the latter and the good conscience of the former; it is in good faith that he assimilates because he has not recognized the difference of others. And it is in quite a coherent manner that in the essay "Of coaches," Montaigne will condemn, not colonization, but the fact that it was undertaken in the name of ideals different from his own: (b) "Que n'est tombée soubs Alexandre ou soubs ces anciens Grecs et Romains une si noble conqueste" (III:6, 910), ["Why did not such a noble conquest fall to Alexander or to those ancient Greeks and Romans?" (694)] It was indeed in the name of high ideals that colonization would be accomplished by Europe in the following centuries.

The shifts of meaning in the word "barbarous" in Montaigne are not caused by distraction or confusion; they are in their own way necessary. The position of radical relativism resulted from the rejection of natural law, a position which turned out to be untenable. Montaigne would like to have his cake and eat it too; barbarism does not exist, and besides we are more barbarous than the others. The polysemy of the word is the price of such a paradoxical position.

But if Montaigne has never perceived others, what is the value of his toleration? Is one still tolerant if one does not even recognize the existence of the other, and if one is merely content to offer him an image of his own ideal, an image which has nothing to do with the other? But perhaps what we took for toleration was only indifference: (b) "La mutation d'air et de climat ne me touche point; tout Ciel m'est un" (III:9, 974). ["Change of air and climate has no effect on me; all skies are alike to me" (744)], and also: (b) "Je sens la mort qui me pince continuellement la gorge ou les reins. Mais je suis autrement faict: elle m'est une par tout" (978). ["I feel death contin-ually clutching me by the throat or the loins. But I am made differently: death is the same to me anywhere" (747).] His is no longer an acceptance of different values but an indifference to values, a refusal to enter the world of others; they don't bother me because they don't count.

II

SELF-SUFFICIENCY

Montaigne used to say that there is no better school than travel and association with people, thus contact with others, whoever they may be. This is the surest way to (a) "frotter et limer nostre cervelle contre celle d'autruy" (I:26, 153), ["rub and polish our brains by contact with those of others" (112)], and it is by exploring the world that one will explore the self: (a) "Ce grand monde . . . c'est le mirouër où il nous faut regarder pour nous connoistre de bon biais" (157). ["This great world . . . is the mirror in which we look at ourselves from the proper angle" (116).] Montaigne's own education seems to have obeyed that very principle: (b) "Pour m'estre, dés mon enfance, dressé à mirer ma vie dans celle d'autruy . . ." (III:13, 1076)

["By training myself from my youth to see my own life in that of others . . ."
(824).] Because the individual has to regulate his life according to the
customs received by society, he first has to take the trouble to learn them.

But it would be an error to attribute to Montaigne a praise of sociability
and human relationships. The mirror can be useful to me; but it reflects an
image of myself, not of the other; the other is only an instrument of self-
knowledge. However an instrument is never indispensable, nor does it have
an end in itself. (b) "Nul plaisir n'a goust pour moy sans communication"
(986) ["No pleasure has any savor for me without communication,"] writes
Montaigne in an essay (III:9, 754), but he promptly adds (b) "Mais il vaut
mieux encore estre seul qu'en compaignie ennuyeuse et inepte" (987). ["But
still it is better to be alone than in boring and foolish company" (755).] Or in
another essay: (c) "Qui ne vit aucunement à autruy, ne vit guere à soy"
(III:10, 1007). ["He who lives not at all unto others, hardly lives unto
himself: (769).] This would be going too far, but the other extreme is even
worse, for it would mean going against nature: (b) "tout de mesme, qui
abandonne en son propre le sainement et gayment vivre pour en servir
autruy, prent à mon gré un mauvais et desnaturé parti" (III:10, 1007). ["even
so he who abandons healthy and gay living of his own to serve others
thereby, takes, to my taste, a bad and unnatural course" (770).] Montaigne's
text is in fact a detailed plea for the autonomy of the subject.

It begins with an attack on the vice of vanity, well within the Stoic
tradition, a vice which seems disposed to assume a mask of generosity or
care for others; by reaction all attention spent on others becomes suspect.
Reputation and glory are (a) "la plus inutile, vaine et fauce monnoye qui soit
en nostre usage" (I:39, 241) ["the most useless, worthless, and false coin that
is current among us" (178)] and our care to acquire them is all the more
dangerous as it is cleverly disguised: (a) "ce beau mot dequoy se couvre
l'ambition et l'avarice: que nous ne sommes pas nez pour nostre particulier
ains pour le publicq" (237) ["that fine statement under which ambition and
avarice take cover—that we are not born for our private selves, but for the
public" (174).] All concern for glory, the most dangerous of pleasures
(volupté) must be renounced. (a) "Quitez avecq les autres voluptez celle qui
vient de l'approbation d'autruy" (247). ["Abandon with the other pleasures
that which comes from the approbation of others" (182).] Besides, one will
avoid, in so doing, many disappointments, for how can such approbation be
guaranteed? (b) "De fonder la recompense des actions vertueuses sur
l'approbation d'autruy, c'est prendre un trop incertain et trouble fonde-
ment" (III:2, 807). ["To found the reward for virtuous actions on the
approval of others is to choose too uncertain and shaky a foundation" (612).]

What on the other hand is certain and solid, is the judgment that each one will find by probing his own mind. (a) "Ce n'est pas pour la montre que nostre ame doit jouer son rolle, c'est chez nous au dedans, où nuls yeux ne donnent que les nostres . . ." (II:16, 623) ["It is not for show that our soul must play its part, it is at home, within us, where no eyes penetrate but our own . . ." (472)]: this is the general rule which Montaigne takes such pride in having so strictly applied: (b) "J'ay mes loix et ma court pour juger de moy, et m'y adresse plus qu'ailleurs" (III:2, 807). ["I have my own laws and court to judge men, and I address myself to them more than anywhere else" (613).] He does not fail to give examples of the exclusive relevance of the internal judgment: (a) "Il faut estre vaillant pour soy-mesmes" (II:16, 623) ["We must be valiant for ourselves" (472)], or be tranquil (c) "mais selon moy" (622). ["According to me" (471).]

One witnesses here a mutation of mentality. The idea that an action should be judged according to criteria that are internal to the individual, and not according to the degree of recognition that society grants it, is already present in Seneca as well as in Saint Paul; but it is indeed in Montaigne's time that it becomes, so to speak, a common good, an *idée reçue*. Here is a radical relativism comparable to that which Montaigne professes with respect to cultural diversity. Just as each society ought to be measured according to its own values (instead of being declared barbarous simply because it is different from us), each individual here becomes his own judge and decides according to his own lights what is good and what is evil.

It is very revealing in this respect to see how for Montaigne the word "honor," which defined the value recognized by the group, almost becomes pejorative; it is in fact displaced from its hierarchical rank by individual and internal values.

> (c) Leur devoir est le marc, leur honneur n'est que l'escorce. . . . (a) Leurs intentions, leur desir et leur volonté . . . sont pieces où l'honneur n'a que voir . . . (c) Toute personne d'honneur choisit de perdre plustost son honneur, que de perdre sa conscience. [II:16, 630]

> Their duty is the pith, their honor is only the rind. . . . (a) their intentions, their desire, and their will . . . are parts in which honor is not concerned . . . (c) Any person of honor chooses rather to lose his honor than to lose his conscience. [478]

The first occurrence of "honor" in this last sentence indicates that the only way of recuperating the word is by identifying it with virtue. A consequence of this installation of conscience as a supreme judge is the erasure of the border between intention and act, because conscience is present in both. (a) "L'offence et envers Dieu et en la conscience seroit aussi grande de le desirer que de l'effectuer" (630). ["The offense, both toward God and in the conscience, would be as great in the desiring as in the doing" (478).]

But one should not stop at this juncture. It does not suffice to disentangle the self from all dependence on the opinion of others; it is also necessary to succeed in liberating the self from any relation with them, because of the uncertainty and confusion of such a relationship. This denial of the relationships that bind us to others on earth does not come about as it does in the Christian tradition, for the sake of the bond to God. Montaigne simply finds it more economical to depend only upon himself. (a) "Faisons que nostre contentement despende de nous, desprenons nous de toutes les liaisons qui nous attachent à autruy, gaignons sur nous de pouvoir à bon escient vivre seuls et y vivre à nostr'aise" (I:39, 240). ["Let us make our contentment depend on ourselves; let us cut loose from all the ties that bind us to others; let us win from ourselves the power to live really alone and to live that way at our ease" (177).] And would it not be more prudent, in anticipation of the eventual disappearance of a dear one, to act as if he were already absent? In this way, his loss will not make us suffer too much! Confined in ourselves, we must (a) "discourir et y rire comme sans femme, sans enfans et sans biens, sans train et sans valets, afin que, quand l'occasion adviendra de leur perte, il ne nous soit pas nouveau de nous en passer" (241). ["talk and laugh as if without wife, without children, without possessions, without retinue and servants, so that, when the time comes to lose them, it will be nothing new to us to do without them" (177).] By this reasoning, one could already lie down in one's coffin in order not to have unpleasant surprises when the moment would come.

We have nothing to fear: thus limited to ourselves, we will lack nothing. (a) "L'homme d'entendement n'a rien perdu, s'il a soy mesme" (I;39, 240). ["A man of understanding has lost nothing, if he has himself" (177).] Nothing! Man is a self-sufficient totality. (a) "Vous et un compagnon estes assez suffisant theatre l'un à l'autre, ou vous à vous-mesmes" (247). ["You and one companion are an adequate theater for each other, or you for yourself" (182)]: one can perfectly do without the other, for the self is multiple. (a) "Nous avons une ame contournable en soy mesme" (241). ["We have a soul that can be turned upon itself" (177).] And Montaigne claims to have made the best of it by keeping to these principles: (b) "Autant que je puis, je m'employe tout à moy" (III:10, 1003). ["As much as I can, I employ myself entirely upon myself" (766).] (a) "Moy, je tiens que je ne suis que chez moy" (II:16, 626). ["As for me, I hold that I exist only in myself" (474).] One could find here a particularly favorable predisposition: (b) "La plus part des esprits ont besoing de matiere estrangere pour se desgourdir et exercer" ["Most minds need foreign matter to arouse and exercise them"], but not his:

> son plus laborieux et principal estude, c'est s'estudier à soy. . . . Il a dequoy esveiller ses facultez par luy mesme. Nature luy a donné, comme à tous, assez de matiere sienne pour son utilité, et de subjects siens assez où inventer et juger. [III:3, 819]

> its principal and most laborious study is studying itself. . . . It has the power to awaken its faculties by itself. Nature has given to it as to all minds enough material of its own for its use, and enough subjects of its own for invention and judgment. [621]

Thus, other minds can follow in this path, if they truly want to.

Thus freed of useless preoccupations, one can concentrate on the essential: the self. Montaigne paraphrases Seneca (a) "La plus grande chose du monde, c'est de sçavoir estre à soy" (I:39, 242). ["The greatest thing in the world is to know how to belong to oneself" (178)], and he transforms it into a precept: (b) "Tu as bien largement affaire chez toy, ne t'esloingne pas" (III:10, 1004). ["You have quite enough to do at home; don't go away" (767).] One always pays too much attention to others: (a) "C'est assez vescu pour autruy, vivons pour nous au moins ce bout de vie. Ramenons à nous et à nostre aise nos pensées et nos intentions" (I:39, 242). ["We have lived enough for others; let us live at least this remaining bit of life for ourselves. Let us bring back our thoughts and plans to ourselves and our well-being" (178).] Once back at home, one should not let others intrude. It is imperative to preserve within the self a space sheltered from foreign eyes:

> (a) Il se faut reserver une arriereboutique toute nostre, toute franche, en laquelle nous establissons nostre vraye liberté et principale retraicte et solitude. En cette-cy faut-il prendre nostre ordinaire entretien de nous à nous mesmes, et si privé que nulle acointance ou communication estrangiere y trouve place . . . [241]

> We must reserve a back shop all our own, entirely free, in which to establish our real liberty and our principal retreat and solitude. Here our ordinary conversation must be between us and ourselves, and so private that no outside association or communication can find a place . . . [177]

Exchanging with others can only estrange us from ourselves, and such is not exactly Montaigne's ideal. (a) "Prenons de bonn'heure congé de la compaignie; despetrons nous de ces violentes prinses qui nous engagent ailleurs et esloignent de nous" (242). ["Let us take an early leave of the company; let us break free from the violent clutches that engage us elsewhere and draw us away from ourselves" (178).] (b) "Aux affections qui me distrayent de moy et attachent ailleurs, à celles là certes m'oppose-je de toute ma force" (III:10, 1003). ["But the passions that distract me from myself and attach me elsewhere, those in truth I oppose with all my strength" (767).] In this respect, Montaigne distinguishes himself from his contemporaries who feel (b) "sans vie quand ils sont sans agitation tumul- tuaire. . . ." (c) "L'occupation est à certaine maniere de gens marque de suffisance et de dignité" (1004 ["without life when they are without tumultuous agitation. . . ." (c) "Occupation is to a certain manner of people a mark of ability and dignity" (767).]

If the spirit of diversion *(l'esprit de divertissement)* is reprehensible, this is because it appertains only to the surface of our being, and not its inner depths. If Montaigne has to accept a degree of unavoidable social communi- cations, he assigns it a rather low place: the essential self is alone; relations with others belong to the accidental.

> (a) Il se faut servir de ces commoditez accidentales et hors de nous, en tant qu'elles nous sont plaisantes, mais sans en faire nostre principal fonde- ment: ce ne l'est pas; ny la raison ni la nature ne le veulent. Pourquoy contre ses loix asservirons nous nostre contentement à la puissance d'autruy? [I:39, 243]

> We should use these accidental and external conveniences, so far as they are agreeable to us, but without making them our mainstay; they are not; neither reason nor nature will have it so. Why should we, contrary to their laws, enslave our contentment to the power of others? [179]

Or in this metaphorical shortcut: we may (a) "aymer ce-cy et cela, mais n'espouser rien que soy" (242) ["love this and that, but be wedded only to ourselves" (178)]: a strange solipsistic marriage. Regarding the affairs of others, Montaigne is willing to (b) "[s]'en charger, non de les incorporer" (III:10, 1004) ["take them on (his) shoulders, not to incorporate them" (767).] Various degrees of engagement in the things of the world should be differentiated; but in true intimacy the mind ends up being alone with itself. (b) "Les unes, il les luy faut seulement presenter, les autres attacher, les autres incorporer. Elle peut voir et sentir toutes choses, mais elle ne se doibt paistre que de soy" (1009). ["Some must be simply presented to it, others attached to it, others incorporated into it. It can see and feel all things, but it should feed only on itself" (771).] After marriage with the self, now we have self-cannibalism *(autophagie)*. One should not confuse these accidents with the (b) "Affaires essentiels, propres et naturels" (1004) ["essential, proper, and natural affairs" (767)] of the subject. Such is the nature of man: (c) "Elle nous dresse pour nous, non pour autruy; pour estre, non pour sembler" (II:37, 761). ["trains us for ourselves, not for others; for being not for seeming" (577).] The self *(Je)* is to the other what being is to seeming.

Henceforth, a subordinate place will be reserved to commerce with others. It is striking to see that, to describe this place, Montaigne often uses an economic metaphor, and even a mercantile one. (c) "Il est temps de nous desnoüer de la societé, puisque nous n'y pouvons rien apporter. Et qui ne peut prester, qu'il se defende d'emprunter" (I:39, 242). ["It is time to untie ourselves from society, since we can contribute nothing to it. And he who cannot lend, let him keep from borrowing" (178).] (a) "Je veux estre riche par moy, non par emprunt. . . . les actions de la vertu, elles sont trop nobles d'elles mesmes pour rechercher autre loyer que de leur propre valeur" (II:16, 625, 629). ["I want to be rich by myself, not by borrowing. . . . the actions of virtue are too noble within themselves to seek any other reward than from their own worth" (474, 477).] What is significant here is not only the opposition borrowing/owning (which corresponds to the opposition internal/external) but the very fact of describing human relations in purely commercial terms: social values, such as honor, having been exhausted, everything has to be converted into an economic exchange between individuals. The essay "Of husbanding your will" (III:10) develops more fully this economic analogy. (b) "Mon opinion est qu'il se faut prester à autruy et ne se donner qu'à soy-mesme" (1003). ["My opinion is that we must lend ourselves to others and give ourselves only to ourselves" (767)] writes Montaigne, again following Seneca. He therefore reproaches those who are too preoccupied with others for their lavish prodigality. (b) "Personne ne distribue son argent à autruy, chacun y distribue son temps et sa vie" (1004). ["No one distributes his money to others, everyone distributes his time and his life on them" (768).] Montaigne thus assimilates without any reservation social values to economic values, whereas (b) "l'avarice nous seroit utile et louable" (1004). ["avarice would be useful to us and laudable" (768).] Sometimes, he will extend further the metaphor:

> (b) les hommes se donnent à louage. Leurs facultez ne sont pas pour eux, elles sont pour ceux à qui ils s'asservissent; leurs locataires sont chez eux, ce ne sont pas eux. Cette humeur commune ne me plaict pas: il faut mesnager la liberté de nostre ame et ne l'hypothequer qu'aux occasions justes. [1004]

Men give themselves for hire. Their faculties are not for them, they are for those to whom they enslave themselves; their tenants are at home inside, not they. This common humor I do not like. We must husband the freedom of our soul and mortgage it only on the right occasions. [767]

Here the psychologist has been replaced by the real estate agent, anxious to protect the interests of landlords from intrusive tenants.

But couldn't we ask: what about friendship? Isn't it an essential and not an accidental relationship, which affects the subject from the inside and not only from the outside? This question is all the more apt since Montaigne has the reputation of having experienced the greatest friendship which he never allows us to forget: (b) "En la vraye amitié, de laquelle je suis expert, je me donne à mon amy plus que je ne le tire à moy" (III:9, 977). ["In true friendship, in which I am expert, I give myself to my friend more than I draw him to me" (746).] The mercantile language is still acceptable, but for once generosity seems more appreciated than avarice.

Montaigne does insist on the exceptional character of friendship. A true friendship is excessively rare, (a) "c'est beaucoup si la fortune y arrive une fois en trois siecles" (I:28, 184). ["it is a lot if fortune can do it once in three centuries" (136).] Therefore what can be said about it cannot be applied to the daily intercourse between men. Under no circumstances should it be confused with the relations between parents and children, or between men and women. It is so exceptional in fact that it is not even a relation to another person. According to Montaigne, what defines friendship is precisely the disappearance of alterity; I become the other, and in so doing I can retain my essential self. (a) "En l'amitié dequoy je parle, elles [nos ames] se meslent et confondent l'une en l'autre, d'un melange si universel, qu'elles effacent et ne retrouvent plus la couture qui les a jointes" (188). ["In the friendship I speak of, our souls mingle and blend with each other so completely that they efface the seam that joined them" (139).] Each of the two souls loses itself in the other: (a) "Je dis perdre, à la verité, ne nous reservant rien qui nous fut propre, ny qui fut ou sien ou mien" (189). ["I say lose, in truth, for neither of us reserved anything for himself, nor was anything either his or mine" (139).] They both constitute just a single whole: (a) "Cette parfaicte amitié, dequoy je parle, est indivisible; chacun se donne si entier à son amy, qu'il ne luy reste rien à departir ailleurs" (191) ["this perfect friendship I speak of is indivisible: each one gives himself so wholly to his friend that he has nothing left to distribute elsewhere" (141)]; so that if the friend dies, (a) "il me semble n'estre plus qu'à demy" (193). ["only half of me seems to be alive now" (143).] Just as confronted with another culture he could only admire it because he found—or thought he did—his own values in it, he makes a friend of the other only because he recognizes himself in him. The other as such has to disappear: the true friend is (c) "celuy qui n'est pas autre: c'est moy" (191). ["the one who is not another man: he is myself" (142).] Friendship is so exceptional a relationship that it ceases to be one at all.

COMMUNICATION

Reviewing the different relationships which occupy the life of a man, Montaigne, in the essay "Of three kinds of association" (III:3), concludes that the most precious is the one we have with books. The reason for that is clear, and again it springs from the owner's reflex: this association *(commerce)* is (b) "plus seur et plus à nous" (827) ["much more certain and more our own" (628)] than the others. Montaigne did not forget the advice of Pliny the Younger, quoted elsewhere: (a) "t'adonner à l'estude des lettres, pour en tirer quelque chose qui soit toute tienne" (I:39, 244). ["to devote yourself to the study of letters, in order to derive from them something that is all your own" (180).] But doesn't this conclusion, which should crown his argumentation as a whole, turn it around suddenly, against him? Montaigne replaced friends by books and he subordinated his entire life to this unique activity: writing. But how can he imagine that by this very activity he has turned his back upon society? Language implies society and there is no speech which is not really an appeal to someone else: one cannot speak *of* something without at the same time speaking *to* someone. "I think" may imply "I am," but "I speak" implies without any possibility of doubt: "you are." If Montaigne were not interested in others, as he claims, he would simply not have written. The contradiction here is no longer between two kinds of texts—such as Montaigne's ideas on the relative and the absolute—it is rather between the virtual totality of his work, on the one hand, and the very purpose *(sens)* of its enunciation *(énonciation)*, on the other, between discourse as meaning and discourse as gesture.

For those reasons we should replace Montaigne's plea in its own terms. He who *writes* "I am not interested in others," cannot really mean it, because of the mere fact of having made such an utterance *(énoncé)* public; he can only mean something like "I am not interested in all the others," or "I am not interested in others in any old way," etc. Montaigne prefers a mediated communication with the authors of the past and with readers of the future to an immediate communication with his contemporaries; but in both cases, there is communication. We have seen the reasons for his preference: herald of the new economic and individualistic ideology,

Montaigne speaks of the psychic life like a small landlord, afraid of big expenditures and lending parcimoniously. One should be careful not to dilapidate one's patrimony; avoid strong attachments for they will provoke useless expenses, affective and others, and nothing would be really gained from them. What counts is what one already has at home. What bourgeois would not be delighted to derive the justifications for his good conscience at such a source?

Sometimes Montaigne thinks of himself as an exceptional person: (a) "Le monde regarde tousjours vis à vis; moy, je replie ma veue au dedans, je la plante, je l'amuse là. Chacun regarde devant soy; moy, je regarde dedans moy: je n'ai affaire qu'à moy, je me considere sans cesse, je me contrerolle, je me gouste. Les autres vont tousjours ailleurs . . . moy je me roulle en moy mesme" (II:17, 657–58). ["The world always looks straight ahead; as for me, I turn my gaze inward, I fix it there and keep it busy. Everyone looks in front of him; as for me, I look inside of me; I have no business but with myself; I continually observe myself, I take stock of myself, I taste myself. Others always go elsewhere . . . as for me, I roll about in myself" (499).] I am alone here and all the others are over there: this is the starting point of the individualist vision (its point of arrival—often reached without the subject's knowledge—is the growing *uniformization* of all individuals). But for the opposition to be real, there should exist inside the self, something different from the outside; otherwise the two ways would lead to the same end. It does not suffice to affirm that the inside is essential and the outside accidental: how can we be sure that a given thing is essence and another accident?

As soon as one tries to analyse Montaigne's own position, one realizes that it implies a conception of the natural and essential man as a solitary being. Considered as a moral and ethical precept, this conception leads directly to individualism and egoism. Taken as a description of facts, such an image is simply false, and even Montaigne's behavior drastically contradicts it. How can the self be constituted without contact with others? As he puts it elsewhere: (a) "Aucune raison ne s'establira sans une autre raison" (II:12, 601). ["No reason can be established without another reason" (454).]

If Montaigne's book is exceptional, this is not because the author is different from all others in that he has no need of them. Its originality resides elsewhere: instead of being subordinated to a transcendent goal, his self-scrutiny is an end in itself; autonomy is not in the origins but in the finality. Montaigne does not portray his life because it exemplifies something, but because it is as it is. The idea itself is not new, but no one before

Montaigne carried it out to the same extent, and no one since has found a comparable resonance. Even if it will never be the truth, solitude can be a program; the proof is that it still has authority, even today.

Montaigne willingly agrees to travel, but only because all skies are alike to him. He doesn't mind rubbing his brain against another's, but it is not particularly out of respect for him. (c) "Je prise peu mes opinions, mais je prise aussi peu celles des autres" (III:2, 814). ["I set little value on my own opinions, but I set just as little on those of others" (618).] In that case indeed one might as well stay at home.

III

INNER DIVERSITY

If man is able to adapt himself to all climates, if he can do without others, it is because he is already multiple in himself; our mind has more than one facet, and the internal dialogue within the self is not fundamentally different from that taking place outside. (a) "Et se trouve autant de difference de nous à nous mesmes, que de nous à autruy" (II:1, 337). ["And there is as much difference between us and ourselves as between us and others" (244).] Can the failure of attributing to the other his essential place in the world be compensated for by the presence of the other within ourselves?

One of the recurrent themes in Montaigne's text is the inner variety of man, an exact counterpart to the diversity of the world. (b) "Jamais deux hommes ne jugerent pareillement de mesme chose, et est impossible de voir deux opinions semblables exactement, non seulement en divers hommes, mais en mesme homme à diverses heures" (III:13, 1067). ["Never did two men judge alike about the same thing, and it is impossible to find two opinions exactly alike, not only in different men, but in the same man at different times" (817).] Nothing is more constant than inconstancy: (b) "Je croy des hommes plus mal aiséement la constance, que toute autre chose, et rien plus aiséement que l'inconstance" (II:1, 332). ["Nothing is harder for me than to believe in men's consistency, nothing easier than to believe in their inconsistency" (239)] he writes in an essay whose very title is "De l'inconstance de nos actions" ["Of the inconsistency of our actions" II:2, 239] we only are (c) "variation et contradiction" (335), ["variation and contradiction" (242).] My opinions change constantly, I am (a) "diversité et division infinie" (II:12, 563) ["infinite diversity and division" (423)]; (b) "je m'entraine quasi où je penche, comment que ce soit, et m'emporte de mon pois" (566). ["I draw myself along in almost any direction I lean, whatever it may be, and carry myself away by my own weight" (426).] All good minds claim my support: (a) "je les trouve avoir raison chacun à son tour, quoy qu'ils se contrarient" (570). ["I find each one right in his turn, although they contradict each other" (429).] Man is a patchwork. (a) "Nostre faict, ce ne sont que pieces rapportées" (II:1, 336). ["Our actions are nothing but a patchwork" (243).] (b) "L'homme, en tout en par tout, n'est que rapiesse-ment et bigarrure" (II:20, 675). ["Man, in all things and throughout, is but patchwork and motley" (511).] But the best image of man is again that of the lawyer: today he defends one cause, tomorrow another, quite different, but always with the same conviction, by which he is finally persuaded: (a) "Les advocats et les juges de nostre temps trouvent à toutes causes assez de biais pour les accommoder où bon leur semble" (II:12, 582). ["The lawyers and judges of our time find enough angles for all cases to arrange them any way they please" (439).]

In these conditions, it would be absurd to strive for fidelity to the self. (b) "Ce n'est pas estre amy de soy et moins encore maistre, c'est en estre esclave, de se suivre incessamment, et estre si pris à ses inclinations qu'on n'en puisse fourvoyer, qu'on ne les puisse tordre" (III:3, 819). ["We are not friends to ourselves, and still less masters, we are slaves, if we follow ourselves incessantly and are so caught up in our inclinations that we cannot depart from them or twist them about" (621).] (c) "Il n'y a que les fols certains et resolus" (I:26, 151). ["Only the fools are certain and assured" (111).] On the contrary, inconstancy is a good and it deserves the highest praise: (b) "C'est estre, mais ce n'est pas vivre, que se tenir attaché et obligé par necessité à un seul train. Les plus belles ames sont celles qui ont plus de variété et de soupplesse" (III:3, 818). ["It is existing, but not living, to keep ourselves bound and obliged by necessity to a single course. The fairest souls are those that have the most variety and adaptability" (621).]

The first reason for this inner diversity is external diversity itself; circumstances change, and we follow them like a weathervane. (a) "Leur ame, estant molle et sans resistance, seroit forcée de recevoir sans cesse autres impressions, la derniere effaçant tousjours la trace de la precedente" (II:12, 571). ["their soul, being soft and without resistance, would be forced to receive incessantly more and more different impressions, the last one always effacing the traces of the preceding one" (429).] But it is because reason, which is inside us, willingly lends itself to such changes: (a) "c'est un instrument de plomb et de cire, alongeable, ployable et accommodable à tous biais et à toutes mesures" (565) ["(it) is an instrument of lead and of wax, stretchable, pliable, and adaptable to all biases and all measures"

(425).] The inconstancy of our behavior comes as much from the changeable world as from our inner instability: (b) "Non seulement le vent des accidens me remue selon son inclination, mais en outre je me remue et trouble moy mesme par l'instabilité de ma posture" (II:1, 335). ["Not only does the wind of accident move me at will, but, besides, I am moved and disturbed as a result merely of my own unstable posture" (242).]

From this state of things there ensues an important consequence for the knowledge of man. Because man is a subject wonderfully (a) "divers, et ondoyant" ["diverse, and undulating"], we read in the very first essay of the book, "il est malaisé d'y fonder jugement constant et uniforme" (I:1, 9), ["It is hard to found any constant and uniform judgment on him" (5).] (c) "Nulle qualité nous embrasse purement et universellement" (I:38, 234–35). ["No quality embraces us purely and universally" (173).] It is impossible to describe the self in terms of a simple category: (b) "Je n'ay rien à dire de moy, entierement, simplement, et solidement, sans confusion et sans meslange, ny en un mot. DISTINGO est le plus universel membre de ma Logique" (II:1, 335). ["I have nothing to say about myself absolutely, simply, and solidly, without confusion and without mixture, or in one word. *Distinguo* is the most universal member of my logic" (242).]

> (c) Non seulement je trouve mal-aisé d'attacher nos actions les unes aux autres, mais chacune à part soy je trouve mal-aysé de la designer proprement par quelque qualité principalle, tant elles sont doubles et bigarrées à divers lustres. [III:13, 1076–77]

> Not only do I find it hard to link our actions with one another, but each one separately I find hard to designate properly by some principal characteristic, so two-sided and motley do they seem in different lights. [825]

But, moreover, since cognitive reason is itself subject to change, it appears as if perfect knowledge is impossible; Montaigne develops the argumentation of this epistemological skepticism particularly in the "Apology for Raymond Sebond" (II:12).

> (a) Finalement, il n'y a aucune constante existence, ny de nostre estre, ny de celuy des objects. Et nous, et nostre jugement, et toutes choses mortelles, vont coulant et roulant sans cesse. Ainsin il ne se peut establir rien de certain de l'un à l'autre, et le jugeant et le jugé estans en continuelle mutation et branle. [II:12, 601]

> Finally, there is no existence that is constant, either of our being or of that of objects. And we, and our judgment, and all mortal things go on flowing and rolling unceasingly. Thus nothing certain can be established about one

thing by another, both the judging and the judged being in continual change and motion. [455]

One way of overcoming the effects of this skepticism would be to deny both to man and to visible things the very category of being and to see them instead as mere conglomerates of attributes which themselves do remain knowable. When Montaigne recalls the diverse and contradictory actions of a single man, he suggests that it would be easier to renounce any categorization of being and to accept a description of the action itself. (c) "Quand, estant láche à l'infamie, il est ferme à la pauvreté; quand, estant mol entre les rasoirs des barbiers, il se trouve roide contre les espées des adversaires, l'action est loüable, non pas l'homme" (II:1, 336). ["When, though a coward against infamy, he is firm against poverty; when, though weak against the surgeons' knives, he is steadfast against the enemy's swords, the action is praiseworthy, not the man" (243).] And at the end of the "Apology," he formulates this general idea: (a) "Ce qui souffre mutation ne demeure pas un mesme, et, s'il n'est pas un mesme, il n'est donc pas aussi. Ains, quant et l'estre tout un, change aussi l'estre simplement, devenant tousjours autre d'un autre" (II:12, 603). ["what suffers change does not remain one and the same, and if it is not one and the same, it also *is* not; but together with its *being the same*, it also changes its simple *being*, from one thing always becoming another" (456).] Changes transform the subject into an other; what is not one, does not exist (and Montaigne strives to draw a proof of God's excellence from this precept).

To prove that one cannot usefully apply to man the distinctions between being and its attributes, essence and its accidents, and to deny all hierarchy within the self, Montaigne uses the same reasoning that helped him before to reject the existence of natural law. If something does not remain the same, it does not exist. (a) "Mais qu'est-ce donc qui est veritablement? Ce qui est eternel, c'est à dire qui n'a jamais eu de naissance, n'y n'aura jamais fin, à qui le temps n'apporte jamais aucune mutation" (603). ["But then what really is? That which is eternal: that is to say, what never had birth, nor will ever have an end; to which time never brings any change" (456).] Isn't this going too far? Montaigne believes in essences and accidents; unable to find in man anything that corresponds to his definition of essence, he declares man accidental and variable through and through; no new distinction gives shape to this magma of attributes—just as the laws of various countries, in the presumed absence of a natural law, were all considered to be equal. But with regard to a comparison between countries, Montaigne's practice did not remain quite consistent with this radical relativism. What is the status then of this other relativism, or rather "variabilism"—psychological and no longer cultural this time, but as radical as the first? Does it hold up better under the test of practice? For Montaigne himself, is man as unstable as he likes to say?

THE RULING PATTERN

When he describes man or when he describes himself, Montaigne likes to have recourse to the opposition between the natural and the artificial, between what is innate in us and what is acquired by education. There are (a) "facultez naturelles qui sont en moy,"; I dispose of "mes propres et naturels moyens" (I:26, 146) ["my own natural resources" (107)], and education should not try to (a) "forcer les propensions naturelles" (149), ["to force natural propensities" (109).] (b) "Les inclinations naturelles s'aident et fortifient par institution; mais elles ne se changent guiere . . ." (III:2, 810) ["Natural inclinations gain assistance and strength from education; but they are scarcely to be changed . . ." (615)] However, the example that he gives to illustrate this maxim is ambiguous; he had first learned Latin, then French; he no longer uses much Latin except in unexpected situations, when Latin words come out of his mouth unexpectedly, (c) "nature se sourdant et s'exprimant à force, à l'encontre d'un long usage" (810–11). ["Nature surging forth and expressing herself by force, in the face of long habit" (615).] Would the "natural" simply be what is a little more ancient than the "artificial"? For Montaigne, the difference remains nevertheless significant between extraneous or acquired desires, and those that are natural even if the former tend to supplant the latter, (a) "ny plus ny moins que si, en une cité, il y avoit si grand nombre d'estrangers qu'ils en missent hors les naturels habitans ou esteignissent leur authorité et puissance ancienne, l'usurpant entierement et s'en saisissant" (II:12, 472). ["neither more nor less than if there were such a great number of foreigners in a city that they put out the natural inhabitants, or extinguished their ancient authority and power, completely ursurping it and taking possession of it" (346).] This is the reason for choosing as an ideal: (b) "Mener l'humaine vie conformément à sa naturelle condition" (III:2, 809) ["Lead the life of man in conformity with its natural condition" (614).]

Other expressions recall the difference between owning and borrowing, being and having. (c) "J'aime mieux forger mon ame que la meubler" (III:3, 819). ["I would rather fashion my mind than furnish it" (622)]. The two activities should not be confused. I know myself from the inside whereas others perceive only the outside: (a) "Les estrangers ne voyent que les evenemens et apparences externes . . . Ils ne voyent pas mon coeur, ils ne voyent que mes contenances" (II:16, 625). ["Strangers see only the results and outward appearances . . . They do not see my heart, they see only my countenance" (474).] The "inner qualities" of man should not then be confused with the "accidents that threaten him" (303) nor further should the mask and the face be confused:

> (b) Il faut jouer deuement nostre rolle, mais comme rolle d'un personnage emprunté. Du masque et de l'apparence il n'en faut pas faire une essence réelle, ny de l'estranger le propre. Nous ne sçavons pas distinguer la peau de la chemise. (c) C'est assés de s'enfariner le visage, sans s'enfariner la poictrine. [III:10, 1011]

> We must play our part duly, but as the part of a borrowed character. Of the mask and appearance we must not make a real essence, nor of what is foreign what is our very own. We cannot distinguish the skin from the shirt. (c) It is enough to make up our face, without making up our heart. [773]

The lawyer must not allow himself to be trapped in his own game, and to forget that, once at home, he has to regain his true nature.

Montaigne did not want to depend upon others but only upon himself: not on what he borrows but on what he owns. (c) "Je n'ay rien mien que moy" (III:9, 968) ["I have nothing of my own but myself" (740)]: the self is what really belongs to me, contrary to the rest. And when he portrays himself, he is far from seeing himself as variegated and unstable as his general propositions would imply. He who had written that man is only composed of patches also declares: (b) "Je fay coustumierement entier ce que je fay, et marche tout d'une piece" (III:2, 812). ["I customarily do wholeheartedly whatever I do, and go my way all in one piece" (616).] He who had declared the inexistence of the subject, identifies being and doing without difficulty, and even envisages the harmony between the two: (b) "Mes actions sont reglées et conformes à ce que je suis et à ma condition" (813). ["My actions are in order and conformity with what I am and with my condition" (617).] He has in his very depth, a (b) "forme universelle," ["nature as a whole"]—a "ruling pattern"—a "teinture universelle" (813), ["tincture with which (he) is stained all over" (617]. The latter is impenetrable by education or by habits: (b) "Il n'est personne, s'il s'escoute, qui ne descouvre en soy une forme sienne, une forme maistresse, qui luicte contre l'institution" (811). ["There is no one who, if he listens to himself, does not discover in himself a pattern all his own, a ruling pattern, which struggles against education" (615).]

So, if we look more closely, Montaigne has not changed that much; in fact, he has not even changed at all. I (c) "trouve que (b) ma raison est celle mesme que j'avoy en l'aage plus licencieux" (815) ["find that (b)it (reason) is the very same I had in my more licentious years" (619)]; (b) "quasi dés sa naissance il [mon jugement] est un: mesme inclination, mesme route, mesme force" (812). ["virtually since its birth it (my judgment) has been one: the same inclination, the same road, the same strength" (616).] Moreover he is sure that the future will ressemble the past: (b) "à circonstances pareilles, je seroy tousjours tel" (813). ["in similar circumstances I should always be the same" (617).] I (b) "en ferois autant d'icy à mille ans en pareilles occasions" (813). ["should do the same a thousand years from now in similar situations" (618).] But what if events and circumstances were to change? The effect would probably not be different, since Montaigne imagines himself identical to himself in the course of a second life: (b) "Je reviendrois volontiers de l'autre monde pour démentir celuy qui me formeroit autre que je n'estois" (III:9, 983). ["I would willingly come back from the other world to give the lie to any man who portrayed me other than I was" (751).] We have reached here the antipodes of protean man.

One cannot explain this contradiction by invoking the evolution of Montaigne's opinions, from the skeptical negation of a nature characteristic of man to the wise and Epicurean acceptance of things as they are. In fact, some texts supporting both the thesis and the antithesis can be found throughout his career. Furthermore, the two positions should not be presented as being radically irreconcilable. In spite of their contradictions, they remain interdependent because of Montaigne's perpetual search for a unique principle which would explain man's behavior. The principle will simply have been changed: in the first instance everything in man is acquired, artificial, external, accidental; in the second, everything is innate, natural, internal, essential. But Montaigne's procedure has remained the same. He only knows all or nothing: either man is immutable, or he is in perpetual mutation: either he is pure essence, or he is nothing but accidents. To the complexity of facts, he answers with a contradiction of theses. And what if man were neither pure motion, nor pure immobility?

But the demonstration would be of little interest if it merely presented Montaigne as an incoherent author, whose utterances were contradictory. If these analyses had only reached this conclusion, they would have merely confirmed one of the theses in question: since man is infinitely changeable, it is natural that he contradicts himself. But this would be to play Montaigne's own game which he wants to impose on us, a game which even dictates to him his form of expression: the essay, a genre opposed to the treatise, lends itself particularly well to the changing mood of the author. Montaigne's text, upon close reading, turns out to be, on the contrary, strikingly monotonous. Take his comparison of cultures. Montaigne enunciates two theses, but the attempt to discover which one is really his is useless; his position depends on their interaction, that is to say, the masking of noncritical universalism as relativism. Likewise, his position emerges from the copresence of both theses, neither one of which really represents his "truth." It is because he has made these shattering declarations on the instability of man, on his radical mutability, that Montaigne can afford to assume the idea of an unchanging human nature with such ingenuity: each thesis clears *(dédouane)* the other.

A few of Montaigne's reflexions permit us to imagine what way he himself would have chosen if he had tried to extricate himself from these contradictions; but one should add immediately that their rarity attests to their marginality in his system.

> (b) L'accoustumance est une seconde nature, et non moins puissante. (c) Ce qui manque à ma coustume, je tiens qu'il me manque. . . . (b) Je ne suis plus en termes d'un grand changement, et de me jetter à un nouveau trein et inusité. . . . Il n'est plus temps de devenir autre. [III:10, 1010]

> Habit is a second nature, and no less powerful. What my habit lacks, I hold that I lack. . . . I am no longer headed for any great change or inclined to plunge into a new and untried way of life, . . . It is too late to become other than I am. [772]

It happens that custom, or usage, ceases to be a simple mask of nature, to become, in the long run, a nature as natural as the first. In the long run; for the time factor comes into play, and what is accidental ends up as essence (we have already seen examples of this); thus, what pertained only to owning, becomes the property of being. (b) "Par long usage, cette forme m'est passée en substance, et fortune en nature" (1011). ["By long usage this form of mine has turned into substance, and fortune into nature" (773).] And in "Of experience":

> (b) Quoy que j'aye esté dressé autant qu'on a peu à la liberté et à l'indifference, si est-ce que par nonchalance, m'estant en vieillissant plus arresté sur certaines formes . . . la coustume a desjà, sans y penser, imprimé si bien en moy son caractere en certaines choses, que j'appelle excez de m'en despartir. [III:13, 1083]

> Although I was trained as much as possible for freedom and adaptability, yet it is a fact that through carelessness, and because I have lingered more

in certain ways as I grow old ... habit, imperceptibly, has already so imprinted its character upon me in certain things that I call it excess to depart from it. [830]

Form can become substance, chance, necessity, and accident essence. But does this really mean a recognition of the nature-custom duality and an attempt to articulate their action in man? Nothing is less certain. In fact, Montaigne situates himself on the "variabilist" side of the question, but he corrects it by introducing within its core a hierarchy between ruling patterns, sanctioned by time, and by subordinate patterns. Instead of the opposition between essence and accident can be found its simulacrum: an opposition between ancient and recent accidents. History has assumed the role of nature.

When the articulation of the universal and the particular is neglected, one runs the risk of claiming that everything is particular, surreptitiously erecting thereby one's own private ideas into a universal system. In my book, Montaigne writes in the foreword, "To the Reader," (a) "je veus qu'on m'y voie en ma façon simple, naturelle et ordinaire, sans contention et artifice," ["I want to be seen here in my simple, natural, ordinary fashion, without straining or artifice,"] and he likes to imagine himself "entre ces nations qu'on dict vivre encore sous la douce liberté des premieres loix de nature" (3) ["among those nations which are said to live still in the sweet freedom of nature's first laws" (2).] But the noble savage does not exist, and that so-called nature is as imaginary as the one that Montaigne attributes to his "fashions" *(façons)*. The ignorance of others is indissolubly tied to the ignorance of the self, and humanist declarations can have grave consequences: for every policy of annexation—whether of countrymen or of alien others—will find its justification in declarations.

Translated by Pierre Saint-Amand

FRANÇOIS RIGOLOT

Montaigne's Purloined Letters

> We are simply dealing with a letter which has been diverted from its path, one whose course has been *prolonged* (literally "purloined") or, to use the language of the post office, an undelivered letter *(lettre en souffrance).*
>
> —Lacan[1]

IN THE BEGINNING WAS DEATH ...

> La mort se promène entre les lettres [Death wanders between letters]
>
> —Derrida[2]

In the morning of Wednesday, August 18th, 1563, Etienne de La Boétie, Montaigne's great friend, died "after living 32 years, 9 months, and 17 days".[3] For Montaigne the man, this death was a terrible blow, a traumatic experience or, as he says himself, a ["human calamity" (1050)]; but for Montaigne the writer, it was the beginning of a literary career.

La Boétie's death is related to us only through a written document, a letter that Montaigne wrote to his father, probably soon after the tragic event. This long and beautiful letter constitutes an extraordinary testimony of love from a man who has painfully recreated the last moments of his friend. The dignified momentum of the scene comes partly from the fact that it is patterned after literary models ranging from Plato's rendition of Socrates's farewell to the *Gospel* account of Christ's *ultima verba.* Montaigne has himself play the central part of the scenario, both as narrator and character. He puts words in La Boétie's mouth that tend to grant Montaigne

1. "C'est bel et bien la *lettre détournée* qui nous occupe, celle dont le trajet a été *prolongé* (c'est littéralement le mot anglais), ou, pour recourir au vocabulaire postal, la *lettre en souffrance." Ecrits I* (Paris: Editions du Seuil, 1966), pp. 39–40. Our translation. For another English version of the same, see: "Seminar on *The Purloined Letter," Yale French Studies,* 48 (1972), p. 59.

2. "Edmond Jabès et la question du livre," in *L'Ecriture et la différence* (Paris: Editions du Seuil, 1967), p. 108. Our translation.

3. The English translation of Montaigne's *Letters* is taken, sometimes with slight changes, from *The Complete Works of Montaigne,* translated by Donald M. Frame (London: Hamish Hamilton, n.d.). The page reference will be given in parentheses (1056), from now on in the body of the text.

a prominent status and make him worthy of this great man's attentive sollicitude. La Boétie calls him "Mon frère" ["My brother"] repeatedly and asks him to get closer and closer to him as death draws near:

"Mon frere, me dit-il, tenez vous au pres de moy, s'il vous plaist." [Pl.1359][4]

He said to me: "My brother, stay close to me, please" [1055]

Estant sur ces destresses il m'appella souvent pour s'informer seulement si j'estois pres de luy. [Pl.1360]

In his distress he often called me simply to know whether I was near him. [1056]

Again and again, this death is described by Montaigne as representing a sense of irretrievable loss: to himself as well as to the world at large. To La Boétie's Stoic statement that death to him is "nothing indeed," Montaigne has himself reply in the letter:

Le *dommage* seroit à moy qui *perdrois* la compaignie d'un si grand, si sage, & si certain amy, & tel que je serois asseuré de n'en trouver jamais de semblable. [Pl.1350]

The *loss* would be mine, for I would *lose* the company of so great, so wise, and so sure a friend, such a friend that I would be certain never to find another like him. [1048]

Then he quotes his friend as worrying about those he will leave behind, specifically his wife, his uncle and Montaigne himself. The words *lose* and *loss* (*perdre* and *perte*) are repeated several times in an obsessive fashion throughout La Boétie's speech.[5]

The same thematic development of the sense of loss can be found in the famous essay "Of Friendship" in which Montaigne returns to the account of his friend's death. At the end of chapter I:28, the exceptional character of his grief is stressed again by the repetitive use of the words *perte* [loss] and *perdre* [lose]:

(a) La *perte* d'un tel amy . . .

4. All references to Montaigne's French letters will be, unless otherwise indicated, to the Pléiade edition of the *Oeuvres complètes*, edited by A. Thibaudet and M. Rat. Appropriate corrections will be made in a few cases. The page number will be given between brackets in the text, preceded by Pl.: (Pl. 1359). The other quotations will be consistent with the rest of the issue.

5. For instance: "bear the loss"; "the consideration of your loss"; "not to lose"; "whatever your loss"; "the grief over losing me". (1048–49).

The *loss* of such a friend . . .

Depuis le jour que je le *perdy* . . . je ne fais que trainer languissant.

Since the day I *lost* him, I only drag on a weary life.

(a) Et les plaisirs mesmes qui s'offrent à moy, au lieu de me consoler, me redoublent le regret de sa *perte*. [143]

And the very pleasures that come my way, instead of consoling me, redouble my grief for his *loss*. [193]

The obsessional use of the vocabulary of *loss* to describe La Boétie's *absence* is matched, earlier in the same essay, by an equally profuse use of a similar vocabulary to describe his *presence* and stress the mutually intense love that bound the friends together. A close textual study of the various layers of discourse is quite instructive in this respect.

The 1580 edition describes this very special friendship as follows:[6]

(a) C'est je ne sçay quelle quinte essence de tout ce meslange, qui ayant saisi toute ma volonté, l'amena se plonger & *se perdre* dans la sienne. Je dis *perdre* à la vérité, ne luy reservant rien qui luy fut propre, ny qui fut sien. [189]

It is I know not what quintessence of all this mixture, which, having seized my whole will, led it to plunge and *lose* itself in his. I say *lose,* in truth, for he never reserved anything for himself nor was anything his. [139]

Between 1580 and 1588 Montaigne made no correction on or addition to this passage. But after 1588, as he was rereading the 1588 edition, he decided to change the wording in order to emphasize more forcefully the reciprocal character of this friendship. On the "exemplaire de Bordeaux" of the *Essays,* the final text reads as follows:[7]

C'est je ne sçay quelle quinte essence de tout ce meslange, (c) qui ayant saisi toute ma volonté, l'amena se plonger & se perdre dans la sienne *qui, ayant saisi [toute] sa volonté, l'amena se plonger et [se] perdre en la mienne d'une faim, d'une concurrance pareille.* (a) Je dis perdre à la vérité, ne *nous* reservant rien qui *nous* fut propre, ny qui fut *ou sien ou mien.* [189]

---

6. The Pléiade edition places the (c) layer of text at the wrong place, and does not mention the emendations that Montaigne made to the 1588 edition.

7. Quoted from Strowski's *Reproduction, en phototypie de l'Exemplaire de Bordeaux* (Paris: Hachette, 1912), vol. I, plate 145. The words placed between square brackets were added by Montaigne above the lines.

> It is I know not what quintessence of all this mixture, which, having seized
> my whole will, led it to plunge and lose itself in his; *which, having seized
> his [whole] will, led it to plunge and lose itself in mine, with equal hunger,
> equal rivalry.* I say lose, in truth, for *neither of us* reserved anything for
> *himself,* nor was anything *either his or mine.* [139]

Whereas in the original version Montaigne had described the "fusion of
souls" from his own, unilateral point of view ["having seized *my* whole will
. . ."], in his personal copy of the 1588 edition he added a parallel subordinate clause to make it clear that his friend had indeed experienced exactly
the same devastating passion, with the same feeling of *losing* himself in the
other ["having seized *his* whole will . . ."]. One should note, incidentally,
that the famous phrase (c) "Par ce que c'estoit luy; par ce que c'estoit moy"
(188) ["Because it was he, because it was I"] is also a late addition with a
characteristically symmetrical structure.

The tautological nature of all these added parallel constructions is
striking. The words used in the 1580 text are reproduced in a mirror-like
fashion, as if the writer was in a position to gain a perfect knowledge of his
dead friend's most intimate feelings and equate them with his own. This is
perhaps the most conscious example of self-appropriation in the *Essays.*
Montaigne has interiorized La Boétie's own consciousness; or, to use the
well-known metaphor, he has made it enter the bee-hive of the book, in
which it has finally become his "miel tout sien," a honey of his own making
(I:26, (a)), [(111).]

Thus there is a counterbalancing effect to this sense of loss, as it is
thematized throughout the text of the *Essays.* First Montaigne expresses
the "ardent affection" of his friendship in a two-tiered textual experience
that takes the form of a mutual loss of self into the other. In another late
addition he writes:

> (c)Le secret que j'ay juré ne deceller à nul autre, je le puis sans parjure,
> communiquer à celuy qui n'est pas autre: c'est moy. C'est un assez grand
> miracle de se doubler. [191]

> The secret I have sworn to reveal to no other man, I can impart without
> perjury to the one who is not another man: he is myself. It is a great enough
> miracle to be doubled. [142]

Second, when the other's physical presence disappears with death, the
androgynous nature of the self must split. The result is a deep sense of being
reduced to one half of one's "original" being: (a) "J'estois desjà si fait et

accoustumé à estre deuxiesme par tout, qu'il me semble n'estre plus qu'à demy" (193). ["I was already so formed and accustomed to being a second self that only half of me seems to be alive now" (143).]

This is why the insecure self must turn to other ways to alleviate his solitude and "counterbalance his loss" ("contrepoiser cette perte"). Unexpectedly, in the chapter "Of Solitude" (I:30), Montaigne tells us that the wise man must build for himself a psychological stronghold against personal calamities. Quoting Seneca's *Letter IX*, he recalls the story of Stilpo who, having lost ("perdu") wife, children and property in a fire, would quietly declare that "thanks to God he had lost nothing of his own" ((a) "il n'y avoit, Dieu mercy, rien perdu du sien"). The Essayist adopts Stilpo's Stoic stance as he comments: "when the time comes to lose them [wife, children, possessions], it will be nothing new to us to do without them" ("quand l'occasion viendra de leur *perte*, il ne nous soit pas nouveau de nous en passer"). Finally, he reverts to the thematics of loss once more in the general statement that serves to introduce the famous passage on the "arrière-boutique" (back-shop): (a) "Certes l'homme d'entendement n'a rien perdu, s'il a soy mesme" (240). [Certainly a man of understanding has lost nothing, if he has himself. (177).

Yet, Montaigne has lost much more than "wife, children and possessions"; he has been deprived of the other half of himself. It is not therefore surprising to see him move from Seneca's Letter to a more relevant piece of writing, Pliny's advice to his friend Cornelius Rufus: (a) "Je te conseille . . . de t'adonner à l'estude des *lettres*, pour en tirer quelque chose qui soit toute tienne" (244). ["I advise you . . . to devote yourself to the study of *letters*, in order to derive from them something that is all your own" (180).] Characteristically, this invitation to turn solitude into a productive activity—the study of letters—is also couched in epistolary form: Pliny the Younger's *Letter* I:1, 3. In Lacanian terms, one might refer at this point to the "insistence of the Letter in the unconscious of the text." The *Letter*, both as literary genre and humanistic study, seems to function as a symbolic substitute for an original, inaugural loss. To counterbalance this loss ("pour contrepoiser cette perte"), Montaigne will quote and refer to Cicero's, Pliny's and Seneca's letters, establishing the priority of the epistolary form as signifier, prolonging it ("purloining" it) and diverting it from its path throughout the *Essays*.

At the beginning was Death. And at the beginning was the letter Montaigne wrote to his father about La Boétie's death. The symbolic sense of the letter, as signifier, possessed the writer from the beginning and sustained itself in displacement throughout his writings. In a way, one could say, to paraphrase Derrida in a literal sense, that "la mort se promène entre les lettres" [Death wanders between letters][8].

THE "PLACE" OF LA BOÉTIE'S "HUMANE LETTERS"

In the letter Montaigne wrote to his father he placed at the midpoint La Boétie's literary legacy. The passage needs to be quoted in its entirety:

"Mon frere, dit-il, que j'ayme si cherement, & que j'avois choisy parmy tant d'hommes, pour renouveller avec vous ceste vertueuse & sincere amitié, de laquelle l'usage est par les vices dés si long temps esloigné d'entre nous, qu'il n'en reste que quelques vieilles traces en la memoire de l'antiquité: Je vous supplie pour signal de mon affection envers vous, vouloir estre successeur de ma Bibliothècque & de mes livres, que je vous donne: present bien petit, mais qui part de bon cueur: & qui vous est convenable pour l'affection que vous avez aux *lettres*. Ce vous sera μνημόσυνον *tui sodalis*." [Pl.1352]

"My brother, whom I love so dearly and whom I chose out of so many men in order to renew with you that virtuous and sincere friendship, the practice of which has for so long been driven from among us by our vices that there remain of it only a few old traces in the memory of antiquity, I entreat you to accept as a legacy my library and my books, which I give you as a sign of my affection toward you: a very small present, but one which comes from a willing heart and which is appropriate for you because of your fondness for *letters*. It will be *a remembrance of your friend*." [1050]

La Boétie's words are prophetic (or *made* prophetic by our narrator) in many ways. Montaigne's "fondness for letters" ("l'affection que vous avez aux lettres") finds its first eloquent expression precisely in this formal letter to the Father, which soon will become a letter to the literary world. Seven years after this death scene, Montaigne will publish his friend's *Works* and he will append this letter to the end of the book. Properly speaking, it will no longer be a "letter to the Father" since, by 1570, Pierre Eyquem had been dead for about two years. The letter has become a pretext for the public manifestation of Montaigne as an epistolary writer. The emotional account of La Boétie's death to the dead father serves quite a different purpose: it is Montaigne's birth certificate as a man of letters.

La Boétie's poems and translations will all be published according to

8. Derrida, loc. cit., p. 108.

the same ritual, i.e. with a dedicatory letter signed by his presumptive literary heir. In the *Notice to the Reader* of the *Translations*, Montaigne expresses the hope that, thanks to this publication, the loss of his friend will be at least partially repaired:

Advertissement au lecteur

Lecteur, *tu me dois tout* ce dont tu jouis de feu M. Estienne de la Boëtie . . .

Reader, *you owe to me all* that you enjoy of the late M. E. de la Boëtie . . .

N'ayant trouvé autre chose dans sa Librairie, qu'il me laissa par son testament, ancore n'ay-je pas voulu qu'il se *perdist*.

Finding nothing else in his library, which he left me in his will, I still did not want this to be *lost*

Asseure toy que *j'y ay faict ce que j'ay peu*, et que, depuis sept ans que nous l'avons *perdu*, je n'ay peu *recouvrer* que ce que tu en vois . . . [Pl. p.1719]

Be assured that *I have done what I could*, and that in the seven years since we *lost* him I have been able to *recover* only what you see here . . . [1061–62]

The thematics of loss are now linked with a definitely self-conscious effort to place the editor (i.e. the letter-writer and publicizer of the translations) at the center of the stage: all these "humane letters," Reader, you owe them to *me* ("Lecteur, tu me dois tout . . .").

Dedicatory letters will be written to friends (Henri de Mesmes for Plutarch's *Rules of Marriage*, Louis de Lansac for Xenophon's *Oeconomicus*) and to his wife (for Plutarch's *Letter of Consolation*). The Latin Poems (*Poemata*) and the book of French Verses (*Vers françois*) will also be prefaced with epistles to Michel de l'Hôpital and Paul de Foix. Indeed one could talk here of *Wiederholungszwang* (repetition compulsion or, as Lacan puts it, *repetition automatism*).[9] For Montaigne's literary production the primal scene was not the referential death scene but the inaugural scene of letter-writing which now repeats itself and only sustains itself in displacement.

On his death bed La Boétie, Montaigne tells us, had praised his uncle ("Mon bon oncle") whom he considered his true father ("Vous estes mon vray pere")' and he had thanked him profusely for training him so well in humane letters:

Tout ce que un tressage, tresbon & tresliberal pere pouvoit faire pour son

9. *Ecrits I*, op. cit., p. 19.

fils, tout cela avez vous fait pour moy, . . . *pour le soing qu'il a fallu à m'instruire aux bonnes lettres.* [Pl.1351]

Everything a very wise, very good, and very liberal father could have done for his son, you have done all that for me, . . . *in the care that was needed to instruct me in humane letters.* [1049]

La Boétie's "bonnes lettres" produced his *Works* which, in turn, produced Montaigne's own letters to accompany their publication. Even if one does not believe that psychoanalysis is indifferent to deep meanings, it is revealing that the latent organization of Montaigne's writings should allow for a *structure of exchange* in terms of signifiers. La Boétie talks to his "vray pere" (true father) who has made it possible for him to be instructed in letters; and this, in turn, is narrated to the reader in the form of a letter to the narrator's own father. One is tempted to think of the Oedipus complex in terms of this structural exchange, with the letter playing the role of "fixative" in the unconscious of the text.[10]

As many critics have shown, Montaigne planned his first book of *Essays* around his friend's major political discourse entitled *Voluntary Servitude*.[11] As early as 1574, when he was probably composing his chapter "Of Friendship" (I:28), Montaigne decided to honor his friend's memory by placing this booklet in the best spot (au "plus bel endroit"), i.e. in the middle (au "milieu") of his first volume of essays. Or, rather, this is what he *says* he decided to do, borrowing a "rich, artistic picture" from La Boétie and filling the space around it with poor, artless "grotesques," namely his "essays" (in the sense of "experimentations"). For the "masterpiece-in-the-center" simile does not seem to function too well when we look closely at the text. First, because anything called "artistic" or "formed according to art" is immediately suspicious in the context of the *Essays*. With Montaigne art has always a bad name; it means artificiality, un-naturalness, hence anything that is deprived of human life. Thus, calling *Voluntary Servitude* a "tableau élabouré" [a picture laboured over] is hardly a compliment. The second reason why the simile does not function is that the description itself

10. Cf. J. Bellemin-Noël, *Vers l'Inconscient du texte* (Paris: Presses universitaires de France, 1979).

11. See, for instance, Donald M. Frame, *Montaigne: A Biography* (New York: Harcourt, 1965); Michel Butor, *Essais sur les Essais,* (Paris: Gallimard, 1968). A. Wilden has examined the function of the essay as "surrogate other," with reference to "psychoanalytic intersubjectivity." "Par divers moyens on arrive à pareille fin: A Reading of Montaigne," *MLN* 83 (1968), pp. 577–97. Richard L. Regosin's more "literary" views on the symbolic value of friendship are also of interest to us here. *The Matter of My Book: Montaigne's Essais as the Book of the Self* (Berkeley: Univ. of California Press, 1977), pp. 9 ff.

of the so-called "masterpiece" contributes to remove it from the code of symbolic plenitude which it is supposed to observe.

At the beginning of the chapter "Of Friendship" Montaigne tells us that La Boétie wrote his political discourse "par maniere d'*essay*" [by way of essay]. This is indeed a curious way to refer to the "masterpiece." Surely it is a "fine thing" ("gentil"), "as full as can be" ("plein ce qu'il est possible"). But it is far from perfection:

> (a) Si y a il bien à dire que ce ne soit le mieux qu'il peut faire; et si, en l'aage que je l'ai conneu, plus avancé, *il eut pris un tel desseing que le mien* de mettre par escrit ses fantasies, nous verrions plusieurs choses rares et qui nous approcheroient bien près de l'honneur de l'antiquité. [184]

> Still, it is far from being the best he could do; and if at the more mature age when I knew him, *he had adopted a plan such as mine,* of putting his ideas in writing, we should see many great things which would bring us very close to the glory of antiquity. [135]

This statement sounds as if Montaigne wished he had taught La Boétie how to write; thus, as if the writer of *grotesques* knew the art of shaping up a *tableau élabouré*. La Boétie's "bonnes lettres" are once again displaced to the periphery: *he* wrote "by way of essay", which implies that the essay-writer, Montaigne, wrote the true literary masterpiece and becomes the rightful heir of the true father's "bonnes lettres."

Similarly, at the end of the same chapter, as Montaigne decides to dislodge *Voluntary Servitude* from his book "Je me suis dédit de le loger icy" (194) ["I have changed my mind about putting it in here" (144)], he explains that his friend treated his topic "par maniere d'exercitation" [by way of exercise]. Montaigne's own chapter "De l'exercitation" (II:6) shows that, in his idiolect, the words "essay" and "exercitation" belong to the same semantic field.[12] La Boétie becomes the real essay-writer as he is the only one who really experienced the only thing that cannot be experienced in life: death. This is actually the pretext for the chapter "De l'exercitation" [Of Practice], in which Montaigne is careful to use the verb "essayer":

> (a) Quant à la mort, nous ne la pouvons *essayer* qu'une fois. [371]

> As for death, we can *try* it only once. [267]

Insidiously, we revert to the death scene once more, because it is the primal scene of writing, the scene of the letter and the scene of the essay at birth.

There is, of course, a well-documented political reason for Montaigne's

12. See, for instance, the opening paragraph of this chapter on "essaying death."

decision not to publish *Voluntary Servitude.* After Protestant activists had used this attack against tyranny for their propaganda, it would have been extremely dangerous for any writer to refer to it positively in his works. Thus Montaigne searched for another "monument" to his friend's memory and switched from prose to poetry. He chose to place twenty-nine of La Boétie's French sonnets at the midpoint of his book, precisely in his chapter 29. These poems, we recall, appeared in all the editions of the *Essays* during Montaigne's lifetime. He crossed them out, however, on his personal copy of the 1588 edition and simply added the following sentence at the end of the dedicatory paragraph to Madame de Grammont: (c) "Ces vers se voient ailleurs" (196). [These verses may be seen elsewhere (145).]

This twice-repeated displacement of La Boétie's works (prose and poetry) by his editor and inheritor cannot be explained away by political (in the case of *Voluntary Servitude*) or editorial reasons (if the sonnets had indeed been published "elsewhere"—which remains to be proven). By the light of what we have said before about Montaigne's ambivalence toward his friend's literary legacy, it is tempting to interpret this double erasure (or, rather, *mise sous rature*) in terms of Montaigne's own search for literary identity. An exchange has taken place that is related to the intersubjective relationship between the "possessor" of the "bonnes lettres" (la Boétie) and the "holder" of these "purloined letters" (Montaigne himself).

A rather simplistic formulation of this required explanation might go as follows. As the years go by and as Montaigne develops his literary self-awareness, a gradual deconstruction of the testator's will takes place within the text of the *Essays.* The language of the Other—albeit the friendliest language of all on the surface—can no longer be allowed to speak as the self-posited origin of Montaigne's language. To use again the words of the chapter "Of Friendship", the writer can no longer accept to regard his essays as "accidental," "nonsequential grotesques" ((a) "crotesques . . . rappiecez de divers membres, sans certaine figure, n'ayants ordre, suite ny proportion que fortuite" (183). In other words, Montaigne comes gradually to the textual realization that his essays have moved from the periphery to the center; that they refuse to be considered as marginal, subsidiary or even subservient *dedicatory letters.* The *Essays* yearn for official, public recognition as full-fledged "bonnes lettres", but they cannot say so overtly. Their utmost singularity comes precisely from the fact that they express negatively the unique object of their desire: to be, but not to appear to be ["a rich, polished picture, formed according to art" (135).]

This logistics of denial is perhaps best expressed in the chapter "Du Dementir" [Of Giving the Lie, II:18]:

(a) Je ne dresse pas icy une statue à planter au carrefour d'une ville, ou dans une Eglise, ou place publique . . . C'est pour le coin d'une *librairie*, et pour en amuser un voisin, un parent, *un amy* . . . [664]

I am not buiding here a statue to erect at the town crossroads, or in a church or a public square . . . This is for a nook in a *library*, and to amuse a neighbor, a relative, a *friend* . . . [503]

Certainly, in the beginning, La Boétie's statue was meant to be erected at the center of Montaigne's own public square, the first book of *Essays*. The fact that he now refers to his writings positively, as a statue *for a nook in a library* and *to amuse a friend*, carries quite a different message. The plastic imagery refers back to the "tableau élabouré" while, at the same time, it denies its artful, polished character. In addition, Montaigne wills his book to a *library* and to a *friend*, and this gesture is not free of guilt: it brings us back to the primal scene, the death scene and the letter scene, in which La Boétie says to his friend: "I entreat you to accept as a legacy my library and my books . . . because of your fondness for letters" (1050).

As he lay half-conscious in bed awaiting death, La Boétie uttered a few sentences that, to this day, have remained rather enigmatic. As related by Montaigne, at the end of his famous letter, they read as follows:

Lors entre autres choses il se print à me prier & reprier avecques une extreme affection, de *luy donner une place:* de sorte que j'eus peur que son jugement fust esbranlé. . . Il redoubla encores plus fort: "Mon frere, mon frere, *me refusez-vous doncques une place?"* Jusques à ce qu'il me contraignit de le convaincre par raison, & de luy dire, que puis qu'il respiroit & parloit, & qu'il avoit corps, *il avoit par consequent son lieu.* "Voire, voire, me respondit-il, j'en ay, mais *ce n'est pas celuy qu'il me faut:* & puis quand tout est dit, *je n'ay plus d'estre"*. [Pl.1359–60].

Then, among other things, he began to entreat me again and again with extreme affection to *give him a place;* so that I was afraid that his judgment was shaken. . . He repeated even more strongly: "My brother, my brother, *do you refuse me a place?"* This until he forced me to convince him by reason and tell him that since he was breathing and speaking and had a body, consequently *he had his place.* "True, true," he answered me then, "I have one, but *it is not the one I need;* and then when all is said, *I have no being left"*. [1055]

This crucial series of statements and interrogations about "finding a place" takes on ironic overtones when confronted with Montaigne's actual treatment of his friend's legacy. La Boétie's *ultima verba* are no longer enigmatic if one considers the "place" occupied by his works within the corpus of the *Essays*. In the letter, the dialogue staged by the narrator between the two friends foreshadows the uneasiness of the writer about "granting a place" to the language of the Other. It also sets the tone for the problematic debate about the "crotesques" and the "tableau élabouré": where is the "best spot" ("le plus bel endroit") whose writings are meant to occupy the center piece of the book ("le milieu de chaque paroy")? In Montaigne's *Essays*, La Boétie "has his place," but it is not "the one he needs." And as Montaigne discovers himself as a unique writer, his friend's last words become more and more prophetic: in the end ("quand tout est dit") he has "no being left" ("je n'ay plus d'estre").

Of course this prophecy is one of Montaigne's own making since he is both the narrator and the writer of the letter. La Boétie's textualized self is made to prophesy his own death *as a writer* by the upcoming writer of the *Essays*. The dying friend's "humane letters" are diverted from their path, "purloined" in Lacan's sense, as they are passed on to the surviving friend. Montaigne seems to have more or less consciously realized this when, toward the end of his chapter "Of Friendship," he writes: (a) "Il me semble que je luy *desrobe* sa part" (194). [It seems to be that I am *robbing* him of his share" (143).] At the outset of his literary career, Montaigne launches into an intense activity of essay-writing, not letter-writing. Yet the letter he wrote to his father sustains itself as some sort of a memory trace; not as the image of the death scene itself, but as a *signifier* that, in the Saussurian sense, takes on meaning through differential oppositions. To paraphrase Lacan, if Montaigne seems to forget letters as a literary genre, the letters, as we will see, will not easily forget him.[13]

ESSAYING SENECA'S LETTERS

Like Horace, Montaigne tells us that he loves literature that mingles "profit with pleasure". In his chapter "Of Books" (II:10) he regards Plutarch's *Moral Essays* and Seneca's *Letters* as two books that precisely serve this purpose:

> (a) Ils ont tous deux cette notable commodité pour mon humeur, que la science que j'y cherche y est traictée à pieces décousues, qui ne demandent pas l'obligation d'un long travail, dequoy je suis incapable . . . [413]

> They both have this notable advantage for my humor, that the knowledge I

13. "Mais la lettre, pas plus que l'inconscient du névrosé, ne l'oublie." *Ecrits I,* op. cit., p. 45.

seek is there treated in detached pieces that do not demand the obligation of long labor, of which I am incapable . . . [300]

This choice is not made at random. As critics have pointed out, Plutarch's *Moralia* are perhaps the closest formal model that shaped the essays as a literary genre.[14] The juxtaposition of Plutarch and Seneca in the form of the opposition *Moral Essays vs Friendly Letters* signals a polarizing effect that needs to be accounted for in terms of Montaigne's own textuality. Whereas, throughout the three books, the *essay* is a consciously and conscientiously developed model and the object of much self-reflexivity, the *letter* seems to occupy the pole of the repressed, unconceded signifier, dreadfully contaminated by the primal scene.

Yet, Montaigne lingers on Seneca's *Epistles* more than on any other piece of writing. As Pierre Villey has remarked, they are our writer's "favourite book".[15] He borrows a lot from them, especially as he prepares the first edition of the *Essays*. Chapters I:14, I:20, I:39, I:42, II:1 and, above all, II:3 are full of *sententiae* from Seneca, translated and arranged like a sophisticated inlaid craft.[16] In the chapter "Of Books" (II:10), Montaigne writes:

> (a) Les *Epistres* de Seneque [sont] la plus belle partie de ses escrits, et la plus profitable. Il ne faut pas grande entreprinse pour m'y mettre; et les quitte où il me plait. Car elles n'ont point de suite des unes aux autres. [413]

> The *Epistles* of Seneca . . . are the finest part of his writings, and the most profitable. I need no great enterprise to get at them, and I leave them whenever I like. For they have no continuity from one to the other. [300]

In the appreciation of the aesthetics of the epistolary genre, Montaigne stresses the lack of continuity and the treatment of topics "in detached pieces." Most probably it is because he finds this stylistic trait closer to the type of informal conversation he will eulogize in his chapter "De l'art de conferer" ["Of the Art of Discussion" (III:8).]

> (b) Le plus fructueux et naturel exercice de nostre esprit, c'est à mon gré la

14. "The *Moralia* . . . , in their mixture of argument, definition, illustration, tall stories, allusions, are not at all unlike the *Essais*, though they seem arid and even banal in comparison." R. A. Sayce, *The Essays of Montaigne. A Critical Exploration* (London: Weidenfeld & Nicolson, 1972), p. 39.

15. *Les Sources et l'Evolution des Essais de M.* (Paris: Hachette, 1908), vol. I, p. 215.

16. The evolution of Seneca's Latin prose within the text of the *Essays* seems to parallel the evolution of Montaigne's recognition of prose writing as a worthwhile medium. There is only one quotation in Latin from Seneca's *Epistles* in 1580. Montaigne at that time, frowns on Latin prose in his book. After 1588, most of the quotations from the *Epistles* are given in the Latin original.

conference. J'en trouve l'usage plus doux que d'aucune autre action de notre vie. [922]

The most fruitful and natural exercise of our mind, in my opinion, is discussion. I find it sweeter than any other action in our life. [704]

As Montaigne depicts the artless art of writing letters, Seneca style, and connects it with spontaneous and animated discussion, the art of discussion itself brings him back, almost necessarily, to a discussion of his unforgettable friendship with La Boétie. In "De l'art de conferer" he continues:

(b)J'ayme une société et familiaritié forte et virile, une amitié qui se flatte en l'aspreté et vigueur de son commerce, comme l'amour, és morsures et esgratigneures sanglantes. [924]

I like a strong, manly fellowship and familiarity, a friendship that delights in the sharpness and vigor of its intercourse, as does love in bites and scratches that draw blood. [705]

The combative excitement of friendship, cherished by Montaigne the man, is immediately after shared by Montaigne the writer who declares that he welcomes any constructive criticism of the *Essays*. In a late addition he writes:

(c) Et, pourveu qu'on n'y procede d'une troigne trop imperieuse et magistrale, je preste l'espaule aux reprehensions que l'on faict en mes escrits; et les ay souvent changez plus par raison de civilité que par raison d'amendement; aymant à gratifier et nourrir la liberté de m'advertir par la facilité de ceder; ouy, à mes despans. [924]

And provided they do not go about it with too imperious and magistral a frown, I lend a hand to the criticism people make of my writings, and have often changed them more out of civility than to improve them, loving to gratify and foster my critics' freedom to admonish me by the ease with which I yield—yes, even at my own expense. [705]

Finally, a few paragraphs further, we find a reminder of a formula to which, by now, we are well accustomed: Montaigne's presentation of his book as his own son: J'aimeroy mieux que mon fils apprint aux tavernes à parler, qu'aux escholes de la parlerie. (926–7). [I would rather have my son learn to speak in the taverns than in the schools of talk (707b).] Montaigne's book is a living person; a person who talks, not a writer, yet, a person who is written into a text. We revert here to the problematics of the letter as a literary genre: it purports to transcribe the art of conversation without art or to paint a "tableau élabouré" in the form of "crotescques."

From the various passages that have just been quoted sequentially it seems possible to reconstruct Montaigne's train of thought between the letter as *point de départ* and the essay as *point d'arrivée*. Graphically, it could be represented roughly like this: (→ = entails)

> *Letter*→ conversational style (Seneca) → art of discussion → friendly discussion; the ideal friendship → friendship welcomes criticism → he welcomes criticism of his *Essays*

Yet there are two missing links in this rather tight metonymic sequence: the *terminus a quo* and the *terminus ad quem*. But then the reader has to move from the textual plane to the plane of referentiality. At the beginning of the chain, the letter as a semiotic sign refers to an absence on the paradigmatic axis. There is no letter possible *in praesentia*; one necessarily writes to absent correspondents. Here in the context of the *Essays*, the letter seems to presuppose the memory-trace of the unreachable Other (the Father addressed, the "Brother" written about, both dead when the letter is published). At the end of the chain, the essay is fantasized as a possible, yet constantly displaced prolongation of the self beyond death. It is posited as a son, the image of a self-appropriated Other moving freely beyond the mirror of the *Aha-Erlebnis*.[17]

The *Essays* thus present themselves both as the negation of the Other's legacy and the affirmation of their own legacy to the others. Writing his book means to Montaigne to change a Son-Father relationship into a Father-Son relationship, while moving at the same time from a past author-reader (La Boétie) to a future reader-author (the "suffisant lecteur.") The movement from "letter" to "essay" in the metonymic sequence of the text is but the formal envelope of a deeper psychological struggle that could also be described as a family romance. The twin ends of the chain never meet. The essay purports to be the equivalent of the letter while, in reality, it is a non-letter, or the ever repetitive exclusion of the letter as a possible model. It writes itself between the written dedicatory letters publicizing the Other's *Works* (La Boétie's prose and verse as well as Sebond's *Theologia naturalis* for that matter) and the unwritten letters inherited from all the *auctores* (Seneca in the first place, but also Pliny and Cicero). The impossibility of finding a common ground for the written and the unwritten letters condemns the *Essays* to a Sisyphus-like fate: they are doomed to become a

17. Cf. Lacan-Köhler's "illuminated mimicry" in "Le Stade du Miroir," *Ecrits I*, op. cit., p. 89.

body of endlessly rewritten texts. As we will soon see, Montaigne wished his essays were letters and he was tempted to use the letter form for some of his chapters.[18] Yet if he never used the letter as a literary genre within the *Essays*, it may be, as Lacan suggests, for fear that its power might be used up. "Avec l'usage de la lettre se dissipe son pouvoir" [with the letter's use its power disappears.] And: "seul nous intéresse l'effet de ce non-usage." Only the effect of the non-use of the letter as signifier is important to Montaigne, and to us.[19]

Returning for a moment to the chapter "Of Books" (II:10) and Seneca's *Epistles*, we notice that Montaigne describes the Latin writer's style as (a) "ondoyant et divers" (413) ["undulating and diverse," (300).] Now this is the very formula that he had used to define the nature of the human being in the first chapter of his first book: (a) "Certes, c'est un subject merveilleusement vain, *divers et ondoyant*, que l'homme" (9). ["Truly man is a marvelously vain, *diverse and undulating* object." (5)]

Then, in the first chapter of the second Book ("Of the Inconsistency of our Actions"), Montaigne develops the "patchwork" theme as the determining trait of the human condition. The French word "piece" is used several times, both alone and in composition, to denote the shapeless and unpredictable nature of man: (a) "Nostre faict, ce ne sont que pieces rapportées" (336) ["Our actions are nothing but a patchwork" (243).][20] Since according to Montaigne, Seneca's letters are characterized by the fact that they deal with topics in detached pieces ("à pieces décousues"), it follows that they mimetically espouse the chief trait of human nature. Seneca is a man *par excellence* ("ondoyant et divers") and his style is human *par excellence* ("à pieces décousues"). It may be time to advance a rather simple hypothesis: namely that in Montaigne's semiotics, the letter is a coded sign for humanness. But humanness in the text of the *Essays* is not a given but a purloined quality, removed from the protagonist's experience by a primal death scene, and which the *Essays* will compulsively attempt to regain *literally.*

ESSAYING EPICURUS'S LETTER

At the beginning of the chapter "De la Gloire" ("Of Glory", II:16), Montaigne notes that all his life Epicurus spoke against what he called

18. Cf. I:26 ("A Madame Diane de Foix . . ."); I:29 ("A Madame de Grammont . . ."); II:8 ("A Madame d'Estissac"); II:37 ("A Madame de Duras"); and even the Apology, II:12, which is most probably dedicated to Margaret of Valois (a) (557; 418).
19. Cf. *Ecrits*, op. cit., pp. 42–43.
20. Cf. also: "r'appiesser" (331); "piece à piece" (332); "pieces" (337); "lopins" (337).

"glory", that is, the search to acquire reputation in the world. Yet, Montaigne goes on, on his death bed, he acknowledged the fact that he felt "pleasure" in remembering his "discoveries" and "teachings," and was somewhat anxious to leave a good reputation behind him after his death.

The contrast between Epicurus's death scene (in II:16) and La Boétie's (in the famous letter) is quite obvious. In what we have called the "primal scene" of the *Essays*, the great friend's attitude is meant to serve as an example of consistency in Stoic self-denial. At the moment of death La Boétie behaves with the same aloof detachment as he had throughout his life without any regard whatsoever for his reputation ("pour l'interest de sa reputation" Pl.1350). He remains cheerful to the end ("il contrefaisoit la chere plus gaye" Pl. 1351) as he wishes to save his relatives from undue grief over losing him (Ibid.).

Only the reputation of Montaigne's family is of concern to La Boétie. When he talks to Michel's brother, Thomas who had espoused the Protestant cause, he advises him to respect the "good reputation" that his family has acquired:

> Et, comme vous estes sage & bon, gardez de mettre ces inconvenients parmy vostre famille, de peur de luy faire perdre la *gloire* & et le bon-heur duquel elle a jouy jusques à ceste heure. [Pl.1356]

> And since you are wise and good, keep from bringing these disturbances into the midst of your family, for fear of making it lose the *glory* and the happiness that it has enjoyed until this hour. [1053]

As a result, Montaigne wishes there had been more people in the room "to witness so many fine proofs of greatness of soul" (1050) and he confesses the zeal that he has had all his life for his friend's "gloire et honneur" ("glory and honor,"|(Pl.1353).

As opposed to Epicurus, whose motto was *"CACHE* TA VIE" (619) ["*Conceal* your life" (469)] but who in the end revealed it somewhat presumptuously to his followers, La Boétie ["always *concealed* from them his opinion that his death was certain" (1049).] ("il leur *cacha* tousjours l'opinion certaine qu'il avoit de sa mort" (Pl.1351). Clearly Montaigne juxtaposes Epicurus's stance with La Boétie's; first, by framing both death scenes around the *ultima verba* motif ("dernieres paroles: (620), (469) and (Pl. 1347), [1046]]; second, by quoting both great men through the device of a *letter*. Epicurus's epistle to Hermachus, quoted at length in the chapter "Of Glory" (620, 469), reveals a self-serving purpose that is obviously meant to contrast with La Boétie's disinterested posture. Yet, there is a major difference between the two instances of the epistolary discourse. La Boétie never wrote a message relating his last moments; instead, he spoke to his friend Michel who narrated the event in a letter. We do have Epicurus's testimony in a written form from the hand of the philosopher himself; we can only grasp La Boétie's through a "truchement" (an interpreter)—like Montaigne himself in the presence of the Cannibals.

In other words, if the parallel is carried all the way, Montaigne plays both the role of Epicurus's friend (as recipient of the letter) and of Epicurus himself (as the writer of the letter). This conflation of roles tells us a great deal about the inception of the essay as a letter in which the sender claims also to be the addressee. Montaigne occupies both ends of the communicative situation. Lacan's and Derrida's disciples would probably argue, at this point, whether the letter Montaigne sends to himself ("s'envoie," in French, has also sexual overtones) ever arrives at its destination. For our purpose, it suffices to note that this doubling-up of the enunciative situation occurs at a crucial moment of the *Essays*, when La Boétie is confronted with the Epiucurean philosopher after whom Montaigne will eventually pattern his life. In this respect, one should note that, just before quoting Epicurus's letter, Montaigne remarks: (a) Nous sommes, je ne sçay comment, doubles en nous mesmes (619). [We are, I know not how, double within ourselves" (469).]

ESSAYING PLINY'S AND CICERO'S LETTERS

In a famous passage of the chapter "A Consideration upon Cicero" (I:40), Montaigne explains why, at the time when he was groping for a literary genre, he chose not to write letters. Specifically, he contrasts himself with Cicero and Pliny the Younger who, out of sheer vainglory, published personal letters they had written to their friends:

> (a) Mais cecy surpasse toute bassesse de coeur, en personnes de tel rang, d'avoir voulu tirer quelque principale gloire du caquet et de la parlerie, jusques à y employer les lettres privées escriptes à leurs amis . . . [249]

> But this surpasses all baseness of heart in persons of such rank: to have wanted to derive some great glory from mere babble and talk, to the point of publishing their private letters written to their friends . . . [183]

Montaigne also criticizes Epicurus and Seneca for similar reasons: namely, because they look upon their letters as means to acquire name and fame (a) (252, 185). Actually there is a long tradition behind this puritanical self-righteousness. Petrarch felt pretty much the same way. Whatever his admiration for the *Familiares*, he was profoundly disturbed by Cicero's motivations. He saw the public stance of the statesman as conflicting shockingly with the supposedly genuine feelings of the private citizen.[21]

Paradoxically, Montaigne comes very close to being guilty of the same crime. The letter about La Boétie's death is probably the most flagrant example of a deliberate infringement upon privacy. But as we have seen, this primal scene was by definition only a beginning. The dedicatory letter is precisely the kind of hybrid genre that requires publication while pretending to be addressed to a father (letters # 2 & 3), a wife (#9) or friends (Henri de Mesmes #4; Michel de l'Hôpital #5; Louis de Lansac #7; Paul de Foix #8).[22]

Of these seven dedicatory epistles, six are meant to introduce one or several of La Boétie's works (Letter #3 is Montaigne's dedication to his father of Sebond's *Théologie naturelle* in his own translation). Thus, La Boétie is almost exclusively the "subject matter" of Montaigne's literary letters. Our epistolarian would probably be quick to disclaim any accusation that he published his letters to gain a reputation in the world; his swift response would be that he did not seek fame for himself but for the great man who happened to be his friend. Yet, as we have found out in our study of the chapter "Of Friendship," there are many traces of ambivalent feelings in the "loyal" friend's attitudes toward his literary legacy.

Between 1580 and 1588 Montaigne added a paragraph to his criticism of famous classical letter writers:

> (b) Sur ce subject de lettres, je veux dire ce mot, que c'est un ouvrage auquel *mes amys* tiennent que je puis quelque chose. [252]

> On the subject of letter writing, I want to say this: that it is a kind of work in which *my friends* think I have some ability. [185]

Obviously, Montaigne considers himself as a very skillful "epistolographer." But somehow he cannot confess his art directly: he needs his "amys" to project indirectly into his text the image of a great letter writer named Montaigne. Once again, we have reverted to the primal letter-scene, as dictated by the Friend who made his literary career possible.

In the 1588 edition, this hardly disguised self-congratulatory remark is

21. Cf. M. Fumaroli, "Genèse de l'épistolographie classique: rhétorique humaniste de la lettre, de Pétrarque à Juste Lipse," *Revue d'Histoire Littéraire de la France*, 78, 4 (July–August 1978), p. 888.

22. This numbering is the one found in Donald M. Frame's translation of the Letters in *The Complete Works*, op. cit.

immediately followed by stylistic comments which tend to emphasize the "disorderly, abrupt, individual" qualities of his writings. The rationale here seems to be that if his style is "inept for public negotiations," it will be all the more appropriate for the "private" activity of letter writing. He goes on:

> (b) "(Je) ne m'entens pas en *lettres ceremonieuses,* qui n'ont autre substance que d'une belle enfileure de paroles courtoises. [252]

> I have no gift for *letters of ceremony* that have no other substance than a fine string of courteous words.

Any critic would be hard put not to place the seven dedicatory letters in this category of "lettres ceremonieuses." After all, isn't this the very definition of a dedicatory letter? Yet for some reason Montaigne does not want to consider them as such. He wrote this addition between 1580 and 1588, i.e. more than ten years after the seven epistles, all composed between 1563 and 1570. It would be too easy to explain away this discrepancy on the account of his legendary "bad memory." Freud and Lacan have given us more sensible reasons for distinguishing between what one *says* about one's (good or bad) memory and how "memory traces" actually function in the writing of a text. If "the unconscious is the discourse of the Other," to Montaigne, any letter he writes or has written *must* be a private affair.[23] It must relate to the most intimate experience of all, as textualized in the primal scene, because it only takes on meaning through its differential opposition to the signifiers of "ceremony":

> (a) Nous ne sommes que ceremonie; la ceremonie nous emporte, et laissons la substance des choses; nous nous tenons aux branches et abandonnons le tronc et le corps. [632]

> We are nothing but ceremony; ceremony carries us away, and we leave the substance of things; we hang on the branches and abandon the trunk and body. [478–79]

This famous passage from the chapter "Of Presumption" (II:17) is a felicitous complement to the commentary on "lettres ceremonieuses." Immediately after this passage, Montaigne makes it a point to relate the question of ceremony with his activity as an essay writer. How can one speak naturally and truthfully of oneself if the laws of ceremony prevent one from saying certain words about certain things? How can a written and published self-portrait be possible?

23. Cf. *Ecrits,* op. cit., p. 24.

(a) Je me trouve *icy* empestré és loix de la ceremonie car elle ne permet ny qu'on parle bien de soy, ny qu'on en parle mal. Nous la lairrons là pour ce coup. [632]

I find myself *here* entangled in the laws of ceremony, for she does not allow a man either to speak well of himself, or to speak ill. We shall let her alone for the moment. [479]

This is the reason why, in the chapter "A Consideration upon Cicero," Montaigne describes his own style as unceremonious, devoid of flattery or insincerity. The *Essays* yearn for a form as close as possible to the idealized "epistolary style," not so much because they want to liberate themselves from the classical and medieval influences of the *artes dicendi*, but because the epistolary style *is* the style of the primal scene. True, in so doing, Montaigne reaffirms his attachment to a tradition that goes back to the great humanists; Petrarch's reading of Cicero's *Familiares* into his own letters, and Erasmus's recommendations in his *De Conscribendis Epistolis* (1522) and *Ciceronianus* (1528).[24] Yet when he says that he writes his letters "posthaste" and "so precipitously" that he can find nobody to copy them, when he claims he is "prone to begin without a plan" and criticizes "the letters of this age" because they "consist more in embroideries and preambles ("bordures et prefaces") than in substance ("matiere") (b) (253), 186–187), the very violence of his statements can be interpreted as a desperate attempt to nullify any act of letter writing that does not conform with the inaugural style of his late Friend.

This hypothesis is borne out by the late addition that Montaigne wrote on his personal copy of the 1588 edition. This *alongeail* sums up in a most forceful way the crucial importance of the connection between essay writing and letter writing in conjunction with the memory-trace of La Boétie's textualized death:

(c) Et eusse prins plus volontiers ceste forme à publier mes verves (= les lettres), si j'eusse eu à qui parler. *Il me falloit, comme je l'ay eu autrefois, un certain commerce qui m'attirast, qui me soustinst et soulevast.* Car de negocier au vent, comme d'autres, je ne sçauroy que de songes, ny forger des vains noms à entretenir en chose serieuse: *ennemy juré de toute falsification.* J'eusse esté plus attentif et plus seur, ayant une addresse forte et amye, que je ne suis, regardant les divers visages d'un peuple. *Et suis deçeu, s'il ne m'eust mieux succédé.* [252]

On the subject of letter writing, I would have preferred to adopt this form to

24. Cf. Fumaroli, op. cit., pp. 888–91.

publish my sallies, if I had had someone to talk to. *I needed what I once had, a certain relationship to lead me on, sustain me, and raise me up.* For to talk to the winds, as others do, is beyond me except in dreams; nor could I fabricate fictitious names to talk with on serious matter, *being a sworn enemy of any falsification.* I would have been more attentive and confident, with a strong friend to address, than I am now, when I consider the various tastes of a whole public. And if I am not mistaken, *I would have been more successful.* [185–186]

The loss of the irretrievable friend means a loss of stylistic plenitude. As late as the last additions on the "exemplaire de Bordeaux," the remembrance of La Boétie's death scene remains associated with the determining signifier of the *Essays.* The *letter* reenters the textual landscape as the guarantor of the nonfictitious *character* (lettre-caractère) of the book. On the page of Montaigne's copy, the words: "ennemy juré de toute falsification" ["being a sworn enemy of any falsification"] are written in a different ink and scribbled between two previously added lines of the *marginalia.* Here again we revert to the fundamental structure of *exchange* between letter and essay: the letter makes the essay the best possible substitute for the symbolically "purloined letter."

Yet, the essay will always remain a second best genre: the anticlimax of the climactic primal scene of letter writing. In the case of Montaigne, essay writing is but a compulsively *unsuccessful* attempt to rewrite the opening death scene ("Et suis deçeu, s'il ne m'eust mieux succédé"). By signaling their vital kinship to the epistolary genre, the *Essays* strive to reproduce the displaced memory-trace of their lost origin. Positing the letter as an impossible (and consciously rejected) medium could be glossed as a demiurgic attempt to bridge the gap between the *ego* and the *imago;* to divert from its path the mirrored image of the self as it is imposed upon the text by the all-powerful Other—all the more powerful since He is dead.

If this were the case, it would be tempting to recognize in this never-ending dilemma (ending only with Montaigne's own untextualized death scene) some sort of a clumsy proto–Cartesian gesture: groping for the primacy of an elusive *Cogito* and at the same time rejecting its reductive appropriateness.

The letter resurfaces all along the *Essays,* as a reef to be cautiously skirted or rather, to be *left far away* (and this is another meaning of "purloin"[25]): because it is too close to the textual unconscious of the primal *scène de l'écriture.*

25. Cf. Norman Holland, "Re-Covering *The Purloined Letter:* Reading as a Personal Transaction," *The Reader in the Text,* ed. by S. R. Suleiman & I. Crosman (Princeton: Princeton Univ. Press, 1980), p. 351.

MARIANNE S. MEIJER

Guesswork or Facts: Connections between Montaigne's Last Three Chapters (III:11, 12 and 13)

The title of chapter III:11, "Of cripples," has baffled many a reader. It is not until the next to last page of this eight-page essay (III:11, 1033; 784–92) that the word cripples appears. It forms the subject of just two paragraphs, less than a page in all, and it is introduced in a rather offhand way by the expression "Apropos or malapropos", as if it were an afterthought. Montaigne helps his puzzled reader by indicating a connection with previously treated matters:

> (b) Ces exemples servent-ils pas à ce que je disois au commencement: que nos raisons anticipent souvent l'effect, et ont l'estendue de leur jurisdiction si infinie, qu'elles jugent et s'exercent en l'inanité mesme et au non estre? [III:11, 1034]

> Do not these examples confirm what I was saying at the beginning: that our reasons often anticipate the fact, and extend their jurisdiction so infinitely that they exercise their judgment even in inanity and nonbeing? [791]

The anecdotes about cripples illustrate and underline an essential point of the chapter, but the subsequent anecdotes, which are not about cripples, serve the same purpose; it therefore seems that Montaigne could as well have entitled his chapter: "On thin legs," or "On the habit of assent" (III:11, 1034–35; 791–92). Why then did Montaigne choose this particular title, what does it signify?

> (b) Les noms de mes chapitres n'en embrassent pas toujours la matiere; souvent ils la denotent seulement par quelque marque. . . . [III:9, 994]

> The titles of my chapters do not always embrace their matter; often they only denote it by some sign. . . . [761]

167

The reader must find the "sign" and try to decipher the message. This chapter's fame rests on its discussion of witchcraft, and "Of witches" would have been an obvious title; indeed, some critics suspect Montaigne of deliberately hiding controversial subjects behind anodine titles.[1] Rather than accuse Montaigne of fearing ecclesiastical authorities, we propose to investigate what the title "Of cripples" might signify, through a close reading of the essay in the context of the last two chapters.

The *Exemplaire de Bordeaux*[2] shows that Montaigne continuously reread his own book and commented on his own text by inserting additions of varying length. Pierre Villey, in the introduction to his 1930 edition of Montaigne's *Essays*,[3] considers these digressions confusing to the reader. But if viewed as Montaigne's reactions to his printed text, they often clarify his thought associations, as we have endeavored to show elsewhere.[4] Even when Montaigne makes merely stylistic changes, or adds a single quotation, this very choice underlines at times a detail that the reader might not otherwise have noticed. We shall therefore pay close attention to the insertions of the (c) layer made between 1588 and 1592.

The essential point discussed in chapter III:11 (and repeated when the examples of cripples come up) is the following:

> (b) Je ravassois presentement, comme je faicts souvant, sur ce, combien l'humaine raison est un instrument libre et vague. Je vois ordinairement que les hommes, aux faicts qu'on leur propose, s'amusent plus volontiers à en cercher la raison qu'à en cercher la verité: ils laissent là les choses, et s'amusent à traiter les causes. [III:11, 1026]

> I was just now musing, as I often do, on how free and vague an instrument human reason is. I see ordinarily that men, when facts are put before them, are more ready to amuse themselves by inquiring into their reasons than by inquiring into their truths. They leave aside the cases and amuse themselves treating the causes. [785]

1. cf. Patrick Henry, "Les titres façades, la censure et l'écriture défensive chez Montaigne," *Bulletin de la Société des Amis de Montaigne,* 5e série, no. 24 (oct.–déc. 1977), 11–28.

2. *Reproduction en phototypie de l'Exemplaire avec notes manuscrites marginales des Essais de Montaigne appartenant à la ville de Bordeaux* publiée avec une introduction par M. Fortunat Strowski (Paris: Hachette & Cie, 1912).

3. Pierre Villey, ed. *Les Essais de Montaigne* (1930). Reprinted by V. L. Saulnier (Paris: Presses Universitaries de France, 1965; third edition 1978), p. xxxi.

4. Marianne S. Meijer, " 'Des postes' et 'Des pouces': plaisanteries ou points de repère?", in *Columbia Montaigne Conference Papers,* edited by Donald M. Frame and Mary B. McKinley (Lexington, Kentucky: French Forum, 1981), and "L'ordre des *Essais* dans les deux premiers livres," to be published in *Actes du Quatriéme Centenaire des Essais de Montaigne,* international conference organized by the Société des Amis de Montaigne and held in Bordeaux, France, in June 1980.

The weakness of human reason is a theme that runs through the whole work but here, however, Montaigne brings out a particular defect: man's mania to search for and discuss causes rather then limit himself to, and establish, facts. The (c) addition, the longest of the eighteen additions in this essay, which starts off with a pun—"plaisants causeurs"—that even Donald M. Frame is at a loss to render into English: "Comical prattlers!," develops this remark: the knowledge of causes belongs to God only, never to man. But man's insatiable desire for knowledge leads him to search for explanations, by resorting, if necessary, to supernatural interpretations. The realm of God and that of man are totally separate, however, and to try to ignore this fundamental difference creates a fallacy. Montaigne illustrates this through his narration of examples of false miracles and his discussion of witchcraft.

He accuses contemporary authors of inciting the persecution of witches:

(b) Les sorcieres de mon voisinage courent hazard de leur vie, sur l'advis de cháque nouvel autheur qui vient donner corps à leurs songes. [III:11, 1031]

The witches of my neighborhood are in mortal danger every time some new author comes along and attests to the reality of their visions. [788]

The most eminent writer on the subject, as Villey and other critics have noted, was Jean Bodin, whose work *De la Demonomanie des sorciers*,[5] was published in 1580 and dedicated to the first president of the Parliament of Paris, Christophle de Thou—father of Montaigne's friend, the historian Jacques-Auguste. The book is a vigorous appeal for strict pursuit of witches, and in his dedication, Bodin writes that he does not expect criticism except from a sorcerer trying to defend his cause ("Or je n'espere pas que personne escrive contre cest oeuvre, si ce n'est quelque Sorcier qui deffende sa cause. . . ."). The various points taken up by sorcerer Montaigne in his essay are the very arguments used by Bodin:
1) the examples of the Bible, used as proof of the existence of witches, 2) the threats and diatribes against doubters, and 3) the belief in all kinds of hearsay testimony. Montaigne agrees that one should believe what happens in the Bible since it is God's word, but to believe an ordinary human being is quite another matter. Belief in the Bible's word does not imply belief in contemporary witchcraft. The same is true as far as other people's testimony is concerned. Montaigne knows how lively our imagination is and how easily one errs; no matter how many people and how often so-called

5. Jean Bodin, *De la Demonomanie des sorciers* (Paris: Jacques du Puys, 1580). All translations of Bodin are mine.

unnatural facts are attested to, one should still doubt, precisely because they seem unnatural. Finally, threats against doubters ("ces maistres doubteurs") called epicurian atheists by Bodin (Bodin, Book I, chapter 1, p. iv) are poor arguments, and do not convince Montaigne whose (b) "belief is not controlled by anyone's fists" (789). This kind of reasoning to prove witchcraft seems unsound—*un raisonnement boiteux*—and the product of unbalanced minds—*esprits boiteux*—:

> (c) Les boiteux sont mal propres aux exercices du corps; et aux exercices de l'esprit les ames boiteuses. . . . [I:25, 141]

> Cripples are ill-suited to bodily exercises, and crippled souls to mental exercises. [104]

Bodin ends his book with a long attack against Johann Wier, a physician who, in his *De Lamiis liber*, published in 1577, defends witches as being mentally ill, and accuses witches and their accusers of having a lively imagination and of being incapable of distinguishing between fantasy and reality; he pleads for medical treatment instead of punishment. Wier uses the authority of Andreas Alciati and quotes him approvingly as saying about witches in Piedmont that most of them should rather be purged with hellebore than purged away by fire ("la plus part desquelles devoyent estre plustost purgees par hellebore que par le feu"),[6] a pun that Montaigne will use in a slightly modified form. This opinion, to which Montaigne subscribes, namely that witches are mentally deranged women, is attacked by Bodin in violent antifeminine terms. Not only does he use all the conventional arguments found in antifeminine works, he adds to them: Minerva, the goddess of wisdom, was born of Jupiter's brain and had no mother, which is meant to show that wisdom never stems from women, who are closer to the nature of wild beasts ("Ce que les Poëtes ont figuré, quand ils ont dit que Pallas Deesse de sagesse estoit nee du cerveau de Jupiter, & qu'elle n'avoit point de mere: pour montrer que la sagesse ne vint jamais des femmes, qui approchent plus de la nature des bestes brutes," Bodin, p. 225r & v). Therefore women cannot possibly suffer from melancholia. If witches are usually women, it is because God planned it that way; God must have wanted women to be punished. It is most interesting to note that Montaigne completely ignores this aspect of Bodin's book; anti-

6. Jean Wier, *Histoires, disputes et discours des illusions et impostures des diables, des magiciens infames, sorcieres et empoisonneurs: des ensorcelez et demoniaques et de la guerison d'iceux: item de la punition que meritent les magiciens, les empoisonneurs et les sorcières. Et deux dialogues de Thomas Erastus* (Paris, 1579) (Paris: Delahaye & Lecrosnier, 1885; reprint New York, N.Y.: Arno Press, 1976), p. 308. All translations of Wier are mine.

feminism does not figure in his essay at all.[7] Particularly noteworthy is the fact that Bodin also builds his exposition on causes and facts, just like Montaigne (cf. above p. 2). Already in the introduction, Bodin writes that

> Il ne faut donc pas s'opiniastrer contre la verité, quand on voit les effects, & qu'on ne sçait pas la cause. Car il faut arrester son jugement à ce qui se faict, c'est à dire ὅτι ἔστι quand l'esprit humain ne peut sçavoir la cause, c'est a dire δι'ὅτι qui sont les deux moyens de monstrer les choses. [Bodin, préface, e iiij]

> one should not hold out against truth when one sees facts, and when one is ignorant of their cause. For one should limit one's judgment to what happens, that is to say *because* it is, when the human mind cannot not know the cause, that is to say *why* it is, which are the two means to see things.

He repeats this statement at the end of his book, in his conclusion against Wier:

> Wier . . . soustient que tout cela n'est qu'illusion. Ce n'est pas faict en Mathematicien, ny en Philosophe, d'asseurer temerairement une chose qu'on n'entend point: Mais il faut en ce cas voir l'effect, & ce qu'on dict, ὅτι ὅτι ἔστι & laisser à Dieu la cause, c'est à dire δι'ὅτι. [Bodin, réfutation des opinions de Jean Wier, p. 244r]

> Wier . . . insists that all this is nothing but illusion. It is not appropriate for a mathematician, or a philosopher, boldly to assert a thing that one does not understand: for one must in that case look at the fact & what one says, *because* it is & leave it to God the cause, that is to say *why* it is.

Montaigne is very conscious of the fact that Bodin uses this premise. In a text from the 1580 edition, he writes:

> (b) Il ne faut pas juger ce qui est possible et ce qui ne l'est pas, selon ce qui est croyable et incroyable à nostre sens, comme j'ay dit ailleurs; et est une grande faute, et en laquelle toute-fois la plus part des hommes tombent. [II:32, 725]

> (b) We must not judge what is possible and what is not, according to what is credible and incredible to our sense, as I have said elsewhere; and it is a great error, and yet one into which most men fall. [548]

---

7. Students of Montaigne's attitude to women should concern themselves not only with actual quotes from the *Essays*, but also with Montaigne's omissions. They should investigate which antifeminine remarks common at the time do *not* appear in the *Essays*.

Significantly, Montaigne adds after 1588: (c) "Ce que je ne dis pas pour Bodin" (II: 32, 725). (c) ["which I am not saying for Bodin" (548).] Bodin's starting point is identical to Montaigne's but his development, reasoning and conclusions are totally divergent; his reasoning is "boiteux," crippled. Although Montaigne respects Bodin as an author, uses him, agrees with him (II: 10, (a) 418; (a) 305), praises him,

(a) Jean Bodin est un bon autheur de nostre temps, et acompagné de beaucoup plus de jugement que la tourbe des escrivailleurs de son siecle, et merite qu'on le juge et considere. [II:32, 722]

Jean Bodin is a good author of our day, equipped with much more judgment than the mob of scribblers of his time, and he deserves to be judged and considered. [546]

he does not hesitate to criticize and contradict him (cf. the same essay, II:32, "Defense of Seneca and Plutarch"). Rereading his reply to Bodin in Chapter III:11 could well have produced this (c)-addition in III:12:

(c) Les autheurs, mesmes plus serrez et plus sages, voiez autour d'un bon argument combien ils en sement d'autres legers, et qui y regarde de pres, incorporels. [III:12, 1039–40]

(c) Authors, even the most compact and the wisest—around one good argument see how many others they strew, trivial ones, and if you look at them closely, bodiless. [795]

The title of Chapter III:11, "Of cripples" may well serve to indicate that the essay is an indictment of unsound reasoning, another demonstration of the (b) "natural infirmity of our mind." (III:13, 817); the common belief in miracles and witchcraft are its products. Montaigne's doubts concerning miracles and witchcraft are the result of his distrust of human reason and man's "hubris." This is supported by the (c)-comments, which stress human ignorance (six additions of a few words or sentences, and four Latin quotations), our tendency to exaggerate when telling or repeating a story (three additional developments and one Latin quotation), and the arrogance of our belief in certitude (three Latin quotations). All of this becomes even more evident when seen in conjunction with chapter III:13, "Of experience."

The beginning of this chapter deals with the judiciary system, that pillar of human society:

(b) un vray tesmoignage de l'humaine imbecillité . . . Combien avons nous descouvert d'innocens avoir esté punis, je dis sans la coulpe des juges;

et combien en y a-il eu que nous n'avons pas descouvert? . . . (c) Combien ay-je veu de condemnations, plus crimineuses que le crime? [III:13, 1070–71][8]

(b) a true testimony of human imbecility, so full it is of contradiction and error . . . How many innocent people we have found to have been punished—I mean by no fault of their judges—and how many there have been that we have not found out about! . . . (c) How many condemnations I have seen more criminal than the crime! [819–20]

When read immediately after chapter III:11, "Of cripples," this lengthy discussion on the inadequacies of the judiciary system emphasizes Montaigne's disgust at man's license to kill, which he has expressed several times in "Of cripples": by his criticism, for example, of the judge of Toulouse who condemned a man to be hanged in an unclear case ((b) 1030; 788); by his insistence that in order to put people to death, one should have absolute evidence of guilt ((b) 1031; 789); by his opinion that one must be wholly arrogant to kill somebody on the basis of uncertain evidence ((b) 1032; 790). This discussion also underlines the uncertainty on which the judicial pursuit of witches is based. It amplifies a point already made, namely the shaky basis of human laws. On rereading chapter III:11, Montaigne was brought to add a longer development; "Of cripples" bore "the seeds of a richer and bolder material . . ." (I:40, (c) 251; 185). By associating the two essays, the condemnation of witchhunting is not so much based on pity for the mentally deranged, but on the broader issue of the basically uncertain assumptions of man's belief in certitude. The combined reading of these two chapter clarifies Montaigne's thought processes: his continual rereading not only produces the additions (which we designate as (b) and (c) layers) but it produces the essays themselves.

Not only is the application of the laws a "testimony of human imbecility," the laws themselves are unjust and are partly responsible for the disorder in the country. Self-study becomes Montaigne's refuge ((b) 1072; 821). The (c)-additions stress man's ignorance: laws are made by fools and they are faulty ((c) 1072; 821) because their authors are "vain and irresolute"; man's quest for knowledge is his undoing. Montaigne, through his (c)-additions, emphasizes the evil of man's "curiosity," that is to say his impertinent desire to pry into God's designs, and he praises ignorance and

8. cf. Emile V. Telle, "Montaigne et le procès Martin Guerre," *Bibliothèque d'Humanisme et Renaissance*, 37, 3 (1975), 387–419, particularly 403–405, concerning Montaigne's use of the verb "voir," especially in connection with the trial in Toulouse mentioned in "Of cripples." "Voir" means: to be present at something.

incuriosity,[9] that is to say resignation to the human condition, life on this earth, being satisfied with not knowing causes (another reference to chapter III:11) and giving up inquisitiveness and impudence. Self-study teaches Montaigne his own ignorance (1074; 882), and from there he arrives at a wider conclusion: (b) "C'est par mon experience que j'accuse l'humaine ignorance, qui est, à mon advis, le plus seur party de l'escole du monde" (III:13, 1075–76). ["It is from my experience that I affirm human ignorance, which is, in my opinion, the most certain fact in the school of the world." (824).] Montaigne's greatest certitude, the acknowledgment of human ignorance, stands in contrast with the certitude of authors and judges about the truth of unnatural deeds and behavior in chapter III:11, but in agreement with Socrates, "the wisest man who ever lived, as attested by gods and men,"[10] "the master of masters" (III:13, (b) and (c) 1076; 824). It is with regard to his bodily health that Montaigne considers himself the least ignorant, and therefore the most useful to his reader as an example (III:13, 1079; 826). He proceeds to give many details about his way of life, in sickness and in health. The many intimate confidences (which Villey considers disgressions from the main theme of the third book, "the entire form of man's estate" (III:2, (b) 805; 611), and a return to his previous aim, his portrait for his family and friends),[11] constitute an impressive list of certitudes "not at all corrupted or altered by art or theorizing" (III:13, (b) 1079; 826). Furthermore, they form a sharp contrast with the content of III:11: Montaigne concerns himself with personal facts, based on lifetime experience, that he can vouch for, as opposed to the hearsay stories and guesswork about causes in the chapter on cripples. It is through this contrast that the uncertainties of chapter III:11 are emphasized, and it gives the minute details of Montaigne's dealings with his body a deeper significance. Montaigne's way of dealing with his illness is a true demonstration of submission to nature and God's will; rather than prying into causes, Montaigne shows how to make the best of it, and that it can be done. Knowing how to deal with one's body is to know how to deal with facts and with nature (rather than causes and the unnatural, always beyond man's grasp), truly man's realm. The culminating of this last chapter into a hymn to nature, through insistence

9. Villey's rendering of "incuriosité" by "insouciance" (p. 1073, note 8) is an example of possible misreading of the text if read as an isolated unit. When seen in conjunction with III:11 and man's assumptions about contacts with the other world, be it saintly (through miracles) or diabolical (through witchcraft), and man's inquisitiveness about causes instead of concern with the facts, it clearly means "noninquisitiveness."

10. This phrase from the 1588 edition was replaced by "the master of masters" in the *Exemplaire de Bordeaux*. The translation is mine. The importance of this change will be discussed below.

11. Villey, *Les Essais de Montaigne*, pp. 3, 1064.

on living one's life according to nature, based on the love of and submission to God's will, seems a final denial of the implausibilities of the chapter on miracles and witchcraft. It is the triumph of facts over guesswork, of tackling "the cases" rather than "the causes." Coupling chapters III:11 and 13 broadens their meaning: it explains why "Of cripples" precedes "Of experience," and it reveals the function of the lengthy description of Montaigne's bodily functions and personal habits in the final chapter.

The question that evidently arises at this point is why, if there is such a strong link between these chapters, they are separated by chapter 12, "Of physiognomy." Again, the title of this essay is a puzzling one and the subject comes up only in the last quarter of the chapter. In an important passage about his use of quotations, Montaigne refers to "this treatise on physiognomy" (III:12, (b) 1056; 808), but it is not until a page later that he begins his treatment of the relationship between the beauty of one's face and the goodness of one's character. In view of the many other points discussed in this chapter, such as the greatness of Socrates, death, the civil wars, the stoicism of the little man, why the choice of this particular title, what brought it about, what does it imply?

Physiognomy, meaning outward features or appearance, is brought up in connection with Socrates, the "perfect model in all great qualities" (III:12, (b) 1057; 809) and Montaigne's fellow believer in the certitude of human ignorance (III:13). He was ugly, in spite of the beauty of his soul, just as was La Boétie. Since witches usually are described as ugly and difformed (cf. III:11, (b)1032; 790), the subject comes up in Bodin's *Demonomanie*. He discusses metoposcopy, the study of physiognomy, the art of trying to judge the character of men by their features:

> . . . la Metoposcopie naturelle n'est point illicite, & de faict en tout l'Orient ils sont fort experimentez en celà. Si est-ce qu'il ne faut pas en faire loy infaillible: car il se trouve des hommes si masquez, & qui sçavent si bien couvrir, & dissimuler leurs naturels, qu'ils sont entierement maistres de leurs visages. . . . C'est pourquoy la Metoposcopie, & les predictions d'icelles sont humaines, pour l'incertitude aussi, quoy qu'on attribue à Aristote le livre de la Physiognomie, qui comprend la Metoposcopie qui n'a rien du style d'Aristote. Et par ainsi en ostant l'asseurance & necessité qu'on met en la Physiognomie & metoposcopie, l'usage natural ne peut estre blasmé. [Bodin, Book I, chapter 5, p. 40 r & v]

> . . . natural metoposcopy is not illicit, & indeed in the entire Orient they are quite adept at it. However one must not make it an infallible law: for there are many people so well disguised, & who know so well how to cover

up, & dissimulate their natural character, that they are entirely master of
their faces. . . . That is why metoposcopy & its predictions are human; also
because of its incertitude, although the book of Physiognomy is attributed
to Aristotle, and this book which includes metoscopy does not resemble
Aristotle's style at all. And thus by taking away the certainty and the
necessity that are attributed to physiognomy & metoposcopy, its natural
use cannot be faulted.

And Bodin uses Socrates as an example of its fallibility (Bodin, p. 40 v).
Indeed, Bodin might be at the origin of the titles of both chapter III:11 and
III:12. When Montaigne dwells on physical beauty and appearance, he
abruptly dismisses metoposcopy: (b) "D'en [des visages] prognostiquer les
avantures futures, ce sont matieres que je laisse indecises" (III:12, 1059), (b)
["As for prognosticating future events from faces, those are matters that I
leave undecided" (811).] Again, he stays with the facts, and refuses guesswork.

The introduction to chapter III: 12, "Of physiognomy," suggesting that
the greatness of Socrates would not have been recognized, had he lived
during Montaigne's time, because simplicity and naturalness are no longer
understood but coupled to stupidity, echoes the complicated unnatural
events and pseudoscientific arguments of the preceding chapter. And while
chapter III:11 had ended with a reminder of man's lack of moderation
(people either believe that man can know all, or that man cannot know
anything), Socrates is the incarnation of moderation: he confines knowledge within purely human bounds, and he expresses himself in everyday
language devoid of learned trappings, the language of peasants and women:
(b) "Ainsi dict un paysan, ainsi dict une femme" (III:12, 1037). ["So says a
peasant, so says a woman" (793)], the very people most often accused of
witchcraft, according to Bodin. The witnesses of Socrates' life are in stark
contrast with those mentioned in connection with witchcraft and their
"conjectures":

> (b) Il a esté esclairé par les plus clair voyans hommes qui furent onques: les
> tesmoins que nous avons de luy sont admirables en fidelité et en suffi-
> sance, [soit pour juger soit pour raporter]. [III:12, 1038]

> We have light on him from the most clear-sighted men who ever lived; the
> witnesses we have of him are wonderful in fidelity and competence, [either
> in judging or in reporting]. [793]

(The part in brackets was struck out in the (c) layer). The beginning of "Of
physiognomy" develops the final remark of the preceding chapter on man's

immoderation by extending it to immoderation even in the desire for knowledge: (b) " . . . son avidité est incapable de moderation. Je trouve qu'en curiosité de sçavoir il en est de mesme" (III:12, 1038). [" . . . his-man's-greed is incapable of moderation. I find that it is the same with the curiosity for knowledge" (794).] This kind of immoderation leads to an insistence on certitude; it does not allow any room for doubt, and that is what Montaigne reproaches the believers in witchcraft. For he does not accuse them

> (b) de faucetéleur opinion; je ne l'accuse que de difficulté et de hardiesse, et condamne l'affirmation opposite, egalement avec eux, sinon si impe-rieusement. (c) Videantur sanè, ne affirmentur modo [Cicero]. [III:11, 1031]

> holding a false opinion; I accuse them only of holding a difficult and rash one, and condemn the opposite affirmation, just as they do, if not so imperiously. (c) Let them appear as probable, not be affirmed positively. [789]

It is this belief in absolute knowledge, a belief encouraged by science and learning, that Montaigne opposes, and increasingly he attacks "art": (b) "Toute cette nostre suffisance, qui est au delà de la naturelle, est à peu pres vaine et superflue" (III:12, 1039). ["All this ability of ours that is beyond the natural is as good as vain and superfluous" (794).] It is not so much the poor witches who go beyond the natural, as the learned among us. The accusers become the accused. Through science, man goes beyond the natural and becomes unwise; Socrates represents the wise man who stays simple and natural. This natural and modest knowledge, available to all, and symbol-ized by Socrates, Montaigne has witnessed at firsthand through events which put him in contact with simple people, and their ways of handling illness, war and death. Their simple ways are in contradiction not only to the fantastic tales related in "Of cripples," but also to the learned but crippled reasoners who believe these tales. Montaigne's recent experiences of the civil war and the plague have provided him with many examples because he has witnessed personally the reactions and the behavior in daily life of the villagers around him. His commentaries on the civil war and the plague are digressions within the digression, brought about by the need to illustrate simplicity and naturalness by actual and contemporary facts. It is not these simple folk but the Ligueurs that Montaigne accuses in a (c) addition of (c) "appellant à [leur] ayde les diables et les furies . . . (III:12, 1043). ["calling the devils and the furies to [their] aid . . . (798).]

Learning gives food to our imagination, and fear is the product of our imagination. The common people suffer and die without fear because they are ignorant. The best way to tame our imagination is to be wary of learning, to stick to the "school of stupidity" and its "teachers, interpreters of the simplicity of nature" (III:12, (b) 1052; 805). One of those teachers is, of course, the "master of masters," Socrates. Socrates' speech to his judges is a perfect example of this lack of fear of death, based on simplicity and naturalness, and of submission to the will of God. The praise of simplicity and ignorance implies criticism of the learning displayed by Bodin and other authors. The description of naturalness as taught by Socrates condemns the learned belief in unnaturalness as described by Bodin in his *Demonologie*.

There is constant interplay between these chapters, and it is this interplay which helps the reader understand the intentions of the author. Montaigne's constant rereading produces new comments, not so much new messages as new formulations of the same message. This very redundancy, this "steady stream of re-statements"[12] is Montaigne's very means of communication. From this abundance, it is for the reader to distill the essence. The contrast between chapters III:11 and III:13 underlines the difference between guesswork and facts: the belief in unnatural phenomena supported by the learned treatises, and the certainty of human ignorance, supported by everyday life experience and natural functions. It pits against man's arrogant belief that God is constantly in need of human assistance the case for man's submission to the will of God: it posits the claims of human justice against the views of the wisest man of all, Socrates. Chapter III:12 develops the figure of Socrates and what he stands for: incuriosity, that is to say satisfaction with the human condition, concentration on the "cases" and renunciation of the "causes." Over and over in III:12, simplicity and naturalness are stressed (more than forty times in some twenty pages), thus reinforcing the impression that to believe that man is able to surpass the limits of his corporeal nature is crippled thinking.

Constant rereading on Montaigne's part leads to many additions and changes in the *Exemplaire de Bordeaux;* to understand their raison d'être, the reader too must reread the work, not simply the immediately surrounding paragraphs, but the surrounding chapters as well. In the context of the two previous chapters, the very last (c) mention of Socrates at the end of "Of experience" takes on additional significance: (c) "rien ne m'est à digerer fascheux en la vie de Socrates que ses ecstases et ses demoneries . . (III:13, 1115). ["nothing is so hard for me to stomach in the life of Socrates as his ecstasies and possessions by his daemon . . ." (856).]

This underlines once more Montaigne's mistrust of man's ability to

12. Jules Brody, "From Teeth to Text in 'De l'experience:' A Philological Reading," *L'Esprit Créateur* 20, 1 (spring 1980), 7–22, p. 16.

communicate with supernatural powers, even if that man is the "master of masters" himself, for, as another (c)-addition on the same page clarifies: (c) "au plus eslevé throne du monde si ne sommes assis que sus nostre cul" (III:13, 1115). ["on the loftiest throne in the world we are still sitting only on our own rump" (857).]

This vivid metaphor, coming as it does on what turned out to be the last pages of the *Essays*, stands as a final reminder of the contrast between the uncertainty of unnatural phenomena and the unarguable evidence of our bodily functions, the one doubtful and unreliable, the other all too realistically persuasive.

MARCEL GUTWIRTH

"By Diverse Means . . ." (I:1)

The "firstness" of the very first chapter of the first book of the *Essais* is in more than one way problematic. Villey established authoritatively the unlikelihood of its having been the first, or perhaps even among the first to be composed. There is much that is supposititious in Villey's method, and we tend nowadays to be little concerned with the order in which writings flow from the pen, more with the order a writer wills, to lend pattern and form to his outpourings. All to the good, therefore, that chapter one of Book One *earned* its primacy, a subdued and well-nigh invisible primacy, to be sure, as clearly befits the earnest of Michel de Montaigne's insistently self-depreciatory outpourings.

Unspectacular as it is, that primacy is not undisputed. In strictest computation, chapter one must be admitted to follow on the heels of that jaunty salutation, titled *Au lecteur*. "He greets him with an adieu," Ruel observed[1]—the book taking its leave of the would-be reader before he can well have it in his grasp. With the act of readership thus forestalled from the onset, (for the book is no sooner set on the market than it appears, in its first page, to be coyly withdrawn), chapter one may duly step forward, reeling a bit one may suppose, under that earlier dismissal.

The matter it has to set forth is of a character very nearly even-handed: submissiveness, propitiation is the standard response of the underdog in a fight, in the often vain hope of saving his skin; a contrary tactic, hopeless defiance, also sometimes works. The unstable balance calls up the image of the scales practically equipoised with Montaigne would, in 1576, have struck on the obverse of a medal bearing his motto *Que scais-je?* True balance lies in the gradually tapering motion of ever diminishing oscillations. What the engraver's art out of necessity left unsaid the pen was to

1. Edouard Ruel, *Du sentiment artistique dans la morale de Montaigne* (Paris, 1901), p. 120.

take up as its proper theme: *mutation et branle* it would call it in the end, so universal that it adds up to a kind of repose. Pairing up uncertainties, for a first step, takes us a fair way on the road to that kind of understanding.[2]

The tactic of submission is not altogether abhorrent in the eyes of one who will announce himself willing to avert the extremity of his fate *soubs la peau d'un veau*, if need be. Yet it is a path as uncertain as it is broadly beaten, apt in fact to be of less use than its direct opposite, preternatural valor in the service of defiance. The scales thus swing widely in a first example. The Black Prince, breathing vengeance, is stopped in the taking of Limoges neither by the sight of a helpless multitude put to the slaughter, nor by the piteous outcry of women and children begging for mercy. The insane courage of three gentlemen taking on the whole thrust of his army gives him pause at last. What pity could not, admiration did: the sight of an ebullience of spirit which the odds could not subdue "first took the edge off his anger," (3) moving him to forgiveness.

The issue then is joined from the first page: it is of life and death. History is the unending chronicle of disasters that stalk us in every nook and cranny of the inhabited globe. The city besieged, shortly to be overwhelmed, is the very image of civil existence falsely secure behind its walls, ever and again fed bleeding to the hounds of war, the unappeasable. Thus it figures in fact, alongside the city still at peace, on the shield forged by Hephaistos for the death-dealing hero Achilles. To escape with your life in a world which your books, both of history and philosophy, paint as perilous beyond belief (the Saint Bartholomew's Day's massacre meanwhile ringing in every one's ears), is the pressing consideration which gets the *Essais* under way from the first. Thus we take the measure of a mind intensely practical, a mind that thirsted mightily after an assurance it knew was not to be had, in the question it chooses to ask at the very onset of a lifelong investigation: "Is there a way out?"

Three times we read of defiance thus unexpectedly rewarded; Edward of Wales, already cited, makes way for Scandenberg who forgives a delinquent soldier when, cornered, he makes a show of fight. To top them both, literally, enter the gentlewomen of Bavaria staggering under the weight of their possessions, as much as they can carry, which a wrathful Conrad III, enraged against their duke, had, as a sole concession, let them haul out of besieged Weinsberg: their husbands, it turns out, their children, and the

---

2. Helène-Hedy Ehrlich, who is alone to my knowledge to have given this same chapter serious consideration, points out that Montaigne's use of exampla goes not, as in classical rhetoric, to prove one proposition true, the other false, but to cast them both into doubt: *Montaigne: La critique et le langage* (Paris: Klincksieck, 1972), p. 31.

duke himself. Female magnanimity wrings tears of forgiveness from the relenting emperor, defiance rising here to an allegorical sublime.

The tears of an emperor are reward enough for a nightingale, in Andersen's well-known tale. Here they call back the reader-of-his-own-book, who by 1588 reenters the essay with an observation which appears to even up the scales: "Either one of these two ways would easily win me," yet the eye no sooner strays beyond the comma than the coordinate clause "for I am wonderfully lax in the direction of mercy and gentleness" (I:14) tilts the balance, in favor this time of compassion. That leniency of his is a fault, he hastens to add, a vice even, in the eyes of the Stoics, for "they want us to succor the afflicted, but not to unbend and sympathize with them." The scales are vibrating still.

Defiance is the way of the strong, and it appeals to the strong, ever ready to reverence greatness in others: thus the text of 1580, the intrusion brushed aside. Pity and compassion are the way to win over women and children, weakness being ever responsive to weakness. The author-reader's self-disparagement is thus carried forward by the earlier text, which offers deceptively retrospective confirmation of his standing amid the weak. But the scales are set in motion once more. Strength may well appeal to stronger natures, but it has also been known to move the fickle mob. The Theban populace were slow to clear Pelopidas, who took to heart the charge of having outstayed his mandate, begging for mercy and pleading extenuation. Epaminondas so stunned them by the proud recital of his high deeds, ramming their cavils down their own throats, "that they did not have the heart even to take the ballots in their hands." (I:4) Holding a mob at bay by the sheer power of the spoken word, a word that speaks of mighty deeds, comes close to enacting Montaigne's headiest dream. Writing for him was, after all, nothing less than putting himself to the proof on every page, backing up every word written with nerve and sinew, fear and hope, admission and resolve. Epaminondas triumphant, moreover, went a long way to dissolving the long shadow thrown by the sire de Moneins, whose misadventure is reported in chapter twenty-four of Book One. That unfortunate official sought by the sheer weight of his presence to outface a mob of tax protesters in the streets of Bordeaux. Alas, he entreated where he should have commanded and in the end let them see him quail: he was rushed and torn asunder under young Montaigne's very eyes. Caesar and Epaminondas, men of quite another stamp, pointedly reverse that Primal Scene of the writer's imagination. True eloquence, at any rate, is so much a matter of sheer character that unarmed Epaminondas winning over his judges may claim pride of place in a chapter where all other instances of defiance paint it arms in hand.

A late rereading, in the last years of the author's life, intervenes at this point in our chapter. A cruel, mean-spirited tyrant had sought to make an example of just the sort of man a greater soul should have honored and spared. The scales swing wildly back. After Epaminondas thundering in righteous indignation at a sovereign assembly he thereby brings to its senses, the spectacle of Dionysius the Elder, impervious to honor or decency, inflicting on the naked person of a noble adversary every form of undeserved injury capable of breaking his spirit. Stripped, flogged, reviled at every street-corner of the town he had once led in resistance Phyto went on "loudly recalling the honorable and glorious cause of his death—that he had refused to surrender his country into the hands of a tyrant." The troops inclining to take to heart such a show of manly defiance, far from resenting it as he had anticipated, "Dionysius had his martyrdom stopped and secretly sent him to be drowned at sea" (I:1, 4).

The inference is clear: defiance brings out the worst in this vilest of rulers. One does not talk back to the Iddi Amins of this world. Common sense might tell us as much; but what common sense does not so easily dispose of is the next, the final whirr of the scales, which returns us to the original text of the essay, there to read what may well be the best-known of Montaigne's characterizations: "Certes c'est un subject merveileusement vain, divers, & ondoyant, que l'homme." [Truly man is a marvelously vain, diverse, and undulating object.] (loc. cit.) The quintessential undependability of human nature, upon which all systematic views run aground, against which no panacea is possible to be devised, lies disclosed on this first approach, this first *assay*, in the shocking contrast exhibited in the last two illustrations of the chapter's point, the forked tail of its argument. For Pompey, great man that he was, did indeed confirm by counter-example the verity exhibited in the somber episode that was one day to be superadded, of Dionysius' revenge. One man, Stheno, taking upon himself the fault of a whole people, the Mamertines, against which the victorious Roman was most incensed, earned the pardon of his fellow-citizens by his great-hearted forwardness. Sylla's host, on the other hand, gained nothing by it—either for himself or for his city—under identical circumstances. Therein, however, does not reside the split. Pompey's graciousness receives no check in that merely parenthetical counter-example, a mere twist in the forward movement of the argument, without so much as a name or a gesture to stamp it in our memory. To force the scales into their last wild motion no less a name than Alexander's is invoked, mildest of conquerors.

Pompey the Great had shown himself great in the episode here instantiated. Alexander, whose claim to greatness of both spirit and achievement is caught up in an appellation familiar to all, Alexander the

Great was to show to no such advantage in a scene that almost smacks of the odiousness of a Dionysius—shattering to the winds what little firm understanding we had begun to build up of the fortunes of defiance. At the taking of Gaza, greatly put out by the uncommon difficulties encountered, among which must be numbered two fresh wounds upon his own person, Alexander, coming upon a man, whose valor he had several times witnessed, carrying on the fight alone, though wounded and his armor cut to pieces, gave notice to the fellow that he was not to die an easy death: all manner of torment awaited him. Further stung by the man's impassivity he then "ordered Betis's heels to be pierced through and had him thus dragged alive, torn, and dismembered, behind a car" (I:1, 5).

Alexander's shattering of his own legend supplies the chapter's conclusion. What better measure could we have asked for of the fluidity of human affairs? How better show that by diverse means we do all indeed come to a bad end? or at any rate that the occasional success of our endeavors need not blind us to the odds that make a mock of both supplication and defiance? The book we are entered upon is not to be a breviary of the way out: it will, in fact, explore faithfully, in its every deceptive meander the labyrinth of experience, fortifying us to live our lives to the full by the very sense of impasse boldly faced up to.

The end is not yet. The chapter in 1580 concluded on a question mark: was valor perhaps so unexceptional in Alexander's scheme of things as to be practically invisible to him? simply of no account? For the nature of true greatness, the kind that makes merely heroic deeds recede into a buzzing as of mosquitoes, is as much the matter of this book—that will resound to the names of Cato, of Caesar, of Socartes, as often as of Alexander and Epaminondas—as is the issue of how life is merely to be held on to and enhanced amid the perils and the distractions of this world. That single question, therefore, elongates into a triad upon a last rereading of the chapter, in the years that saw the preparation of the text for what was to be—final irony of that so nearly endless meditation upon one's own mortality—a posthumous edition. Was it a matter of high possessiveness? of resistless impetuosity? Alexander's unaccountable betrayal of his own idealized self-image in that haunting scene goes on puzzling the aging rereader. In Proustian fashion, *avant la lettre,* he offers, while he carefully refrains from a settled conclusion, three alternative readings of the incident. Valor does not signify in the eyes of the prince of valor, hence naked defiance is left alone to account for his rage. Valor is so much a part of Alexander's self-conception that he bitterly resented seeing it raised to such a pitch in another. The impetuosity of his wrath could suffer no check:

Alexander enraged was more than a match for the rational faculties, for the self-control even of an Alexander.

Epaminondas and Alexander thus vie for our admiration from the very first pages of the *Essais*, the one unambiguously heroic, the other darkly complex. They will figure again, alongside Homer, in a chapter straight-forwardly titled "Des plus excellens hommes." (II: xxxvi) Epaminondas there will again gain the edge: "The third, and the most outstanding, to my mind . . ." and his superiority to Alexander in that chapter is specified in the very terms suggested by their initial confrontation in the opening pages of Montaigne's probationary enterprise:

> En cettuy-cy l'innocence est une qualité propre, maistresse, constante, uniforme, incorruptible. Au parangon de laquelle elle paroist en Alexandre subalterne, incertaine, bigarrée, molle et fortuite. [I:36, 756]

> In this man innocence is a key quality, sovereign, constant, uniform, incorruptible. In comparison, it appears in Alexander as subordinate, uncertain, streaky, soft, and accidental. [573]

A full consecration—practically an apotheosis—of the Theban general awaits the first chapter of the Third Book, "De l'utile et de l'honneste." There his scrupulous observance of the laws of friendship and hospitality in the heat of battle—the victor of unvanquished Sparta not fearing to observe the niceties of private intercourse amid the clash of arms—offers a model for the discrimination of private duty from public necessity:

> Ne craignons point, apres un si grand precepteur, d'estimer (c) qu'il y a quelque chose illicite contre les ennemis mesmes, (b) que l'interest commun ne doibt pas tout requerir de tous contre l'interest privé . . . [III:1, 802]

> Let us not fear, after so great a preceptor, to consider (c) that there are some things illicit even against an enemy; (b) that the common interest must not require all things of all men against the private interest . . . [III:1, 609]

How grimly contrastive with the closing lines—the product of the latest of Montaigne's afterthoughts (Ed. municipale, I:7 n. 1)—that expatiate in our own chapter one, on the theme of Alexander's wrath:

> De vrai, si elle eust receu la bride, il est à croire qu'en la prinse et desolation de la ville de Thebes elle l'eust receue, à veoir cruellement mettre au fil de l'espée tant de vaillans hommes perdus et n'ayans plus moyen de desfense publique." [I:1, 10]

> In truth, if it could have been bridled, it is probable that it would have been in the capture and desolation of the city of Thebes, at the sight of so many valiant men, lost and without any further means of common defense, cruelly put to the sword. [5]

Six thousand were slaughtered, who far from crying mercy or seeking to save their lives sought out occasions to die an honorable death. None were spared but the old, the women and children—to furnish thirty thousand slaves.

The annihilation of Thebes—we savor the irony that it is the self-same Thebes that Epaminondas briefly roused to greatness—is the destruction of a free Greece, homeland of Montaigne's idea of virtue. The wrath of Alexander, that awesome force of nature, exacts on a mass basis the sacrifice of that defiant virtue, that unwillingness to give in to defeat, to acknowledge oneself flesh and bone merely, liable to be crushed by superior force, of which the compiler of these examples rejoiced to note that, on occasion, it could preserve life and limb as well as bestow undying honor. Fallen Thebes crushed by a heedless Alexander exhibits all at once the vanity, the grandeur, the instability of the human condition. It is vain to bank on either admiration or compassion from even the most unsullied of world-historical figures. A whole nation gone down unbowed gives notice, just the same, that mortality can be outfaced, if not eluded. An Alexander so spectacularly untrue to the image of Alexander launches us upon the treacherous waters of our own bottomless incertitude.

What lesson is to be learned from a consideration of the chapter Montaigne chose for his first clearly outstrips the mere recognition afforded it by Villey—who stands alone, I believe, in giving it any serious thought whatever; it takes up the theme of *diversity*, to the end that, in the first edition at least, Montaigne's book may make that "notion capitale" both the first and the last word of its wisdom (I:1, 7). Pompey and Dionysius, Alexander and Epaminondas, the Black Prince and Conrad III, mangled Betis and honored Stheno weave a web not so easily unraveled. We have our backs at all times to the wall: that much is clear. No easy prescription exists to cure the human predicament. Virtue, though it may save us, more often than not earns itself—and us—a crown of thorns. The ways of greatness are a bafflement mostly, and only very occasionally satisfy the legitimate craving of our famished spirit, although a relatively obscure Theban general may one day supplant the dashingly heroic, spectacularly humane master of the world as the repository of that elusive radiance. Thus, in the small compass of three pages, some of Montaigne's most pressing, most inalterable concerns crowd upon us *in nuce*. And whether to fight to the last and beyond or trust to mercy is an issue that quietly fades into nonresolution, as the scales settle at last and lie even, though not before the lesson sinks in that theirs is to be no idle repose—a balance, rather, spiritedly won, not meekly or, Lord knows, dully received.

CATHERINE DEMURE

Montaigne: The Paradox and the Miracle—Structure and Meaning in "The Apology for Raymond Sebond" (Essais II:12)

From this essay to the *Essays*, there is neither any shortcut possible nor any implication from a principle to a consequence: the refusal of an organizing system in this fundamentally open work makes the circle which goes from the whole to its parts interminable. But doubtless it is not unimportant, nor without implications for the reading of the entire work, to be able to show, throughout a text as considerable as the "Apology," the coherence of a system of thought which is the rigorous expression of the possibilities and limits of the philosophical enterprise at the dawn of modern times.

The goal of this study is to bring to light the structure of one chapter of the *Essays*, the "Apology for Raymond Sebond," whose importance the most divergent readings acknowledge in spite of the conflict of interpretations. We know that Villey[1] sees in the "Apology" the high point of a "skeptical crisis" which Montaigne was then to transcend and repudiate; as for Brunschvicg,[2] he uses the "Apology" as a constant, central reference point for his reading of the *Essays*, but he blurs its tension in order to demonstrate the powers of balance and happiness of a moral subject on the far side of skepticism. We have been obliged to recall these conclusions before proposing a structural reading of the "Apology," that is, very simply, a reading which bases meaning on the formal organization of the text in its literalness and integrality.

We shall show, thus, counter to a "humanist" or moderate reading, that

This article is a translation of "Montaigne: Le Paradoxe et le Miracle. Structure et sens dans l'"Apologie de Raymond Sebon' (*Essais*, II, 12)" which first appeared in French in *Les Etudes Philosophiques*, no. 4/1978. It is reprinted here with the kind permission of the author Catherine Demure.

1. Cf. his brief but very clear presentation of the "Apology" in his edition of the *Essays*, op cit.

2. Léon Brunschvicg, *Descartes et Pascal, lecteurs de Montaigne* (Paris: La Baconnière, 1945).

the coherence of Montaigne's thought appears here in the rigor of a maintained contradiction: the model of this paradox, which makes up the very heart of the text, is constituted by the status of theology, a knowledge which is both necessary and impossible.

But inversely, against an "antihumanist" reading such as Jean-Yves Pouilloux's,[3] we affirm the existence of an "ideological content": in dealing with knowledge and action, Montaigne affirms both the distinction and contradiction of the two orders, and, with a dual fidelity to Christianity and Socrates, asserts that true knowledge is awareness of ignorance: a goal to regain, where all the possibilities of philosophical endeavor are inscribed.

I. IN ORDER TO READ, ONE MUST READ EVERYTHING

We know that, following his presentation of the "Apology," Villey proposes an outline of it. Without going into detail, we can note from the start that the opening of the text is excluded from the outline, which Villey thereby relegates to the inessential; now, this opening is a rapid presentation of Montaigne's relationship to knowledge and of the conditions of his access to Sebond's text. Speaking in it of knowledge in general, of "letters," Montaigne indeed writes here: (a) "Moy, je les ayme bien, mais je ne les adore pas" (439). (a) ["Myself, I like them well enough, but I do not worship them" (319).]

Even if we reserve an understanding of this text, it is clear that it has a slightly different ring from certain affirmations of a total, definitive rejection of knowledge which the ulterior text will present. But Villey also presents the end of the text as a mere prolongation, without connecting it in any way with the context; as for Pouilloux, he says nothing about this ending.[4] Is it innocuous, then, or repetitive? Not at all: what is involved is a quotation from Seneca which is difficult and paradoxal in itself: (a) "O la vile chose, dit-il, et abjecte, que l'homme, s'il ne s'esleve au dessus de l'humanité!" (604) [(a) "O what a vile and abject thing is man," he says, "if he does not raise himself above humanity!" (457)] and which Montaigne's commentary takes up again—especially strengthening its paradoxical, even contradictory, aspect—in two additions dating from the (c) manuscript; the two moments of this commentary are in fact the following: the first moment: (c) "Voylá un bon mot, et un utile desir, mais pareillement

3. Jean-Yves Pouilloux, *Lire les "Essais" de Montaigne* (Paris: Maspero, 1969).

4. Hugo Friedrich, on the other hand, dwells on this conclusion at length; we shall return to this commentary. Hugo Friedrich, *Montaigne* (Paris: Gallimard, 1968 for the French translation), p. 107.

absurde" (604). [(c) "That is a good statement and a useful desire, but equally absurd" (457)]; and the second moment—and this sentence definitively closes the text of the "Apology": (c) "C'est à nostre foy Chrestienne, non à sa vertu Stoique, de pretendre à cette divine et miraculeuse metamorphose" (604). [(c) "It is for our Christian faith, not for his Stoical virtue, to aspire to that divine and miraculous metamorphosis" (457).] Here again, this difficult text—a real appeal to understanding and a quite manifest return to the problematics of the "Apology" as to the true place of man and his powers in the world—cannot be evaded.

Without anticipating the ulterior reading of the text, we can then already affirm that these two texts, the opening and closing of the "Apology," must be understood within and through the context, which will doubtless be illuminated by them in its turn. Limits of a very long text which they enclose, these passages may find in it their meaning, or perhaps a confirmation of their meaning by reflection. One must affirm, then, the absolute necessity of first respecting the external form of the text, which really begins with this opening and which really ends with this conclusion. *In short, in order to read, one must read everything.* No matter what the "situation" of a text which it claims to reveal and activate, no rigorous reading can abandon what constitutes the material boundaries of that text.

This methodological requirement, moreover, is not based only on these criteria of the exhaustiveness of the reading. Every partial reading reaches a second stopping point when it encounters a new difficulty, in this case one so obvious that it is all but forgotten in the most precise readings, and this difficulty will also lead us to problems of meaning.

II. WHY THIS SUBJECT: "THE APOLOGY FOR RAYMOND SEBOND"?

We know that Pouilloux shows, rightly, that for Montaigne there is "an intellectual, philosophical innovation which makes all subjects possible for him."[5] Granted, all subjects are possible for him, but: the longest *Essay* on a text which Montaigne literally destroys! On a text about which he says (a strange compliment for a theological work) that he finds "belles les imaginations" ["the ideas of this author fine"] and that "beaucoup de gens s'amusent à le lire, et notamment les dames" (440); ["many people are busy reading it, and especially the ladies" (320),] on a text which he judges doubly vain, first because no theology is possible for man—a sufficient argument in itself!—and secondly because reason is particularly unsuitable for this task

5. Pouilloux, p. 59.

(which is impossible, besides . . .) There is, at the very least, a problem here: why then does Montaigne devote such a long discourse to this work which he could sufficiently refute in a few lines? In other words, *why "The Apology for Raymond Sebond"*? How can we not see an anomaly, an incoherence, in taking as the object of his reflection a text of which Montaigne will show only the weaknesses, when we know that, no matter how critical, even subversive, his thought may be, it is never polemical?

It seems that on one level, however, this contradiction may be, if not completely removed, at least made comprehensible by its presuppositions. First of all, Montaigne tells us, the text is dear to him because he translated it and worked on it, which confers upon it at least a subjective importance, especially since this work was undertaken for Montaigne's father, and at his request:

> Or, quelques jours avant sa mort, mon pere, ayant de fortune rencontré ce livre soubs un tas d'autres papiers abandonnez, me commanda de le luy mettre en François. [439]

> Now some days before his death, my father, having by chance come across this book under a pile of other abandoned papers, commanded me to put it into French for him. [320]

This father had died several years before (in 1568), and Montaigne loved him. This is what permits us to understand his choice of Sebond's text among other theological essays. But there is more. In this era of conflicts and religious wars (and we know how overwhelmed Montaigne was to learn of their atrocity, and that this atrocity appealed on both sides to evangelical truth), and even though in other respects Montaigne believes theology to be impossible and dangerous, he still thinks that after the "nouvelletez de Luther" (the "innovations of Luther") Sebond's text could reasonably appear capable of combatting "un execrable atheisme" ("an execrable atheism") which the "maladie" ("malady") of free examination "aysément" ("easily") risked bringing about (439) (320).]

But if Montaigne's choice of Sebond's text becomes comprehensible in this way, the essence of the difficulty remains, since the text, dear to Montaigne's heart and possibly useful on the religious and social plane, will nevertheless be totally ruined by him. But this is because we had only seen a superficial difficulty, so to speak historical, which masked a *contradiction that will dominate the whole text, to which we shall have to refer the text in its entirety.*

This dominant contradiction is announced and confirmed by the opening and closing texts of the "Apology," whose importance we have already emphasized. Radical and definitive, it is presented in the sixth paragraph of the "Apology" when Montaigne takes up an examination of the theological project.

What does Montaigne affirm in fact? First of all (and this thesis will be abundantly developed in the continuation of the text, notably at the criticism of anthropomorphic conceptions of God) *the radical impossibility of all theology;* it is a knowledge which is absolutely out of our power and grasp:

> Toutefois je juge ainsi, qu'à une chose si divine et si hautaine, et surpassant de si loing l'humaine intelligence, comme est cette verité de laquelle il a pleu à la bonté de Dieu nous esclairer, il est bien besoin qu'il nous preste encore son secours, d'une faveur extraordinarie et privilegée, pour la pouvoir concevoir et loger en nous; et ne croy pas que les moyens purement humains en soyent aucunement capables. [440–41]

> However, I think thus, that in a thing so divine and so lofty, and so far surpassing human intelligence, as is this truth with which it has pleased the goodness of God to enlighten us, it is very necessary that he still lend us his help, by extraordinary and privileged favor, so that we may conceive it and lodge it in us. And I do not think that purely human means are at all capable of this. [321]

Human intelligence, therefore, cannot gain access to God or theology; only faith in the revealed word enables us to attain the mysteries of religion, but not to understand them, or perhaps even to express them (441). And this determining thesis will weigh on the whole text. Montaigne will conclude his account of philosophical contradictions concerning the soul's immortality with these words: "Confessons ingenuement que Dieu seul nous l'a dict, et la foy: car leçon n'est ce pas de nature et de nostre raison" (554). ["Let us confess frankly that God alone has told us so, and faith; for a lesson of nature and of our reason it is not" (415)], words which he had founded earlier with the affirmation that "c'est à Dieu seul de se cognoistre et d'interpreter ses ouvrages" (499). ["It is for God alone to know himself and to interpret his works (369)].

Why then doesn't Montaigne stop there, why this detour through Sebond's theology, through the conflict of philosophical and religious beliefs? Why, if only to demonstrate its inanity, pursue at such length the road of theology? Because this impossible knowledge is nevertheless necessary to man; it is even the highest, most valorized human enterprise;

so that *after* having posited the impossibility of theology, Montaigne affirms that

> [c'est] une tresbelle et tresloüable entreprinse d'accommoder encore au service de nostre foy les utils naturels et humains que Dieu nous a donnez. Il ne faut pas douter que ce ne soit l'usage le plus honorable que nous leur sçaurions donner . . . [441]

> it is . . . a very fine and very laudable enterprise to accommodate also to the service of our faith the natural and human tools that God has given us. There can be no doubt that this is the most honorable use that we could put them to . . . [321]

Therefore we see Montaigne conclude the paragraph in this way, by legitimating the attempt at thought about the divine which must "accompaigner nostre foy" [accompany our faith"] even though he knows that "ny . . . nos efforts et arguments puissent atteindre à une si supernaturelle et divine science" (441). ["our efforts and arguments can[not] attain a knowledge so supernatural and divine" (321)].

In such a way is this fundamental contradiction stated. It refers to a paradox of which neither term will be removed or modified. The whole development of the "Apology," as it has often and truly been said, aims at ruining any claim to establish certain knowledge; the senses and reason, experience and discourse *(discours)*, are deceptive, and human privilege doubtful. Like any other realm of knowledge and more than any other, theological knowledge is impossible. What has been seen less often is the situation of this apology for skepticism in a paradoxical problematics: even if it is impossible, knowledge about God is still necessary. The whole "Apology" testifies relentlessly to the vanity of human knowledge, but *we shall only be able to understand this "apogee of skepticism" by enclosing it within the paradox which governs the whole text and which alone permits it to function.*

This schema of a paradoxical thought is close to the one which Lucien Goldmann presented as constitutive of Pascal's philosophy in *Les Pensées*[6] and which he related to the notion of "tragic vision" borrowed from the young Lukács. The proximity of Montaigne's and Pascal's approaches and the difference between them thus become the instrument of a vaster theological enterprise seeking to reveal, before and after the emergence of the Cartesian system, the meaning of this contestation of a rationalist vision of man and the world.

6. Lucien Goldmann, *Le dieu caché* (Paris: Gallimard, 1955).

III. STRUCTURE AND MEANING IN "THE APOLOGY FOR RAYMOND SEBOND"

1) The "Apology" fits into a criticism of learning: more restricted than limited (plus bornée que limitée)

Montaigne's reflection begins with an affirmation of principles whose bearing could be vague or could betray an inconsequential "skepticism" were it not for the context and argumentation which support it:

> C'est, à la verité, une tres-utile et grande partie que la science, ceux qui la mesprisent, tesmoignent assez leur bestise; mais je n'estime pas pourtant sa valeur jusques à cette mesure extreme qu'aucuns luy attribuent, comme Herillus le philosophe, qui logeoit en elle le souverain bien, et tenoit qu'il fut en elle de nous rendre sages et contens [438]

> In truth, knowledge is a great and very useful quality; those who despise it give evidence enough of their stupidity. But yet I do not set its value at that extreme measure that some attribute to it, like Herillus the philosopher, who placed in it the sovereign good, and held that it was in its power to make us wise and content. [319]

Such are the first lines of this essay which situate us, it seems, in that moderation, that equilibrium to which it would be Montaigne's mission to bear witness.[7] Will he not reinforce his moderate and somewhat distant, attitude towards "letters," which are the very body of all knowledge, by writing at the end of this same paragraph: "Moy, je les ayme bien, mais je ne les adore pas"? ["Myself, I like them well enough, but I do not worship them"?] But do we understand the text correctly? It is a question here of nuances, of moderation, of equilibrium? Can one accept a flat, anodyne reading of these lines of exordium when they lead to one of their author's most important essays?

Let us go back. And first of all, in order to point out the unexpectedness of this praise of knowledge on the threshhold of one of Montaigne's most violently skeptical texts; what is written (*l'écrit*) remains, as well as the totality of the text. Being ignorant of knowledge is "bestise" ("stupidity"); loving philosophy and knowledge,[8] on the contrary, goes without saying; to

7. Cf. for example Brunschvicg, op. cit., p. 87: "The simply human ideal of balance and harmony has never been expressed more exquisitely."

8. On the sciences and scholastic intellectual techniques, and on the content designated by the vocables "letters," "philosophy," etc., reference to Gilson's works remains irreplaceable. On the French humanist movement in the sixteenth century, and on innovations in matters of education in particular, reference to the works of Robert Mandrou (*Introduction à la France moderne*, Albin Michel, 1961 and 1974) permits a synthesis which the bibliographical references in Chapter V, section D, complete, especially François de Dainville, *Les Jésuites et*

be unaware of them is to deprive oneself of thought itself. *No matter what the limits of factual knowledge, they are contested by a movement of thought which is a philosophy and a search for a possible learning.* It is the manifest character of the statement—Montaigne being the intellectual that he is—and not any scorn or irony on his part, which makes it so brief and so little argued here: the "will to know" *(le "vouloir-savoir")* is legitimate if not in its results, at least in its intention to learn and to organize learning into a body of knowledge. Thus when the text turns back upon itself and Montaigne refuses to take this love of knowledge to the "extresme", it is not in order to exhibit a skeptical argumentation on the impotence of reason or the opacity of reality. If he refuses the type of life which will be Descartes', the one which the true moral maxim of the *Discours de la Méthode* expresses: "to spend my whole life in cultivating my reason, and to advance as much as I can in the knowledge of truth . . ."[9] it is not at all that he "moderates" adoration into simple affection; the difference is not quantitative, but qualitative. To love the sciences rather than to worship them, no matter how great the effort which leads Montaigne toward intellectual reflection, is not to be moderate but divided. The postulate which underlies Montaigne's reticences here is neither methodological nor skeptical: it refers to the irreducible difference of orders. What Montaigne refuses is adoration owed to God, to the signifying totality of the world; and he is gently ironical toward his father, infatuated with learned personages;

> recueillant leurs sentences et leurs discours comme des oracles, et avec d'autant plus de reverence et de religion qu'il avoit moins de loy d'en juger, car il n'avoit aucune connoissance des lettres . . . [439]

> collecting their savings and discourses like oracles, and with all the more reverence and religion as he was less qualified to judge them; for he had no knowledge of letters . . . [319]

More versed than him in letters and intellectual life, Montaigne does not ask for moderation, but the distinction of genres: life cannot be inscribed in a single register which would be that of knowledge. Science—no matter what its scope, rigor, and possibilities are in other respects—cannot "nous rendre sages et contens" (p. 438); ["make us wise and content" (p. 319);] he does not believe, he says, "ny ce que d'autres ont dict, que la science est mere de toute vertu, et que tout vice est produit par l'ignorance (438);

l'éducation de la société française, la naissance de l'humanisme moderne (Paris: Duchesne et ses fils, 1940).

9. Descartes, *Discours de la Méthode*, 3rd part. Ed. Gilson (Paris: Vrin, 1926 and 1967), p. 27.

["what others have said, that knowledge is the mother of all virtue, and that all vice is produced by ignorance (p. 319).]

Such is the postulate of Montaigne, who refutes what one may call the search for a theoretical confirmation, an epistemological legitimation of action. Happiness and virtue remain real finalities of human life, different from knowledge. This postulate is clear, and its understated formulation should not deceive us: its position preliminary to the whole development of the chapter marks a refusal of rationalism—if one means by the word, in its Cartesian sense, not the belief in a possible and necessary usage of rigorous reason, but the affirmation of the homogeneity of the world as knowable reality,[10] and hence, the homogeneity of learning *connaissance* itself, completely identified with knowledge *savoir*, whose model is mathematical science.

Thus for Montaigne, beyond any skeptical argumentation, including the one which he himself will develop in the "Apology," the first insufficiency of all knowledge is that it is *only* knowledge, and for this reason never concerns us entirely as such. For the rupture between orders is first of all a rupture in me; I am a being of mobility and conflict, diverse in the long run *(durée)* as well as during the moment, and a being whose unity is always in question; so much so that in the first chapter of the second book, Montaigne writes:

> Cette variation et contradiction qui se void en nous, si souple, a faict qu'aucuns nous songent deux ames, . . . une si brusque diversité ne se pouvant bien assortir à un subjet simple. [335]

> These supple variations and contradictions that are seen in us have made some imagine that we have two souls . . . for such sudden diversity cannot well be reconciled with a simple subject. [242]

Montaigne discovers this shattered subject in himself, such that

> je n'ay rien à dire de moy, entierement, simplement, et solidement, sans confusion et sans meslange, ny en un mot. DISTINGO est le plus universel membre de ma Logique. [335]

> I have nothing to say about myself absolutely, simply, and solidly, without confusion and without mixture, or in one word. *Distinguo* is the most universal member of my logic. [242]

This is why learning *(connaissance)* is not knowledge *(savoir)* here, but first of all description, "recitation"; and it is because I am—like the world—a

10. Without wishing to develop this point here, let us say in a word that we do not mean to reduce Cartesian "philosophy" to Cartesian "rationalism."

"branloire perenne" (III:2, 804); ["perennial movement" (p. 610)] that "je ne puis asseurer mon object" (p. 805) ["I cannot keep my subject still" (p. 610)]. Located here is the origin, in Montaigne, of resistance to (rather than refusal of) the rationalist hypothesis: for the truth can be contradictory: "Tant y a que je me contredits bien à l'adventure, mais la verité . . . je ne la contredy point" (805). ["So, all in all, I may indeed contradict myself now and then; but truth . . . I do not contradict (611).]

One sees where this modest introductory paragraph leads us and what a permanent counterpoint it will bring to bear on the whole ulterior argumentation of the text; under no circumstances can the skeptical argumentation of the "Apology" be considered the sole foundation of Montaigne's criticism of knowledge. The refusal to worship letters, the (real) distance with regard to organized knowledge,[11] are not primarily skeptical attitudes putting the quality of knowledge into question, but the expression of a mistrust whose foundation is *practical*;[12] wisdom and happiness are of a different order, which nothing permits me to reduce or subordinate to that of knowledge. If it is conceivable, such a dependence is at least "subject à une longue interpretation" (p. 438) ["subject to a long interpretation" (p. 319).] Montaigne, for his part, does not believe in it, and the skeptical argumentation will have to be reread in this perspective, which allows us to save the interest of the text beyond that of a rather superficial criticism of organized knowledge which one century would render obsolete. Pascal's thought will also violently express this mistrust and this affirmation of the hetereogeneity of orders without the slightest intrusion of skepticism. Copernicus, Galileo, Descartes will produce a new, rigorous knowledge; but this triumphant reason will stir up in Pascal (who is, however, a beneficiary of its rise) a protestation of all the more forceful in that it is more divided: he goes so far as to write against Descartes: "And even if that were true, we do not consider all philosophy to be worth one hour of pain."[13] ["Even if that were true . . ."]

This introduction allows us then to affirm that the criticism of knowledge in Montaigne cannot be reduced to mere skepticism: the plurality of human finalities and the impossibility of reducing the subject to unity are here, explicity or implicity, the point of departure of the reflection. And this contradiction prepares and grounds the paradoxical

11. Cf. H. Friedrich who recalls "the distancing of the contemporary sciences" in Montaigne and who sees there, rightly, not so much the cause as the very effect of his mistrust in regard to human, intellectual, and technical claims to master nature (pp. 151–55).

12. One can see therefore that if we accept with Pouilloux that what is given in Montaigne is "the confusion of orders" (p. 107), we must refrain from concluding with him that there is a renunciation of any search for an "objective reference" (p. 81) to philosophical discourse.

13. Pascal, *Les Pensées*, ed. Brunschvicg (Paris: Hachette, 1959), fragment 79.

structure of the text: it is a divided subject, perhaps even rife with conflict, which touches upon his entire relationship to knowledge in general, and to theology in particular. This major contradiction organizes the argumentation of the whole ulterior development; it will establish the coherence of a thought which is necessarily in conflict with all unifying dogmatisms. Skeptical argumentation properly speaking—multiform and uneven, besides—is thus only second in relation to this first, irremediable break of which the subject is the bearer.

2) Theology, Exemplary Knowledge

Thus we can understand the strange series of reversals which Montaigne effects in his evaluation of the theological enterprise, which is the knowledge under consideration here. Montaigne's whole art here consists in encountering theology through personal paths, thereby merging reflection on an essential knowledge with his own story—which seems to be the inessential, the anecdotal, or even the insignificant.

For therein, first of all, lies the privilege of theology in relation to Montaigne's project: history confronted him and his father, like all men of their time, and much more than others, with religious problems. Faced with the reality of contrary arguments, and with the reality of actions which take their inspiration from these arguments or which claim to, theology becomes a personal matter for Montaigne. By choosing Sebond's theological work as the theme of a text as long and important as the "Apology," Montaigne chooses first of all, in accordance with his philosophical project, to speak himself (de se dire lui-même),[14] a theme which is doubly his, both through his personal history and through History itself. No matter what the difficulties or the impossibility for me to invest myself totally in an enterprise of knowledge, I feel myself (me, Montaigne, a Christian, a Catholic and a politically responsible figure) entirely concerned by a problem to which, beyond the properly intellectual interest which it can inspire, the necessities of action and the attempt to live happily lead me back incessantly, and often tragically. The first privilege of theology resides then in the fact that this "knowledge" is, in the sixteenth century, like the locus where all the possibilities of action and happiness converge—or from which they arise. And even though this is not the place to speak of "Montaigne's religion,"[15] let us simply remember that the historical reality

14. Cf. "Au lecteur" ("To the Reader"): "Ainsi, lecteur, je suis moy-mesmes la matiere de mon livre . . ." (3); ["Thus, reader, I am myself the matter of my book . . ." (p. 2).]

15. First of all because this would be anticipating what only the reading of the "Apology" and then of the *Essays* can allow us to perceive. Then because theology and religion are obviously not equivalent.

of the religious wars, the strange metamorphoses of the legitimacy throughout the relationships between the royalty and the Catholic and Protestant
religions, only serve to dramatize the fundamental importance of the
religious question for the whole sixteenth century, and force us—us,
belated readers—to take this question into consideration as a constant
horizon of this century, as Lucien Febvre has admirably shown in *Le
problème de l'incroyance au XVIe siècle*.[16]

But theology is privileged in another way—theology which causes
Montaigne to choose it as the model of knowledge for and against which he
will argue. This privileged status is not made any more explicit than the
preceding one and, unlike the other, is not even alluded to. We feel it
necessary, however, to bring it to light because it allows us, among other
things, to perpetuate a contemporary reading of this text of Montaigne, and
not just a historical one.

What is theology for Montaigne, at least the one he discusses, and
which he judges here in order to illustrate, let us not forget, a reflection on
knowledge? It is a work of reason, entirely separate from the revelation and
faith which certainly ground it, give rise to it, and control it, but which
never mingle with it. Theology is a human science, an implementation of
"utils naturels et humains" (441) ["natural and human tools" (321)], of
"moyens purement humains" (441); ["purely human means" (321)]; it is a
work of "raison" ("reason") by means of "efforts et argumens" ("efforts and
arguments"); in short, it is the realm of reason, and of human reason alone.
It is therefore homogeneous with mathematics or logic and can thus
perfectly illustrate the powers and the shortcomings of our capacity for
knowledge. But in contrast to the other sciences, it allows us to attribute all
its successes and failures to that reason alone; for, unlike all the other
sciences, *it has all its possible experience behind it:* no progress to come, no
discovery, no accumulation of results can occur to improve it or to modify
it. Founded on revelation alone—which came about historically and was
handed down to the man completely in definitive texts—it cannot look to
the future for anything. Its field is that of reason alone.

This is why skeptical argumentation takes on such a particular tone in
this text, one so disdainful of the specific divisions of the sciences. This is
not due to a misunderstanding *(méconnaissance)* of these sciences, but
justifies rather this argumentation, as we have already said. For what reason

16. Ed. Albert Michel, 1942 and 1968: "Claiming to make the sixteenth century a skeptical
century, a libertine century, a rationalist century, and glorifying it as such is the worst of errors
and illusions. Through the will of its best representatives, it was, quite on the contrary, an
inspired century. A century which, first of all, sought a reflection of the divine in all things" (p.
427).

cannot do is speak for happiness and the good. It it could, where could we see it better than in theology, a knowledge which, by its very essence, as the French historical context of the sixteenth century demonstrates dramatically, is the constant theoretical referent of men's lives?

Then Montaigne's entire perspective turns back on itself indefinitely, for this impossible knowledge still remains just as necessary, and reason is its only instrument. And this is why Montaigne's attitude will be paradoxical when he chooses—as he does choose to love, not worship, knowledge in general—to attempt this inevitable but unrealizable search for God through reason:

> (a) Il . . . faut . . . accompaigner nostre foy de toute la raison qui est en nous, mais tousjours avec cette reservation de n'estimer pas que ce soit de nous qu'elle dépende, nÿ que nos efforts et argumens puissent atteindre à une si supernaturelle et divine science. [441]

> (a) We must . . . accompany our faith with all the reason that is in us, but always with this reservation, not to think that it is on us that faith depends, or that our efforts and arguments can attain a knowledge so supernatural and divine. [321]

We have sufficiently shown that Sebond's text is not a simple pretext here by linking theology as a model of knowledge to Montaigne's global philosophical project and to the general subject of this essay. The fact still remains that the whole ulterior text will ruin the very claims of Sebond: is it to ridicule him? Could this be the real reason behind Montaigne's choice: a text too naive to resist skeptical argumentation?[17]

Such a hypothesis is necessarily reductive, not only because it shows us a cynical Montaigne including his father in his derision, which is highly improbable and would be somewhat distressing, but especially because it masks the very tension of the text—and therefore its meaning, such as the paradoxical structures already pointed out allow us to foresee. For the truth is that Montaigne is both "for" and "against" Sebond, and not only in the relative, manageable harmony of good and bad arguments or of laudable intentions and mediocre results: even if real, these reasons remain absolutely accessory to Montaigne's observation. He is totally for and against Sebond, throughout, in contradiction and paradox—in the coherent but contradictory affirmation that we must approach the theological quest as perhaps the most urgent, fundamental pursuit, while at the same time we are convinced of the aporetic result of such a quest. So that no theological

17. Cf. Brunschvicg, op cit., p. 56: "The Apology, which appears to answer *for* Sebond, never stops talking and fighting *against* him."

text other than Sebond's, even if it were infinitely superior to his, could have escaped Montaigne's criticism—nor be destroyed by it, either, however.

In order to see this better, we must take a closer look at the "responses" given by Montaigne to objections to Sebond. We find it particularly interesting to give the text here its complexity and movement against all simplification. Let us follow Montaigne, then:

> La premiere reprehension qu'on fait de son ouvrage, c'est que les Chretiens se font tort de vouloir appuyer leur creance par des raisons humaines, qui ne se conçoit que par foy et par une inspiration particuliere de la grace divine. [440]

> The first criticism that they make of his work is that Christians do themselves harm in trying to support their belief by human reasons, since it is conceived only by faith and by a particular inspiration of divine grace. [321]

In answer to this objection, Montaigne gives the response in which he defines the difficult and paradoxical relationship of man to theology. We shall not return to this response except to emphasize that it does not "ridicule" Sebond in any way;[18] it *maintains* the legitimacy of its (theological) attempt even while *affirming* the impossibility of reaching God through human means.

But there is more. For Montaigne's text continues beyond this paragraph upon which we have commented at length; and Montaigne adds to this first response a much more extensive text covering several pages. What we find there is surprising, to say the least: *Montaigne legitimates theology by the very absence in which we find ourselves of any contact with God.* Only revelation can found and give rise to theology, he says, thus clearly defining the distinct fields of religion and theological knowledge. But here this human, rational approach to the subject of God is made all the more urgent and legitimate by the fact that we no longer seem to be able to actualize revelation: theology lets the very essence of the divine escape, but the faith which would exempt us from it, or which is at least able to found it,

---

18. We can only recall here how Lucien Febvre (op. cit.), after having meticulously and rigorously refuted the very possibility of an atheist Rabelais, and after having rejected all theories of "the masked author," finally exclaims: "One would have to say, without admiration—contrary to the custom of our contemporaries, who are always delighted to show us, in the "rationalists" of yesterday, so many liars and cowards—one would have to say, not without scorn: "He was a scoundrel." But one would have to add, also: "And a proud imbecile." For he went beyond the goal" (p. 244). It is the same with Montaigne: by attributing so much subtlety or cynicism to him, one denies his very thought in its original effort.

is no longer in us. Our only personal and present access to God is therefore, undoubtedly, this path of reasoning, the reference to the divine word remaining more historical than personal. For this knowledge of God,

> (a) si elle n'entre chez nous par une infusion extraordinaire; si elle y entre non seulement par discours, mais encore par moyens humains, elle n'y est pas en sa dignité ny en sa splendeur. Et certes je crain pourtant que nous ne la jouyssions que par cette voye. [441]

> (a) if it does not enter into us by an extraordinary infusion; if it enters, I will not say only by reason, but by human means of any sort, it is not in us in its dignity or in its splendor. And yet I am afraid that we enjoy it only in this way. [321]

Faith is difficult and rare; does it really exist? Are there men, even among Christians, other than those whom Montaigne divides (in a surprisingly Pascalian expression) into two equally inauthentic categories:

> (c) Les uns font accroire au monde qu'ils croyent ce qu'ils ne croyent pas. Les autres, en plus grand nombre, se le font accroire à eux mesmes, ne scachants pas penetrer que c'est que croire. [442]

> (c) Some make the world believe that they believe what they do not believe. Others, in greater number, make themselves believe it, being unable to penetrate what it means to believe. [322]

Thus theology, Sebond's as much as any other, will open up a whole propaedeutic to faith, not by proving the existence of God or by revealing him, but by showing at least "comment il n'est piece du monde qui desmante son facteur" (447) [how there is no part of the world that belies its maker (326)], and in this way theology will serve "d'acheminement et de premiere guyde à un apprentis pour le mettre à la voye de cette connoissance" (447); [as a start and a first guide to an apprentice to set him on the road to this knowledge (327)] so that theological arguments at least

> le façonnent aucunement et rendent capable de la grace de Dieu, par le moyen de laquelle se parfournit et se perfet apres nostre creance. [447]

> fashion him to some extent and make him capable of the grace of God, by means of which our belief is afterward completed and perfected. [327]

Montaigne, far from ridiculing Sebond in these responses to the first objection made against him, shows that this objection itself gets carried away in criticizing theology in the name of the powers of a faith which never appears—and which none of us, Christians, including me, Montaigne, can manifest. And yet, against Sebond, the fact remains that theology is impossible—at least if its object really is God.[19]

It is of capital importance to see here how Montaigne evades the tragic conflict to which his paradoxical argumentation seems to lead him: this is because the possibility remains of going around the irreducible opposition between God and man, between faith and reason, between necessary and impossible theology, through action—including the intellectual act which is theology. Only true faith, which I do not have, leads to God. And yet, theology is inevitable, *de facto* and *de jure*. *Montaigne finds a way out of this double, contradictory affirmation which he maintains:*

1. by changing the object of theology, which becomes a simple account of the marks of the divine in the world, and even more modestly, of the marks of the possibility of the divine in the world. From knowledge about God we pass then to a purely human propaedeutic to possible belief;

2. by recalling a faith in Christian revelation which is certainly formal—since it is not acted upon by the subject—but nevertheless real. Faith remains, historical, as an acquisition of humanity, even if each particular man today fails to recapture it and live it.

There is, therefore, a displacement between the philosophical—or metaphysical—aporia which we unmasked and the possibility—minimal, hazardous, but real—of bridging this gap between the divine and the human, for our forces are not absolutely null, nor God absolutely hidden:

> Ce seroit faire tort à la bonté divine, si l'univers ne consentoit à nostre creance. Le ciel, la terre, les elemans, nostre corps et nostre ame, toutes choses y conspirent: il n'est que de trouver le moyen de s'en servir. [447]

> It would be doing a wrong to divine goodness if the universe did not assent to our belief. The sky, the earth, the elements, our body and our soul, all things conspire in this; we have only to find the way to use them. [326]

One of the actualizations of this precarious path in the search for a way out of the theological dilemma is precisely the work of Raymond Sebond.

19. We must note two points here (briefly) in order to state the limits of our recourse to the work of Lucien Febvre already cited: 1) This work, centered on Rabelais, studies above all the first half of the sixteenth century—and therefore encompasses a religious life before the religious wars (in France). 2) L. Febvre—like so many philosophers or historians—seems to be unaware of Montaigne as a philosopher. Which is confirmed by this affirmation that sees little but a void from Rabelais to Descartes: "And it is not chance," he says, "if it is only around 1600 that philosophy counted two important men expressing themselves in French, Du Vair and Charron. True philosophy came afterwards: René Descartes" (p. 341).

The response to the second objection to Sebond remains to be examined: "Aucuns disent que ses argumens sont foibles et ineptes à verifier ce qu'il veut, et entreprennent de les choquer aysément" (448). ["Some say that his arguments are weak and unfit to prove what he proposes, and undertake to shatter them with ease" (327).]

Montaigne does not answer this objection, as much as if to say that he would willingly accept this thesis, and we know moreover that he will be opposed to Sebond's arguments in favor of the powers of reason and human supremacy in the world.[20] But this is not the essential point. Montaigne's answer will be a radical argument which to be sure also subverts Sebond's thesis, but which aims first at the dangerous naiveté of an objector sure of the powers of his reason. Montaigne's argumentation will in fact constitute the rest of the *Essay*. The whole "Apology" will now be devoted to the criticism of reason, and this so-called "skeptical" development will hold true for the totality of knowledge—thus justifying the choice of the theme announced by the introduction.

We see what form the paradoxical coherence of Montaigne's thought takes here: it does not save the value of Sebond's work; it merely confuses its detractors, who are assimilated to Sebond himself and to all humanity in a common misery (how can we avoid using the Pascalian term here?). But this tactical victory is a strategic rout since it carries Sebond with it. What does it matter? What does it matter if we have read well, if we remember that theology cannot aim at a true knowledge—its object is incommensurate with knowledge, and no progress can bring it closer to this object; if we also remember that theology was not so much a theoretical possibility as a practical solution to the conflict between the necessity and the impossibility of a relationship with God? If we understand, finally, that theology is valuable for the practice of humility and the search for God which it initiates, and which can only prepare us to believe? And this is why the skeptical tornado which follows will sweep away real or possible knowledge much more than a theology already disproved as theoretical knowledge. What does it matter whether or not it is rich or even rigorous, if it can be of use to me—or if it can help anyone to reconcile his abstract belief with Christianity through a real faith? The important thing is for me to live in spite of my powerlessness; life implicates me completely, and not only as the subject of knowledge—as a transcendental consciousness or soul: and this is what this theology—a propaedeutic, good or bad—will be useful for: living. Montaigne affirms indeed that

20. On this point—and, in general, on the relationship between Sebond's text and the reading which Montaigne proposes of it—reference to H. Friedrich's text, chapter 3, paragraph 2, will be useful.

nous ne nous contentons point de servir Dieu d'esprit et d'ame; nous luy devons encore et rendons une reverence corporelle; nous appliquons nos membres mesmes et nos mouvements et les choses externes à l'honorer. [441]

we do not content ourselves with serving God with mind and soul, we also owe and render him a bodily reverence; we apply even our limbs and movements and external things to honor him. [321][21]

So that what is under attack is not so much the result of theology—that of Sebond or any other—as its claim to be a science, testifying as much to the powers of man as to divine nature. This is why we must understand the position of Montaigne, who both accepts and refuses theology, and who, even while ruining Sebond's argumentation, considers it just as convincing as any other: for the question no longer has to do with the content—the argumentation and results—of theology, but only with the *need* for theology, which paradoxically stems from a deficiency of faith but derives its value only from its anchoring in faith. From personal—absent—faith to revealed faith—in the form alone of dogma.

Thus we can, at least schematically, situate the problematic "religion" of Montaigne and his religious "conservatism": without this real and personal faith, by which "nous remuerions les montaignes de leur place" (442) ["we should move mountains from their place" (322)], our belief does not even attain the level of a "simple belief" (une "simple croyance") such as one grants a "story" ("histoire"); religion is but the never really attained horizon of our acts; only dogma permits us to keep its form and possibility. Let us be conservative, then, but tolerant: we have neither true faith nor the intellectual means of attaining it or ruining it.[22] Playing the role of a Catholic here is neither hypocritical nor facile; it is becoming entirely accustomed to the possibility of encountering personal faith; theology, on the condition that it remains in conformity with dogma, is an element like any other of this preparation of the self for God; all the same, it must know its limits.

21. "Learn from those who have been bound like you," Pascal will say. "Follow the way in which they began: it is by doing everything as if they believed, by taking holy water, by having masses said, etc. Naturally even that will make you believe and will make you stupid" (Brunschvicg, fragment 233).

22. The "we" here refers to an experience which obviously goes beyond Montaigne's, and which renders it exemplary: to escape this collective which includes me in a community where conservatism is a means and tolerance an obligation, I would have either to argue my real faith— and for what purpose, since our actions then "auroient quelque chose de miraculeux comme nostre croyance" (442); ["would have something miraculous about them like our belief" (332)] or prove that reason can attain everything and understand everything, in me and outside of me: which the rest of the "Apology" explicitly refutes.

IV. THE PARADOX AND THE MIRACLE

This reading of the first pages of the text of the "Apology for Raymond Sebond" has allowed us to bring out a paradoxical structure, that is, a form accounting for a signification which cannot be reduced to either one of the opposing terms constituting it. We have shown that this structure also governs the conclusion of the essay—thus giving shape to a homogeneous and coherent text through the additions of the manuscript. We shall not return to the quotation from Seneca or to the commentary which Montaigne makes on it, "utile desir, mais pareillement absurde" ("useful desire, but equally absurd") which now allow us to encompass in a concise form, the very movement of the text. [Let it suffice to point out that Montaigne's so-called disorderly writing demonstrates here a masterful—and durable—organization of free reflection: there is nothing more satisfying, on the level of esthetics as well as on the level of meaning, than this conclusion which offers, in the form of a maxim, the model of the whole preceding argumentation and which strengthens the expression both of the contradictions justifying the opening's reservations—to "love," not "worship" knowledge—and of the particular paradox at the very heart of the text: necessary and impossible theology. Neither our personal faith nor the powers of reason enable us to go beyond humanity:

> Car (a) de faire la poignée plus grande que le poing, la brassée plus grande que le bras, et d'esperer enjamber plus que de l'estanduë de nos jambes, cela est impossible et monstrueux. Ny que l'homme se monte au dessus de soy et de l'humanité. [604]

> For (a) to make the handful bigger than the hand, the armful bigger than the arm, and to hope to straddle more than the reach of our legs, is impossible and unnatural. Nor can man raise himself above himself and humanity. [457]

But we can seek to rejoin the impossible, the living God who must ground revealed texts, so that the paradox moves towards a transcendence: I cannot raise myself above the human condition, either by my faith or by my reason. And yet the whole meaning of the text refers back to this desire which is unrealizable except through the miraculous intervention of God: man

> s'eslevera si Dieu lui preste extraordinairement la main; il s'eslevera, abandonnant et renonçant à ses propres moyens, et se laissant hausser et soubslever par les moyens purement celestes. [604]

> will rise, if God by exception lends him a hand; he will rise by abandoning and renouncing his own means, and letting himself be raised and uplifted by purely celestial means. [457]

Man is not himself the subject of the transcendence, but is acted upon by God. The paradox is due to the personal and collective displacement between the particular and the historical which traverses this "form" of the human condition from one end to the other, causing man to hope beyond his human possibilities; and therein, for Montaigne, lie man's fragile humanity and his emergence—purely potential—out of nature and animality.

Dogma renders such a transcendence, if not comprehensible, at least expressible. The illusion lies in believing that it is humanly or even intellectually realizable. Against Seneca—but also against all theology which believes it is speaking of God—and against all rationalism which would mask our immersion in nature and its multiple orders, Montaigne, to conclude, appeals therefore "à nostre foy chrétienne" ("to our Christian faith") for this true "métamorphose" ("metamorphosis") which he describes as "divine" and "miraculeuse" ("divine" and "miraculous") in order to show fully that we are perhaps its beneficiaries, but under no circumstances its origin or author.

Only a miracle, then, permits us to get out of the paradox. Only dogma affirms—and founds—the irruption of the miracle in the order of nature. So that the very situation of paradox is paradoxical, which is to say, human: necessary and impossible for man and for him alone, theology becomes possible and useless if he surpasses himself, if God frees him from his contradictions and his limits,[23] which "la foy chrestienne" ("Christian faith") allows us to hope (and maybe even forces us to hope).[24]

Translated by Dianne Sears

23. We know the position Montaigne takes on the question of miracles (cf. especially *Essays* III:2, "Of repentance") and the works of Pascal: "Montaigne against miracles. Montaigne for miracles" (Brunschvicg, fragment 814). We should not be surprised by this convergence, but invest it with all its meaning. H. Friedrich (op. cit., p. 151) points out this convergence but makes it problematic by including Montaigne's position under the sole rubric of skepticism: "Skeptical, Montaigne knocks down the wall of illusory certitudes from both sides and opens the vast horizon of possibility." In fact, Pascal would not have approved of this any more than Montaigne even if he did find Montaigne "skeptical" (and in fact, he is not skeptical, but paradoxical, both for and against)—the only legitimate attitude according to Pascal, who writes (Brunschvicg, fragment 813): "How I hate those who pretend to doubt miracles! Montaigne talks about it in the right way, in both places" (probably I:27 and III:2). One can obviously add to these references the conclusion of "The Apology for Reymond Sebond": "On voit, en l'un [endroit] combien il est prudent; et néanmoins, il croit en l'autre [endroit], et se moque des incrédules" (Pascal, *Les Pensées*, ed. Brunschvicg, fragment 813) ["We see how careful he is in one place, and yet in the other he believes and makes fun of unbelievers."]

24. H. Friedrich, in the chapter which he devotes to the study of the "Apology" ("Man humiliated") is perfectly attentive to the very nuances and contradictions of Montaigne's text; but he greatly attenuates their paradoxical character. For Friedrich both questions the seriousness of the object of the text—namely the meaning and scope of the theological enterprise: "Dealing with Christianity . . . he uses it in order to reject it later" (p. 108) and refuses

to give full weight to the tension revealed by the conflict between the privilege of human reason and the derision of its acquirements. Rather close to Pouilloux on this point, he affirms (p. 138) that Montaigne gives up the idea of progress in the search for truth, contenting himself with inducing contradictions of reason from the contradictory nature of reason. This is to forget—at least—this text of Montaigne in which first appear the idea that obscurity and ignorance are not uniform and identical for everyone, always, and secondly, the idea of possible progress, if not in knowledge, at least in the formulation of problems: "ce qui estoit incogneu à un siecle, le siecle suyvant l'a esclaircy . . ." etc. (560) ["what was unknown to one century the following century has made clear . . .", etc. (421).]

JOSHUA SCODEL

The Affirmation of Paradox: A Reading of Montaigne's "De la Phisionomie" (III:12)

C'est une absolue perfection, et comme divine, de sçavoyr jouyr loaillement de son estre. Nous cherchons d'autres conditions, pour n'entendre l'usage des nostres, et sortons hors de nous, pour ne sçavoir quel il y fait [III:XII, 1115]

It is an absolute perfection and virtually divine to know how to enjoy our being rightfully. We seek other conditions because we do not understand the use of our own, and go outside of ourselves because we do not know what it is like inside [857].[1]

This affirmation of human life rightly occurs near the conclusion of Montaigne's *Essays*, for it represents the true *perfectio* of both Montaigne's life and his consubstantial book. This "savoyr jouyr" implies a full acceptance of man's contradictions, since for Montaigne man is above all "la mixtion humaine" (II:XX, 674). In "De la Physiognomie" Montaigne's acceptance of the paradoxes inherent in the human condition reveals itself through his playful building and overturning of categories. Inner and outer, past and present, knowledge and ignorance, medicine and poison, pleasure and pain, life and death, nature and art, nature and reason—all these polarities collapse and supposed opposites fuse. *Concordia discors* reigns throughout.[2] The essay plays most centrally—and elusively—with the

1. Pierre Villey, ed. *Les Essais de Montaigne* (Paris: Presses Universitaires de France, 1924), p. 1115; Donald M. Frame, tr. *The Complete Essays of Montaigne* (Stanford: Stanford University Press, 1948), p. 857. All citations of Montaigne's essays are from these two editions. If the citation is not from the essay "De la Physionomie," I have given the essay number as well as the page. I have used Villey's appendix on sources (pp. 1223–33) without footnote. All citations from classical sources, unless otherwise stated, are from the Loeb Classical Library series. I would here like to thank M. Gerard Defaux, under whose patient and inspiring guidance I wrote the initial version of this essay.

2. On paradox and *discordia concors* in Montaigne, see Rosalie L. Colie, *Pardoxical Epidemica* (Princeton: Princeton University Press, 1966), pp. 374–95 and Alfred Glauser, *Montaigne Paradoxal* (Paris: A. G. Nizet, 1972). M. Baraz well conveys Montaigne's sense of a cosmic unity of opposites in "Sur la Structure d'un Essai de Montaigne (III:12 *De l'Experience*)," *BHR*, vol. 23, (1961), pp. 265-81 and "Les Images dans les *Essais* de Montaigne," *BHR*, vol. 27, no. 2 (May, 1965), pp. 361–95.

209

opposition of self and other as embodied in the figures of Montaigne and Socrates. Montaigne's Socrates is neither the "traditional" Socrates of the numerous ancient sources[3] nor a self-portrait of Montaigne, but a kind of *tertium quid* one critic has described as "the impact of the personality of Socrates on Montaigne's personality."[4] Montaigne is indeed very conscious of constructing his Socrates, a Socrates both self and other, but Montaigne is equally conscious of constructing himself in terms of this Socrates, so that Montaigne himself becomes a mixture of self and other. In the course of the essay Socrates and Montaigne are implicitly compared, explicitly contrasted, and paradoxically made to exchange roles. The essay may be read as a dialogue between two figures whose final unity-within-difference mirrors the *condordia discors* of the whole essay.

The major portion of the essay has a chiasmic structure: 1) Praise of Socratic ignorance and attack on the "curiosité" of the philosophers and their "arts et sciences" (1037–40); 2) Praise of the peasants' ignorance (pp. 1040–41); 3) Description of Montaigne's character and conduct during the civil war and plague: Montaigne as a Socratic figure; 4) Praise of the peasants' ignorance (1048–49); 5) attack on the "curiosité" of the philosophers and praise of Socratic ignorance (1049–54).[5] Montaigne thus places himself at the center of a chiasmic structure which begins and ends with a praise of Socrates. This structure suggests the balancing of self and other that occurs throughout the essay: if the praise of Socrates frames the major portion of the essay, it is nevertheless Montaigne himself who stands as a modern Socrates at the center of this *laus inscientiae*.

The opening section of the essay contrasts Socratic self-reliance and self-examination with the (other) philosophers' self-alienating reliance on philosophical dogma. Socrates leads men to themselves: "Il a faict grand

3. For the ancient sources on Socrates, see W. K. C. Guthrie, *Socrates* (Cambridge: Cambridge University Press, 1971) and Herbert Spiegelberg and Bayard Quincy Morgan, ed. *The Socratic Enigma: A Collection of Testimonies Through Twenty-Four Centuries* (Bobbs-Merrill Company, 1964). There is no canonical ancient portrayal of Socrates, of course, and thus to speak of the "traditional" Socrates is misleading insofar as the ancient philosopher and his teaching have remained a mystery. For modern attempts to reconstruct true Socratic teaching, see Guthrie, op. cit., Laslo Versenyi, *Socratic Humanism* (New Haven: Yale University Press, 1972) and Gregory Vlastos, ed. *The Philosophy of Socrates* (Garden City, New York: Anchor Books, 1971).

4. Friedrich Kellerman, "Montaigne's Socrates," *Romanic Review*, vol. 45, no. 2 (April 1954), p. 171. For general treatments of the relationship between Montaigne and Socrates, see, in addition to Kellerman's article, Hugo Friedrich, *Montaigne* tr. Robert Rovini (Paris: Gallimard, 1968), pp. 63–67 and Margaret M. McGowan, *Montaigne's Deceits* (Philadelphia: Temple University Press, 1978), pp. 150–63 (Chapter 8: "Montaigne and Socrates").

5. I have adopted with minor modification the structure proposed in Baraz, "Sur la Structure. . . ," op. cit., p. 268.

faveur à l'humaine nature de montrer combien elle peut d'elle mesme"
(1038). ["He did a great favour to human nature by showing how much it can
do by itself" (794).] The philosophers and their books, on the other hand,
lead men to lose themselves in the vain quest of superfluous knowledge:
"on nous dresse à l'emprunt et à la queste: on nous duict à nous servir plus
de l'autruy que du nostre" (1038). ["we are trained to borrow and beg; we are
taught to use the resources of others more than our own" (794).]

Montaigne's contrast between Socratic ignorance and philosophical
dogma exploits commonplaces of Erasmian humanism. Socrates is associated with humility, the philosophers with overweening pride.[6] Erasmus'
discussion of the adage "Nosce teipsum" reveals the close connection
between Socratic ignorance and humility:

> Know Thyself. In this there lies a recommendation to be modest and
> moderate . . . For every disease of life arises from the fact that each man
> flatters himself . . .
> Socrates thus interpreted the fact that he alone was judged wise by the
> oracle of Apollo when Greece had so many "wise men," that he was
> superior to the others who claimed that they knew something which they
> did not know in that he claimed that he knew nothing and that this alone
> he knew.[7]

To know oneself is humbly to know that one knows nothing; self-flattery,
by making men believe that they are better than they are, causes every
disease of life. Montaigne speaks of philosophical dogma as self-flattery
("cette complaisance voluptueuse qui nous chatouille par l'opinion de
science" (1039) ["that voluptuous complacency which tickles us with the
notion of being learned" (794)], and as a disease "excez fievreux" (1039)
["feverish excesses" (794)] to be contrasted with the "allegre et nette santé"
(1038) ["blithe and clear health" (793)] of the humble Socrates. Montaigne
similarly follows the Christian humanists in associating Socratic humility
with an earth-bound state to be contrasted with the philosophers' attempts
to ascend "au delà."[8] Erasmus cites with approval the Socratic dictum
"What is above us, need not concern us" and relates it to Paul's "Knowledge

6. On Socrates and the Christian humanists, see Gérard Defaux, "Au Coeur du
Pantagruel: Les Deux Chapitres IX de l'Edition Nourry," Kentucky Romance Quarterly, vol. 21,
no. 1 (1974), pp. 78–79.

7. Erasmus von Rotterdam, Augewählte Shriften (Darmstadt: Wissenschaftlich Buchge-
sellschaft, 1972), vol. 7, p. 416 (translation mine).

8. On knowledge, pride, and vertical imagery of high and low, see Carlo Ginzburg, "High
and Low: The Theme of Forbidden Knowledge in the Sixteenth and Seventeenth Centuries,"
Past and Present, vol. 73 (November, 1976), pp. 28–41.

puffeth up, but charity edifieth."[9] Montaigne notes Socrates's refusal to investigate "What is above us": "C'est luy qui ramena du ciel, où elle perdoit son temps, la sagesse humaine" (1038). ["It is he who brought human wisdom down from heaven, where she was wasting her time" (793).] In his *Convivium Religiosum*, Erasmus contrasts Socratic humility with Cato's Stoic pride in the face of death,[10] and Montaigne makes a similar contrast:

> aux braves exploits de sa vie, et en sa mort, on le [sc. Caton] sent toujours monté sur ses grands chevaux. Cettuy-cy [sc. Socrates] ralle à terre, et d'un pas mol et ordinaire traicte le plus utile discours . . . [1037–38]

> in the brave exploits of his [sc. Cato's] life and in his death we see very clearly that he is always mounted on his high horse. The other [sc. Socrates] always walks close to the ground, and at a gentle and ordinary pace treats the most useful subjects . . . [793]

Montaigne's portrait of Socrates is highly indebted to the Socrates-as-Silenus presented in Plato's *Symposium* and taken up most noticeably in the Renaissance by Erasmus and his disciple Rabelais.[11] Montaigne notes that he and his contemporaries have a "veuë grossiere" (1037) ["a sight so gross" (793)] that misses the hidden beauty of Socratic discourse, which he describes as follows:

> il faut la veuë nette et bien purgée pour descouvrir cette secrette lumiere . . . Socrates faict mouvoir son ame d'un mouvement naturel et commun. Ainsi dict un paysan, ainsi dict une femme. (c) Il n'a jamais en la bouche que cochers, menuisiers, savetiers et maçons. (b) Ce sont inductions et similitudes tirées des plus vulgaires et cogneues actions des hommes; chacun l'entend. Soubs une si vile forme nous n'eussions jamais choisi la

9. From a letter to John Carondelet, cited in Guido Calogero, *Erasmo, Socrate e il Nuovo Testamento* (Rome: Accademia Nazionale dei Lincei, 1972), p. 7. On Erasmus' use of Socrates, see also Lynda Gregory Christian, "The Figure of Socrates in Erasmus's Work," *Sixteenth Century Journal*, vol. 3, no. 2 (October 1972), pp. 1–10.

10. Erasmus of Rotterdam, *Colloquia* (Batavia: Hackiana, 1664), pp. 148–49.

11. On the Silenus figure in Plato, see Elizabeth Belfiore, "Elenchus, Epode and Magic: Socrates as Silenus," *Phoenix*, vol. 34, no. 2 (1980), pp. 128–37. For the Silenus in Erasmus, see, amongst many, Peter G. Bietenholz, *History and Biography in the Work of Erasmus of Rotterdam* (Geneva: Libraire Droz, 1966), pp. 24–25 and *passim.*; Marjorie O'Rourke Boyle, *Erasmus on Language and Method in Theology* (Toronto: University of Toronto Press, 1977), p. 147; Christian, op. cit., pp. 3–10; Arthur Rabil, Jr. *Erasmus and the New Testament: The Mind of a Christian Humanist* (San Antonio: Trinity University Press, 1972), pp. 80–83. For Rabelais's use of the Silenus figure, see M. A. Screech's note in François Rabelais. *Gargantua* intro. and comm. M. A. Screech (Geneva: Librairie Droz, 1970), pp. 10–11. For bibliography and discussion of the Silenus motif, I am indebted to Daniel Kinney.

noblesse et splendeur de ses conceptions admirables, nous . . . qui n'aper-
cevons la richesse qu'en montre et en pompe [1037]

we need a clear and well-purged sight to discover their secret light . . .
Socrates makes his soul move with a natural and common motion. So says
a peasant, so says a woman. (c) His mouth is full of nothing but carters,
joiners, cobblers, and masons. (b) His are inductions and similitudes drawn
from the commonest and best known actions of men; everyone understands him. Under so mean a form we should never have picked out the
nobility and splendour of his admirable ideas, we . . . who perceive
richness only in pomp and show. [793]

In the *Symposium*, Alcibiades compares Socrates's appearance and his
discourse to the statuettes of Silenus, which have an ugly and ridiculous
exterior but contain beautiful images of the gods within. Alcibiades's praise
of Socrates's words is clearly the basis for Montaigne's similar praise:

his discourses are like Sileni that are opened. For if anyone listens to his
discourses, they seem at first sight to be excessively absurd. For his nouns
and verbs present themselves with the external appearance, indeed, of
some abusive satyr. For he always speaks of asses, smiths, shoemakers, and
tanners . . . so that every inexperienced and ignorant person might laugh at
his words. But if one should look inside his discourses, then first indeed
one would find that they alone of all others have a profound sense . . .[12]

Alcibiades suggests that one needs to "look inside" Socrates's words in
order to discover their hidden profundity, but he does not explain exactly
how this movement from outer to inner is to be made. He remarks that he
has seen the "real" Socrates only once, but he speaks of being possessed by a
philosophical *furor*, asserting that the other symposiasts have had a similar
experience: "we have all alike been corrupted by a single *furor* and
Dionysian infatuation for philosophy . . ."[13] It would seem that an understanding of Socrates, based on the movement from outer to inner, depends
upon a philosophical *furor* that distinguishes the philosophical few from
the vulgar many. In his *Seleni Alicibiadis* Erasmus applies the Silenus
analogy not only to Socrates himself but to a number of virtuous figures—
including Christ—as well as to the Sacraments and the Bible. He too
stresses the need to move from outer to inner for an understanding of
Socrates: "But once you have opened out this Silenus, absurd as it is, you

12. *Divini Platonis opera* (Lyon: A. Vincetium, 1567), p. 299 (translation mine). I have
translated from the Latin of Ficino's Plato throughout the essay on the basis of Villey's claim
that Montaigne himself used the Ficinian translation (Pierre Villey, *Les Sources et l'Evolution
des Essais de Montaigne* (Paris: Librairie Hachette, 1933), vol. 1, pp. 212–14).
13. Ibid.

find a god rather than a man, a great, lofty, and truly philosophic soul . . ."[14] But Erasmus Christianizes this movement from outer to inner by identifying it with the allegorical hermeneutic of the Church Fathers.[15] One reaches the inner core of the Silenus by moving from letter to spirit, body to soul; a passage from the *Enchiridion*, in which Erasmus suggests that tests be treated as Sileni, makes this spiritualizing process clear:

> you should observe in all your reading those things consisting of both a surface meaning and a hidden one—comparable to body and spirit—so that, indifferent to the merely literal sense, you may examine most keenly the hidden. Of this sort are the works of all the poets and the Platonists in philosophy. But especially do the Holy Scriptures, like the Silenus of Alcibiades, conceal their real divinity beneath a surface that is crude and almost laughable.[16]

Rabelais's comparison of his *Gargantua* to the Silenic Socrates and his assertion that his text must be read allegorically to reveal its inner profundity clearly derives from the Erasmian treatment of the Silenus.[17] But Montaigne's treatment of the Silenic Socrates differs vitally from the treatments of Plato, Erasmus, and Rabelais in its total neglect of the *spiritualizing* movement from outer to inner. If Alcibiades has his *furor*, Erasmus and Rabelais their Christian hermeneutic of faith, what does Montaigne have to lead him to understanding?

Montaigne in fact rejects the movement from body to soul normally associated with the Silenus figure. He sees the bodily, exterior aspect of Socrates and Socratic discourse *not* as something to be transcended but as something to be *viewed* in order that one may learn the unity of outer and inner, body and soul, which is the human condition. Erasmus speaks of the Silenus showing its inner treasure to "the purified eyes of the soul,"[18] and Montaigne strikes a superficially similar note when he writes that only a "veuë nette et bien purgée" (1037) ["a clear and well-purged sight" (793)] can see Socrates's inner worth. But for Montaigne this "sight" is highly physical, for he expounds a radical empiricism in his faith that the eye of man—once purged of the philosopher's vain dogmas—can in fact *see* the good and the bad. He *visualizes*—or asks his reader to visualize—concrete, physical *exempla* of the good, natural life and of the false, philosophical life:

14. Margaret Mann-Phillips, *Erasmus on his Times: A Shortened Version of the "Adages" of Erasmus* (Cambridge: Cambridge Univ. Press, 1967), p. 79.

15. For a good general treatment of Erasmus' Christian hermeneutic, see Rabil, op. cit.

16. Desiderius Erasmus, *The Enchiridion of Erasmus*, tr. Raymond Himelick (Bloomington: Indiana University Press, 1963), p. 105.

17. Rabelais, loc. cit.

18. Phillips, *Erasmus*, op. cit., p. 79.

Car, en Caton, *on void bien à clair* que c'est une alleure tendue bien loing
au dessus des communes . . . *Voyez* le plaider [Socrates] devant ses juges,
voyez par quelles raisons il esveille son courage aux hazards de la guerre . . .
A voir les efforts que Seneque se donne pour se preparer contre la mort, à le
voir suer d'ahan pour se roidir et pour s'asseurer . . . j'eusse esbranle sa
reputation . . . A quoi faire nous allons nous gendarmant par ces efforts de
la science? *Regardons* à terre les pauvres tens que *nous y voyons* espandus
. . . de ceux là tire nature tous les jours des effects de constance et de
patience . . . [1037–40]

For in Cato *we see very clearly* that his is a pace strained far above the
ordinary . . . *See* him plead [Socrates] before his judges, *see* by what
reasonings he rouses his courage in the hazards of war . . . *To see* the trouble
to which Seneca puts himself to be prepared for death, *to see* him sweat
from the exertion of steeling and reassuring himself . . . would have shaken
his reputation with me . . . To what end do we keep forcing our nature with
these efforts of learning? Let us *look* on the earth at the poor people *we see*
scattered there . . . From them Nature every day draws deeds of constancy
and endurance . . . [793–95] [All italics mine].

Montaigne suggests that true knowledge is corporeal. He advises against
excessive curiosity for knowledge with an appeal to the corporeal eye and
its powers of judgment: "C'est un bien, *à le regarder d' yeux fermes*, qui
a . . . beaucoup de vanité et foiblesse . . ." (1039) [*"Looked at steadily*, it is
like men's other goods; it has in it much . . . vanity and weakness . . ." (794,
italics mine).] He reads books not for any allegorical, spiritual meaning but
for a physical substantiality that books all too often lack: "Les autheurs . . .
voiez autour d'un bon argument combien ils en sement d'autres legers et,
qui y regarde de pres, incorporels" (1039–40;) ["Authors . . . around one
good argument *see* how many others they strew, trivial ones, and *if you look
closely at them, bodiless*" (795, italics mine).] To look closely at the books
of the philosophers leads to a disappointing realization of their bodiless-
ness; to look closely at the Silenic Socrates, on the other hand leads to an
understanding of corporeal man's "spiritual"—because "virtually divine"
(857)—greatness.

Montaigne ends this opening *laus inscientiae* praising the peasants,
who know "ny exemple, ny precepte" (1040) ["neither example nor precept"
(795)] but rely on themselves and on nature in the face of calamity and
death. But Montaigne and his educated readers are irremediably cut off from
this idealized portrait of pure self-reliance and natural simplicity. For them,
self-reliance can be reached only through the mediation of Socratic
example—"le plus digne homme d'estre cogneu et d'estre presenté au

monde pour *exemple"* (1038) ["the man most worthy to be known and to be presented to the world as *an example"* (793, italics mine)]—and simplicity only through the mediation of Socratic precepts—*"preceptes* qui reelement et plus jointement servent à la vie" (1037) [*"precepts* that serve life really and more closely" (793, italics mine).] Their ignorance is necessarily a highly paradoxical "learned ignorance," for the Socratic attack on book learning is indissolubly linked to the study of books. Montaigne begins the essay with the problem of Socrates and books:

> Quasi toutes les opinions que nous avons sont prinses par authorité et à credit. Il n'y a point de mal: nous ne sçaurions pirement choisir que par nous, en un siecle si foible. Cette image des discours de Socrates que ses amys nous ont laissée, nous ne l'approuvons que pour la reverence de l'approbation publique; ce n'est pas par nostre cognoissance . . . [1037]

> Almost all the opinions we have are taken on authority and on credit. There is no harm in this: we could not make a worse choice than our own in so feeble an age. The version of the sayings of Socrates that his friends have left us we approve only out of respect for the universal approval these sayings enjoy, not by our own knowledge. [782]

Socrates is mediated by the writings of his friends and disciples.[19] The men of Montaigne's times do not know true Socratic teaching but only have "opinions . . . on authority and on credit" based on the written "version of the sayings of Socrates." But to accept the written Socratic teachings "on authority and on credit" is to run the risk of self-loss inherent in the "curiosity for knowledge" and the study of books. In his essay on education Montaigne writes of book learning: "Nostre ame ne branle *qu'à credit,* liée et contrainte à l'appetit des fantasies d'autruy, serve et captivée soubs *l'authorité* de leur leçon" (I:26, 151) ["Our mind moves only *on faith,* being bound and constrained to the whims of others' fancies, a slave and a captive under *the authority* of their lesson" (111, italics mine).] The pursuit of Socratic self-sufficiency is from the first paradoxically mingled with dependence upon the otherness of texts and thus with the ever present danger of self-loss.

Montaigne suggests that one should trust the texts portraying Socrates because of their remarkable reliability:

> nous ayons plus certaine cognoissance [de Socrates]. Il a esté esclairé par les plus clair voyans hommes qui furent oncques: les tesmoins que nous avons de luy sont admirables en fidelité et en suffisance [1038]

19. Terence Cave, *The Cornucopian Text* (Oxford: Clarendon Press, 1979), p. 305. Cave's "deconstructive" approach to the problem of textuality in Montaigne's essay (pp. 302–12) in many places parallels my own.

we have most certain knowledge [of Socrates]. We have light on him from the most clear-sighted men who have ever lived; the witnesses we have of him are wonderful in fidelity and competence." [793]

Montaigne's irony seems to be at work here. At the beginning of the essay Montaigne denies that men of his time have "knowledge" (792) of Socrates, but here he contradicts his earlier statement and suggests that the disciples of Socrates left "most certain knowledge" (793) concerning the great Athenian. Montaigne implicitly contrasts his own "feeble age" (793), filled with men of "gross" vision (793), with the ancient times of "the most clear-sighted men" (793), and suggests that somehow the men of his times can reach the "true" Socratic teaching by relying on ancient "witnesses" (793). But to rely on the ancients' authority is precisely *not* to discover one's own powers and is thus to perpetuate one's weakness vis-à-vis the powerful past of Socratic self-reliance. Montaigne in fact tries to obliterate the distinction between a powerful past and an enfeebled present. His own portait of Socrates constantly moves back and forth in time in order to suggest that Socrates is not only the past figure of the ancient texts but also the present creation of Montaigne's own text:

> Socrates faict . . . Cettuy-cy ne se propose point . . . sa fin fut . . . Il fut . . . et se monta . . . il ne monta rien, mais ravala . . . et ramena . . . Cettuy-cy ralle . . . et . . . traicte . . . et se conduict . . . Il . . . represente . . . il dressa . . . C'est luy qui ramena . . . Voyez . . . voyez . . . il esveille . . . Il a faict . . . [1037–38]

> Socrates makes . . . this man did not propose to himself . . . his aim was . . . he raised nothing, but rather brought . . . down and back . . . The other walks . . . and . . . treats . . . and behaves . . . He shows . . . he constructed . . . It is he who brought . . . back down . . . See . . . see . . . he rouses . . . He did [793–94]

This mingling of past and present leads naturally to the mingling of Socrates and Montaigne. Montaigne makes his own text the true "voice" of Socrates:

> Il ne nous faut guiere de doctrine pour vivre à nostre aise. Et Socrates nous aprend qu'elle est en nous, et la manière de l'y trouver et de s'en ayder . . . Recueiellez vous; vous trouverez en vous les arguments de la nature contre la mort . . . [1039]

> We need hardly any learning to live at ease. And Socrates teaches us that it is in us, and the way to find it and help ourselves with it . . . Collect yourself: you will find in yourself Nature's arguments against death . . ." [794]

The final direct address to the reader comes from Montaigne acting as the modern Socratic spokesman. Montaigne thus avoids undue reliance on others by appropriating the Socratic message and making it his own, by not simply *reading about* Socrates but instead *writing as* Socrates. Montaigne finds himself by recreating Socrates.

There is a further irony in Montaigne's discussion of the reliability of the "witnesses" (793) concerning Socrates. Although Montaigne seems to imply that his portrait of Socrates is based on the eyewitness accounts of Socrates's disciples, he is in fact highly aware that his portrait of Socrates is mediated by the very philosophical tradition that he attacks. But he uses the texts of the philosophers to portray the philosophers' opponent to Socrates. Thus he borrows from *Tusculan Disputations* V:4, 10 the description of Socrates bringing wisdom down from heaven (793) while singling out this Ciceronian dialogue as an example of philosophy's inutility in the face of death "Fussé je mort moins allegrement avant qu'avoir veu les Tusculanes? J'estime que non" (1039) ["Should I have died less cheerfully before having read the *Tusculans?* I think not" (794).] Just before declaring the superiority of Socrates to the Stoic Cato, Montaigne takes precepts Lucan uses to describe Cato and applies them to Socrates: *"servare modum, finemque tenere, naturamque sequi"* (1037) Lucan's *Pharsalia* II:381) ["To keep the mean, to hold our aim in view,/And follow nature" 793).] Thus Montaigne declares that Socrates—and not the histrionic Stoic Cato—is the true follower of nature. Montaigne's use of texts shows a mastery that substantiates his claim, "Les livres m'ont servi non tant d'instruction que d'exercitation" (1039) ["Books have served me not so much for instruction as for exercise" (795).] He shows an erudite independence from the philosopher's books, a learning dedicated to Socratic ignorance.

There is yet another tradition that Montaigne manipulates in making his portrait of Socrates: the humanist tradition of Christ the teacher. In "De la Phisionomie" Montaigne differs from such Christian sceptics as Erasmus and Cornelius Agrippa in his almost total neglect of Christ and Christian faith as the ultimate solution to the problem of learning and ignorance. For Erasmus and Agrippa, Socrates is but a shadow or type of the true redeeming teacher Christ; Socrates leads men to humility, but it is Christ who restores men to themselves.[20] Montaigne's claims for Socratic teaching are strikingly similar to the Erasmian description of the *philosophia Christi*:

20. In the *Paraclesis*, Erasmus calls on Christians to return to Christ instead of studying only imperfect classical philosophers such as Socrates, Diogenes and Epictetus (see Desiderius Erasmus, *Christian Humanism and the Reformation* ed. John C. Olin (New York: Fordham University Press, 1975), pp. 100–02. Socrates is the *first* Silenus of the adage *Sileni Alcibiadis*, but Christ is the "most extraordinary." For Agrippa's call to abandon worldly knowledge and return to Christ, see Cornelius Agrippa, *The Vanity of Arts and Sciences* (London, 1684), Chapter C ("Of the Word of God"), pp. 348–56.

il n'y a rien d'emprunté de l'art et des sciences; les plus simples y recognoissent leurs moyens et leurs force; il n'est possible d'aller plus arriere et plus bas. Il a faict grand faveur à l'humaine nature de montrer combien elle peut d'elle mesme [1038]

There is nothing borrowed from art and the sciences; even the simplest can recognize in him their means and their strength; it is impossible to go back further and lower. He did a great favour to human nature by showing how much it can do by itself. [794]

here there is no requirement that you approach equipped with so many troublesome sciences. The journey is simple, and it is ready for anyone . . . This doctrine in an equal degree accommodates itself to all, lowers itself to the little ones . . .[21]

To follow nature in simplicity and without the burden of great learning is for the Christian humanist based on the *philosophia Christi*, for Montaigne on the *philosophia Socratis*. For both thinkers the true way represents a simple *oneness* opposed to the *diversity* of learned and contentious opinions. The contrast between "so many troublesome sciences" and the single and simple way of Christ, between the diversity of sects and the concord of the divine *Logos*, indeed runs throughout Erasmian thought.[22] In "De la Phisionomie" the contrast between what Montaigne calls the "diversité et nouvelleté" (1049) ["diversity and novelty" (803)] of man's overcurious reason and the simple Socratic way—"un et pareil" (1037) ["one and the same" (793)]—is no less central. Montaigne's use of the unifying Socrates in place of the unifying *Logos* is easily explained both by his essentially pagan moral vision and by his religious conservativism in the face of Protestantism and religious civil war.[23] The Erasmian hope that a return to the *Logos* would bring "pax et unanimitas" to Christendom had by Montaigne's time proved disastrously misguided, and Montaigne would instead call his contemporaries back to a purely human ignorance that knows itself as such and does not attempt to escape "outside of ourselves" (857).

Imagery of disease helps to unify the chiastic structure of the major portion of the essay.[24] The opening attack on learning's "feverish excesses" (794) is balanced by the closing attack on the "fiévre" (1050) ["fever" (803)]

21. Desiderius Erasmus, "The *Paraclesis*," in Olin, op. cit., p. 96.
22. Boyle, op. cit., pp. 94–95.
23. On Montaigne's combination of a *morale païenne* and an allegiance to the Catholic church, see Frieda S. Brown, *Religious and Political Conservatism in the Essais of Montaigne* (Geneva: Libraire Droz, 1963), especially pp. 46–47.
24. See also Cave, op. cit., p. 306, for the equally pervasive motif of "borrowing."

of learning. The central narrative section concerns the "maladie/s/populaire/s/" (1041) ["epidemic/s/" (796)] of civil war and what seems but a logical accompaniment, the plague. And if Socrates is the man of "blithe and clear health" (793) as opposed to the feverish philosophers, Montaigne portrays himself as a healthy Socratic figure in the face of civil war and plague. He maintains his health, both physical "ma santé tint bon ce temps là outre son ordinaire . . ." (1047) ["my health for that time was unusually good" (801)] and moral. Like Socrates, who follows the precept "to keep the mean" (793), Montaigne retains his moderation against the disease of fanatical religious war: "J'encorus les inconveniens que la moderation aporte en telles maladies" (1044) ["I incurred the disadvantages that moderation brings in such maladies" (798).] Like Socrates, who displays great patience in the face of misfortune ". . . voyez . . . quels arguments fortifient sa patience contre la calomnie, la tyrannie, la mort . . ." (1038) [". . . see . . . what arguments fortify his patience against calumny, tyranny, death . . . (794)] in the civil war Montaigne learns "patience . . . contre la fortune" (1047) ["endurance . . . against Fortune" (801)] and during the plague has his "preservatifs, qui sont resolution et souffrance" (1048) ["preservatives, which are resolution and patience" (802).]

Yet the opposition between health and disease is complicated by yet another pervasive image, that of the poisonous medicine. In the attack on the philosophers Montaigne notes that dangerous kinds of knowledge can poison the self while seeming to cure it: "sous tiltre de nous guerir, nous empoisonnent" (1039). ["under color of curing us, poison us" 794).] The civil war is a similar poisonous medicine: "Nostre medicine porte infection . . ." (1041) ["Our medicine carries infection" (796)] "Mais est-il quelque mal en une police qui vaille estre combatu par une drogue si mortelle [la sedition]?" (1043) ["But is there any disease in a government so bad that it is worth combatting with so deadly a drug [rebellion]?" (797).] But Montaigne displays his Socratic resolution by converting the poisonous medicine of civil war into a healing poison:

> Et me résolus que c'estoyent utiles inconveniens. D'autant premierement qu'il faut avertir à coups de foyt les mauvais disciples, quand la raison n'y peut assez . . . Je me presche il y a si long temps de me tenir à moy, et separer des choses estrangeres; toutesfois je tourne encores tousjours les yeux à costé: l'inclination, un mot favorable d'un grand, un bon visage me tente . . . Or à un esprit si indocile il faut des bastonnades [1045–46]

> And I resolved that these were useful troubles. First, because bad students must be instructed with the rod when reason cannot do the job . . . I have

long been preaching to myself to stick to myself and break away from outside things; nevertheless I still keep turning my eyes to one side. Inclination, a favorable word from a great man, a pleasant countenance, tempt me. . . . Now a spirit so indocile needs some beating . . . [799–800]

It is no accident that Mongaigne's relationship to civil strife is that of a pupil to his necessarily cruel teacher, for Montaigne thus makes the civil war a modern substitute for Socrates's presence as teacher. In his praise of Socrates, Alcibiades claims that Socratic "poison" alone leads him back to himself:

[Socrates] forces me to confess that although I am deficient in many respects, I neglect myself, and instead engage in the affairs of Athens. . . . For I am aware that I cannot defend myself from doing what he orders me to do; but when I leave him I am overcome by political ambition . . . In addition I am affected like one whom a viper bites . . . I am wounded by the bite of philosophy, stronger than any other. . . . stricken with the love of philosophical discourse, which bites sharper than a viper . . .[25]

In his commentary on The Symposium, Ficino calls Socrates a "veneficus" [poisoner],[26] but Socrates is a "poisoner" who heals. Montaigne finds a similarly healing poison in the "venin" (1041) ["venom" (796)] of civil war, for just as Socrates forces Alcibiades to stop losing himself in public affairs and to return to self-examination, so the civil war forces Montaigne to separate himself from "outside things" (800) and to return to himself. Montaigne now claims, in fact, that the discord of civil war leads his contemporaries and himself to develop their own self-sufficient powers:

D'autant faut-il tenir son courage fourny de provisions plus fortes et vigoureuses. Sçachons gré au sort de nous avoir fait vivre en un siecle non mol, languissant, ny oisif: tel, qui ne l'eut esté par autre moyen, se rendra fameux par son malheur [1046]

Therefore we must keep our courage supplied with stronger and more vigorous provisions. Let us be grateful to destiny for having made us live in an age that is not soft, languid, and idle. Many a man who could never have been famous by any other means will make himself famous by his misfortune. [800]

Montaigne can become a great man like Socrates through the "misfortune" (p. 800) of civil strife. It is in fact the civil war which prevents Montaigne's

25. Plato, op. cit., p. 299.
26. Marcile Ficin, Commentaire sur le Banquet de Platon trans. Raymond Marcel (Paris: Les Belles Lettres, 1978), p. 244.

own time from being the "feeble . . . age" (p. 792) he claimed it to be at the opening of the essay; discord has made his age "not soft, languid, and idle" (p. 800) but a *powerful* age that can produce its own great men independently of the ancients.

Montaigne's reflections on war's usefulness leads in the (c) additions to a profound consideration of human life's mixing of opposites:

> ainsi faict ma curiosité que je m'aggrée aucunement de veoir de mes yeux ce notable spectacle de nostre mort publique, ses symptomes et sa forme. . . . Si cherchons nous avidement de recognoistre en ombre mesme et en la fable des Theatres la montre des jeux tragiques de l'humaine fortune. Ce n'est pas sans compassion de ce que nous oyons, mais nous nous plaisons d'esveiller nostre desplaisir par la rareté de ces pitoyables evenemens. Rien ne chatouille qui ne pince. Et les bons historiens fuyent . . . des narrations calmes, pour regaigner les seditions, les guerres, ou ils sçavent que nous les appellons [1046]

> so my curiosity makes me feel some satisfaction at seeing with my own eyes this notable spectacle of our public death, its symptoms and its form. . . . Thus do we eagerly seek to recognize, even in shadow and in the fiction of the theatres, the representation of the tragic play of human fortune. Not that we lack compassion for what we hear; but the exceptional nature of these pathetic events arouses a pain that gives us pleasure. Nothing tickles that does not pain. And good historians avoid peaceful narratives . . . in order to get back to the seditions and wars to which they know that we summon them. [800]

Montaigne earlier condemned the "curiosity for knowledge" and the excessive "study of books" (794), but here he accepts his own "curiosity" (800) and treats his own experience as if it were a history book to be read or a tragic drama to be seen. If the philosophers' books lead one away from natural experience, sometimes it is best to distance such experience by converting it into a book. And by means of an essentially Aristotelian conception of the spectators' experience of tragedy, Montaigne collapses the opposition of pleasure and pain: "Nothing tickles that does not pain" (800). Montaigne in fact makes his own writing and our reading of "De la Phisionomie" exemplify the paradoxical mixture of pleasure and pain in human life: he is himself one of the "good historians" who give their readers "seditions and wars" (800) that they desire. If Montaigne is in a sense mocking his readers, letting them know that they are more interested in the bittersweet narrative concerning the civil wars than in the edifying discourses on ignorance, he is also expounding his version of Socratic teaching. In the last essay Montaigne refers to Socrates's discussion of the "alliance" of pleasure and pain: "[Socrates] se resjouit à considerer l'estroitte alliance de la douleur a la volupté, comme elles sont associées d'une liaison necessaire . . ." (III:XIII, 1093). ["he [Socrates] rejoiced to consider the close alliance between pain and pleasure, how they are associated by a necessary link . . ." (838).] The Platonic Socrates in fact notes this interdependence of pleasure and pain as the sign of the corporeal life's imperfections and of the need for the philosopher to abandon the body and to reach for a transcendental, spiritual realm (Phaedo 60B:83A–E). But Montaigne and his body-affirming and life-accepting Socrates would have man accept such "imperfections" as essential parts of man's being.

Critics have long noted that Montaigne's Socrates is indeed very different from the Platonic Socrates.[27] Montaigne's second presentation of Socratic ignorance, though based on passages from Plato's Apology, creates by omission and adaptation a very different picture of Socrates from that of Plato's text. Montaigne begins his borrowings from the Apology with a declaration that he is paraphrasing from his (notoriously faulty) memory "de ce qu'il m'en souvient, il parle environ en ce sens" (1052) ["For as far as I can remember, he speaks in about this sense . . ." 805).] By claiming to be relying solely on his memory, Montaigne establishes his right to paraphrase independently and without an excessive reliance on "the study of books" (794).[28] His Socrates lacks the transcendental beliefs and aspirations of the Platonic Socrates. He begins with a paraphrase of the Platonic Socrates' claim that to fear death is to pretend that one knows what death is, omitting the Platonic Socrates' claim that he has a divinely-ordained duty to continue philosophizing no matter what the cost (1052–53) [805–06] compare to Apology 28D–29A). Montaigne portrays a Socrates whose argument against the fear of death springs from pure "simplicité naturelle" (1052) ["simplicity of nature" (805)] and he therefore rejects the Platonic Socrates' exceptional sense that he has a unique divine mission from which not even the fear of death can deter him. Montaigne similarly has no interest in the Platonic Socrates' fervid espousal of the soul's immortality

27. On the difference between Montaigne's Socrates and the Platonic Socrates, see Friedrich, op. cit., p. 63, Kellerman, op. cit., p. 173, and McGowan, op. cit., pp. 152–53. Kellerman notes the importance of Socrates the skeptic for Montaigne, and it should be pointed out that the ancient skeptics had long distinguished between the dogmatic Plato and the original, more skeptical Socrates (see, e.g., Diogenes Laertius, Lives of the Philosophers III:35 for an anecdote in which Socrates accuses Plato of writing lies about him).

28. Cave, op. cit., p. 305.

(*Phaedo* 105E); for Montaigne Socrates is "courageux en la mort, non parce que son âme est immortelle, mais parce qu'il est mortel" (1059) ["courageous not because his soul is immortal but because he is mortal" (811).] He therefore tones down the *Apology's* references to the possible blessedness of the afterlife. While in the *Apology* Socrates suggests that the afterlife might be the greatest of blessings ("For nobody knows whether death is the greatest of all blessings to befall man . . ."[29]), Montaigne's Socrates states that death is merely "[a] l'avanture . . . indifferente, à l'avanture desirable" (1053;) ["perhaps . . . indifferent, perhaps desirable" (806).] Though a (c) addition gives the Platonic Socrates' two suggestions concerning the nature of the afterlife—either it is a complete annihilation or a transmigration—Montaigne drastically reduces the Platonic Socrates's vivid closing evocation of the blessed afterlife and has his Socrates end instead with an emphasis upon death as annihilation. Montaigne's non-Platonic Socrates views death—as he views man—"d'un visage ordinaire. . . . Il ne cherche point de consolation hors de la chose" (III:IV, 833;) ["with an ordinary countenance. . . . He seeks no consolation outside the thing itself" (632).]

Though Montaigne ends his presentation of Socratic ignorance with close translations of the Platonic text, Socrates' views in part echo those already expressed by Montaigne in *propria persona* in the preceding narrative section of the essay, and thus remind the reader how much the Socrates being presented is *Montaigne's* Socrates. Socrates ironically suggests that he should not be executed but instead should be kept at public expense for his services to the state, and he explains that stooping to beg for mercy would be inappropriate to his age and reputation and that he disdains being pardoned "par ma honte" (1053) ["by my shame" (806).] Socrates' attitude recalls Montaigne's own, for Montaigne has a tendency "de fuir à me justifier, excuser et interpreter, estimant que c'est mettre ma conscience en compromis de playder pour elle" (1044) ["avoiding justifying, excusing, and interpreting myself, thinking that it is compromising my conscience to plead for it" (799).] But if it is clear that the Socratic "defense" reflects the concerns and attitudes of Montaigne rather than those of Plato, Montaigne's "defense" of his choice of passages further emphasizes the way in which the borrowings from Plato reveal Montaigne himself: "Si quelqu'un estime que, parmy tant d'autres exemples que j'avois à choisir pour le service de mon propos és dicts de Socrates, j'aye mal trié cettuy-cy . . . je juge autrement . . ." (1054)["If anyone thinks that among the many examples of the sayings of Socrates that I might have chosen to serve my purpose I selected this one badly. . . . I judge otherwise . . ." (807).] The presentation of

29. Plato, op. cit., pp. 322–23.

Socrates reflects Montaigne's own *judgment*, the faculty he considers most inward and indicative of the true, essential self.[30] If Montaigne begins his borrowings with his faulty memory, he ends them with his most cherished and self-affirming possession, his independent judgement. Socrates is both self and other, the product of Montaigne's judgement and an ideal *exemplum*.

Montaigne praises Socrates for dying in the same manner as he lived and thus providing man with an exemplary lesson of how to live and die:

> Il feit tres-sagement, et selon luy, de ne corrompre une teneur de vie incorruptible et une si saincte image de l'humaine forme, pour allonger d'un an sa decrepitude et trahir L'immortelle memoire de cette fin glorieuse. Il devoit sa vie, non pas a soy mais a l'exemple du monde . . . [1054]

> ["He did very wisely, and like himself, not to corrupt an incorruptible tenor of life and such a saintly image of human nature in order to prolong his decrepitude by a year and betray the immortal memory of that glorious end. He owed his life not to himself but to the world as an example. [807].

The exemplary continuity of Socrates' life and death should reveal to man that he need not fear death, since "C'est [la mort] une partie de nostre estre non moins essentielle que le vivre" (1055) "It [death] is a part of our being no less essential than life" (807).] Montaigne's vision of the unity of life and death leads to a discussion of how death in nature engenders life, but a Latin quotation not only continues this theme but also obliquely suggests the powerful effect of Socrates' great sacrifice for man: *"Mille animas una necata dedit"* (1055, Ovid's *Fasti* 1:380). ["From one death come a thousand lives" (807).] The quotation refers to Aristaeus' sacrifice for the regeneration of his bees, but a Renaissance reader would have known that "Aristaeus" etymologically and allegorically signifies "the best man,"[31] and Montaigne thus obliquely suggests that Socrates is "the best man" giving new life to mankind through edifying self-sacrifice.

The motif of Socrates' sacrifice for the regeneration of man is indeed Montaigne's naturalized version of the transcendent Christ's sacrifice for man. M. Mann-Phillips argues that Montaigne's oxymoronic praise of Socrates betrays the influence of the Erasmian praise of Christ in the *Sileni*

---

30. On Montaigne's notion of judgement, see Raymond C. la Charité, *The Concept of Judgment in Montaigne* (The Hague: Martinus Nijhoff, 1968). Charité succinctly expresses the essential point: "Judgement is [for Montaigne] the inner part of man and the most important of his faculties" (p. 16).

31. See, for example, the *explicatio nominis* in the highly influential mythographic handbook, Natalis Comes, *Mythologiae* (original: Venice, 1567; facsimile reproduction: New York and London: Garland Publishing Company, 1976), p. 331.

Alicibiadis and *Dulce bellum.*[32] Indeed the two encomia show a parallel use of the oxymoron in order to suggest the reversal of values by which the base becomes sublime:

> (b) Voylà pas un plaidoyer sec et sain, (c) mais quand et quand naïf et bas, (b) d'une hauteur inimaginable, (c) vertible, franc et juste au delà de tout exemple.... Cette superbe vertue eust-elle calé au plus fort de sa montre? ... C'est un discours en rang et en naifveté bien plus arriere et plus bas que les opinions communes ... [1054]

> Is that not a sober, sane plea, but at the same time natural and lowly, inconceivably lofty, truthful, frank, and just beyond all example. ... Should that proud virtue have quit at the height of its display? ... it is a speech which in its naturalness ranks far behind and below common opinions. [806–07]

> in such service to mankind, there is a pearl of great price, in such humility, what grandeur! in such poverty, what riches! in such weaknesses, what immeasurable strength! in such shame, what glory! in such labors, what utter peace! And lastly in that bitter death there is the source of everlasting life.[33]

Mann-Phillips sees an essential continuity from Erasmus to Montaigne and avoids the full significance of Montaigne's substitution of Socrates for Christ. She speaks of the Erasmian conception of a "renversement des valeurs" based on "l'énigme de la croix."[34] But certainly at the time Montaigne was writing such a conception of Christianity would have seemed tainted by reformist doctrine.[35] If Montaigne recalls Erasmus' Christ-as-Silenus in portraying his Socrates, he is nevertheless strikingly different from his humanist predecessor in using a purely human "transvaluator" and rejuvenator of man in order to propound a man-affirming ignorance that could avoid the disputations of both the learned philosophers and their modern counterparts, the rebellious Protestants. In place of the cross as transcendent "source of everlasting life" stands Montaigne's and his Socrates' consolation, based on the "simplicity of nature" (805), that life and death are inextricably linked.

Montaigne praises Socrates as the natural man whom art cannot reach: "il n'est aisé de parler et vivre comme Socrates. Là loge l'extreme degré de

32. M. Mann-Phillips, "Erasme et Montaigne," in *Colloquia Erasmiana Toronensi* ed. Pierre Mesnard (Paris: Librairie Philosophique J. Vrin, 1972), vol. 1, p. 500.
33. Phillips, *Erasmus*, op. cit., pp. 79–80.
34. Phillips, "Erasme," loc. cit.
35. On Luther's *theologia crucis*, see Regen Prenter, *Luther's Theology of the Cross* (Philadelphia: Facet Books, 1971).

perfection et de difficulté: l'art n'y peut joindre" (1055)["to talk and live like Socrates. There lies the extreme degree of perfection and difficulty; art cannot reach it" (808).] Yet the following sections of the essay radically undermine the validity of this nature-art contrast. Montaigne's oxymoronic praise of Socrates' apology itself begins subtly to blur the distinctions:

> (c) Vrayement ce fut raison qu'il le preferast à celuy que ce grand orateur Lysias avoit mis par escrit pour luy, excellemment façonné au stile judiciaire, mais indigne d'un si noble criminel. . . . Et sa riche et puissante nature eust elle commis à l'art sa défense, et en son plus haut essay renoncé à la verité et naïfveté, ornemens de son parler, pour se parer du fard des figures et feintes d'une oraison apprinse? [1054]

> (c) Truly he was right to prefer it to the one the great orator Lysias had put in writing for him, excellently fashioned in the forensic style, but unworthy of so noble a criminal. . . . And should his rich and powerful nature have committed his defense to art, and, in its loftiest test, renounced truth and sincerity, the ornaments of his speech, to bedeck itself with the make-up of the figures and fictions of a memorized oration? [807]

Villey notes that Montaigne borrows from Diogenes Laertius this anecdote of Socrates' rejecting the overly rhetorical defense written for him by Lysias (*Lives of the Philosophers* II:40–41). But the contrast between truth and rhetoric, spontaneity and memorization, comes from Socrates' opening remarks in the *Apology* itself:

> I confess indeed that I am a rhetorician, though not of their [Socrates' accusors] kind. . . . From me indeed you are about to hear the whole truth. Nor, by Jove, Athenian gentlemen, will you hear from me an oration painted in their manner, or in any way adorned, but instead you will hear from me an oration composed of those words which come to me by chance and at random.[36]

Socrates and Montaigne both contrast Socratic truthfulness with the rhetoricians' "painted" discourse, Socratic spontaneity with the rhetoricians' elaborate preparations. But for both Socrates and Montaigne truthfulness is itself rhetorical. Socrates calls himself a rhetorician, and indeed his claim to truth is a rhetorical *captatio benevolentiae*.[37] Montaigne oxy-

36. Plato, op. cit., p. 318.
37. John Burnet, after noting that Socrates' exordium is extremely close to that of contemporaneous rhetoricians, suggests that Socrates is not simply following but rather parodying the orators' style: "We have the usual τόποι here, but they are all made to lead up to the genuinely Socratic paradox that the function of a good orator is to tell the truth" (Plato, *Euthyprho, Apology of Socrates, and Crito* ed. with notes by John Burnet (Oxford: Clarendon

moronically calls Socrates' "truth and sincerity" the "ornaments of his speech (807), and he thus suggests the rhetorical nature of a speech not "in any way adorned." And if Montaigne reveals his own judgement and thus himself in his choice of Socratic speeches, it is also true that his seemingly independent expression of judgement concerning Socrates is here based not on his self-affirming judgment but on the Platonic text. "Naturalness" becomes itself a rhetorical style, and the "spontaneous" judgement of Montaigne is mediated by a reading of the Platonic Socrates.

In the apparent digression following the praise of Socrates, Montaigne further reveals the breakdown of the nature-art distinction. Montaigne defends his own writing against the charge of borrowing from and relying on others, an activity associated with bad "art" and opposed to natural Socratic self-reliance. He imagines some reader condemning his use of "fleurs estrangeres" (1055;)["other people's flowers" (808)], but he insists that it is only as a concession to the times that he avails himself of these "parements empruntez" (1055;)["borrowed ornaments" (808).] He himself desires nothing more than to write a natural, self-reliant text: "[je]ne veux faire montre que du mien, et de ce qui est mien par nature" (1055)["I who wish to make a show only of what is my own, and of what is naturally my own" (808).] But a (c) addition gives a highly paradoxical defense of Montaigne's intertextual activity:

> Parmy tant d'emprunts je suis bien aisé d'en pouvoir desrober quelqu'un les desguisant et difformant à nouveau service. Au hazard que je laisse dire que c'est par faute d'avoir entendu leur naturel usage, je luy donne quelque particuliere adresse de ma main à ce qu'ils en soient d'autant moins purement estrangers. . . . Nous autres naturalistes estimons qu'il y aie grande et incomparable preferance de l'honneur de l'invention a l'honneur de l'allegation [1056]

> "I, among so many borrowing of mine, am very glad to be able to hide one now and then, disguising and altering it for a new service. At the risk of letting it be said that I do so through failure to understand its original use, I give it some particular application with my own hand, so that it may be less purely someone else's. . . . We naturalists judge that the honor of invention is greatly and incomparably preferable to the honor of quotation.[809].

Montaigne argues that he deliberately changes, disguises and deforms the borrowings he makes in order to make them "less purely someone else's"

Press, 1924), p. 67. If Socrates is parodying the orators, he is nevertheless using their rhetorical art to attack the art of rhetoric. On the general issue of "the rhetoric of anti-rhetoric," see Paolo Valesio, *Novantiqua: Rhetorics as a Contemporary Theory* (Bloomington: Indiana University Press, 1980), pp. 41–60.

and thus revealing of himself rather than of another. But if he thus claims to avoid the self-loss inherent in "the study of books" (794), he makes explicit that he does not do so naturally but only through a highly artful "deformation" of the borrowings' *natural* meanings "leur naturel usage" (1056) [its original use" (809).] "Deformation" and its cognates appear in three other (c) additions to the essay, all of them describing negative *exempla* of the *unnatural*. The reformers cause "la derniere des difformations" (1043)["the worst of deformations" (798),] the Stoic philosophers attempt to "difformer" (1051)["make inconsistent" 805)] life and death, and true ugliness is "une laideur *desnaturée* et difformité de membres" (1057)["*unnatural* ugliness and deformity of limbs" (809).] If Montaigne claims to be among the naturalists, he also implies that a naturalist must use (a morally dangerous) art in order to follow nature.

In the description of his writing style, Montaigne speaks of the essay as a "traicté de la phisionomie" (1056)["treatise on physiognomy" (808), and he thus ironically introduces the putative topic of the essay in what seems a digression from the tight chiasmic structure framed by the two encomia of Socrates. With the air of a complete nonsequitur, in fact, Montaigne introduces the subject of Socrates' physiognomy: "Socrates, qui a esté un exemplaire parfaict en toutes grandes qualitez, j'ay despit qu'il eust rencontre un corps et un visage si vilain . . ." (1057)["About Socrates, who was a perfect model in all great qualities, it vexes me that he hit on a body and face so ugly . . ."(809)]. But this apparently casual, digressive structure is itself an example of art hiding art. Montaigne begins the essay discussing Socrates' Silenic discourse and here he abruptly resumes this theme by discussing Socrates' Silenic physiognomy. In so doing he is simply reversing the order of Alcibiades' drunken, rambling praise of Socrates the Silenus. Alcibiades begins his comparison of Socrates and Silenus by praising Socrates' Silenic appearance, but towards the end of his encomium he adds the disconnected afterthought that Socratic discourse is itself like a Silenus: "I also had omitted to mention before that his discourses are like Sileni that are opened."[38] The true irony is not the devious structure of Montaigne's text, which has a basis in the Platonic text, but the fact that Montaigne once more supplants Socrates as the center of interest. Montaigne has stolen— and deformed!—the Platonic praise of Socrates.

The last section of the essay contrast Socrates and Montaigne in two ways. Socrates is ugly, while Montaigne has "un port favorable" (1059)["a favorable bearing" (819).] More importantly, Socrates corrects himself through reason and art, while Montaigne simply follows nature:

38. Plato, op. cit., p. 299.

> Comme Socrates disoit de la sienne [sa laideur] qu'elle en accusoit justement autant en son ame, s'il ne l'eust corrigée par institution.
>
> J'ay pris . . . bien simplement et cruement pour mon regard ce precepte ancien: que nous ne sçaurions faillir à suivre nature, que le souverain precepte c'est de se conformer à elle. Je n'ay pas corrigé, comme Socrates, par force de la raison mes complexions naturelles, et n'ay aucunement troublé par art mon inclination. Je me laisse aller . . . [1058–59]

> So Socrates said of his ugliness that it betrayed what would have been just as much ugliness in his soul, if he had not corrected it by training.
>
> . . . I have very simply and crudely adopted for my own sake this ancient precept: that we cannot go wrong by following nature, that the sovereign precept is to conform to her. I have not, like Socrates, corrected my natural disposition by force of reason, and have not troubled my inclination at all by art. I let myself go . . . [810–11]

The anecdote concerning Socrates's physiognomy comes from the *Tusculan Disputations* (IV:80), and thus the passage which gives the whole essay its title comes from the very work attacked by Montaigne as philosophical superfluity (1039; 794). But Montaigne once more uses the books of the philosophers to attack them. Cicero tells this tale concerning Socrates in a passage espousing the Stoic doctrine of the continuity of nature and reason: "is anything in accordance with nature which is done in opposition to reason?" (*Tusculan Disputations* IV:79).[39] Montaigne, rejecting this continuity, distinguishes Socrates' use of reason and art from his own true following of nature. Thus Socrates becomes an example of the bad Stoic philosopher who tries to go beyond the natural, and it is now neither Cato nor Socrates who correctly interprets the Stoic precept embodied in Lucan's "follow nature" (793), but only Montaigne himself. Montaigne is the authentic natural man, though even *his* naturalism is mediated by the tradition and texts of Stoic "precept" (811); but Socrates, until now the ideal *exemplum* of the natural man, joins his erstwhile opponents the misguided philosophers.[40]

Yet in a (c) addition that follows the contrast between the natural Montaigne and the reasonable Socrates, Montaigne abandons his contrast between nature and reason:

39. On the Stoic doctrine of natural reason, see Maryanne Cline Horowitz, "The Stoic Synthesis of the Idea of Natural Law in Man: Four Themes," *Journal of the History of Ideas*, vol. 35, no. 1 (January–March 1974), pp. 3–16.

40. For a general discussion of the shift from the Stoic conception of "following nature" to Montaigne's "naturalistic" conception, see Hiram Haydn, *The Counter-Renaissance* (New York: Harcourt, Brace, and World, 1950), pp. 468–97.

Je l'aime [la vertue] telle que les loix et religions non facent mais parfacent et authorisent . . . née en nous de ses propres racines par la semence de la raison universelle empreinte en tout homme non desnaturé. Cette raison, qui redresse Socrates de son vicieux ply . . [1059]

What I like is the virtue that laws and religions do not make but perfect and authorize . . . born in us from its own roots, from the seed of universal reason that is implanted in every man who is not denatured. This reason, which straightens Socrates from his inclination to vice . . . [811]

Man's virtue should be based on "the seed of universal reason" planted in every natural man, and Socrates's virtuous self-correction is no longer a negative example of "unnatural" art but a wholly legitimate use of "natural" reason. Montaigne is now in fact expounding Stoic doctrine, for his "universal reason" is equivalent to the Stoics' "highest reason, implanted in Nature, which commands what ought to be done and forbids the opposite" (Cicero, Laws 1:18). And one cannot but feel that the blatant contradiction between Montaigne's initial anti-Stoic stance contrasting nature and reason and his final adoption of the Stoics' reconciliation of the two is meant to suggest his fundamental conviction that following nature includes and requires accepting one's own contradictions. When Montaigne writes "Je ne combats rien" (1059)["I combat nothing" (811)], he suggests his assent to the collapse of all his distinctions.

In his discussion of physiognomy, indeed, Montaigne wholly destroys his contrast between nature and art by presenting a truly legitimate art of following nature. Montaigne gives credence to a modified form of physiognomic science according to which there is some conformity between a man's appearance and the nature of his soul: "Et crois qu'il y a quelque art a distinguer les visages debonnaires des nyais, les severes des rudes . . ." (1059). ["And I think there is some art to distinguish the kindly faces from the simple, the severe from the rough . . ."(811).] At the beginning of the essay Montaigne expounds a belief in the unity of outer and inner, but here Montaigne the physiognomist transforms this belief into an art. In the Renaissance, physiognomic lore was associated with such an "art" as astrology,[41] which Montaigne might condemn as an excessive "curiosity for knowledge" (794). But the "art" of physiognomy is also a way of following

41. Note the titles of two representative Renaissance books on physiognomy: *Absolutissimae Chyromantiae Libri Octo. In quibus quidquid ad chyromantiae, physiognomiae, et naturalis astrologiae perfectionem spectat, continetur* (1563); *Introductiones apotelesmatice elegantes, in chyromantiam, physiognomiam, astrologiam naturalem* (1566). Cited in Walter Clyde Curry, *Chaucer and the Medieval Sciences* (New York: Oxford University Press, 1926), p. 243. (I am indebted to Clarence H. Miller for this reference.)

nature, or attending to what Montaigne calls nature's "propre visage" (1050) ["Her [nature's] own countenance" (803) and "les promesses que nature . . . [a] plantées au front" (1058)["the promises that nature . . . implanted on . . . brows" (811).] Once more Montaigne aligns himself with his erstwhile opponents the philosophers. Thus in a section of the *Laws* expounding the doctrine that arts follow "the teachings of nature," Cicero provides the same natural basis for physiognomic lore by discussing how "nature among her many gifts to many has imprinted man's inner character upon his face: "she [nature] has so framed his features as to portray therein the character that lies hidden deep within him" (1:26).

Montaigne tells two final anecdotes of his civil war experiences that ostensibly show how he has been saved by his (naturally-implanted) outward appearance: "Il m'est souvant advenu que, sur le simple credit de ma presence et de mon air, des personnes qui n'avoyent aucune cognoissance de moy s'y sont grandement fiées . . ." (1060) ["It has often happened that on the mere credit of my presence and manner, persons who had no knowledge of me have placed great trust in me . . ." (811–12).] One expects that the two anecdotes will thus confirm the correspondence of outer and inner as embodied in the exemplary figure of Montaigne himself. The first anecdote, indeed, does so: enemy soldiers take over Montaigne's home, but the enemy chief calls his men away because of Montaigne's good-nature "visage" and "franchise" (1060) ["face" and "frankness" (813).] The second anecdote, however, in which Montaigne is taken prisoner by enemy soldiers but then set free, is more problematic. Montaigne states that he still does not know *why* he was set free:

> La vraye cause d'un changement si nouveau et de ce ravisement, sans aucune impulsion apparente, et d'un repentire si miraculeux . . . certes je ne sçay pas bien encores quelle elle est. Le plus apparent, qui se demasqua et me fit cognoistre son nom, me redict lors plusieurs fois que je devoy cette deliverance à mon visage, liberté et fermeté de mes parolles . . . (1062)

> The true cause of so unusual an about-face and change of mind without any apparent motivation, and of such a miraculous repentance . . . I truly do not even now well know. The most conspicuous among them, who took off his mask and let me know his name, repeated to me several times that I owed my deliverance to my face and the freedom and firmness of my speech . . . [813–14]

Montaigne does not know the true cause of his good fortune despite the captor's "revelation" of his unmasked face and his explanatory discourse. If the captor *appears* to be himself a believer in physiognomy and the correspondence of Montaigne's outer and inner nature, Montaigne himself is now unsure of his physiognomic "art" and thus cannot *in-terpret* the man's face and his words in order to determine the "inner" truth of the situation. In a passage from the 1588 edition, Montaigne underscores his desire to know the captor's true character: "(j'essayerois volontiers à mon tour, quelle mine il feroit en un pareil accident)" (1062) ["(I would like to find out in my turn what kind of countenance he would have in a similar accident" (814).] But the use of "countenance" suggests all the difficulties of outer and inner, for it too refers to the merely external aspect of a man and thus suggests the impossibility of ever truly seeing "into" another man's character.

Montaigne's abandonment of the unity of outer and inner is further revealed in a (c)-addition concerning Socrates' visage. While in the (b)-edition Montaigne accepts at "face value" Socrates's contention that his soul would have been as ugly as his face wtihout the "training" of reason and art, Montaigne now suggests that Socrates' statement is ironic and that the ancient philsopher's soul was naturally beautiful: "Mais en le disant je tiens qu'il se mocquoit suivant son usage, et jamais ame si excellent ne se fit elle mesme" (1058) ["But in saying this I hold that he was jesting according to his wont. So excellent a soul was never self-made" (810).] It now appears that Socrates's face *hides* his excellent soul, and that his ironic discourse is so devious that it leads Montaigne into contradictory interpretations of its "inner" meaning.

Both the captor, whose discourse is about Montaigne, and Socrates, whose mission is to teach men to know themselves, should lead Montaigne to self-knowledge; and if Montaigne cannot fully interpret these men, at the end of the essay he reveals that he also cannot fully interpret himself. After emphasizing his handsome exterior, Montaigne ends the essay with a discussion of his more ambiguous moral interior. If the section defending physiognomy attempts to establish the close connection of beauty and goodness ("je la [la beauté] considere comme à deut doits près de la bonté" (1058) ["I consider it [beauty] within two finger's breadth of goodness" (810)], Montaigne concludes by raising anew the whole question of the relationship between these two qualities. Montaigne states his unwilling-ness to punish criminals, and he records contradictory judgements as to whether or not such leniency is morally sound:

À moy . . . peut toucher ce qu'on disoit de Charillus, roy de Sparte: Il ne sçauroit estre bon, puis qu'il n'est pas mauvais aux meschants. Ou bien ainsi, car Plutarque le presente en ces deux sortes, comme mille autres

choses, diversement et contrairement: Il faut bien qu'il soit bon, puisqu'il
l'est aux meschants mesme [1063]

To me . . . may apply what they said about Charillys, king of Sparta: 'He
could not possibly be good, since he is not bad to the wicked.' Or else thus,
for Plutarch presents it in these two ways, as he does a thousand other
things, variously and contrastingly: 'He must certainly be good, since he is
good even to the wicked.' " [814]

Montaigne here employs one of his favorite devices, the radical skeptics'
method of opposing "judgement to judgement" in order to show the
impossibility of certain truth (cf. Sextus Empiricus, *Outlines of Pyrrhonism*
I.9). Since these judgements concern Montaigne's own moral status, Montaigne confesses that he does not know himself. Montaigne does not know
the most important thing about himself (whether he is "good" or "bad"), but
the ultimate paradox would seem to be that to know one does not know
oneself is truly to know that one knows nothing . . . and thus to fulfill
absolutely the requirements of Socratic self-knowledge. Yet Montaigne
ends the essay not with epistemological paradoxes but with a simple
statement concerning his own character:

Comme aux actions legitimes je me fasche de m'y employer quand c'est
envers ceux qui s'en desplaisent, aussi, à dire verité, aux illegitimes je ne
fay pas assez de conscience de m'y employer quand c'est envers ceux qui y
consentent [1063]

As I do not like to take a hand in legitimate actions against people who
resent them, so, to tell the truth, I am not scrupulous enough to refrain
from taking a hand in illegitimate actions against people who consent to
them. [814]

Montaigne moves from an ignorance that is a kind of self-knowledge to a
self-description that implies a self-acceptance. Though Montaigne may
know only that he knows nothing, though he may never be sure whether he
does good or bad, he simply *is* as he is. Radical skepticism based on the
"diversity" (803) of reason leads to a noncombative ethic of ignorance and
acceptance, to a state of simple self-affirmation.

Montaigne's self-portrait as the *modern* exponent of Socratic ignorance, as a *new* kind of Socrates, presupposes a distance and independence
from Socrates and the texts that portray him, since the dependence on
others and on books is radically antithetical to the true Socratic spirit.
Montaigne, as we have seen, meets this challenge by displaying a remarkable independence and creative spirit in his use of the Socratic texts and by

describing the civil war as a useful evil that leads him to his own authentically independent Socratic stance. Towards the end of the essay Montaigne argues that he is never condemned for what he says if people hear it directly from his own mouth, and he adds the gnomic utterance: "Les paroles redictes ont, comme autre son, autre sense" (1063) ["Words when reported have a different sense, as they have a different sound" (814).] Although Montaigne is clearly presenting a *captatio benevolentiae*, trying to win over his readers by suggesting the inadequacy of his text as a full presentation of the living, speaking Montaigne, this assertion of the radical historicity of any linguistic utterance grants Montaigne his independence of Socrates and his legitimate place as a new Socratic spokesman. For when Montaigne repeats words of or about Socrates—even when he repeats them with the utmost fidelity—the new context and the new "voice" of Montaigne's own essay gives them a new meaning.[42] Perhaps Montaigne's repetition of Lucan's "follow nature" presents the clearest example of the change in meaning that occurs through repetition: the phrase originally describing Cato's Stoicism becomes first a description of Socrates' ignorance (1037; 793) and then a description of Montaigne's ignorance and self-acceptance (1059; 811). Montaigne's assertion of the historicity of discourse may in fact be a deliberate denial of the Platonic claim that Socratic discourse transcends the drift inherent in linguistic repetition. Alcibiades praises Socrates' discourse for being repeatable without losing any of its power: "But if anyone of us listens to you, *or to your words repeated by someone else, even by one inept at speaking* . . . we are struck dumb . . ."[43] Montaigne denies this transtemporal power and is thus able to "appropriate" Socratic teaching in the flux of meaning and to find his own authentic voice *à travers* Socratic discourse.

It would certainly be wrong, however, to emphasize the asserted difference between Socrates and Montaigne without recognizing the powerful bonding of the two figures. After his discussion of Socrates' "corps et . . . visage si vilain" (1057) ["body and face so ugly" (809) and "la beauté de son ame" (1057) ["the beauty of his soul"),] Montaigne makes a (c)-addition revealing the full intensity of his relationship to Socrates:

> Cettuycy [Cicero] parle d'une laideur desnaturée et difformité des membres. Mais nous appellons laideur aussi une mesavenance au premier regard, qui loge principallement au visage . . . La laideur qui revestoit une ame tres-belle en La Boitie estoit de ce predicament [1057]

42. Cave, op. cit., p. 309.
43. Plato, op. cit., p. 297.

> This man [Cicero] is speaking of an unnatural ugliness and deformity of limbs. But we also call ugliness an unattractiveness at first glance, which resides chiefly in the face. . . . The ugliness which clothes a very beautiful soul in La Boetie was in this category." [809–10]

Since the discussion of la Boétie's external ugliness and internal beauty occurs right after the discussion of Socrates' ugliness, one notes a mingling in Montaigne's mind of his deceased friend and the ancient philosopher. Both are for Montaigne part of the ancient past, since Montaigne considers la Boétie not a modern contemporary but an ideal ancient: "Il avoit son esprit moulé au patron d'autres siecles que ceux-cy" (I:XXVIII, 194) ["His mind was molded in the pattern of other ages than this" (144).] But the introduction of la Boétie into "De la Phisionomie" suggests that the relationship between Montaigne and Socrates is analogous to that complicated unity-within-difference described so feelingly in "De l'Amitié" (I:XXVIII).[44] In that essay Montaigne suggests that there is a self-loss inherent in true friendship: "Je dis perdre, à la verité, ne nous reservant rien qui nous fut propre, ny qui fut ou sien ou mien" (189) ["I say lose, in truth, for neither of us reserved anything for himself, nor was anything either his or mine" (139).] In his relationship to Socrates, Montaigne once more risks losing the "propre" by relying on Socrates and the texts concerning Socrates instead of relying without mediation on himself and on nature. After la Boétie died, Montaigne registers his feeling that his own life is a kind of theft from his friend: "il me semble que je luy desrobe sa part" (193) ["it seems to me that I am robbing him of his share" (143).] There is clearly a similar way in which Montaigne steals from Socrates in suggesting that he is the modern living representative of Socratic teaching. That Montaigne indeed feels that he is to some extent "betraying" both friend and philosopher seems clear from the contrast between la Boétie's—and presumably Socrates'—"laideur superficielle" (1057) ["superficial ugliness' (810),] an ugliness which is neither unnatural nor associated with "deformity" (809) and the unnatural ugliness of Montaigne's own text, which makes its borrowings from Socrates "propre" by an act of "difformation" (". . . difformant à nouveau service" 1056). But the instability of the relationship between Montaigne and Socrates, the oscillations between self-loss and self-assertion, should not hide what is never directly asserted

44. On Montaigne's friendship with la Boétie and its role in the *Essays*, see Anthony Wilden's Lacanian analysis, "*Par divers moyens on arrive à pareille fin*: A Reading of Montaigne," *Modern Language Notes*, 83, no. 4 (May 1968) pp. 577–97 and Barry L. Weller, "The Rhetoric of Friendship in Montaigne's *Essais*," *New Literary History*, IX (1977–1978), pp. 503–23.

in "De la Phisionomie" but is suggested throughout in the balancing of the French essayist and the Greek philosopher: the unity-within-difference of the two figures, the perhaps elusive sense in which Montaigne could say of Socrates, as he said of la Boétie, "c'est moy" (191).

JULES BRODY

"Du repentir" (III: 2): A Philological Reading

I

> Un auteur paradoxal ne doit jamais dire son mot, mais
> toujours ses preuves: il doit entrer furtivement dans l'âme de
> son lecteur, et non de vive force. C'est le grand art de
> Montaigne, qui ne veut jamais prouver, et qui va toujours
> prouvant, et me ballottant du blanc au noir, et du noir au
> blanc.
>
> —Diderot

It is generally agreed that the essays first published in the edition of 1588, those of the so-called "Epicurean" or "naturalistic" last period, differ markedly in form and substance from the earlier, shorter, "impersonal" essays of 1580. "Book III," so Donald Frame observes, "is full of a new sense of human unity and solidarity and of the confidence in man that goes with it." Frame alleges a number of biographical facts in support of this generalization and then concludes: "His new feeling is best expressed in the formula, 'Each man bears the entire form of man's estate' " (xiii). This last comment, specifically the words *his, new* and *feeling,* is typical of the normal or predominant way, in academic circles, of interpreting Montaigne. This approach consists in decontextualizing certain particularly pregnant, provocative *dicta* in an effort to correlate them with those events, situations, emotions or ideas that could plausibly have determined the tendencies or the content of a complete, all-enveloping *mens montaneana* that is presumed to exist somewhere behind the printed page. To read Montaigne in this manner is to view his writing in what I have called "the hypothetical perspective of the *destinateur.*"[1] The philological reader, by

1. For other examples of "philological" readings, see my *Lectures de Montaigne,* Jules Brody, *Lectures de Montaigne* (Lexington, Ky; French Forum, Publishers, 1982), pp. 107–08. The attempts to grapple with the complexities of *Du repentir* have been surprisingly few. Outstanding among these are: Erich Auerbach, *Mimesis,* trans. by Willard Trask (Princeton, N. J.: Princeton University Press, 1953), pp. 285–311; *Trois essais de Montaigne (I:34, II:1, III:ii),* expliqués par Georges Gougenheim et Pierre-Maxime Schuhl (Paris: Vrin, 1951), pp. 62–146; Floyd Gray, *Le Style de Montaigne* (Paris: Nizet, 1958), *passim;* Lawrence D. Kritzman,

238

contrast, situates his activity resolutely and exclusively in what I believe is "the objective perspective of the destinataire." To such a reader as this, the statement, *chaque homme porte la forme entiere de l'humaine condition*, belongs inalienably to a verbal environment, whose existence and specificity are a matter of incontrovertible evidence, whence my calculated use of the word *objective*. With respect to its immediate—and ultimately to its total—context, Montaigne's much-quoted maxim raises several precise and difficult questions, these among others: what is its function on the page where it appears, its relation to the essay in which it figures, its connection with the announced subject, repentance? And finally: what are we to make of the fact that Montaigne's self-congratulatory claim to exemplarity, as bearer of "the entire form" of the human condition, contradicts roundly the general thrust of his self-depreciating initial sentence?

> (b) Les autres forment l'homme; je le recite et en represente un particulier bien mal formé, et lequel, si j'avoy à façonner de nouveau, je ferois vrayement bien autre qu'il n'est. [804]

> Others form man; I tell of him and portray a particular one, very ill-formed, whom I should really make very different from what he is if I had to fashion him over again. [610]

Whether the reader's first impulse is to view the marked opposition *forment/mal formé* as ironic, devious, sincerely or strategically modest, it will only be a question of time, once he has reached the expression *forme entiere*, before he begins to suspect that the prominence of this lexical item may indicate the presence of a thematic constant or a structure. For on the next page, he will notice the sentence:

> (b) Icy, nous allons *conformément* et tout d'un trein, mon livre et moy. [806]

> In this case we go hand in hand and at the same pace, my book and I. [611–12]

Midway through the essay, he will find the word *forme*, made conspicuous once again by its redundancy, in the following reflection:

Destruction/Découverte: le fonctionnement de la rhétorique dans les Essais de Montaigne (Lexington, Ky: French Forum, Publishers, 1980), pp. 126–38; Yaskuaki Okubo, "Essai sur le mécanisme de la pensée de Montaigne: pour une interprétation globale du troisième livre des *Essais*," *Etudes de Langue et de Littérature Françaises* (Tokyo), 36 (1980), 24–27; Francois Rigolot, "La *Pente* du 'repentir': un exemple de remotivation du signifiant dans les *Essais* de Montaigne," *Columbia Montaigne Conference Papers*, ed. Donald M. Frame and Mary B. McKinley (Lexington, Ky.: French Forum, 1981), pp. 119–34.

(b) il n'est personne, s'il s'escoute, qui ne descouvre en soy une *forme* sienne, une *forme* maistresse, qui luicte contre l'institution, et contre la tempeste des passions qui luy sont contraires. [811]

There is no one who, if he listens to himself, does not discover in himself a pattern of his own, a ruling pattern which struggles against education and against the tempest of the passions that oppose it. [615]

The *forme* that Montaigne invokes at this point, like the earlier *forme entiere*, is of universal attribution, but with the added nuance: all lives are essentially of a type, all people are the same in that they share, in their difference, a fundamental selfhood which is intractable to change, or as specified here, to *institution* or education in the sense of moral improvement or "reform." And in this respect, the parallel expressions *une forme sienne, une forme maistresse* betray more than a passing connection, when read in retrospect, with Montaigne's jibe, just ten lines above, at the "reformers" of what we now know as the "Reformation":

(b) Ceux qui ont essaié de r'aviser les meurs du monde, de mon temps, par nouvelles opinions, *reforment* les vices de l'apparence . . . [811]

Those who in my time have tried to correct the world's morals by new ideas, reform the superficial vices . . . [615]

Such *reformations externes* ("external reforms"), Montaigne concludes, never touch *les vices naturels consubstantiels et intestins* (811) ["the natural, consubstantial, and internal vices," 615]. By an inner logic, modulated at the level of the lexicon around the radical *forme*, Montaigne is repeating here the essential message of his opening page: we all have—not only I—a constant, guiding inner "form," *une forme maistresse qui luicte contre l'institution*, that will not and cannot be "re-formed".[2] Although

2. M. Baraz notes: "la forme maistresse est, sinon l'expérience directe de l'être, du moins l'être entrevu comme but idéal et qui fait naître dans l'âme l'inspiration vers un état aussi voisin que possible de la constance et du calme des passions." "Le Sentiment de l'unité cosmique chez Montaigne," *Cahiers de l'Association Internationale des Etudes Françaises*, 14 (1962), 221; according to Y. Bellanger, "forme maistresse" is a synonym for "nature." *Nature* et *naturel* dans quatre chapitres des *Essais*," *Bulletin de la Société des Amis de Montaigne*, 25–26 (1978), 37–49. No one, to my knowledge, has ever noted that *forme maistresse* is a veiled Latinism (= *forma magistra*), generated intertextually from a passage in Lucan alleged by Montaigne just a page earlier in support of the assertion: *Les inclinations naturelles s'aident et fortifient par institution, mais elles ne se changent quiere et surmontent* (810). ["Natural inclinations gain assistance and strength from education; but they are scarcely to be changed and overcome," 615.] In the Latin verses that follow, the passions (= *inclination naturelles*) are pictured as bloodthirsty wild beasts on the verge of revolt against their "master" (= *institution*): *Admonitaeque tument gustato sanguine fauces;/Fervet, et a trepido vix abstinet ira magistro*

removed by several pages from Montaigne's entry into his subject, this proposition will be recognized as a mere re-writing of his initial sentence: the others—the teachers, moralists and sundry "re-formers"—"form" or educate man; they try to shape and mold him, bring his character and behavior into conformity with an external pattern.[3] I, at the outset, renounce such ambitions; I may be "ill formed," but it is too late for me to "re-form" (= *façonner de nouveau = faire . . . autre*).

As its first and most gratifying reward, philological reading offers the occasion to make connections and to perceive constants within a given essay that will be obscured, if anything, by perusal of the content, analysis of the ideas, or extratextual reference to the abstraction, "Montaigne."[4] In the present case, the apparent generative power of the word and the idea of a dominant, universal inner *forme*—in the sense of the individual's "character," "make-up," or "nature"—brings into sharp focus, as the reader travels back in memory from the words *forme maistresse* to *Les autres forment l'homme*, a vital aspect of the essay's nominal subject.[5] At just a few lines distance from the signpost *Du repentir*, we are made to understand that "repentance"—at least in the deep and far-reaching sense of a self-scrutiny capable of producing effective change—is a profound illusion. In those later parts of the essay, actually quite few in number, which deal specifically with repentance, in personal, historical, theoretical and theological terms, the same conclusion will recur: the examples that we see around us are more verbal than actual, more apparent than real; what passes for repentance is superficial and will not measure up to the deep implications of the word. Montaigne applies systematically to others what he says of the instances alleged from his own life: (b) *Cela ne s'appelle pas repentir* (814). ["that is not to be called repentance," (618).] The opening sentence of *Du repentir* had made this clear. To "repent" is to reshape and remake personality, with the incidental irony that will acquire increasing prominence and pertinence as the writing unfolds: to "re-form" people is equally

["Excited by the taste of blood, their jaws swell, and seething with rage, they come close to turning on their trembling master," *Pharsalia*, IV: 237–42, my translation.] In this light, the *forme maistresse, qui luicte contre l'institution et contre la tempeste des passions* may be read as a metaphor for a posited innate tendency towards stability and order that resists both external coercion and internal sedition.

3. Gougenheim and Schuhl (above, n. 1) gloss the words *Les autres forment l'homme* as equivalent to "donner une formation morale" (p. 63).

4. In this study, I use the proper name, Montaigne, with exclusive reference to the author of the *Essais*, in the limited sense of the person who put the words on the pages.

5. On the vagaries of the radical *forme* in *Du repentir*, see Kritzman's illuminating discussion (above, n. 1), pp. 127–31.

futile and absurd as the claim to "form" them in the first place. In short, when we read the initial sentence of *Du repentir* philologically, as a series of periphrases of the unspoken identity *repentir* = *re-former,* we understand that Montaigne has begun, in a more than usually provocative way, by evacuating his announced subject and by inviting us therewith to wonder and to ponder what his essay is really "about."

Montaigne's statements, individually taken, are always clear, but in context they are never simple. This is why scholars have always found it so difficult to decide what he "really" believed or what he "intended" his reader to infer with respect to his personal opinions. Whatever other-directed ironies we may eventually be able to see in the opening sentences of *Du repentir,* our first, linear reading must yield a powerful quotient of self-disparagement: they "form," I "tell"; they deal with the general (= noble), I with the individual (= common), and a pretty sorry specimen at that, sorely in need of repair. Both the object and the mode of my discourse, Montaigne stresses at great length and at great pains, are lacking in dignity and importance. And in the next couple of pages, he will refer to his undertaking variously as deficient in consistency, order, information, and artistry; this series of faults that were implicit in the initial contrastive pair *forment/recite,* is recapitulated a bit farther along in the echo-sentence: (b) *Je n'enseigne poinct, je raconte* (806). ["I do not teach, I tell." (612).]

Much of the charm and a great deal of the difficulty of Montaigne's writing lies in his favorite habit of taking back from the reader the previously given only to present it to him again from another angle, suffused with a different light. Thus, negative and positive visions and versions of the same phenomenon are often placed side by side with no immediate indication as to their interconnection or their relative value. This, exactly, is the eventual status of Montaigne's liminal self-effacement and self-disparagement, which on closer inspection turn out to be no more sustained or convincing than his ostensibly respectful attitude vis-à-vis the "others."[6] The ill-formed individual that I portray may be unworthy of the effort expended, the result may be paltry in comparison with the works of the professional moralists and the educators of mankind, but—at this precise point a shift from pejorative to meliorative occurs—the portrait itself is true to life;

6. Margaret McGowan rightly sees Montaigne's "modesty" as functioning within a self-serving didactic strategy. *Montaigne's Deceits: the Art of Persuasion in the* Essais. (Philadelphia, Pa.: Temple University Press, 1974), pp. 1–19.

(b) Or les traits de ma peinture ne forvoyent point, quoy qu'ils se changent et diversifient. Le monde n'est qu'une branloire perenne. Toutes choses y branlent sans cesse: la terre, les rochers du Caucase, les pyramides d'Aegypte, et du branle public et du leur. La constance mesme n'est autre chose qu'un branle plus languissant. Je ne puis asseurer mon object. Il va trouble et chancelant, d'une yvresse naturelle. Je le prens en ce point, comme il est, en l'instant que je m'amuse à luy. Je ne peints pas l'estre. Je peints le passage: non un passage d'aage en autre, ou, comme dict le peuple, de sept en sept ans, mais de jour en jour, de minute en minute. [804–05]

Now the features in my portrait are faithful; they do not stray from the original although they change and vary. The world is but a perpetual see-saw.[7] All things in it are in constant motion—the earth, the rocks of the Caucasus, the pyramids of Egypt—both with the common motion and with their own. Stability itself is nothing but more languid motion. I cannot keep my subject still. It goes along befuddled and staggering, with a natural drunkenness. I take it in this condition, just as it is at the moment I give my attention to it. I do not portray being: I portray passing. Not the passing from one age to another, or, as the people say, from seven years to seven years, but from day to day, from minute to minute. [610–11]

It deserves to be stressed that this celebrated paean to human mutability and cosmic flux takes place under the banner of constancy, negativly stated in the words *ne forvoyent point*, but positively marked by virtue of a process of retrieval and valorisation that is continued throughout the passage. Because it honors the principle of variety and change, my portrait stays close not only to its original but to the order of the universe and to the very rhythm of life. Human instability, although a sign of imperfection and finitude, also reflects the cosmic dispensation. In its natural debility, our condition is at one with the splendor of the Caucasus and the grandeur of the Pyramids with which it shares a shifting existential mode. The world order, inversely, is trivialized and humanized by means of the metaphor *branloire* (= modern French, *balançoire*), a child's swing or seesaw.[8] As each detail is added, great and small are brought closer and closer to their common focus: I, like all men, like the physical universe itself, am unstable, labile and oscillatory, but I am constantly, continuously so, in the same manner and for the same reasons that the *branloire* is *perenne*

7. I adapt and expand Frame's rendering of these two sentences ("The lines of my painting do not go astray . . . The world is but a perennial movement") in order to accommodate the metaphoric power of the words *forvoyent* and *branloire*.

8. See Edmond Huguet, *Dictionnaire de la langue française au XVIè siècle*, s.v. *branloire*. Both Trechmann and Cohen translate *branloire* as "see-saw"; Fausta Garavini, likewise, gives "altalena."

(=eternal, immutable, perpetual). Even *passage,* a lowly and relativistic word by contrast with the august, absolute *estre,* assumes positive resonance from the way it is expanded contextually. Rather than completely adversative, *passage,* when translated into a temporal rather than a movemental code, relates to *estre* as becoming to being, as process to product (*Werden* and *devenir,* in the philosophers' language).[9] Man, like the world in which he moves, is part of what Montaigne was to call with elaborate praise a (b) *condition mixte* (III:xiii, 1087):

> (b) C'est un contrerolle de divers et muables accidens et d'imaginations irresoluës et, quand il y eschet, contraires; soit que je sois autre moy-mesme, soit que je saisisse les subjects par autres circonstances et considerations. Tant y a que je me contredits bien à l'adventure, mais la verité, comme disoit Demades, je ne la contredy point. [805]

> This is a record of various and changeable occurrences, and of irresolute and, when it so befalls, contradictory ideas: whether I am different myself, or whether I take hold of my subjects in different circumstances and aspects. So, all in all, I may indeed contradict myself now and then; but truth, as Demades said, I do not contradict. [611]

This last sentence, of course, is but another, more aggressive way of saying that the features in the portrait, although they change and vary, do not "stray from the original." Contradiction here is but a hyperbolic form of variety, an extreme statement or an exaggerated version of difference. Within the confines of human instability and cosmic flux, Montaigne makes a valid claim to sameness, coherency and wholeness. The self-portrait is accurate because it is mutable, it is true to life because it is contradictory.

The opening page of *Du repentir* may indeed be read, as many critics want to read it, as an exposition of Montaigne's "ideas" concerning human nature or as an elaboration of the "theme of inconstancy."[10] When viewed from the angle of its specific contextual function, however, as opposed to its presumed ideological intention, this development serves to prepare and organize a muted but exultant tribute to a rare kind of wholeness that is not incompatible with lowness, inconsistency, or deviance:

> (b) Je propose une vie basse et sans lustre, c'est tout un. On attache aussi bien toute la philosophie morale à une vie populaire et privée que à une vie

9. Thus, Gougenheim and Schuhl, p. 65. They also see in the expression *de sept ans en sept ans* an allusion to the Hippocratic theory of the "seven ages of man," best known to readers of English from the passage in Shakespeare's *As You Like It,* II:vii, 143–66.

10. See, for example, McGowan (above, n. 6), p. 53 and Richard A. Sayce, *The Essays of Montaigne: a Critical Exploration* (London: Weidenfeld and Nicolson, 1972), pp. 99, 109.

de plus riche estoffe; chaque homme porte la forme entiere de l'humaine condition. [805]

I set forth a humble and inglorious life; that does not matter. You can tie up all moral philosophy with a common and private life just as well as with a life of richer stuff. Each man bears the entire form of the human condition. [611]

This passage, perhaps the most celebrated in all of Montaigne, has the effect of reversing the thrust of the seminal first sentence of the essay in which it appears. The words *Je propose une vie basse et sans lustre* rewrite and, in the end, replace the original description of the essayist's undertaking: *je le recite et en represente* (= *Je propose*) *un particulier bien mal formé* (= *une vie basse et sans lustre*). What had been described as valueless has been valorized. The humble, lusterless life that is now advanced by way of synecdoche as representative of mankind in its totality, projects a series of qualities, parallel to its faults, that are both consistent with them and compensation for them: my self-portrait, says Montaigne, is shifting but continuous, deviant but dynamic, contradictory but true, common but typical, undistinguished but complete. In this essay about repentance, my life, my being and my writing constitute a *felix culpa*; its every defect is balanced and redeemed by a contingent virtue.

In a post–1588 edition, Montaigne carries his rewriting of the *incipit* one step farther and makes the turnabout complete:

(c) Les autheurs se communiquent au peuple par quelque marque particu-liere et estrangere; moy, le premier, par mon estre universel, comme Michel de Montaigne, non comme grammairien, ou poete, ou juriscon-sulte. Si le monde se plaint de quoy je parle trop de moy, je me plains de quoy il ne pense seulement pas à soy. [805]

Authors reveal themselves to the public by some special extrinsic mark;[11] I am the first to do so by my entire being, as Michel de Montaigne, not as a

11. None of the current English translations does justice to *Les autheurs se communiquent au peuple:* "Authors communicate with the world" (Cohen), "Authors communicate with the people" (Frame), "Authors communicate themselves to the world" (Trechmann). Trechmann, who acknowledges the existence of the reflexive pronoun *se,* comes close to the nuance that is correctly conveyed by Garavini's "Gli autori *se presentano* al popolo." This is an archaic use of *se communiquer* in the sense of "se donner, se rendre accessible" (Huguet, *Dictionnaire,* s.v.). In Montaigne's context, this expression is relayed by the synonyms, *me rendre public* and *je produise au monde* (805). In Robert's *Dictionnaire de la langue française, se communiquer,* listed as "rare," is defined as "se confier, se livrer, s'ouvrir, parler," with this example from Montesquieu: "Je me communique fort peu," which might be translated as "I keep pretty much to myself."

grammarian or a poet or a jurist. If the world complains that I speak too
much of myself, I complain that it does not even think of itself. [611]

The opposition *Les autres forment/je . . . recite,* from which Montaigne's
initial self-depreciating argument had been generated, undergoes a double
transformation: *Les auteurs/moi,* followed by the similarly marked antithesis *Le monde/je.* But this is not all. It is now the others who are presented
as partial, marginally inauthentic, tarnished, as it were, by *quelque marque
particuliere et estrangere;* it is now the narrating *Moi* that speaks in the
name of integrity and generality *(estre universel < forme entiere).* Inferior
has become superior and vice-versa; *Les auteurs* are deficient, *I* am
complete. In yet another inverted derivation from the *incipit,* the words *je
parle . . . de moi* (< *je le recite*) are delivered of all negative associations,
coupled as they are here, as effect to cause, with the idea of thought. I write
about myself and from the depths of my selfhood because I am a thinking
man. Self-scrutiny—the very condition, by the way, of repentance—
generates a higher level of discourse than the mere transmission of
knowledge or the establishment of moral norms. The relaxed, casual *oratio*
that I practice in this essay, Montaigne implies, is the expression of surer,
more fundamental *ratio.*

However emphatic or persuasive they may appear, Montaigne's affirmations, like his hesitations, are never sustained, at least not in the short
run. His narrative and rhetorical strategy inevitably involves him in a
counter-process of qualification and withdrawal, if only temporary, in the
course of which the original doubts or the original certainties are brought
once again into tandem in such a way as to produce, often within a very
small interval, a second and more comprehensive set of assertions. This is
exactly what happens in the passage that begins:

> (b) Mais est-ce raison que, si particulier en usage, je pretende me rendre
> public en cognoissance? Est-il aussi raison que je produise au monde, où la
> façon et l'art ont tant de credit et de commandement, des effects de nature
> crus et simples, et d'une nature encore bien foiblette? [805]

> But is it reasonable that I, so fond of privacy in actual life, should aspire to
> publicity in the knowledge of me? Is it reasonable too that I should set forth
> to the world, where fashioning and art have so much credit and authority,
> some crude and simple products of nature, and of a very feeble nature at
> that? [611]

The redundancy of this passage is complete: *La façon et l'art* throw back to
Les autres forment l'homme and *façonner de nouveau,* just as *crus, simples*

and *foiblette* relay and replay the deficiency theme launched by *bien mal formé*. Similarly, the synonymous verb forms *me rendre public* and *produise au monde* stand on the same semantic line as the expressions *je parle trop de moy, se communiquent au peuple, je propose une vie, mon histoire* and ultimately, at its origin, *je le recite*. Once again, however, true to the characteristic undulating diversity of his argument, Montaigne reclaims for his book the positive status that he appeared to be in the process of trading away, as he now prepares to undermine anew the foregoing supposition of lowness and proceeds to revalorize what he has just devalued: although my book lacks learning and artistry, it offers a plenitude not found in any other; no man has ever known his subject better than I, no man has ever treated it more thoroughly, or spoken of himself as openly or faithfully. It is the power of Montaigne's exclusions *(jamais homme, jamais aucun)* and his comparatives *(plus avant, plus particulierement, plus exactement, plus sincere, plus de liberté)* to infuse the dry bones of his lexicon and syntax with the full semantic substance of the crucial expressions *estre universel*, and *forme entiere:* my discourse is artless but exhaustive, common but consistent, I describe myself crudely but completely.

This latest undulation rises to a new crest that is marked graphically by the sentence: (b) "Icy, nous allons conformément et tout d'un trein, mon livre et moy" (806). ["In this case we go hand in hand and at the same pace, my book and I (611–12).] I am *mal formé*, inadequate, imperfect, different from the way I ought to be; so is my inartistic, haphazard book, whose only redeeming feature is to have been written in strictest conformity with its model:

> (b) Ailleurs, on peut recommander et assurer l'ouvrage à part de l'ouvrier; icy, non: qui touche l'un, touche l'autre. [806]

> In other cases one may commend or blame the work apart from the workman; not so here; he who touches the one, touches the other. [612]

The unspoken message here, which fairly bursts out of the sequence of juxtapositions *livre/moi, ouvrage/ouvrier, l'un/l'autre*, is one of identity, continuity, coherency. This writer, although deficient in the standard virtues, claims as his sole but inimitable distinction a symbiotic relation to his subject. Both are ill-formed, but both are true to the same inner form, both are representations of the same original. In this light, the sentence: *Icy, nous allons conformément . . . mon livre et moy* will be perceived as an emphatic transformation of the earlier: *Or les traits de ma peinture ne forvoyent point.* But with this new wrinkle: if book and man go hand in hand together in this happy conformity, it is also given as true, (although the reader has not yet been told in just what way this truth obtains) that the human sample incorporated by the author in his book carries within it *la forme entiere de l'humaine condition,* and displays an exemplary humanity.

Several pages later, in an entirely different context, Montaigne has occasion to rephrase in almost identical language the paradoxical relationship on which this essay and the book of *Essais* are founded. We are all alike, the small and the great. *C'est tout un.* Not even the most marvellous of men are admired by their wives and servants; familiarity breeds contempt:

(c) Nul a esté prophete non seulement en sa maison, mais en son païs, dict l'experience des histoires. De mesmes aux choses de neant. Et en ce bas exemple se void l'image des grands. [808–09]

No man has been a prophet, not merely in his own house, but in his own country, says the experience of history. Likewise in things of no importance. And in this humble example you may see an image of greater ones. [614]

What follows is a detailed and complex illustration of the way(s) in which the *vie basse et sans lustre* typifies the human condition. The example, both humble and ambiguous, is this: in Gascony where I live and where people know me, my writing is considered a joke *(on tient pour drolerie de me veoir imprimé)*; elsewhere they take my book more seriously, or, to invoke Montaigne's left-handed and self-serving insult, I may just be, then again, the proverbial prophet who happens to live in the wrong country. The principal thrust of this example, however, has essentially little to do with Montaigne himself or with his literary reputation. He advances his *bas exemple* in this post–1588 insertion in retrospective support of the proposition, developed at length in the (b) text, that the same phenomenon will look different depending on whether it is viewed from within or from without. At issue here and in what follows is a studied contrast between surface and substance, appearance and reality. How seldom in human affairs does external performance reflect inner being. His own example now gives rise, as Montaigne had promised, to a greater one. An important public figure quits his functions and his robes and is escorted home by a cheering crowd: (b) "il en retombe d'autant plus bas qu'il s'estoit plus haut monté; au dedans, chez luy, tout est tumultuaire et vile" (809). ["the higher he has hoisted himself, the lower he falls back; inside, in his home, everything is tumultuous and vile" (614).]

As we are led from outside to inside—*chez luy* can be referred both to the man's residence and his private life or innermost self—as high becomes low and splendor becomes misery, Montaigne's humble example begins to loom far larger in retrospect than when it was first advanced.[12] In words that pointedly evoke his own *bas exemple*, he goes on now to specify that the orderly, ceremonious demeanor of those in public life often covers over a horrible disarray, immediately visible in their (b) *actions basses et privées* ["humble private actions"]. Besides, "order" is a (b) *vertu morne et sombre* ["a dull and somber virtue"], far less striking and appealing than the (b) *actions esclatantes* ["dazzling actions"] that are involved in winning battles and governing nations. The more outwardly brilliant, so the paradox develops, the less inwardly worthy. Or, to put it the other way around—this time with all the support of Aristotle's prestige—private individuals (c) "rise higher . . . in the service of virtue than those in authority" *(plus hautement . . . que . . . ceux qui sont en magistrats)*. Alexander the Great, in this respect can hardly hold a candle to the lowly Socrates:

> (b) Et la vertu d'Alexandre me semble representer assez moins de vigueur en son theatre, que ne fait celle de Socrates en cette exercitation basse et obscure. Je conçois aisément Socrates en la place d'Alexandre; Alexandre en celle de Socrates, je ne puis. [809]

> And Alexander's virtue seems to me to represent much less vigor on his stage[13] than does that of Socrates in his lowly and obscure activity. I can easily imagine Socrates in Alexander's place; Alexander in that of Socrates, I cannot. [614]

At this point, the foregoing series of tautological polarities—outside/inside, high/low, brilliant/somber, public/private, orderly/tumultuous, noble/vile—is subsumed in the proper names, Alexander the Great and Socrates, the man of action par excellence and the archetypal man of contemplation. The confrontation of these two quasi-mythical figures transposes into the register of ancient heroism the paradox that had been advanced at the beginning of this development, in modern workaday terms, with the examples of Montaigne as unrecognized prophet and of the public

12. In Montaigne's discourse the word *chez* often signalizes a powerful domiciliary metaphor, which is used in *Du repentir* to illustrate the activity of the *forme maistresse*. The quality of our souls (*les ames vicieuses/vertueuses*) must be judged *quand elles sont chez elles, si quelque fois elles y sont* (810) ["when they are at home, if ever they are," 615]; *je me trouve quasi tousjours en ma place . . . Si je ne suis chez moy, j'en suis tousjours bien pres* (811) [("I am nearly always in place . . . If I am not at home, I am always very near it," 615).] The entire essay *De mesnager sa volonté* (III:1 is built around this metaphor. See Brody, *Lectures*, pp. 28 ff.
13. Frame's "in his theater" (of activity?) sacrifices an important figure.

eminence whose private life is a bleak shambles, or, to focus on the specifics of Montaigne's language, whose impressive qualities fall from him the minute he doffs his official garb: (b) *il laisse avec sa robbe ce rolle* ["He drops his part with his gown."] By virtue of this histrionic metaphor, Montaigne invites the attentive reader to equate Alexander *en son theatre*, strutting vainly across the *theatrum mundi*, with the robed magistrate or politician marching home exultantly to the applause of the servile crowd.[14] Once this connection has been made, a second equation, parallel to the one that identifies Alexander with the magistrate/politician, imposes itself upon our attention, an equation built on the inverse paradigm: low = high, small = great, dark = bright. Montaigne's statement *Je propose une vie basse et sans lustre* (= *obscure*), which had appeared at first glance to be entirely self-referential and at least marginally pejorative, emerges in retrospect as the complete proleptic model for the *exercitation basse et obscure* (= *sans lustre*) of Socrates (cf. *l'ordre est une vertu . . . sombre*). Each, standing as he does at the center of the same descriptive system, becomes the allomorphic double of the other;[15] each in his way—Socrates with respect to Alexander *(Je conçois aisément Socrates en la place d'Alexandre*, etc.), Montaigne with respect to Socrates—illustrates to perfection and with equal pertinence the apparently anodyne comment that seemed, when we first heard it, to apply to Montaigne alone: (c) *en ce bas exemple se void l'image des grands.* "I," proclaims Montaigne by verbal indirection, "I, *mutatis mutandis*, am Socrates."

In terms of Montaigne's original argument, the equation *low* = *high* brings with it one further corollary: as the common locus of his own *exercitation basse et obscure* and Alexander's *actions esclatantes*, the image of Socrates, in keeping with his mythic Silenic nature, superimposes itself once again on Montaigne's "self-portrait"; it can and, indeed, it will be said in so many words of this masterpiece of ambiguity that he too carries within him "the entire form of the human condition." This much is at least implicit in the maxim that Montaigne invented expressly for the purpose of representing for his reader the epitome of Socratic wisdom: ask Alexander what he knows how to do, he will say: *"Subjuguer le monde"* [" 'Subdue the world' "]; put the same question to Socrates, he will reply: (b) *"Mener*

14. On the preceding page, the motif of the world-as-stage had already been brought into view: *Chacun peut avoir part au battelage et representer un honneste personnage en l'eschaffaut, mais au dedans et en sa poictrine*, 808, etc. ["Any man can play his part in the side show and represents a worthy man on the boards; but to be disciplined within, in his own bosom, etc." 613].]

15. I use the term "descriptive system" as defined and illustrated by Michael Riffaterre, *The Semiotics of Poetry* (Bloomington, Ind.: Indiana University Press, 1978), pp. 39–46.

l'humaine vie conformément à sa naturelle condition" [" 'Lead the life of man in conformity with its natural condition.' "] In its immediate impact, this pseudo-Socratic gnomic version of the *exercitation basse et obscure,* replicates, by reshuffling them in another order, the essential components in Montaigne's earlier defense and valorization of his own *vie basse et sans lustre: chaque homme porte la forme entiere* (= *"Mener . . . conforme-ment) de l'humaine condition* (= *l' humaine vie, naturelle condition"*). All lives, mine and Socrates', the humble and the glorious alike, are equal and complete in that they all obey the same essential pattern. My lowly and obscure existence, Montaigne had been proclaiming before the fact, bears the same stamp of humanity as does the life of Socrates. In a way that is perhaps less obvious, Socrates' attributed credo concerning the good life coincides at the word *conformément* with Montaigne's avowed credo as a writer: *Icy, nous allons conformément . . . mon livre et moy.* Although it is less than completely congruent, this additional superimposition may be taken to imply something along these lines: my book bears the same relation to my own nature as does Socrates' behavior to universal human nature; in both cases existence mirrors essence. Man and book will look the same whether viewed from within or from without; what you see is what there is. In the course of repeated re-readings, however, these two isolated occurrences of the word *conformément,* along with the two superficially disparate utterances in which that word appears, will sooner or later conflate in our memory of the text's details as an anticipation of a subsequent statement in which the subterranean assertion, "I am Socrates," comes at long last into sharp focus: (b) *"Mes actions sont reglées et conformes à ce que je suis et à ma condition."* (813). ["My actions are in order and conformity with what I am and with my condition," (617).] Here, the Socratic paradigm, recapitulated metonymically by the words *con-formes* and *condition,* has been fully absorbed into the so-called "self-portrait" and vice versa. My life exhibits the same dignity and coherency as the life of Socrates, he whose wisdom I earlier summed up in the motto: *"Mener l'humaine vie conformément à sa naturelle condition."*

So tight is the verbal web in which Montaigne wraps these two allomorphic, exemplary lives that any significant word common to their shared descriptive system is capable of symbolizing and communicating the entire unspoken message: "I am Socrates." The word *reglées* provides a particularly handy and striking example. A bit farther down on the page where we met the expression *actions reglées et conformes,* etc., we read the following reflection by Montaigne on his *deportemens* ["behavior"] as a young man: (b) *je les ai ay communément conduits avec ordre, selon mov* (813) ["I have generally conducted myself in orderly fashion, according to my lights," [617]. In this utterly tautological observation, *ordre* supplants the earlier *reglées*, just as *selon moy* replicates *conformes à ce que je suis et à ma condition.* This intersection of the ideas "order" and "conformity," which stands at the very heart of the equation Montaigne = Socrates, will bring us right back, along the same line of force that led us through the sequence *conformément . . . mon livre et mov* > *conformément à sa naturelle condition* > *conformes à . . . ma condition,* to that seminal page where Alexander and the magistrate, Socrates and Montaigne were counterposed in antithetical pairs representing the inverse relationships: lowness = greatness, darkness = light. In the magistrate's interior (= home and/or soul) everything, we recall, was *tumultuaire;* there was no *reglement* in his *actions basses et privées.* How could there be? For *l'ordre est une vertu morne et sombre* (= *sans lustre* = *obscure,* typical of "lowly" people like me and Socrates); the *éclat* of his actions is all superficial, with no correlation between outer and inner, no connection between what he does and what he is. This notion of organic "conformity," although contained in *in nuce* in the predominant semes of *reglement* and *ordre* (= consistency, coherency, continuity), will not fully claim our attention until it surfaces as the consummate jewel in the Socratic crown: *"Mener l'humaine vie conformément a l'humaine condition,"* where the word *conformément* turns out to be synonymous, *ante litteram,* with *ordonnéement* and antonymous with *haut: Le pris de l'ame ne consiste pas à aller haut,* Montaigne now concludes, *mais ordonnéement* (809) ["The value of the soul consists not in flying high but in an orderly pace,"] (614).

The "philological circle," to evoke Leo Spitzer's picturesque but astonishingly accurate expression, is now complete.[16] It also becomes apparent at this point that we could have begun our search for the thematic constants in *Du repentir* by following out any single one of its several redundancies; whatever the initial choice, whatever detail had first happened to attract our attention or arouse our curiosity, whether we had started our reading with the word *condition, conformément, bas, haut, sombre, ordre,* or *lustre* the terminal point would have coincided inevitably with the point of departure. The philological circularity of Montaigne's writing is in fact so relentless and so total that it will take us back and forth through the same semantic fields whether we read cursively, as everyone was obliged to do before the existence of the modern critical editions or

16. Spitzer, *Linguistics and Literary History* (Princeton, N.J.: Princeton University Press, 1948), p. 25.

vertically, as it is now possible to do, charting the progressive stages in Montaigne's layering of his text. In this respect, the passage at hand on Socratic "conformity" is particularly illuminating. In a post–1588 addition, the polarity *aller haut/ordonnéement* gives rise to a lengthy tautological expansion of the earlier Socrates/Alexander confrontation:

> (b) Le pris de l'ame ne consiste pas à aller haut, mais ordonnéement. (c) Sa *grandeur* ne s'exerce pas en la *grandeur*, c'est en la *mediocrité*. Ainsi que ceux qui nous jugent et touchent au *dedans*, ne font pas grand recette de la *lueur* de noz actions *publiques* et voyent que ce ne sont que filets et pointes *d'eau fine* rejaillies d'un *fond* au demeurant *limonneux* et *poisant*, en pareil cas, ceux qui nous jugent par cette brave *apparance*, concluent de mesmes de nostre constitution *interne* . . . [809–10]

> The value of the soul consists not in flying high, but in an orderly pace. Its greatness is exercised not in greatness, but in modesty.[17] As those who judge and touch us inwardly make little account of the brilliance of our public acts, and see that these are only thin streams and jets of water spurting from a bottom otherwise muddy and thick; so likewise those who judge us by this fine appearance draw similar conclusions about our inner constitution . . . [614]

Although Alexander and Socrates have disappeared from view, the antithetical kinds of *grandeur* symbolized by their respective names remain opposed to each other and defined in terms of the presence or absence of an unstated, hypogrammatical relationship between external deportment and inner being; each of the italicized words in the foregoing quotation figures in a sequence that illustrates one or the other of these polarities, both as they were previously described in the original text and as they are developed in the later insertion. In addition to continuing the contrasts from inner to outer and light to dark, reinforced by parallel comparisons between water and mud, thinness and thickness, the passage before us points back to Montaigne's earlier argument in an even more concrete and compelling way: the single word *s'exerce* locates the exact point of articulation between the (b) and (c) textual layers in such a way as to remind the reader

---

17.   Frame translates *mediocrité* as "mediocrity"; Trechmann gives "a middle state" and Cohen an "intermediate state"; I prefer "modesty" as a meeting-ground for the cluster of positive and contextually pertinent notions: measure, awareness, order and control. In sixteenth- and seventeenth-century French, *mediocrité* is often neutral (= average, medium); but never pejorative; as an affirmative value it is associated with the *aurea mediocritas* or golden mean; Huguet, s.v., defines it as a "juste milieu." Gougenheim-Schuhl (p. 95) gloss *mediocrité* as "la condition moyenne qui est celle de l'homme privé." At the end of this passage, I substitute "fine appearance" for Frame's unnecessarily ambiguous "brave appearance."

with renewed insistence that Socrates' *exercitation basse et obscure,* and Montaigne's *vie basse et sans lustre* along with it, is to be understood as signifying the opposite of what it seems to say.[18] Montaigne's casual and marginally pejorative "self-portrait," like his parallel, low-keyed moral portrait of Socrates, must be read, inversely, as a militant statement of unity, coherency and harmony: *les traits de ma peinture ne forvoyent point; nous allons conformément et tout d'un trein, mon livre et moy . . . qui touche l'un, touche l'autre; mes actions sont reglées et conformes à ce que je suis et à ma condition.* As I live, so do I write, in strict observance of the Socratic model: *"Mener l'humaine vie conformement à l'humaine condition."*

Unlike those other authors who reveal themselves only partially, or those people whose behavior masks or belies the real self, Montaigne/ Socrates presents only one face, a composite shape that always appears the same, viewed from within as from without. We all have but *one* form to which, inevitably, we must con-form; to do otherwise, to repent or to re-form is to betray, to de-form our *forme maitresse,* one of Montaigne's several equivalent periphrases, along with *humaine condition, condition naturelle,* and *constitution interne,* for the idea of "human nature."[19] Or, in the terms of an alternate version of the *re-form/de-form* identity, to live unrepentant is to live "uniformly," according to the same inner *forme* in youth as in age, in public as in private, in the present and future as in the past:

> (c) Je ne me suis pas attendu d'attacher monstrueusement la queuë d'un philosophe à la teste et au corps d'un homme perdu; ny que ce chetif bout eust à desadvouer et desmentir la plus belle, entiere et longue partie de ma vie. Je me veux presenter et faire veoir par tout *uniformément.* Si j'avois à revivre, je revivrois comme j'ay vescu; ny je ne pleins le passé, ny je ne crains l'advenir. Et si je ne me deçoy, il est allé du *dedans* environ comme du *dehors.* C'est une des principales obligations que j'aye à ma fortune, que le cours de mon estat corporel ayt esté conduit chasque chose en sa saison. J'en ay veu l'herbe et les fleurs et le fruit; et en vois la secheresse. Heureusement, puisque c'est naturellement. [816]

18.   There is a similar doubleness in the language that Montaigne uses to extend his praise of Socratic "modesty." Note how the sentence, *ainsi que ceux qui nous jugent et touchent au dedans,* etc. echoes Montaigne's earlier comment on the conformity between his book and himself: *qui touche l'un, touche l'autre* (806): with me, as with Socrates, outer and inner are one, behavior mirrors character.

19.   See above, n. 2.

I have made no effort to attach, monstrously, the tail of a philosopher to the head and body of a dying man;[20] or that this sickly remainder of my life should disavow and belie its fairest, longest, and most complete part. I want to present and show myself uniformly throughout. If I had to live over again, I would live as I have lived. I have neither tears for the past nor fears for the future. And unless I am fooling myself, it has gone about the same within me as without. It is one of the chief obligations I have to my fortune that my bodily state has run its course with each thing in due season. I have seen the grass, the flower, and the fruit; now I see the dryness—happily, since it is naturally. [619–20]

This passage is built on a series of studied oppositions between two groups of polarized words denoting conformity, consistency, uniformity, continuity and wholeness on the one hand *(teste/corps, belle, entiere, longue, uniformément)*, and disjunction, contradiction, fragmentation and disparity on the other *(queue, chetif, bout, desadvouer, desmentir)*. The passage is bounded at either end, moreover, by two adverbs of manner, each of which subsumes completely one of these polar sequences: *monstrueusement*, in its standard, older sense of "unnaturally," "contrary to the way of nature," and its antonym, *naturellement*. These two words, in turn, point contextually to a deeper cleavage and focus attention once again on the ubiquitous latent equation: *re-form = de-form*. In the unreformed, life, by contrast, *dedans* and *dehors*, *passé* and *avenir* will be contained together in a well-formed, undifferentiated unit; conducted with integrity and in conformity with "nature," this unrepentant life, described also as a relentless march forward, comparable to the revolutions of the seasons *(le cours de mon estat corporel*, etc.), represents in microcosm the larger dispensation that Montaigne had alluded to a page earlier as (b) *le grand cours de l'univers et . . . l'encheineure des causes Stoïques* (815) ["the great stream of the universe and . . . the chain of Stoical causes," (619).] My life, all life is one; what has once been done can neither be undone nor redone. The flow of time, the movement from youth to age, the passage of the seasons, the laws that govern the cosmic order, all the manifestations of Nature, in a word, proclaim the same subjacent message of unbroken and unbreakable unity.

This message, which was apparent in Montaigne's first uses of *forme* and its compounds, traverses *Du repentir* under a number of guises in such a

20. Frame renders *un homme perdu* as "a dissipated man." Although *perdu* can carry overtones of moral decline or "perdition," the dominant sense here has more to do with mortality than morality. Cf. the cliché *le malade est perdu = sa mort est certaine.* (Robert).

way as to saturate the text from beginning to end with words, images, expressions and constructions denoting the ideas of coherency, similarity, integrity, regularity, consistency, continuity, harmony and their opposites. So fundamental, so powerful and pervasive is this hypogrammatic constant that it may be discerned in the most desultory, seemingly insignificant details and traced from them through the essay's length along any one of several lexical axes. In the text just quoted, where Montaigne vaunts his "unrepentant uniformity," it might be observed further that the words *desadvouer* and *desmentir* stand on a continuous semantic/thematic line which attracts to it, like metal particles to a magnetic rod, a cluster of other words, also built on the Latin *de-* prefix, whose function in the essay is to develop some aspect of the matricial *de-formity/con-formity* opposition:

I.   (b) On peut *desavouër* et *desdire* les vices qui nous surprennent . . . Le repentir n'est qu'une *desditte* de nostre volonté . . . qui nous *pour-mene à tout sens*. Il faict *desadvouër* à celui-là sa vertu passée et sa CONTINENCE . . . C'est une vie exquise, celle qui se MAINTIENT en ORDRE jusques en son privé . . . Chacun peut . . . representer un honneste personnage en l'eschaffaut, mais au dedans et en sa poictrine . . . d'y estre REGLÉ, c'est le poinct. Le voisin degré c'est de l'estre EN SA MAISON . . . [808]

We can disown and retract vices that take us by surprise . . . Repentance is nothing but a disavowal of our will . . . which leads us about in all directions. It makes this man disavow his past virtue and his continence. . . It is a rare life that remains well ordered even in private. Any man can represent a worthy man on the boards; but to be disciplined within, in his own bosom . . . —that's the point. The next step to that is to be so in your own house . . . [613]

II. (b) CONVERSER AVEC les siens et AVEC soymesme . . . ne *relacher* point, ne se *desmentir* poinct, c'est chose plus rare . . . [809]

to deal . . . with our households and ourselves, not to let ourselves go, not to be false to ourselves, that is a rarer matter . . . [614]

III. (b) De moy . . . je me trouve quasi tousjours EN MA PLACE . . . Si je ne suis CHEZ MOY, j'en suis tousjours BIEN PRÈS. Mes *débauches* ne m'emportent pas *loing*.

For my part . . . I am nearly always in place . . . If I am not at home, I am always very near it. My excesses do not carry me very far away. [615]

IV. (b) Je fay coustumierement entier ce que je fay et MARCHE TOUT
D'UNE PIECE; je n'ay guere de mouvement qui se cache et *desrobe* à
ma raison et qui ne se CONDUISE . . . par le CONSENTEMENT de
toutes mes parties . . . Et en matiere d'opinions universelles, dés
l'enfance je me LOGEAY au poinct où j'avois à me TENIR. [812]

I customarily do wholeheartedly whatever I do, and go my way all in
one piece. I rarely experience a desire that eludes or escapes my
awareness,[21] and that is not guided more or less by the consent of all
parts of me . . . And in the matter of general opinions, in childhood I
established myself in the position where I was to remain. [616]

V. (b) je puis condamner et me *desplaire* de ma FORME UNIVERSELLE
. . . Mais cela, je ne le doits nommer repentir . . . non plus que le
desplaisir de n'estre ny Ange, ny Caton. Mes actions sont REGLÉES et
CONFORMES à ce que je suis et à ma CONDITION. [813]

I may condemn and dislike my nature as a whole . . . But this I ought
not to call repentance . . . any more than my displeasure at being
neither an angel nor Cato. My actions are in order and conformity with
what I am and with my condition. [617]

VI. (c) les raisons *estrangeres* peuvent servir à m'appuyer, mais peu à me
destourner . . . Selon moy, ce ne sont que mousches et atomes qui
promeinent ma volonté . . . [814]

other peoples' reasons can serve to support me, but seldom to deter me
. . . If you ask me, they are nothing but flies and atoms that distract my
will. [618]

VII. (c) me laissant là, on faict selon ma profession qui est de m'ESTABLIR et
CONTENIR tout EN MOY: ce m'est plaisir d'estre *desinteressé* des
affaires d'autruy et *desgagé* de leur gariement. [814–15]

by leaving me alone, they treat me according to my professed
principle, which is to be wholly contained and established
within myself. To me it is a pleasure not to be concerned in

21. For *je n'ay guere de mouvement*, etc. Frame translates: "I scarcely make a motion that
is hidden and out of sight of my reason." My preference for "desire" takes account of the fact that
mouvement, a Latinate metaphor, stands for *mouvement de l'âme*, equivalent to the Ciceronian *motus animi*. On this point see my *Lectures*, p. 81. My recourse, in the same sentence, to
"awareness" leads on the implicit distinction between rational and irrational, conscious and
unconscious.

other people's affairs and to be free of responsibility from them. [618]

Whether the individual texts in this series deal specifically with repentance (I; V), keeping to oneself (II), the solicitations of passion and desire (III, IV), heeding other people's advice or involvement in their affairs (VI, VII), they all refer at the level of their deep semantic structure to the phenomenon of *dis-traction* in the etymological sense of that word: a divisive force, located within the self or outside it, that threatens or injures its wholeness by *drawing* it *away* from its rightful, proper or natural place. In each of the foregoing quotations, a kernel *de-* word attracts into its orbit one or more other negative markers, printed in italics, from the semantic fields of dis-junction, di-stance, dis-location and the like. Only when directed outwardly, in protection of the self, as in passage VII, will *de-* words *(desinteressé, degagé)* acquire positive force. By the same token, these same kernel *de-* words generate simultaneously a countervailing series of expressions, printed in capitals, which denote stability, proximity, con-stancy and co-herency. Nor is it by any means an accident that this latter group contains a preponderant number of words built on the Latin prefix *cum: converser*, supported by the double *avec* (= *cum*) (II), *conduise, consentement* (IV), *conformes, condition* (V), *contenir* (VII).[22] It would also be pertinent to observe in this connection that each and every one of the statements in the foregoing cross-sectional anthology may be read as a negative or positive transform, at a lesser or greater degree of removal, of the image of coherency that informs the matricial sentences, *les traits de ma peinture ne forvoyent point* and *nous allons conformément et tout d'un trein, mon livre et moy*: the features in my portrait do not go astray—*forvoyer* (<*fors* = *hors* + *voie*) is, after all, the etymological doublet of *dévier*—they do not de-viate or de-part from the original, they con-form to it.

Sometime after 1588, as Montaigne reread his original reflections on the "conformity" between himself and his book, he was prompted to rewrite this same idea in terms of another conformity, the self-consistency of the impenitent man:

22. The contextual functioning of the *de-* and *cum-* words in *Du repentir* provides a striking example of what Spitzer, in his history of the *concordia discors* topos, has labeled "prefixal leitmotivs." See his *Classical and Christian Ideas of World Harmony: Prologomena to an Interpretation of the word "Stimmung,"* ed. Anna G. Hatcher (Baltimore, Md.: Johns Hopkins Press, 1963), pp. 148–52, 193–94. On Montaigne's treatment of this topic see Robert D. Cottrell, *Sexuality/Textuality: a Study of the Fabric of Montaigne's Essais* (Columbus, Ohio: University of Ohio Press, 1981), pp. 93–95.

(b) Excusons icy ce que je dy souvent, que je me repens rarement (c) et que ma *conscience* se *contente* de soy, non comme la *conscience* d'un ange ou d'un cheval, mais comme la *conscience* d'un homme . . . [806]

Let me here excuse what I often say, that I rarely repent and that my conscience is content with itself—not as the conscience of an angel or of a horse, but as the conscience of a man . . . [612]

In this passage, justly celebrated as quintessential Montaigne, the entire meaning of the essay *Du repentir* is contained in shorthand within the opposition *je me repens*—surrogate for all the *de-* words that saturate the text—and the series of *cum-* words that are generated contextually from the noun *homme* and the concept of "humanity" as a comprehensive middle ground between bestial and angelic, previously indicated by the polarity high/low. This exultant conformity on the part of the (non-repentant) speaking subject between spirit and being may be read as yet another variant of the Socratic model, founded *en la mediocrité* and recapitulated in the maxim *"Mener l'humaine vie conformément à sa naturelle condition."* The rare capacity that is required to conduct one's life "humanly," in self-conscious, self-consistent and self-centered impenitence, defines the kind of mind and character, Socrates' or Montaigne's interchangeably, that are, as we say in the vernacular, "with it"; to live in conformity with one's natural condition is, in a word, to get or to have it all "together," or less elegantly still, to be a "together" person.

This, in Montaigne's idiolect, is the precise force of the adjective *entier:*

Je fay coustumierement *entier* ce que je fay et marche tout d'une piece; je n'ay guere de mouvement qui se cache et desrobe à ma raison, et qui ne se conduise à peu près par le consentement de toutes mes parties, sans division, sans sedition intestine; mon jugement en a la coulpe ou la louange entiere et la coulpe qu'il a une fois, il l'a tousjours, car quasi dès sa naissance il est un: mesme inclination, mesme route, mesme force. Et en matiere d'opinions universelles, dès l'enfance je me logeay au poinct où j'avois à me tenir. [812]

I customarily do wholeheartedly whatever I do, and go my way all in one piece. I rarely experience a desire that eludes or escapes my awareness and that is not guided more or less by the consent of all parts of me, without division, without internal sedition. My judgment takes all the blame or all the praise for it; and the blame it once takes, it always keeps, for virtually since its birth it has been one; the same inclination, the same road, the same strength. And in the matter of general opinions, in childhood I established myself in the position where I was to remain. [616]

This passage, which we already had occasion to note as a prime locus of *de-* and *cum-* words, provides a striking example of Montaigne's characteristic way of developing and reinforcing an idea by means of the kind of tautological derivation normally associated with "poetic" composition.[23] There is no lexical item here, down to the anaphoric utility words *sans* and *mesme*, that does not propel forward the predominant seme of *entier* in its root sense of "integrity" or indivisibility.[24] The word *entier*, bracketed by the redundant *Je fay/je fay*, launches a powerful assertion of wholeness *qua* sameness; in the sentences that follow, this assertion will be underscored by a battery of synonymous expressions, each of which illuminates an aspect of integrity or division as a moral category: *tout d'une piece > toutes mes parties > sans ... sans > louange entiere > tousjours > un > mesme ... mesme ... mesme ... This sequence speaks to the same end as Montaigne's parallel description of his psychic life as a continuous journey, that may be represented in skeletal fashion as follows: marche > mouvement > conduise > inclination > route.* At the word *mouvement*, however, there occurs a notable semantic bifurcation. This "movement" derives its surface meaning from the word *marche*, but by its double opposition first to *raison* and then to *jugement*, it soon becomes identified as the standard periphrasis for feeling, impulse or desire, as in the stock expression *mouvement de l'âme*, the usual translation of the Latin cliché *motus animi*. In its new metaphoric capacity (= deviance from conscious, rational control), the word *mouvement* generates the redundant series: *desrobe > division > sedition [< sed + ire =* "to go one's separate way," "deviate"] > *inclination.* At the word *intestine*, moreover, the affirmed collusion between reason and passion acquires the additional resonance outer/inner; this polarity will be transposed, in turn, beginning with *tousjours*, into temporal code as a continuity between before and after, youth and age. From their earliest origins, my judgmental faculty *(dès sa naissance)* and my general outlook *(dès l'enfance)* were complete, formed in their entirety as they were to remain to this day. Of one as of the other, Montaigne can now say, in a further retake of *Je fay ... entier: il est un.* Finally, with the equivalence *logeay = tenir* the idea of integrity as sameness and self-conformity, expressed now in locative code, precludes even more forcefully the possibility or even the admissibility of any infraction of life's unity or any deviation from its forward course.

With each successive stroke in the "self-portrait" that shifts in and out

23. See Riffaterre, *Semiotics of Poetry*, pp. 20–21 and *passim.*

24. For an illuminating discussion of this motif in the *Essais*, see M. Baraz, "Montaigne et l'idéal de l'homme entier," *O un amy! Essays on Montaigne in Honor of Donald M. Frame*, ed. Raymond La Charité (Lexington, Ky: French Forum, Publishers, 1977), pp. 18–33.

of focus over the pages of this essay, the *particulier bien mal formé* of the opening comes across increasingly as being singularly well-fashioned and marvellously intact. This perception is one of the many satisfactions that will reward the patience of the philological reader. For it is the peculiar power of Montaigne's words to lead us back repeatedly and relentlessly to a constant sub-text that parallels the surface text, in a series of equivalent or complementary versions, in much the same way as the parallel voice lines that make up a musical score. Thus it is that a vital part of the content of *Du repentir*, the subliminal statement, "I am Socrates," is subsumed and fully conveyed by the progression, "I am deficient" *(mal formé)* > "I am whole" *(entier)*.

This claim to integrity and unity is the ultimate destination, the signifying center, at which all the major verbal axes that traverse this essay will inevitably converge. Had we plotted our reading along the line marked out by the occurrences of the word *entier*, our point of arrival would have been the same:

I.   (b) chaque homme porte la FORME *entiere* de l'humaine condition.

II. (b) Il n'est vice veritablement vice qui n'offence, et qu'un jugement *entier* n'accuse; car il a de la laideur et incommodité si apparente, qu'à l'adventure ceux-là ont raison qui disent qu'il est principalement produict par bestise et ignorance. [806]

     There is no vice truly a vice which is not offensive, and which a sound judgment does not condemn; for its ugliness and painfulness is so apparent that perhaps the people are right who say it is chiefly produced by stupidity and ignorance. So hard it is to imagine anyone knowing it without hating it. [612]

III. (b) Je fay coustumierement *entier* ce que je fay et marche tout d'une piece, etc. [812]

     I customarily do wholeheartedly whatever I do, and go my way all in one piece. [616]

IV. (b) Quant à moy, je puis desirer en general estre autre; je puis condamner et me desplaire de ma FORME universelle, et supplier Dieu pour mon *entiere* REFORMATION et pour l'excuse de ma foiblesse naturelle. Mais cela, je ne le doits nommer repentir, ce me semble, non plus que le desplaisir, de n'estre ny Ange, ny Caton. Mes actions sont reglées et CONFORMES à ce que je suis et à ma condition. [813]

As for me, I may desire in a general way to be different; I may condemn and dislike my nature as a whole, and implore God to reform me completely and to pardon my natural weakness. But this I ought not to call repentance, it seems to me, any more than my displeasure at being neither an angel nor Cato. My actions are in order and conformity with what I am and with my condition. [617]

V. (c) Je ne me suis pas attendu d'attacher monstrueusement la queuë d'un philosophe à la teste et au corps d'un homme perdu; ny que ce chetif bout eust à desadvouer et desmentir la plus belle, *entiere* et longue partie de ma vie. Je me veux presenter et faire veoir par tout UNIFORMEMENT. [816]

I have made no effort to attach, monstrously, the tail of a philosopher to the head and body of a dying man; or that this sickly remainder of my life should disavow and belie its fairest, longest, and most complete part. I want to present and show myself uniformly throughout. [619–20]

VI. (b) L'homme marche *entier* vers son croist et vers son décroist. [817]

Man grows and dwindles in his entirety [620]

The first and most immediate fruit of this conspectual *découpage* is a feeling of *déjà vu*. It cannot fail to be obvious now, since three of the six passages reproduced above (I, IV and V) forced themselves on our attention for other reasons, that the word *entier* and the concept of "wholeness" are systematically drawn together, as if in irresistible verbal company, with the prominent family of *forme*-based words. Only the occurrences of *entier* in quotations II and VI seem adventitious and unrelated to any other significant or memorable theme in the essay. The real bearing of the first of these two passages begins to come fully into view, however, once we recognize that those whom Montaigne cites with approval—those who equate vice with "stupidity and ignorance—are none other than the disciples of Socrates; the reference of this ostensibly anodyne statement is clearly to the famous "Socratic paradoxes": virtue is knowledge, vice is ignorance, no one does wrong intentionally, etc.[25] To have a judgment that is "sound" or *entier* is to imitate the "integrity" and approach the moral perfection of Socrates.

25. See E.R. Dodds, *The Greeks and the Irrational* (Berkeley, Cal.: University of California Press, 1971), p. 17; cf. Plato, *Protagoras* 345d, *Gorgias* 509de, *Laws* 731c, 860d.

The appearance of *entier* in conjunction with *marcher* in passage VI speaks to the point of human integrity from a position adjacent to the one taken in passage III. In the earlier instance, Montaigne credits his own inner life with the kind of consistency and coherency that obtain when judgment and feeling operate in unison; on this aspect of the "self-portrait" the maxim *L'homme marche entier vers son croist et vers son décroist* superimposes the larger but complementary vision of human existence in general as a continuum, a relentless progression from life to death. The sixteenth- or seventeenth-century reader, who, like Montaigne, had been nurtured on Latin literature, would have been in a position to see in the provocative antithesis *croist/décroist* a recasting of the Senecan aphorism: *cum crescimus, vita decrescit* ("as we grow up, we grow old," *Ep. ad Luc.* 24: 20).[26] Although not indispensable to a satisfactory decoding of the passage at hand, the perception of this intertext enables us to identify *L'homme marche entier* as a variant in human, physical terms of the relation between past and future events that Montaigne had described earlier as a cosmic and metaphysical dispensation: (b) *les voylà dans le grand cours de l'univers et dans l'enchaineure des causes Stoïques.* Even the reader who does not share Montaigne's cultural code or who misses the specific connection between Seneca, the archetypal Stoic philosopher, and the generalized description of the Stoic world-view, will be able, nonetheless, to react to each of them independently of the other as vehicles of a constant message: the parallel phrases *vers son croist/vers son décroist,* illustrate verbally and syntactically, like the links in the chain of "Stoic causes," the same identity paradigm as the combination *cours/enchaineure.* To die, as I do, unrepentant and unreformed, ever true to the thoughts and values that guided me throughout, Montaigne suggests, is to imitate in one's mental and moral life the very organicity of Nature. The modern reader, who has been sensitive to the several verbal constants that thread their way through this essay, will take the statement *l'homme marche entier* etc., at the very least, as an invitation to reevaluate Montaigne's earlier, casual, presumably self-

26. I happened to stumble upon this reminiscence while looking for something else in Seneca. Montaigne's first readers might easily have encountered the aphorism in the indexes to the editions of Seneca's works or in one of the contemporaneous anthologies or commonplace books where it is routinely cited as an example of the familiar Pauline/Senecan topic of the *mors vitalis.* For example: Erasmus, *Senecae . . . lucubrationes omnes* (Basel, 1515), p. 117; Pierre Grosnet, ed., *Les Authoritez, sentences et singuliers enseignemens . . . [de] Seneque, tant en latin comme en françoys* (Paris, 1534) f° K vii, v° : "lorsque nous croissons nostre vie descroist"; *Epistres de Seneque, traduictes en François, par Pressac* [Montaigne's brother-in-law] (Paris, 1582), p. 80: "à mesure que nous croissons la vie nous descroit." In the 1587 Paris edition of Seneca's complete works, we find this comment in Muret's annotations to the passage in question: "Saepe tractatur hic locus a Seneca" (p. 243, n. 6). I am grateful to my research assistant, Christine Brousseau-Beuermann for having gathered this information.

referential comment: *Je fay coustumierement entier ce que je fay et marche tout d'une piece.* The move, at several pages distance, from *Je fay . . . entier . . . marche* to *L'homme marche entier*—from the anecdotal and the particular to the general and the philosophical—re-enacts and re-valorizes at the close of this essay the liminal and, as it turns out, seminal equation: *une vie basse et sans lustre = la forme entiere de l'humaine condition.* Or: I am Everyman.

This, however, is only part of the final message conveyed by the Senecan maxim. Equal and parallel to it is the implicit proposition: "I am Socrates." As Montaigne reread the first published version of this essay he made the following insertion right after the word *décroist:*

> (c) A voir la sagesse de Socrates en plusieurs circonstances de sa condamnation, j'oseroy croire qu'il s'y presta aucunement luy mesme par prevarication, à dessein, ayant de si près, aagé de soixante et dix ans, à souffrir l'engourdissement des riches allures de son espirit et *l'esblouissement de sa clairté accoustumée.* [817]

> Seeing the wisdom of Socrates and several circumstances of his condemnation, I should venture to believe that he lent himself to it to some extent, purposely, by prevarication, being seventy, and having so soon to suffer an increasing torpor of the rich activity of his mind, and the dimming of its accustomed brightness. [620]

Here, as the italicized words so eloquently proclaim, we are presented with a final modulation of the equation I = Socrates. In this epiphanous vision of Socratic wisdom, Montaigne amplifies one of the earlier variants of his dominant paradox: dark = bright, just as small = great and low = high. The *clarté* of Socrates in his last and finest hours sends the reader back in memory yet one more time to the essay's first page, to the narrator's ambiguously exemplary *vie basse et sans lustre* (805), and from there to its reprise in the equally ambiguous evocation of Socrates' *exercitation basse et obscure.* At this juncture, we see the "philological circle" close once again, and, as we move back from its center to its periphery, from the intratextual reference of Socrates' *clarté* to its contextual reverberations, another network of relationships begins to fall into place. Montaigne's decision to represent Socrates at the moment of his *condamnation (= condamnation à mort)* extends and recapitulates the most prominent associations of the word *décroist:* decline = deterioration = death. The placement at the end of this addition of two further metaphors for death, *engourdissement* and *esblouissement,* works, of course, to the same purpose. In death as in life, Montaigne suggests by indirection, Socrates—like the *homo sene-*

canus, like my humble self—was *entier*, his *croist* and his *décroist* were of a piece. This desire for "integrity" was so intense with Socrates, Montaigne speculates, that he may actually have collaborated in his own conviction *par prevarication*, that is, by refusing to recant (= repent), in order to maintain to the very end, without alteration or decline, in age as in youth, in death as in life, the mental powers and the spiritual qualities *(esprit, clarté)* that were the distinguishing characteristics of his *sagesse* or his *forme maistresse*. The exemplary Socratic *exercitation*, depicted earlier in terms of "con-formity" between outer and inner *("Mener l'humaine vie conformément à sa naturelle condition")* emerges now as a matter of continuity between before and after. And in this respect the *sagesse* attributed to the impenitent Socrates *en plusieurs circonstances de sa condamnation*, the "integration" of his *croist* with his *décroist*, proves to be no more than a redundant version of the "wisdom" that Montaigne claims for himself, twice on the same page. The first of these occurrences is a post–1588 addition, contemporaneous with the insertion concerning *la sagesse de Socrates:*

> (c) Pareillement ma *sagesse* peut bien estre de MESME taille EN L'UN ET EN L'AUTRE TEMPS . . . Je renonce donc à ces reformations casuelles et douloureuses.

> Likewise my wisdom may well have been of the same proportions in one age as in the other . . . Therefore I renounce these casual and painful reformations. [620]

This transposition into temporal code of the *croist/décroist* motif was already present in almost identical language in the original (b) text. I remain now, Montaigne had claimed as if in anticipation of the Socratic example, just as I was then, true to myself, unrepentant, undivided, *entier*. What I say now, I said then; my way, again in anticipation of Socrates' *prevarication*, is to belie the so-called "wisdom" that allows for discontinuity between mind and body and thereby denies human "integrity":

> (b) Je le disois ESTANT JEUNE; lors on me donnoit de mon menton par le nez. Je le dis encores À CETTE HEURE que mon poil (c) gris (b) m'en donne le credit. Nous appellons *sagesse* la difficulté de nos humeurs, le desgoust des choses presentes. [816–17]

> I used to say so when I was young; then they taunted me with my beardless chin. I still say so now that my gray hair gives me authority to speak. We call "wisdom" the difficulty of our humors, our distaste for present things. [620]

Such as I was in my *croist,* thus have I remained in my *décroist.*

The respective *sagesses* of Socrates and Montaigne occupy the high
point and the middle ground in the didactic strategy of *Du repentir.* At the
low end of the scale, this essay presents us with yet another *vie basse et sans
lustre,* which stands in the same relative position to Montaigne as Montaigne to Socrates. This is the person whom Montaigne calls the Thief *(le
larron).* His story, although comprehensible at the point in the essay where
it appears, takes on its fullest meaning when read in retrospect as still
another variant on the paradigm of unrepentant integrity. Born a beggar
[*estant né mandiant*], he soon learned that hard work would never remedy
his plight and decided to become a thief [*il s'advisa de se faire larron*]. He
spent all his vigorous years [*toute sa jeunesse*] reaping other people's
harvests, but took care [*avoit soing*] to equalize the damage by not stealing
inordinate amounts from any individual. Now, in his old age [*en sa
vieillesse*], he openly admits his misdeeds, makes what restitution he can to
the heirs of his victims, and has instructed his own heirs to continue these
payments for as long as is necessary after his death. He is sorry for what he
has done, but since he despises theft less than poverty he remains unrepentant, whence Montaigne's conclusion:

> (b) Cela, ce n'est pas cette habitude qui nous incorpore au vice et y
> conforme nostre entendement mesme, n'y n'est ce vent impetueux qui va
> troublant et aveuglant à secousses nostre ame et nous precipite pour
> l'heure, jugement et tout, en la puissance du vice. [812]

> This is not that habit that incorporates us with vice and brings even our
> understanding into conformity with it; nor is it that impetuous wind that
> comes in gusts to confuse and blind our soul, and hurls us for the moment
> headlong, judgment and all, into the power of vice. [616]

This is as close as Montaigne will ever come to asserting that repentance, as
it is commonly known and practiced, is incompatible with rational
behavior. The Thief is unrepentant because he is and always has been in full
command of his faculties; his decisions and actions are independent both of
ingrained habit (*cette habitude qui nous incorpore au vice*) and of the
tyranny of passion (*ce vent impetueux qui va troublant et aveuglant à
secousses nostre ame*). In other words, this exemplary Thief has lived in
"conformity" with what Montaigne had called earlier on the same page *une
forme sienne, une forme maistresse:*

> (b) il n'est personne, s'il s'escoute, qui ne descouvre en soy une forme
> sienne, une forme maistresse, qui luicte contre l'institution, et contre la

tempeste des passions qui luy sont contraires. De moy, je ne me sens guere agiter par secousse, je me trouve quasi tousjours en ma place, comme font les corps lourds et poisans. Si je ne suis chez moy, j'en suis tousjours bien pres. Mes debauches ne m'emportent pas loing. Il n'y a rien d'extreme et d'estrange; et si ay des ravisemens sains et vigoureux. [811]

There is no one who, if he listens to himself, does not discover in himself a pattern all his own, a ruling pattern, which struggles against education and against the tempest of the passions that oppose it. For my part, I do not feel much sudden agitation; I am nearly always in place, like heavy and inert bodies. If I am not at home, I am always very near it. My excesses do not carry me very far away. There is nothing extreme or strange about them. And besides I have periods of vigorous and healthy reaction. [615]

Upon comparison and reflection, Montaigne's epiloque to the story of the Thief (*Cela, ce n'est pas cette habitude, etc.*) turns out to be the complete transform of what has always been hailed as the central feature in his own "self-portrait." As the following synoptic table makes clear, Montaigne's moral description of the Thief attracts the same cluster of attributes that comprises the descriptive system of the famous *forme maistresse*; in each case, the rational mind is depicted as beset on either side by subversion, whether from the constraints of culture or those of nature:

	Montaigne	Thief
RATIONAL MIND	forme sienne	nostre entendement
	forme maistresse	jugement
		nostre ame
CONSTRAINTS OF CULTURE (= HABIT)	luicte contre l'institution	ce n'est pas cette habitude
CONSTRAINTS OF NATURE (= PASSION)	tempeste des passions	vent impetueux
	agiter par secousse	troublent
	debauches	à secousse
	emportent	aveuglant
	extresmes/estranges	precipite
		puissance du vice

The superimposed, parallel reading of these two disparate "portraits" produces a composite, layered message: the Thief is like me, to the extent that each of us acts with characteristic deliberation, rationality and impenitence; we both approach the wholeness of Socrates, to the extent that we are at peace and at one with our respective *forme maistresse*. All three of us testify to the sameness of man and illustrate, each of us in his own register, *la forme entiere de l'humaine condition*.

The correspondences between the "self-portrait" and the Thief's "portrait" do not end here, however. The note of intentionality and control on which Montaigne concludes his comments on his own *forme maistresse*, recapitulated in the final sentence by the single word *ravisemens* (= reactions = reassessments, as opposed to reformation = repentance), finds a sharp verbal echo in the conduct of the Thief, who in "assessing" his own situation, decided or found it "advisable" *(s'advisa)* to live off the labor of others. In old age, as in his youth *(jeunesse/vieillesse)*, in pursuing a career of larceny as in indemnifying his victims, his behavior is the result of undeterred rational choice. His "review" and "reassessment" of his past actions lead him to make restitution, but without regret:

> (b) cettuy-cy regarde le larrecin comme action deshonneste et le hayt, mais moins que l'indigence; s'en repent bien simplement, mais, en tant qu'elle estoit ainsi contrebalancée et compencée, il ne s'en repent pas. Cela, ce n'est pas, etc. [812]

> this man regards theft as a dishonorable action and hates it but hates it less than poverty; he indeed repents of it in itself, but in so far as it was thus counterbalanced and compensated he does not repent of it. This is not, etc. [616]

Although in no way edifying, the Thief's impenitence, like Montaigne's and like Socrates', provides at the bottom of the social and moral scale a striking example—and this is why it is presented at such great length—of "integrity" or "wholeness" in the basic sense that underpins this essay at all its crucial junctures: consistency between the outer and inner man. Or, to use the term that Montaigne goes on to apply to himself, as the "self-portrait" resumes in the wake of the Thief's example: whatever this man did, he was *entier*. And so am I:

> Je fay coustumierement entier ce que je fay et marche tout d'une piece; je n'ay guere de mouvement qui se *cache* et desrobe à ma raison, et qui ne se conduise à peu près par le consentement de toutes mes parties, sans division, sans sedition intestine; mon jugement en a la coulpe ou la louange entiere; et la coulpe qu'il a une fois, il l'a tousjours, car quasi dés sa naissance il est un: mesme inclination, mesme route, mesme force. Et en matiere d'opinions universelles, dés l'enfance je me logeay au poinct ou j'avois à me tenir. [812]

We have already observed how, at one end of the moral spectrum, this seminal passage points proleptically to a crossroads where Stoic philosophy—*L'homme marche entier vers son croist et vers son décroist*—and the glorious, unrepentant death of Socrates converge. Now, at the other extreme, we see how this same passage leads the reader back to the inglorious unrepentant Thief and, through him, to a fuller vision of Montaigne's also inglorious and equally unrepentant self. In my case, as in his, Montaigne asserts once more, mind and heart, sense and passion, work and move in unison. I, like him, remain today as I have always been. With reference to the tabular scheme printed above, Montaigne's description of his own "integrity" may now be viewed as a re-writing and systematic transform of the earlier equation between himself and the Thief: *coustumierement*, now become a positive marker, repeats the words *institution* and *habitude; raison, jugement* and *consentement* replicate the essential meaning of *forme maistresse* and its counterparts in the description of the Thief; finally, each element in the sequence *mouvement* > *division* > *sedition* > *inclination* designates, interchangeably with the others, the impetuosities and the tempestuous violence of unreflective passion. Even in the description of his guilt, Montaigne's "self-portrait" parallels the Thief's psychological motives and the movement of his career. Neither of them evolves; youth and age reveal the same man, equally guilty, equally aware of that guilt—and that *quasi dés sa naissance*. Montaigne's general concepts and values follow the same pattern; the opinions that he holds today are such as they were *dés l'enfance*. At the end of the circuitous itinerary, along which this philological reading of *Du repentir* has led us, we are returned on yet another byway to the essential but—as we now see—superficial and transparent paradox of this essay's first sentence and its first page: like the Thief, I am *mal formé* but whole, and, if only in the consciousness and completeness of my humanity, I approximate the wholesomeness of the Stoic sages and of Socrates.

II

To read Montaigne philologically is to be ready at every moment to obey a double solicitation, the contextual and the intratextual. Alongside—and at certain times simultaneously with—the "normal" effort to relate successive sentences or blocks of material logically or thematically to what precedes and what follows, the philological reader, once he has been through the text linearly, will be drawn to pursue and compare observed lexical recurrences, synonymies or on occasion even sizeable passages which continue to impinge on one another in his memory even at several pages' distance. At the level of its language, Montaigne's writing is replete with signals of this kind. The reader who perceives any one of a given essay's formal redundancies will be led sooner or later—but inevitably if he dwells long enough on the actual, observable properties of Montaigne's text—to the intersection of this first set of signals with a second and a third, etc. To the degree that this process of verbal tracking can be described as having an end, it will reveal to the reader, finally, the absolutely uncanny way in which Montaigne's words respond to one another, in the Baudelairean sense, across the pages of the essay; in the process of following out these intratextual "correspondences," the reader will find it possible to chart the stages and detail the movement of Montaigne's argument far more clearly and completely than has ever been feasible through the conventional paraphrasings of Montaigne's explicit "theories" or "ideas".

We are all free in the privacy of our thoughts to do what we wish with an author's words. In the case of Montaigne, there will always be readers who cannot resist the lure of trying to grasp and define in its totality the brilliant intellectual personality that haunts the pages of the *Essais.* Those who succumb to this impulse should be aware, however, that, like any attempt to enclose the fullness of a human career within the necessarily artificial and arbitrary limits of a historico-biographical scheme, the altogether grandiose project of reconstructing the psyche of a deceased genius will never yield more than a partial distillation of the essence that it seeks to capture. In purely practical terms, any reading that claims access to a reality or a unity located outside the pages of Montaigne's book imposes an enormous sacrifice and exacts an exorbitant price, namely, the palpable, objective reality and unity constituted by the unbroken string of words which spans the textual space of each individual essay. This is the price that must be paid and the sacrifice that must be made, *nolens volens,* by those readers who choose to dismantle Montaigne's pages, decontextualize his words, rearrange the *disjecta membra* of his presumed "ideas" in patterns of their own devising, and who thus rewrite what Montaigne himself has so carefully and so magnificently written. Some such process of textual disagregation is indelibly inscribed, moreover, in the very notion of Montaigne's book as host to a "self-portrait": the "portrait," a mimetic artifact, is by definition a picture *of* the genuine article; it is the shadow, as in a world of Platonic forms, *of* a full, living "self" that lurks somewhere behind it or hovers somewhere above it. Reading the book becomes a quest for the reality of which the "portrait" is a copy.

The philological reader, by extreme contrast, ever mindful of the fact that Montaigne composed each essay individually by grafting new words onto words already there, will be satisfied to refer the words in the "self-portrait," to other words that figure along with them in the same essay, and with which they show some evident connection. When studied as a function of the verbal clusters generated by *forme, entier, lustre, bas,* etc. the sum of Montaigne's first-person interventions in *Du repentir* demands to be described not as a "self-portrait," but as the *literary representation* of an authorial Self that turns out to be coordinate at every point, in choice of language and in rhetorical effect, with literary representations of other people in that same essay: an anonymous magistrate, Alexander the Great, Socrates and a common thief.

At the end of his long, often roundabout inquiry, the philological reader finds reason to question the standard maxim, quoted earlier in Donald Frame's hyperbolic version, "the book is the man," and to propose in its place the more modest, objective statement: "the man is *in* the book," in exactly the same way, moreover, that Socrates, Alcibiades and Epaminondas are *in* Montaigne's book: not as mimetic or even approximate pictures of the way they really were, or the way they must or may have been—what ancient authority ever credited Socrates with anything resembling the statement, *"Mener l'humaine vie conformément à sa naturelle condition"?*—but as allegorical, symbolic, semiotic lives, assigned to clear roles in an overall didactic enterprise and designed to solicit a reader's attention as the incarnation of specific psychological attitudes or moral stances. Montaigne can be said to portray himself for precisely the same reason that he portrays the Thief and Socrates: as part of a rhetorical strategy designed to persuade his reader of the value of his opinions and the truth of his beliefs. The *peinture du Moi,* when examined in its relation to other "portraits" in any given essay, emerges not as an end in itself, or a chance by-product of the business of essay writing, but as a means to an end: as one of several parallel, exemplary lives that concur in the elaboration of a unified epistemic model.

To subordinate *Du repentir,* in the present instance, or the *Essais* in general to an overriding didactic purpose, is certainly not to reduce one or the other to their mere ideological content. There is, after all, more than one way to be didactic. Some writers may actually tell people what to believe and how to behave. Such was at least the guiding spirit if not the expressed motive that gave rise to the reductive, anthological reading of the *Essais* in

Pierre Charron's unititular *De la sagesse*.[27] And then, there is Montaigne's way, the one that Charron and his progeny of ideological readers have always ignored and betrayed; this was the way of Plato and Lucretius, as it was to be the way of Pascal and La Bruyère. Rather than tell us what to do, didactic writers of this temper make it their business to involve our minds, our feelings and our imaginations, through a dazzling variety of verbal detours and maneuvers, in a personal, poetic, and seductive vision of how things are. *De rerum natura:* no matter what his actual subject, *this* is Montaigne's constant theme, the matter of his book and the intimate message of every significant word that it contains. This is also the conclusion, in all its banality, to which each successive element in the foregoing philological reading has been bringing us progressively closer. The semantic line projected by the sentence, *Les autres forment l'homme*, the word *entier*, the group *lustre/sombre/obscure/clarté*, the vocabulary of separation and conjunction—every single marked property of the text, whatever its immediate or apparent reference, points eventually, but infallibly, to some crucial aspect of the continuity and coherency of Nature, and, from there, to yet another consideration of what it means in that light to be (impenitently) human.

27. In an unadorned statement, worth thousands of pages of subsequent Montaigne criticism, Marie de Gournay distinguishes for all time between the author of the *Essais* and his *epigonoi:* "ses compagnons enseignent la sagesse, il désenseigne la sottise," "Préface," *Les* Essais *de Michel, Seigneur de Montaigne*, ed. Pierre Coste (Paris: Par la Société, 1725), pp. xli–xlii.

JEAN STAROBINSKI

The Body's Moment

1. THE ELOQUENT CUP-BEARER

In regard to the two realms which constitute man—body and soul—
Montaigne is determined to follow *(écouter)* intimate and direct experience
in preference to what the specialized arts say (and promise) about them:
theology and philosophy for the soul; medicine for the body. Let us take up
here our reading of the essay *Of experience* [All italics are those of Jean
Starobinski]

> (b) Les arts qui promettent de nous *tenir le corps en santé et l'ame en santé,*
> nous promettent beaucoup; mais aussi n'en est il point qui tiennent moins
> ce qu'elles promettent. Et en nostre temps, ceux qui font profession de ces
> arts entre nous en montrent moins les effects que tous autres hommes. On
> peut dire d'eus pour le plus, qu'ils vendent les drogues medecinales; mais
> qu'ils soyent medecins, cela ne peut on dire. [1079][1]

> The arts that promise *to keep our body in health and our soul in health*
> promise us much; but at the same time there are none that keep their
> promise less. And in our time those who profess these arts among us show
> the results of them less than any other men. The most you can say for them
> is that they sell medicinal drugs; but that they are doctors you cannot say.
> [827]

Montaigne is going to devote himself to reversing these roles. In place of the
medical arts, which transform life into their *object* and claim to govern it,
he substitutes life such as he himself directly experiences it—life elevated

---

1. Cf. W.G. Moore, "Montaigne's Notion of Experience" in *The French Mind: studies in
honour of Gustave Rudler*, (Oxford 1952), p. 000; M. Baraz, "Sur la structure d'un essai de
Montaigne (III:13, *De l'experience), BHR,* 123 (Genève: E Droz 1961), pp. 265–81; Jules Brody,
"From Teeth to Text in 'De l'experience'. A Philological Reading," *L'Esprit Créateur,* Kansas, 20,
No. 1, Spring 1980, p. 7–22.

to the rank of art. "Mon mestier et mon art, c'est vivre" (379) ["My trade and my art is living" (274).] The individual subject frees himself from the prevailing discourse which concerns him and demands for himself, and for himself alone, the *authority* of knowing *(savoir)*, of another kind of knowing which, as we have seen, was almost merged with feeling *(le sentir)*.

Montaigne declares himself convinced that in regard to the body, this knowledge *(savoir)*, born of one's *own* experience, renders superfluous any outside prescription; that this rivalry with medical science does not frighten him: that he can find support for his position among ancient authorities—Tiberius, or better yet, the Socrates of the *Memorabilia* and the Plato of the *Republic*, who maintain that one's personal experience with illness, diet and therapeutics is the necessary and sufficient condition for maintaining one's health:

> (b) L'experience est proprement sur son fumier au subject de la medecine, où la raison luy quite toute la place. Tibere disoit que quiconque avoit vescu vingt ans se debvoit respondre des choses qui luy estoyent nuisibles ou salutaires, et se sçavoir conduire sans medecine. (c) Et le pouvoit avoir apprins de Socrates, lequel, conseillant à ses disciples, soigneusement et comme un tres principal estude, l'estude de leur santé, adjoustoit qu'il estoit malaisé qu'un homme d'entendement, prenant garde à ses exercises, à son boire et à son manger, ne discernast mieux que tout medecin ce qui luy estoit bon au mauvais. (b) Si faict la medecine profession d'avoir tousjours l'experience pour touche de son operation. Ainsi Platon avoit raison de dire que pour estre vray medecin, il seroit necessaire que celuy qui l'entreprendroit eust passé par toutes les maladies qu'il veut guarir et par tous les accidens et circonstances dequoy il doit juger. C'est raison qu'ils prennent la verole s'ils la veulent sçavoir penser. [1079][2]

> Experience is really on its own dunghill in the subject of medicine, where reason yields it the whole field. Tiberius used to say that whoever had lived twenty years should be responsible to himself for the things that were harmful or beneficial to him, and know how to take care of himself without medical aid. (c) And he might have learned this from Socrates, who, advising his disciples, carefully and as a principal study, the study of

2. What is involved here is an argumentation that, from its origin, medical writings (for example, the Hippocratic book *Ancient Medicine*) try to combat in order to legitimize the superior knowledge of the health specialist, saying that individual experience does not have the certainty of a *technè*. Only the doctor, having had to compare a large number of cases, knows how to reason about their differences and similarities: medicine is reasoned experience, *(tribè méta logon.)*

their health, used to add that it was difficult for an intelligent man who was careful about his exercise, his drinking, and his eating not to know better than any doctor what was good or bad for him.

(b) And indeed, medicine professes always to have experience as the touchstone for its workings. So Plato was right in saying that to become a true doctor, the candidate must have passed through all the illnesses that he wants to cure and all the accidents and circumstances that he is to diagnose. It is reasonable that he should catch the pox if he wants to know how to treat it. [826–27]

The ancient authorities invoked by Montaigne were concerned with a medicine whose modes of treatment consisted primarily in dietetics (to be understood in the wider sense, as a regulating of the ensemble of one's nutrition and activities). They could easily argue for the primacy of self-observation and self-medication.

Rousseau will still remember this passage in which health corresponds closely with the *original (primitives)* conditions of existence:

(a) Il n'est nation qui n'aist esté plusieurs siecles sans la medecine, et les premiers siecles, c'est à dire les meilleurs et les plus heureux . . . Et parmy nous le commun peuple s'en passe heureusement . . . toute chose qui se trouve salubre à nostre vie se peut nommer medecine. [766–67][3]

There is no nation that has not been without medicine for many centuries, and those the first centuries, that is to say the best and happiest . . . and among us the common people get along happily without it . . . everything that is found to be salubrious for our life may be called medicine. [581]

Montaigne takes up anew the old, anti-technician objections and directs them against a medical discourse which had acquired an institutional force under the auspices of the University. In search of allies, he does not step outside the boundaries of the culture that he has inherited: he plays off the authority of some (Tiberius, Plato, Socrates) against the authority of others. He is therefore not alone in his rebellion. But in a time of literary renaissance, when respect surrounds the works of the ancient scientists *savants*, the transferal of authority from the professional *l'homme de l'art* to the "layman," to the mere "private individual," implies a challenge nevertheless. It disavows the right of a consecrated "science" to speak and to decide (a "science" already contested from within by its dissident

3. Rousseau develops these ideas in the first part of the *Discours de l'Inégalité* and in *Emile*, book I.

representatives, its reformers and its heretics, of whose esistence Montaigne is at least aware: "Paracelse, Fioravanti, Argentevius" (772; 586)[4], so that it can listen instead, and in an immediate way (d'une écoute immédiate) to *that of which* "science" speaks haphazardly and which can speak just as well in its stead: our body. Montaigne proposes, for his personal use first of all, but with the intention of winning us over to his cause, an anti-medicine which is to be grounded on what he himself can say about his own body and not on what professional medicine *(l'art)*, which has granted itself an expertise in the matter, has to say about it. Knowledge *(science)* of the body can and must be understood as knowledge which issues *from* the body and not as knowledge which aims *at* the body.

This reversal, as we have already indicated, transforms the entire epistemological perspective: the body is no longer willing to be the *object* of an external knowing *(connaissance)* capable of being confirmed by health-producing effects: it is necessary that our body, aided by our judgement, become itself the *subject* of its own knowledge.

This appeal to intimate experience and to the body's wisdom—a wisdom both spontaneous and premeditated *(réfléchie)*—enters into opposition with an entire trend of the renaissance of science which, through observation, dissection, and detailed pictorial representation, refines and reinforces the knowing of the human body as a natural *object*. The progress made in anatomy, since da Vinci and Vesalius, had transformed the body into a *spectacle*—but in the form of a nameless cadaver exposed to the observers who fill up the bleachers of an "anatomical theater." In the more or less long term, this exactness of observation will contribute to the increase in the powers and capabilities *(pouvoirs)* of a science whose promises Montaigne holds to be illusory. Further, everything leads one to think that Montaigne, not content with disputing the validity of traditional medicine, remains indifferent to the objective corrections that medical science, in its new and rapid rise, had applied to the old and commonplace ideas *(idées reçues)*. While the anatomists are outdoing Galenic science *(savoir)* in precision, Montaigne goes back, beyond Galen, to a Socratic discourse which confers on the living individual the responsibility for governing the habits of his material, as well as his spiritual, life. In view of this, Montaigne's thought, rebelling against the temptation to master more completely the body in its spatial attributes, as an object, may seem

4. Men of science *(savants)* themselves liked to note down the contradictions of the different medical discourses. Cf. Jérome Cardan, *Contradicentium Medicorum libri duo* (Paris, 1564–1565).

"reactionary" in comparison with the nascent scientific movement. But it is appropriate to remind ourselves that the extension of an objectifying knowledge *(savoir)*, which treats the human body as a machine or as one of a number of structures around which extended substance is organized, would necessarily provoke a protest on behalf of a spontaneous subjectivity and the tangible act of repossession *(saisie sensible)* by means of which the individual assures himself of his own presence *(présence à soi)*. This protest became apparent in the eighteenth century, notably in Rousseau and Biran. . . . And, as Rousseau's antimedical arguments are, for a large part, dependent on Montaigne, we are not, in a modern reconsideration of the evolution of ideas, precluded from thinking that Montaigne, far from exhibiting a backward-looking tendency, was heralding (unintentionally and without foreseeing it) the claims of the individual anxious to confide in the dictates of his actual *(vécue)* experience and trying to preserve within himself an irreducible realm that would be sheltered from the invasions of an objectifying knowledge *(connaissance)*.

This type of reversal is not the only example of its kind. At different times in history, the development of rational, objective science has provoked an uneasiness among those who felt that such a knowledge *(savoir)*, through its excessive generalizations, was exerting its *rigor* against the profound essence and originality of its object. Whether it is a question of the natural world or of man himself, the defensive riposte lies in restoring this object to the dignity and prerogatives of a *subject* capable of apprehending itself immediately within an intuitive and truthful knowledge *connaissance*—and equally capable of allowing itself to be understood by another type of science which is closer to a respectful listening than to a reductive explanation. In Montaigne's time, Parcelsus holds that nature can surrender her secret to the few individuals privileged to know how to read her "signatures" and to lend their ears to her mysteries[5]; in the eighteenth century, the hypothesis of sensibility, indeed of a thought inherent in inanimate matter retaliates against the ambitions of a geometrized physics[6]; we know that analogous moments have not been lacking in our own time in the "social sciences"; phenomenology speaks out against a "psychologism" which borrows its methods from the natural sciences; a psychoanalysis which sought to draw up a cartography and dynamometry of the

5. Cf. Walter Pagel, *Paracelsus* (Bâle-New York, 1958); *Paracelse*, French tr. by Michel Deutsch, (Arthaud, 1963); see in particular the second part which is devoted to the philosophy of Paracelsus.

6. The most remarkable document in this respect is *Le Rêve de d'Alembert*.

unconscious sees itself opposed by another psychoanalysis in which truth resides in the very language of the unconscious and which evicts any discourse modeled after the natural sciences.

It goes without saying that this type of reversal always ends up with reinstating the experience of the individual (or with making this individual experience the starting-point for new generalizations) and opposing it to the claims of universal value heard in the language used by objective knowledge *(savoir)*. For Montaigne, the importance accorded to the *self (moi)* and the attention of which it is the object necessarily called for the epistemological primacy of knowledge *(connaissance)* through "feeling"—with regard to the body as well as to the soul. The body-subject, such as it feels itself to be, demands a legitimacy superior to that of science's discourse *on* the body. Better yet, the enterprise of speaking the body *(dire le corps)* ends up in granting the body permission not only to *express itself (se dire)* (through the living voice, gestures, movements) but also to provide the necessary metaphorical repertoire by means of which all the acts of thought will be represented in the writing of the book. To speak the body is, in a way, to return to the source, when so many objects—and, possibly, everything which can be spoken—are capable of being spoken *by* the body . . .

What Montaigne will reveal of his bodily health will therefore be an anti-medicine but which is entitled to resist medicine because it can more justly claim the guarantee of experience which medicine—as we have seen—has made into the "touche de son opération" (1079); the ["touchstone of its workings" (827).] The author-reader relationship, insofar as it is more individual, will be the vehicle of this rebel science. The experience of a single individual will be trusted; and this individual will choose as his addressee *(destinataire)* another individual subject, symetrically: to the essay, as practised by Montaigne, a supplementary meaning is added by means of a metaphor (that could also be legitimately called a metonymy) in which the bodily act of *tasting* is a figure for the experience of the body in its entirety:

> (b) J'ay assez vescu, pour mettre en compte l'usage qui m'a conduict si loing. *Pour qui en voudra gouster, j'en ay faict l'essay, son eschançon.* [1080]

> I have lived long enough to give an account of the practice that has guided me so far. *For anyone who wants to try it I have tasted it like his cupbearer.* [827]

The metaphor of taste is doubled here with a banquet metaphor: Montaigne has tried out *(a fait l'essai)* before the reader, who will perhaps decide to imitate him, the dishes and drinks of life's banquet. He invites the reader to drink following him. Montaigne's antimedicine can be defined as a "dietetics" established from the user's—the patient's—point of view, and no longer from the point of view of the practice exercized by the agent—the doctor—who is in possession of a universalized knowledge *(savoir)*.

In the narration of the fall from his horse and of his fainting, Montaigne had spoken the bodily *event* in its uniqueness and non-repeatability (II:vi): afterwards, he interpreted it as a trial which foreshadowed a more decisive loss: death.

But how shall one express the habitual practices *(l'usage)* of life, the things which the body becomes accustomed to? Narrative *(récit)* is no longer fitted to this task. A detailed description of these habits is necessary and, even if one were determined to speak in a nonchalant fashion, it is necessary to adopt a certain order in order to present them. Where is this order to be found except in common descriptive usage such as it was itself influenced by the discourse of medicine? One's attention becomes drawn to an arrangement whose importance and stamp of reality have been developed from generation to generation by the influence of concepts determined by doctors. Montaigne announces that he will furnish the "articles" ["items"] of the "usage qui [l']a conduict si loin," "comme la souvenance les [lui] fournit" (1080) ["practice that has guided (him) so far," "as remembrance* supplies (him) with them" (827)[7]; but remembrance itself does not surrender *(livrer)* everything and has not retained everything; it has chosen the materials which it deemed worthy of being surrendered up. And in its choice, in its very perception, remembrance has been guided by a language wherein the categories of medicine play a greater role than it presumes or recognizes. In order to speak the body better than medicine does, it is necessary to find a language that is both intelligible and suited to the purpose; every day language is willing to offer its services—yet it is entirely wrought with medical reminiscences, wherein lies the difficulty of abandoning medical language in order to, in this case, speak against medicine.

The reader will notice (were he only to glance at the medical books of the time) that Montaigne cannot narrate his own being *(se raconter)* except by appropriating the language of the doctors, by *making use* of their

---

*In view of J. Starobinski's distinction between "souvenance" and "mémoire" (see note 7), I have changed D. Frame's rendering of "souvenance" from "memory" to "remembrance."— Trans.

7. Note that Montaigne here writes "souvenance" and not "memory" (NT: these are translated respectively by "remembrance and "memory"). This is not by chance. On this point, see Michel Beaujour, *Miroirs d'encre* (Paris, 1980, p. 113–31).

categories, by diverting them, according to the rule he applies to all of his borrowings, for his own benefit.

In the conclusion of the essay *Of repentance* (III:2), an excellent example is given both of this recourse to the concepts of medicine and of this modification that Montaigne, by inserting them into his personal remarks, imposes on them. Montaigne could have read in Ambroise Paré: "La vieillesse, quelque gaillarde qu'elle soit, est de sa nature *comme une espece de maladie.*"[8] ["Old age, however full of life it be, is by its very nature *like a species of malady . . .*"] And Paré concluded from this that it "semble meilleur la nourrir des viandes contraires à son tempérament, sçavoir chaudes et humides, pour tousjours retarder les causes de la mort, frigité et siccité, qui la talonne de bien pres"; ["seems better to nourish it with foods of the opposite temperament, namely those which are hot and fluid, in order to always defer the causes of death—coldness and dryness—which follow closely on its heels."] In the last paragraph of the essay *Of repentance*, Montaigne echoes this, but according to his own rhythm, in an élan of personal expression in which moral reflection is poeticized:

> (b) Il me semble qu'en la vieillesse nos ames sont subjectes à des maladies et imperfections plus importunes qu'en la jeunesse . . . *C'est une puissante maladie*, et qui se coule naturellement et imperceptiblement. Il y faut grande provision d'estude et grande precaution pour eviter les imperfections qu'elle nous charge, ou aumoins affoiblir leur progrets. Je sens que, nonobstant tous mes retranchemens, elle gaigne pied à pied sur moy. Je soustien tant que je puis. Mais je ne scay en fin où elle me menera moy-mesme. A toutes avantures, je suis content qu'on sçache d'où je seray tombé. [816–17]

> it seems to me that in old age our souls are subject to more troublesome ailments and imperfections than in our youth . . . *It is a powerful malady*, and it creeps up on us naturally and imperceptibly. We need a great provision of study, and great precaution, to avoid the imperfections it loads upon us, or at least to slow up their progress. I feel that, notwithstanding all my retrenchments, it gains on me foot by foot. I stand fast as well as I can. But I do not know where it will lead even me in the end. In any event, I am glad to have people know whence I shall have fallen. [620–21]

As for the therapeutic value of *warmth* (as opposed to the "coldness and dryness" of old age), Montaigne will not forget it either. But, as we shall see, it is in the chapter *On some verses of Virgil* (III:v) that he will speak of it, not insofar as it has anything to do with "foods" but with the warming aroused

---

8. Ambroise Paré, *Les Oeuvres*. "Premier livre de l'introduction à la chirurgie," ch. 17. I quote from the eighth edition, Paris, 1628, p. 29.

by love, which could be approved of by medical art as an appropriate medication.

2. THE SIX NON-NATURALS

The long exposition that Montaigne devotes to his "bodily health" in *Of experience* can be included nearly entirely under the heading of what is called, in medicine, "non-naturals": this name is applied to them because they are not directly linked to the individual's own nature (humors, temperament), but to the way in which the individual modifies or yields to his conditions of existence. The non-naturals are in themselves neutral but the *use* that individuals make of them can influence their health. In this area—hygiene—the doctor takes into account the life-style of his patient and asks him questions about his habits. Here again, Paré exhibits superlatively the reigning opinion; we will not hesitate to quote from him at length:

> Telles choses . . . sont comprises en la seconde partie de la medecine, dite Hygiaine, c'est à dire garde de santé: non parce qu'aucunes d'icelles soient telles, qu'elles soient tousjours salubres, autres insalubres de leur nature, mais seulement pour ce qu'elles sont faites et rendues telles par *usage* commode ou incommode.
>
> Tel usage consiste en quatre conditions, sçavoir en quantité, et qualité, en l'occasion et en la manière d'user: lesquelles si tu observes, tu feras que ces choses qui de soy sont indifférentes, seront tousjours salubres: car de ces quatre dependent toutes les regles et preceptes de ceste partie de Medecine, qui a esgard à la conservation de la santé. Ces choses non naturelles, comme dit Galien au premier livre *De sanitate tuenda*, sont comprises entre quatre genres et dictions universelles, que l'on nomme *sumenda, admovenda, educenda, facienda. Sumenda*, c'est-à-dire, choses qui se prennent au dedans soit par la bouche, soit autre part, sont l'air, boire et manger. *Admovenda*, c'est à dire, choses qui s'appliquent par dehors, sont tous medicamens, et toute autre chose que l'on approche tant au corps qu'à quelque partie que soit. *Educenda*, c'est à dire ce qui est tiré dehors, sont tous excremens qui sortent hors du corps, toutes choses estranges que l'on tire d'iceluy. *Facienda*, c'est à dire ce qu'il faut faire, sont travail, repos, dormir, veiller, et autres: toutes fois communément on les divise en six, qui sont,
>
> L'air.
> Boire et manger.
> Travail, ou exercice et repos.
> Dormir et veiller.

> Excretion et retention, ou repletion et inanition.
> Les perturbations de l'ame.[9]

Such things (i.e. non-naturals) . . . are included in the second part of medicine, called Hygiene, or the keeping of one's health: not because any of these things are such that they are always salubrious, while others are insalubrious by nature, but only because they are so made and rendered by proper and improper *use*.

Such use consists of four conditions, namely: in quantity, in quality, in the occasion, and in the manner, of use: if you observe the said conditions, you will make these things, which in themselves are neutral, become always salubrious: for all the rules and precepts of Medicine, which look to the conservation of health, depend on these four conditions. These non-naturals, as Galen says in the first book of *De sanitate tuenda*, are grouped into four classes and universal dictions, which are named: *sumenda, admovenda, educenda, facienda*. *Sumenda*, namely things which are taken within, whether through the mouth or elsewhere, are the air, drinking, and eating. *Admovenda*, namely things which are applied from the outside, are all the medicines, and any other thing that one brings to the body or anywhere else. *Educenda*, namely that which is led outside, are all the excrements which leave the body, all foreign matter which one leads out of it. *Facienda*, namely the things one must do, are work, repose, sleeping, waking, and other things: although, commonly, these conditions are divided into six categories, which are

> Air,
> Drinking and Eating,
> Work, or Exercise and Rest,
> Sleeping and Waking,
> Excretion and Retention, or Repletion and Inanition,
> The Perturbations of the Soul.

Paré is careful to add that in all of these areas, and notably, in that which concerns nutrition, one must take into account, above all, custom, which contributes to the specific (*propre*) temperament of the individual (idiosyncrasy):

> Ce n'est pas assez seulement d'avoir cogneu la quantité et qualité des viandes, mais aussi il faut entendre la *coustume* et maniere de les prendre, s'il est ainsi que selon le dire des principaux Medecins, *la coustume (c'est à dire, maniere de vivre) est une autre nature.* Car icelle aucunes fois change le propre temperament naturel, et en laisse un autre acquis: partant la coustume non seulement est à garder és sains, mais aussi és malades: car si

9. Ambroise Paré, op. cit., p. 26.

promptement vous la voulez changer de pire en meilleure, vous tenez
certainement plus de mal que de bien.[10]

> It is not enough to know only the quantity and quality of the foods, but
> one must also know the *custom* and manner of taking them, if it is correct
> that, according to the sayings of the principal Doctors, *custom (i.e. manner
> of living) is a second nature.* For custom sometimes changes one's own
> natural temperament, and leaves behind another, acquired one: therefore,
> not only the healthy, but also the sick must keep to their customary habits:
> for if you wish immediately to change these habits from poor to better
> ones, you receive, to be sure, more bad than good.

Should one be surprised to see Montaigne, in beginning the exposition on
"bodily health" in *Of experience,* emphasize the imperious power of
custom? Is this—from the point of view of a man who wants to free himself
from the tutelage of medicine—the sign of an excessive docility towards the
very language of medical men?

> (b) Ma forme de vie est pareille en maladie comme en santé: mesme lict,
> mesmes heures, mesmes viandes me servent, et mesme breuvage. Je n'y
> adjouste du tout rien, que la moderation du plus ou du moins, selon ma
> force et mon appetit. Ma santé, c'est maintenir sans destourbier mon estat
> accoustumé . . .
>
> C'est à la coustume de donner forme à nostre vie, telle qu'il lui plaist;
> elle peut tout en cela; c'est le breuvage de Circé, qui diversifie nostre
> nature comme bon luy semble [1080]

> (b) My way of life is the same in sickness as in health; the same bed, the
> same hours, the same food serve me, and the same drink. I make no
> adjustments at all, save for moderating the amount according to my
> strength and appetite. Health for me is maintaining my accustomed state
> without disturbance . . .
>
> It is for habit to give form to our life, just as it pleases; it is all-powerful
> in that; it is Circe's drink, which varies our nature as it sees fit . . . [827]

There follows the list of the surprising examples of the effects of custom.
The epistemological critique of custom, which prevents our minds from
grasping the natural *(native)* truth, now gives way to the established
medical fact of the necessity, for whomever wishes to keep one's health, of
not interrupting his accustomed train of life.

To be sure, Montaigne did not want to make himself a slave of his own

10. Ambroise Paré, op. cit., p. 29. Fernel speaks of *necessary causes (quae necessario nobis
ferendae sunt, et sine quibus vivere non liceat). Universa Medicina,* 1567, "Pathologia," I,xii.

habits: "La meilleure de mes complexions corporelles c'est d'estre flexible et peu opiniastre: j'ai des *inclinations* plus propres et ordinaires et plus agreables que d'autres; mais avec bien peu d'effort je m'en destourne, et me coule aiséement à la façon contraire" (1083) ["The best of my bodily qualities is that I am flexible and not very stubborn. I have inclinations that are more personal and customary, and more agreeable to me, than others; but with very little effort I turn away from them, and easily slip into the opposite habit" (830).] But, with age, custom has become more domineering, and the list of those habits that Montaigne cannot give up is long: (b) . . . "La couŝtume a desjà, sans y penser, imprimé en moy son caractere en certaines choses, que j'appelle excez de m'en despartir.[11] Et sans m'essaier, ne puis ny dormir sur jour, ny faire collation entre les repas, ny desjeuner, ny m'aller coucher sans grand intervalle, (c) comme de trois bonnes heures, (b) apres le soupper, ny faire des enfans qu'avant le sommeil, ny les faire debout, ny porter ma sueur, ny m'abreuver d'eau pure ou de vin pur, ny me tenir nud teste long temps, ny me faire tondre apres disner; et me passerois autant malaiséement de mes gans que de ma chemise, et de me laver à l'issuë de table et à mon lever et de ciel et rideaux à mon lict, comme de choses bien necessaires . . . Je dois plusieurs telles mollesses à l'usage" (1083–84). ["habit, imperceptibly, has already so imprinted its character upon me in certain things that I call it excess to depart from it. And I cannot, without an effort, sleep by day, or eat between meals, or breakfast, or go to bed without a long interval, (c) of about three full hours, (b) after supper, or make a child except before going to sleep, or make one standing up, or endure my sweat, or quench my thirst with pure water or pure wine, or remain bareheaded for long, or have my hair cut after dinner; and I would feel as uncomfortable without my gloves as without my shirt, or without washing when I leave the table or get up in the morning, or without canopy and curtains for my bed, as I would be without really necessary things . . . (b) I owe many such weaknesses to habit." (830–31)]

11. In the chapter *Of husbanding your will* (III:10), Montaigne lets us know this even more explicitly; (b) "Si ce que nature exactement et originellement nous demande pour la conservation de nostre estre est trop peu . . . dispensons nous de quelque chose plus outre; taxons nous, traitons nous à . . . cette mesure, estandons nos appartenances et nos comptes jusques là. Car jusques là il me semble bien que nous avons quelque excuse. L'accustumance est une seconde nature et non moins puissante. (c) Ce qui manque à ma coustume je tiens qu'il me manque." ["(b) If what Nature flatly and originally demands of us for the preservation of our being is too little . . . then let us grant ourselves something further: . . . let us rate and treat ourselves according to this measure, let us stretch our appurtenances and our accounts that far. For in going thus far we certainly seem to me to have some justification. Habit is a second nature, and no less powerful. (c) What my habit lacks, I hold that I lack."] Custom becomes acceptable at the cost of an appropriation that makes it cease from being a foreign influence: it has thus become "mine," it is my "appartenance" ["appurtenance."]

As one can see, Montaigne does not here contradict medical practice *(la médecine)* through his individual example: he confirms it by multiplying the details which characterize him in the individuality of his existence. And when Montaigne generalizes, he again comes upon, in a more finely wrought *(frappé)* style, the generalities of medical discourse. It is worth the trouble to compare them again. Let us listen to Paré: "Suivant le dire d'Hippocrate . . . les mutations subites et repentines sont dangereuses. A ceste cause, si nous voulons changer la maniere de vivre accoustumée, qui est vicieuse, ou qui engendre mal, ou l'entretient, peu à peu faut faire ce *changement*, afin que nature ne se fasche, et que sans grande perturbation elle puisse prendre nouvelle coustume: car encore qu'une viande ne soit de soy-mesme de bon nourissement, elle sera moins ou plus tard cuitte et digerée qu'une autre pire et accoustumée. Qu'ainsi soit, nous voyons que gens rustiques cuisent plustost lard ou boeuf, desquels ordinairement ils usent, qu'une perdrix ou chappon, ou autre viande de bon suc"[12] ["According to Hippocrates's saying . . . sudden and rapid alterations are dangerous. For this reason, if we wish to change an accustomed way of life which is harmful, or leads to illness, or makes it last, one must make this *change* little by little, so that nature is not upset and can acquire, without being greatly disturbed, new habits; for, although one meat may be in itself proper nourishment, it will be warmed and digested either less, or later, than another one that is of poorer quality and customary. That this is so, is apparent when we see that country people cook bacon and beef rather than pheasant and capons or other meat of good quality." Montaigne will say it more succinctly: "Je ne juge . . . poinct . . . où les malades se puissent mieux estre en seurté qu'en se tenant quoy dans le train de vie où ils se sont eslevez et nourris. Le *changement*, quel qu'il soit, estonne et blesse. Allez croire que les chastaignes nuisent à un Perigourdin ou à un Lucquois, et le laict et le fromage aux gens de la montaigne" (1085). ["I have no idea . . . where sick men can better place themselves in safety than in keeping quietly to the way of life in which they have been brought up and trained. *Change* of any sort is disturbing and hurtful. Go ahead and believe that chestnuts hurt a native of Périgord or of Lucca, or milk and cheese the mountaineers." (832).]

In summary, Montaigne, beginning from his personal experience, is filling in, so to speak, the questionnaire that professional medicine formulates in general terms, and whose headings he had himself enumerated in the last essay of Book II, when he had evoked the diverse considerations of which the medical profession should keep itself informed, at the risk,

12. Paré, op. cit., p. 29.

otherwise, of "se mesconter"; ["making a mistake,"] if one of these considerations is poorly grounded: "la complexion du malade, sa tempera-ture, ses humeurs, ses inclinations, ses actions, ses pensemens mesmes et ses imaginations"; . . . the "circonstances externes," la "nature du lieu, condition de l'air et du temps" (773) ["(the) patient's constitution, his temperament, his humors, his inclinations, his actions, his very thoughts and fancies"; . . . the "external circumstances," the "nature of the place, the conditions of the air and weather" (586).] Montaigne cannot, of course, provide answers for all the questions with which he sees the medical profession preoccupied: the "assiette des planettes et leur influance"; [the "position of the planets and their influences"]—so remote, so conjectural—leaves him indifferent. As for his illness, its "causes," "signes," "affections," "jours critiques"; ["causes," "symptoms," "effects," "critical days,"] he had conversed with the reader about these in due course, in the essay *Of the ressemblance of children to fathers,* in dwelling on the almost miraculous phenomenon of hereditary transmission: "Il y a és ouvrage de nature aucunes qualitez qui nous sont imperceptibles, et desquelles nostre suffi-sance ne peut discouvrir les moyens et les causes . . . Quel monstre est-ce, que cette goute de semence dequoy nous sommes produits, porte en soy les impressions, non de la forme corporelle seulement, mais des pensemens et inclinations de nos peres? Cette goute d'eau, où loge elle ce nombre infiny de formes?" (763)[13] ["(T) here are in the works of nature certain qualities and conditions that are imperceptible to us and whose means and causes our capacity cannot discover . . . What a prodigy it is that the drop of seed from which we are produced bears in itself the impressions not only of the bodily form but of the thoughts and inclinations of our fathers! Where does that drop of fluid lodge this infinite number of forms?" (578).] By indicating that the *necessary cause* of his illness is in the paternal "goute de semence"; ["drop of seed,"] Montaigne does not fail to underline the limits of our comprehension which is incapable of grasping, beyond the necessary cause, the true and sufficient causes. In the field of pathology, the *patient* knows full well that he is not given access to the knowledge of the causes (but he rightfully doubts that the professional man *(l'homme de l'art)* knows more than he). What he will say, for having put to the *test* illnesses, is that they themselves are like "animaux" (1088)[14]; ["animals" (834)] that have a

13. In Fernel one reads: *"Quocumque enim morbo pater quum generat tenetur, eum semine transfert in problem." Universa Medicina,* 1567, "Pathologia," I:11.

14. As Villey reminds us, Montaigne here takes up anew an idea formulated by Plato in his *Timaeus* (89, b): "diseases . . . unless they are very dangerous should not be irritated by medicines, since every form of disease is in a manner akin to the living being, whose complex frame has an appointed term of life . . ." (translation of B. Jowett in *The Collected Dialogues of*

limited life-span. This is an *ontological* conception of illness, which Montaigne has found in the philosophers and doctors, but for which he gives credit to his own experience:

> (b) L'experience m'a encores appris cecy, que nous nous perdons d'impatience. Les maux ont leur vie et leurs bornes, (c) leurs maladies et leur santé. [1088]

> (b) Experience has further taught me this, that we ruin ourselves by impatience. Troubles have their life and their limits, (c) illnesses and their health. [834]

As for his "complexion," his "temperature," his "humeurs"; [his "constitution," his "temperament," his "humors," Montaigne had displayed them in the essay II:xvii, *Of presumption,* in the very language of the medical profession: his constitution is "(b) entre le jovial et le mélancholique, moiennement (a) sanguine et chaude" (641). ["(b) between the jovial and the melancholy, moderately (a) sanguine and warm" (486).] He will not need, therefore, to come back and dwell on it at length later on. What he still has left to say in the conclusive essay of the entire book of *Essays,* concerns the "inclinations" and the "actions," the "pensemens," the "imaginations;" the ["inclinations" and the "actions," the "thoughts," the "fancies,"] and above all the series of behaviorisms and experiences which belong to the group of the "six non-naturals."

These confidences may have seemed frivolous or indecent to readers who were not aware of the matters that the doctor's investigation *(enquête)* would systematically encompass. Taking a closer look, one sees that there is nothing that Montaigne reveals—without limiting himself in appearance to any systematic procedure—which does not fall under the headings already provided by the medical profession's classification and which does so without omitting any. What about these "six non-naturals"? Let us follow here the order in which they are set forth by Ambroise Paré:

Air. Montaigne almost let himself be persuaded that the "serain" (1084) ["dew (831)] is more dangerous before sunset. "Je crains un *air* empesché et fuys mortellement la fumée . . . J'ai la respiration libre et aisée . . . L'aspreté de l'esté m'est plus ennemie que celle de l'hyver" (1104–05). ["I fear a stuffy *atmosphere* and avoid smoke like the plague . . . My breathing is free and easy . . . The rigor of summer is more of an enemy to me than that of winter" (848).]

Plato, Including the Letters, ed. Edith Hamilton and Huntington Cairns, Bollingen Series, (Princeton: Princeton U. Press, April 1978.)

Eating and drinking

Montaigne will speak of these matters on several occasions, according to his pace which proceeds "à sauts et à gambades" (944) ["by leaps and gambols" (761)]: "Et sain et malade, je me suis volontiers laissé aller aux appetits qui me pressoient" (1086) ["Both in health and in sickness I have readily let myself follow my urgent appetites" (832).] But it is still only a matter of the ensemble of the passions (or bodily appetites), wherein the pleasures of eating and sexual pleasures[15] can be enumerated side by side. The more specific question of eating and drinking, interrupted by digressions, begins with the declaration: (b) "Je ne choisis guiere à table" (1099); ["I make little choice at table" (843).] And Montaigne continues: "(b) Les longues tables me (c) faschent et me (b) nuisent" (1100); ["Long sessions at table (c) annoy me and (b) disagree with me" (844) . . .] Although the loss of a tooth becomes a pretext for a long exposition on the inevitability of death imperceptibly slipping within, Montaigne does not forget his primary discussion: (b) "Je ne suis excessivement desireux ny de salades ny de fruits, sauf les melons" (1102); ["I am not excessively fond of either salads or fruits, except melons" (846).] The questions of fasting, of the quantity of food, of the interval between meals take up the paragraphs which follow: (b) "Dés me jeunesse je desrobois par fois quelque repas . . . Je croys qu'il est plus sain de menger plus bellement et moins et de menger plus souvent" (1103); ["Ever since my youth I have occasionally skipped a meal . . . I think it is healthier to eat more slowly and less, and to eat more often" (846).]

As for *drinking*, which should, according to correct method, be coupled with the question of *eating*, the exposition is delayed by Montaigne's insertion of a short paragraph devoted to *clothing* (the consideration of which is traditionally a part of medical hygiene, under the heading of the *admovenda* or of the *applicata)*: (b) "Je ne porte les jambes et les cuisses non plus couvertes en hyver qu'en esté, un bas de soye tout simple" (1103); ["I do not keep my legs and thighs any more covered in winter than in summer: silk hose, nothing else" (847).] Montaigne comes back for a moment to considerations on the hour for meals at the end of the day, then finally treats the subject of beverages to drink: (b) "Je ne suis guiere subject à estre alteré,

15. According to medical classification, sexuality can be assigned to the category of the "appetites," or in the less important one of the *excreta*, or even in the category of the "passions of the soul." I will have occasion to speak of this again when I examine the essay III:5, *On some verses of Virgil*, which is entirely devoted to the recollection of love. In *Of experience*, Montaigne, in speaking of his sexual life, adopts a line of reasoning which seeks to prove that that which is the object of a desire, a sexual satisfaction, or nourishment, could not be harmful to the body. One will note that the avowals which are the most indiscreet are relegated to Latin quotations which are inserted into a long sentence (1086; 833). As we shall see, it will be the same in the essay III:5.

ny sain ny malade" (1104) ["I am not much subject to thirst, either in health or in sickness" (847)] On this subject likewise Montaigne praises custom: "(b) "La forme de vivre plus usitée et commune est la plus belle: toute particularité m'y semble à eviter, et haïrois autant un aleman qui mit de l'eau au vin qu'un françois qui le boiroit pur. L'usage publiq donne loy à telles choses" (1104). ["(b) The most usual and common way of living is the best; all particularities seem to me things to be avoided; and I should hate as much to see a German putting water in his wine as a Frenchman drinking it pure. Public usage lays down the law in such things" (848).]

On the question of *sleeping and waking*, then of *work, exercise* and *rest*, Montaigne has a great deal to tell us: it is not unimportant that the first of the actions he mentions is that of "le parler" ["talking"]: "J'ay aperceu qu'aux blessures et aux maladies, le parler m'esmeut et me nuit autant que desordre que je face. La voix me couste et me lasse, car je l'ay haute et efforcée ... Le ton et mouvement de la voix a quelque expression et signification, de mon sens; c'est à moy à le conduire pour me representer. Il y a voix pour instruire, voix pour flater, ou pour tancer. Je veux que ma voix, non seulement arrive à luy [mon auditeur], mais à l'avanture qu'elle le frape et qu'elle le perse" (1087–88). ["I have noticed that when I am wounded or sick, talking excites me and hurts me as much as any irregularity I may commit. It is costly and tiring for me to use my voice, for it is loud and strained ... The tone and movement of my voice express and signify my meaning; it is for me to guide it to make myself understood. There is a voice for instructing, a voice for flattering, a voice for scolding. I want my voice not only to reach my listener, but perhaps to strike him and pierce him" (834).] Much later in the text, the subject of exercise will be taken up again fully, with Montaigne beginning by mentioning the experiences of sleep and of wakefulness:

(b) Il n'est rien qu'on doive tant recommander a la jeunesse que l'*activeté* et la *vigilance*. Nostre vie n'est que mouvement. Je m'esbranle difficilement, et suis tardif par tout: à *me lever*, à *me coucher*, et à mes repas; c'est matin pour moy que sept heures ... [1095]

There is nothing that should be recommended so much to youth as *activity* and *vigilance*. Our life is nothing but movement. I have trouble getting under way, and am late in everything: *getting up, going to bed*, at meals. Seven o'clock is early for me ... [840]

Since the question of wakefulness and sleep is traditionally tied to that of exercise, one is not surprised that Montaigne, after having admitted his "propension paresseuse" (1096) ["lazy propensity" (841)], goes to the other extreme: his aptitude of applying himself, when necessary, to sustained effort by sacrificing the eight or nine hours that he habitually devotes to sleeping. He insists on reminding us that he bravely undertook his share of military details:

> (b) Je me retire avec utilité de cette propension paresseuse, et en vauts evidemment mieux; je sens un peu le coup de la mutation, mais c'est faict en trois jours. Et n'en vois guieres qui vive a moins quand il est besoin, et quis s'exerce plus constamment, ny à qui les corvées poisent moins. Mon corps est capable d'une agitation ferme, mais non pas vehemente et soudaine. Je fuis meshuy les exercices violents, et qui me meinent à la sueur: mes membres se lassent avant qu'ils s'eschauffent. Je me tiens debout tout le long d'un jour, et ne m'ennuye point à me promener . . . Et ay aymé à me reposer, soit couché, soit assis, les jambes autant ou plus hautes que le siege. [1096]

> I am weaning myself profitably from this lazy propensity, and am obviously the better for it. I feel the impact of the change a little, but in three days it is done. And I hardly know anyone who can live with less sleep when necessary, or who stands up better under exercise, or who is bothered less by military duties. My body is capable of steady but not of vehement or sudden exertion. These days I shun violent exercises which put me into a sweat; my limbs grow tired before they grow warm. I can stay on my feet a whole day, and I do not weary of walking . . . and I have always liked to rest, whether lying or sitting, with my legs as high as my seat or higher. [840–41].

All is not yet said concerning exercise. Several pages later, after having treated eating, drinking, air, and a slight visual fatigue, Montaigne adds some more information: "Mon marcher est prompt et ferme" (1105) ["My walk is quick and firm" (848).] But already it is now a question of the more particular problem of the relationships between body and soul: "Et ne sçay lequel des deux, ou l'esprit ou le corps, j'ay arresté plus mal-aiséement en même point" (1105); ["(a) and I know not which of the two, my mind or my body, I have had more difficulty in keeping in one place" (848).] Montaigne admits the difficulty he experiences in remaining attentive and calm ("Je ne suis jamais venu à bout que quelque piece des miennes n'extravague tousjours" (1105) ["I have never succeeded in keeping some part of me from always wandering" (848)).] Likewise, immediately after, the confiding of his greedy way of eating—although this belongs, once again, under the heading of eating and drinking—introduces the question of competition between *eating* and *speaking* (1105–06); (848–49). There is now a new rivalry between bodily and spiritual activities: "Il y a de la jalousie et envie entre nos plaisirs" (1106); ["There is jealousy and envy between our pleasures . . ." (849).] Montaigne, again treating of the non-naturals, is already preparing the theme of the accepted interdependance between body and soul which will take up the conclusive pages of the essay. The slipping from one subject to another is so frequent that it renders unrecognizable a construction that is nonetheless very well traced out in its larger outlines. Thus, one can relate what Montaigne says about the expressivity of one's physionomy to the category of exercise (of movement in general): (b) "Mon visage me descouvre incontinent" (1097) ["My face immediately betrays me" (842).] In the present case it is a question of medical symptomatology, as the question of moral symptomatology—of the relationship between character and physionomical signs (indices)—has been duly treated in the final pages of the essay Of Physiognomy (III:xii); the face is now considered to reflect, like a mirror, health and sickness: (b) "Tous mes changemens commencent par là, et un peu plus aigres qu'ils ne sont en effect; je faits souvent pitié à mes amis avant que j'en sente la cause" (1097) ["(All) my changes begin there, and seem a little worse than they really are. I often move my friends to pity before I feel the reason for it" (842).] Would it, then, be possible to read upon his face, as though it were an open book, his state of health? Not in the least. Whenever Montaigne's complexion changed its natural color, the doctors remained puzzled and, unable to uncover either an organic or humoral cause, they retreated to the sixth of the non-naturals, the "passions de l'âme" ["the passions of the soul,"] without succeeding in seeing things more clearly:

> (b) Mon miroir ne m'estonne pas, car, en la jeunesse mesme, il m'est advenu plus d'une fois de chausser ainsin un teinct et un port trouble et de mauvais prognostique sans grand accident; en maniere que les medecins qui ne trouvoient au dedans cause qui respondit à cette alteration externe, l'attribuoient à l'esprit et à quelque passion secrete qui me rongeast au dedans; ils se trompoient. Si le corps se gouvernoit autant selon moy que faict l'ame, nous marcherions un peu plus à nostre aise. [1097–98]

> My mirror does not alarm me, for even in my youth I have more than once found myself thus wearing a muddy complexion and an ill-omened look, without any serious consequences; so that the doctors, finding inside me no cause responsible for this outward change, attributed it to the spirit and to some secret passion gnawing me within. They were wrong. If my body obeyed my orders as well as my soul, we should get along a little more comfortably. [842]

The signs *(indices)* that have as their object one's physical state are therefore dealt with like those of character *(moralité)* discussed in the essay on "phisionomie" ["physiognomy"] and, more generally, like any presumed causality . . . "Ce traict et façon de visage, et ces lineaments par lesquels on argumente aucunes complexions internes et nos fortunes à venir, est chose qui ne loge pas bien directement et simplement soubs le chapitre de beauté et de laideur. Non plus que toute bonne odeur et serenité d'air n'en promet pas la santé, my toute espesseur et puanteur l'infection en temps pestilent. Ceux qui accusent les dames de contre-dire leur beauté par leurs meurs ne rencontrent pas tousjours: car en une face qui ne sera pas trop bien composée, il peut loger quelque air de probité et de fiance; comme au rebours, j'ay leu par fois entre deux beaux yeux des menasses d'une nature maligne et dangereuse . . . C'est une foible garantie que la mine: toutesfois elle a quelque consideration" (1058–59). ["the cast and formation of the face and those lineaments from which people infer certain inward dispositions and our fortunes to come, are things that do not fall very directly and simply under the heading of beauty and ugliness; any more than every good odor and clear air promises health, or every closeness and stench promises infection, in time of pestilence. Those who accuse the ladies of belying their beauty by their character do not always hit the mark. For in a not too well formed face there may dwell an air of probity and trustworthiness; as, on the contrary, I have sometimes read between two beautiful eyes threats of a malignant and dangerous nature . . . The face is a weak guarantee; yet it deserves some consideration" (810–11).]

But before reaching the passions of the soul, the list that we have read in Montaigne mentioned *excretion and retention*. On this point, Montaigne fills in scrupulously the spaces of the questionnaire *(répond scrupuleusement au questionnaire)*.[16] There is no reason for him to leave this space blank: (b) "Et les Roys et les philosophes fientent, et les dames aussi . . . Parquoy je diray cecy de cette action" (1085) ["Both kings and philosophers defecate, and ladies too. . . . Wherefore I will say this about that action" (831).] And there too, it is necessary for a custom to be imposed: this action has to be put off until later: "a certaines heures prescriptes et nocturnes"; ["certain prescribed noctural hours";] one must "s'y forcer par coustume et assubjectir" (1085) ["force and subject ourselves to them by habit" (831).] Indiscretion? Immodesty? To be sure. By why—if one wants to oppose doctors point by point—leave out a subject to which they themselves attach so much importance?

16. I will come back to this: the activity of recording, which constructs the book of the *Essays*, depends from time to time on the metaphor of excrement. This is a rhetorical device, pertaining to *humilitas*.

As for his stones, which are also in the category *(domaine)* of excretions, Montaigne devotes a long exposition to them. Of all his "conditions corporelles"; ["bodily qualities,"] it is in this one alone that illness intrudes. Everywhere else, habitual practices reestablish a healthful equilibrium. Here, on the contrary, is where the internal menace appears. Now it is precisely on this very point that Montaigne insists, once again, on declaring—as he had done in the essay III:37—his antagonism toward the procedures and behavior of doctors. The best solution he can find, he declares, is that of resignation: "C'est injustice de se douloir qu'il soit advenu à quelqu'un ce qui peut advenir à chacun . . . La goutte, la gravelle, l'indigestion sont symptomes des longues années, comme des longs voyages la chaleur, les pluys et les vents . . . Il faut apprendre à souffrir ce qu'on ne peut éviter" (1089). ["It is unjust to complain that what may happen to anyone has happened to someone . . . The gout, the stone, indigestions, are symptoms of length of years, as are heat, rains, and winds of long journeys . . . We must learn to endure what we cannot avoid" (835).] Once this principle is established, what need is there to resort to doctors, especially when their treatment is limited to the formulation of alarming predictions?

(b) Je consulte peu des alterations que je sens, car ces gens icy sont avantageux quand ils vous tiennent à leur misericorde: ils vous gourmandent les oreilles de leurs prognostiques; et me surprenant autre fois affoibly du mal, m'ont injurieusement traicté de leurs dogmes et troigne magistrale, me menassant tantost de grandes douleurs, tantost de mort prochaine. Je n'en estois abbatu ny deslogé de ma place, mais j'en estois heurté et poussé; si mon judgement n'en est ny changé ny troublé, au moins il en estoit empesché; c'est tousjours agitation et combat. [1090]

I do little consulting about the ailments I feel, for these doctors are domineering when they have you at their mercy. They scold at your ears with their forebodings. And once, catching me weakened by illness, they treated me insultingly with their dogmas and magisterial frowns, threatening me now with great pains, now with approaching death. I was not floored by them or dislodged from my position, but I was bumped and jostled. If my judgment was neither changed nor confused by them, it was at least bothered. It is still agitation and struggle. [835–36]

"Agitation et combat"; ["agitation and struggle"]: these are among the passions of the soul. The sixth of the non-naturals is, in this way, found to be closely tied to the illness which is due to the excretory difficulty. There is nothing surprising here: according to the medical doctrine generally taught, the passions of the soul can sometimes produce illness and sometimes, inversely, be affected by illness. For Montaigne, saying how he refused his gravel does two things at once: he continues to give an account of his excretions, and he reveals to us what his passions are when he is confronted with the "maladie pierreuse" ["stony disease"] wherein he knows full well that death awaits him.

As one can see, the importance of the subject demands an extremely idiosyncratic way of exposing it. How does Montaigne go about it? First of all, he assigns to this matter a central position, in the middle of the median part of the essay devoted to his bodily habit. Moreover, he is going to dramatize the question, all the while devoting to it a considerable exposition which is out of proportion with the other subjects considered. Thus, immediately after having evoked the doctors' "troigne magistrale" ["magisterial frowns"] and their inconsiderate verdicts, he resorts to a long prosopopeia in order to give voice to another discourse which goes against the professionals. The procedure will consist of *quoting* (of course: or pretending to quote) the words that his *mind (esprit)* customarily addresses to his *imagination* to help and comfort it:

> (b) Or je trete *mon imagination* le plus doucement que je puis et la deschargerois, si je pouvois, de toute peine et contestation. Il la faut secourir et flatter, et piper qui peut. *Mon esprit* est propre à ce service: il n'a point faute d'apparances par tout; s'il persuadoit comme il presche, il me secourroit heureusement.
>
> *Vous en plaict-il un exemple?* Il dict que c'est pour mon mieux que j'ay la gravele; que les bastimens de mon aage ont naturellement à souffrir quelque goutiere . . . que la compaigne me doibt consoler . . .[Ibid.][17]

> Now I treat *my imagination* as gently as I can, and would relieve it, if I could, of all trouble and conflict. We must help it and flatter it, and fool it if we can. *My mind* is suited to this service; it has no lack of plausible reasons for all things. If it could persuade as well as it preaches, it would help me out very happily.
>
> *Would you like an example?* It tells me that it is for my own good that I have the stone; that buildings of my age must naturally suffer some leakage . . .—That the company should console me . . . [Ibid]

This "exposing" *(mise en évidence)* takes then the form of a discourse within a discourse. Just a moment ago, at the beginning of the description of his "habits", Montaigne had made an appeal to the reader: "Pour qui en voudra gouster, j'en any faict l'essay, son eschanson"; ["For anyone who wants to try it I have tasted it like his cupbearer."] Now the reader is again

17. The quoting of the arguments that Montaigne addresses to himself take up pages 1090–95 in the Villey edition (Frame: 836–37).

called upon, still more directly: "Vous en plaict-il un exemple?"; ["Would you like an example?"] In the middle of the diverse items furnished by his "remembrance" (souvenance), Montaigne gives another speaker the right to speak—the mind—who comes forward to take Montaigne's place and who requires the redoubled attention of the reader. In this apostrophe of the mind to the imagination there is an internal debate which is being reported to us in an allegorical form: this debate unfolds between two of the faculties which, according to traditional doctrine, constitute the *sensus internus*. (There are three of these faculties in all: reason or mind, imagination or fantasy, memory: the third faculty, memory, is not left idle because, right from the beginning of the description of the body's experience, Montaigne relied on "remembrance" in order to retrace the pertinent details.)

The instances of the self *(moi)* have divided themselves. A *he*, which is the mind, preaches to and tries to persuade a *you* which is the imagination, i.e. the being who risks becoming frantic and allowing itself to be overcome by troubles and suffering. In the hierarchy of the functions of the *sensus internus*, mind holds the superior rank. Montaigne invites us to listen to a discourse which proceeds from the most authoritative internal resource:

> (b) La crainte de ce mal, faict-*il*, *t'*effraioit autresfois, quand il *t'*estoit incogneu: les cris et le desespoir de ceux qui l'aigrissent par leur impatience *t'*en engendroient l'horreur. C'est un mal qui *te* bat les membres par lesquels tu as le plus failly; *tu és* homme de conscience.

> *Quae venit indigne poena, dolenda venit*

> Regarde ce chastiement; il est bien doux au pris d'autres, et d'une faveur paternelle. Regarde sa tardiveté: il n'incommode et occupe que la saison de ta vie qui, ainsi comme ainsin, est mes-huy perdue et sterile, ayant faict place à la licence et plaisirs de ta jeunesse, comme par composition. La crainte et pitié que le peuple a de ce mal te serte de matiere de gloire; qualité, de laquelle si tu as le jugement, purgé et en as guery ton discours, tes amys pourtant en recognoissent encore quelque teinture en ta complexion. Il ya a plaisir à ouyre dire de soy: Voylà bien de la force, voylà bien de la patience. On te voit suer d'ahan, pallir, rougir, trembler, vomir jusques au sang, souffrir des contractions et convulsions estranges, degouter par foys de grosses larmes des yeux, rendre les urines espesses, noires, et effroyables, ou les avoir arrestées par quelque pierre espineuse et herissée qui te pouinct et escorche cruellement le col de la verge, entretenant cependant les assistans d'une contenance commune, bouffonnant à pauses avec tes gens, tenant ta partie en un discours tendu, excusant de parolle ta douleur et rabatant de ta souffrance. [1091][18]

18. The Latin quotation is from Ovid (Heroïdes, V:8): "Le mal immérité vaut seul qu'on s'en plaigne." ["Punishment undeserved gives pain."]

"Fear of this disease, says my *mind*, "used to terrify you, when it was unknown to *you*; the cries and despair of those who make it worse by their lack of fortitude engendered in you a horror of it. It is an affliction that punishes those of *your* members by which you have most sinned. *You are* a man of conscience:

Punishment undeserved gives pain. OVID

Consider this chastisement; it is very gentle in comparison with others, and paternally tender. Consider its lateness; it bothers and occupies only the season of your life which in any case is henceforth wasted and barren, having given way, as if by agreement, to the licentiousness and pleasures of your youth.

"The fear and pity that people feel for this illness is a subject of vainglory for you; a quality of which, even if you have purged your judgment and cured your reason of it, your friends still recognize some tincture in your makeup. There is pleasure in hearing people say about you: There indeed is strength, there indeed is fortitude! They see you sweat in agony, turn pale, turn red, tremble, vomit your very blood, suffer strange contractions and convulsions, sometimes shed great tears from your eyes, discharge thick, black, and frightful urine, or have it stopped up by some sharp rough stone that cruelly pricks and flays the neck of your penis; meanwhile keeping up conversation with your company with a normal countenance, jesting in the intervals with your servants, holding up your end in a sustained discussion, making excuses for pain and minimizing your suffering. [836–37]

All the same, this apostrophe, in which all the resources of rhetoric are deployed (interrogation, admonitions, maxim, dialogismus, hypotyposis, etc.), does not exhaust all the arguments which are addressed by the mind to the imagination: there is still a lot to say. But Montaigne changes his tone. Remarks in the first person, in which it seems that Montaigne—as he did before—begins to speak again, follow the apostrophe: "Je suis obligé à la fortune de quoy elle m'assaut si souvent de mesme sorte d'armes: elle m'y façonne et m'y dresse par usage, m'y durcit et habitue" . . . (1092) ["I am obliged to Fortune for assailing me so often with the same kind of weapons. She fashions and trains me against them by use, hardens and accustoms me" (837).] We might think that Montaigne, once again, speaks to us directly, as he does elsewhere in the *Essays*. But three pages further on, we learn that what we read was still a self-quotation, i.e., a continuation of the discourse within the discourse:

(b) Par tels *argumens*, et forts et foibles, comme Cicero le mal de sa vieillesse, j'essaye d'endormir et d'amuser *le mal de mon imagination*, et gresser ses playes. Si elles s'empirent demain, *demain nous y pourvoy-erons d'autres eschapatoires.* [1095]

> By such *arguments,* both strong and weak, I try to lull and beguile my *imagination** and salve its wounds, as Cicero did his disease of old age. If they get worse tomorrow, *tomorrow we shall provide other means of escape.* [839]

The exemplary argumentation concerning the gravel which is offered to the reader in the central part of the inventory of the body has been prolonged up to this kind of conclusion. In the meantime, Montaigne will tell us in an "allongeail" ["extension"] that he "se forge" ["makes" a memory] "de papier" ["of paper"] (1092; 837), and that in leafing through "ces petits brevets" ["these little notes"] he can find [à se] "consoler de quelque prognostique favorable en [son] experience passée" (1092). ["grounds for comfort in some prognostic from [his] past experience" (838).] The nature of the argument is changing: previously moral, when the mind was scolding the imagination, the argument does not hesitate to mimic medical language in order to construct a favorable hypothesis concerning the outcome of the trouble. The lines of reasoning elaborated by Montaigne seem astonishingly like those of the doctors, yet do so only to contradict them: the possible (*vraisemblables*) hopes with which he lulls himself are certainly equal in value to the menaces they throw at him:

> (b) L'aage affoiblit la chaleur de mon estomac; sa digestion en estant moins parfaicte, il renvoye cette matiere cruë à mes reins. Pourquoy ne pourra estre, à certaine revolution, affoiblie pareillement la chaleur de mes reins, si qu'ils ne puissent plus petrifier mon flegme, et nature s'acheminer à prendre quelque autre voye de purgation? Les ans m'ont evidemment faict tarir aucuns reumes. Pourquoy non ces excremens, qui fournissent de matiere à la grave. [1093]

> Age weakens the heat of my stomach; its digestion being thereby less perfect, it sends on this crude matter to my kidneys. Why cannot the heat of my kidneys be likewise weakened, at some other turn, so that they can no longer petrify my phlegm, and nature may take steps to find some other way of purgation? The years have evidently made some of my rheums dry up. Why not these excrements that provide material for the gravel? [838]

But what need is there of forming physiological hypotheses on the favorable evolution of the illness? Why not also consider the pleasure *(jouissance)* that one feels at the abatement of the illness, once the crisis is over?

*I have altered Frame's translation slightly to make it conform more closely to the original text.—Trans.

(b) Mais est-il rien doux au pris de cette soudaine mutation, quand d'une douleur extreme je viens, par le vuidange de ma pierre, à recouvrer comme d'un esclair la belle lumiere de la santé, si libre et si pleine, comme il advien⁺ en nos soudaines et plus aspres choliques? Y a il rien en cette douleur soufferte qu'on puisse contrepoiser au plaisir d'un si prompt amandement? De combien la santé me semble plus belle apres la maladie, si voisine et contigue que je les puis recognoistre en presence l'une de l'autre en leur plus haut appareil, où elles se mettent à l'envy comme pour se faire teste et contrecarre! Tout ainsi que les Stoyciens disent que les vices sont utilement introduicts pour donner pris et faire espaule à la vertu, nous pouvons dire avec meilleure raison et conjecture moins hardie, que nature nous a presté la douleur pour l'honneur et service de la volupté et indolence. Lors que Socrates, apres qu'on l'eust deschargé de ses fers, sentit la friandise de cette demangeson que leur pesanteur avoit causé en ses jambes, il se resjouyt à considerer l'estroitte alliance de la douleur à la volupté, comme elles sont associées d'une liaison necessaire, si qu'à tours elles se suyvent et s'entr'engendrent . . . [1093]

But is there anything so sweet as that sudden change, when from extreme pain, by the voiding of my stone, I come to recover as if by lightning the beautiful light of health, so free and so full, as happens in our sudden and sharpest attacks of colic? Is there anything in this pain we suffer that can be said to counterbalance the pleasure of such sudden improvement? How much more beautiful health seems to me after the illness, when they are so near and contiguous that I can recognize them in each other's presence in their proudest array, when they vie with each other, as if to oppose each other squarely! Just as the Stoics say that vices are brought into the world usefully to give value to virtue and assist it, we can say, with better reason and less bold conjecture, that nature has lent us pain for the honor and service of pleasure and painlessness. When Socrates, after being relieved of his irons, felt the relish of the itching that their weight had caused in his legs, he rejoiced to consider the close alliance between pain and pleasure, how they are associated by a necessary link, so that they follow and engender each in turn. [838]

While the attack of lithiasis was represented for us in its most acute phase by the prosopopeia of the mind, the new argumentation relies on the lull following the attack. The experiencing of relief, such as we have just read, undoubtedly corresponds to something the body has authentically lived *(à un vécu corporel authentique)*, and its transposition into the metaphor of the "belle lumière" ["beautiful light"] is both a figure of language and a transcription of a deeply experienced synesthesia. All the same, Montaigne insists on reinforcing his remarks with the authority of the Stoics and of

Socrates. (All the while declaring that he scorns all "foreign" science, he cannot overlook witnesses who are so important for the confirmation of what he has felt himself: "l'estroitte alliance de la douleur à la volupté." ["the close alliance between pain and pleasure".] After all, he has to reckon with the reader's resistance or skepticism when faced with the individual experience of one Michel de Montaigne: "ceux qui ne la [l'humaine ignorance] veulent conclurre en eux par un aussi vain exemple que le mien ou que le leur, qu'ils la recognoissent par Socrates, (c) le maistre des maistres" (1076). ["Those who will not conclude their own ignorance from so vain an example as mine, or as theirs, let them recognize it through Socrates, (c) the master of masters" (824).]

With these considerations, the argumentation has not yet reached its end: it still has other resources: "J'argumente que les vomissemens extremes et frequens que je souffre me purgent . . . Voicy encore une faveur de mon mal, particuliere: c'est qu'à peu prez il faict son jeu à part et me laisse faire le mien . . . Je remarque encore cette particuliere commodité que c'est un mal où nous avons peu à diviner. Nous sommes dispensez du trouble auquel les autres maus nous jettent par l'incertitude de leurs causes et conditions et progrez, trouble infiniement penible. Nous n'avons que faire de consultations et interpretations doctorales: les sens nous montrent que c'est, et où c'est" (1094–95). ["I argue that the extreme and frequent vomitings that I endure purge me . . . Here is another benefit of my illness, peculiar to it: that it almost plays its game by itself and lets me play mine . . . I notice also this particular convenience, that it is a disease in which we have little to guess about. We are freed from the worry into which other diseases cast us by the uncertainty of their causes and conditions and progress—an infinitely painful worry. We have no concern with doctoral consultations and interpretations; the senses reveal to us what it is, and where it is" (839).] We can thus live with the stone, in the present, in feeling, without retrospective speculation as well as without divination of the future.

If the privilege of the stone is that with it one can live in the absence of any "prévoyance ennuyeuse" ["bothersome precaution,"] Montaigne's argumentation is careful to furnish us proof by occupying all temporal positions. It goes back to the past, remembers attacks that have passed and which were followed by the return of health. In the long self-quotation, the first part (prosopopeia of the mind) resorts in vain to the present indicative: the *representation* of the discourse spoken by the mind confers on the latter a completed, remembered aspect. The second movement, in which Montaigne again resorts to the *I* and expresses himself in his own name, is more clearly expressed in the present (but in a present for which a "mémoire de papier" is necessary). Finally, Montaigne warns us that his argumentation is not finished. He will, in the future, address to himself if necessary other exhortations of the same type. We have already encountered this hypothetical anticipation: "Si mes playes s'empirent demain nous y pourvoyerons d'autres eschapatoires." ["If (my wounds) get worse tomorrow, tomorrow we shall provide other means of escape."] Further, the composition of the *Essays* in successive layers allows Montaigne here, in one of the rare passages in which he himself calls attention to an addition, to confirm his promise in the form of a postscriptum or of an updating:

> (c) Qu'il soit vray. Voicy depuis, de nouveau, que les plus legers mouvemens espreignent le pur sang de mes reins. Quoy, pour cela je ne laisse de me mouvoir comme devant et picquer apres mes chiens d'une juvenile ardeur, et insolente. Et trouve que j'ay grand raison d'un si important accident, qui ne me couste qu'une sourde poisanteur et alteration en cette partie. C'est quelque grosse pierre qui foule et consomme la substance de mes roignons, et ma vie que je vuide peu à peu, non sans quelque naturelle douceur, comme un *excrement* hormais superflu et empeschant. [1095]

> (c) Here is proof. Now it has happened again that the slightest movements force the pure blood out of my kidneys. What of it? I do not, just for that, give up moving about as before and pricking after my hounds with youthful and insolent ardor. And I think I come off well from such an important accident when it costs me nothing but a dull heaviness and uneasiness in that region. It is some big stone that is crushing and consuming the substance of my kidneys, and my life that I am letting out little by little, not without some natural pleasure, as an *excrement* that is henceforth superfluous and a nuisance. [839–40]

The illness has reappeared. And if this new relapse were announcing the arrival of death itself? From this point of view, death would not be so formidable, it would not be too costly . . .

3.   FROM PAIN TO PLEASURE: ART IN DEATH

In the course of the consolation that Montaigne addresses to himself and that he offers to us as a spectacle, the heading of urinary excrement (and of the other evacuations which are its consequence: vomiting) has been, on the way, completed in due form; and the passions of the soul have been revealed as the mind attempts to bring them under its domination. For it is in this precise area of the bodily functions that the mind's brotherly assistance must be manifested. As one has seen, thought is expended lavishly and uses every means at its disposal to arrive at its ends, from the penitential interpretation of sickness [it is a "chastiement" ["chastise-ment"] but "bien doux au prix d'autres" ["very gentle in comparison with others"], to the reassuring ideas about its evolution: through the effects of age and of a general *cooling;* the warmth of the kidneys which "petrifie le flegme" ["petrify (the) phlegm"] can be weakened, as has the stomach's heat already: the vital fire dwindles, the restoration of health can accompany the advancement of old age. And then, whatever the sharpness of the pain may have been at certain moments, this evacuation, of which only a "sourde poisanteur" ["dull heaviness"] is left, is that by which life itself—not without pleasure—is evacuated. Let us reread this astonishing sentence: "C'est quelque grosse pierre qui foule et consomme la substance de mes roignons, et ma vie que je vuide peu à peu, non sans quelque naturelle *douceur,* comme un *excrement hormais superflu et empeschant.*" ["It is some big stone that is crushing and consuming the substance of my kidneys, and my life that I am letting out little by little, not without some natural *pleasure,* as an *excrement that is henceforth superfluous and a nuisance.*"] How can one not compare this sentence with several other passages of the *Essays* in which the text of the *Essays* is metaphorically designated as an excrement: "Ce sont ici . . . des excremens d'un vieil esprit dur tantost, tantost lache et toujours indigeste" (946).[19] ["Here you have . . . some excrements of an aged mind, now hard, now loose, and always undigested" (721).] At the end of the essay III:5 *On some verses of Virgil,* Montaigne speaks in a condescending and deprecatory way of the pages he has just written: this "notable commentaire [lui est] eschappé d'un *flux de caquet,* flux impetueux parfois et nuisible." ["notable commentary has escaped from (him) in a *flow of babble,* a flow sometimes impetuous and harmful"—.] The metaphor of the body places the flow of life and the flow of the text on an equal footing: the individual's body is being dissipated and dispersed in emptying itself of the substances it had "digérées" and "cuites." (Let us remember that the digestive simile is found again, but this time in regard to absorption, in the image of pedagogy being made effective through the assimilation and imbibation of foreign fluids, as well as in the frequent evocation of thought as *rumination . . .)*

As for the "naturelle douceur" ["natural pleasure"] that Montaigne feels at the very moment he "vuide [sa] vie peu à peu," ["lets out [his] life little by little,"] this reminds us of the insistence with which Montaigne, in

19. This comparison was suggested by Terence Cave *The Cornucopian Text* (Oxford: at the Clarendon Press, 1979), pp. 293–94.)

his narration *(récit)* of the fall from his horse, speaks of the "douceur" accompanying the condition in which he feels himself slipping toward a state that, upon reflection, perfectly ressembles death. He recognizes in this the "douceur que sentent ceux qui se laissent glisser au sommeil" (374)[20] ["sweet feeling that people have who let themselves slide into sleep" (270).] When Montaigne speaks of the unexpected "exercitation" ["practice"] which had made him familiar with death, he does not forget that breath, from the viewpoint of the medical profession, also comprises an "excretory" element: "Il me sembloit que ma vie ne me tenoit plus qu'au bout des levres: je fermois les yeux pour ayder, ce me sembloit, à la *pousser hors* . . . (374) ["It seemed to me that my life was hanging only by the tip of my lips; I closed my eyes in order, it seemed to me, to help *push it out* . . . (269).] It seems as if the last sigh is both evacuation and deliverance. And Montaigne does not tire of evoking the "douceurs" ["pleasures"] of this experience: "mon assiete estoit à la verité *tres-douce* et paisible . . . Quand on m'eust couché, je senty une *infinie douceur* à ce repos . . . Je me laissoy couler *si doucement* et d'une façon *si douce* et si aisée que je ne sens guiere autre action moins poisante que cella-là estoit" (376–77). ["Meanwhile my condition was, in truth, *very pleasant* and peaceful . . . When they had put me to bed, I felt *infinite sweetness* in this repose . . . I was letting myself slip away *so pleasantly*, in such an easy and *pleasant* way,* that I hardly did anything with less of a feeling of effort" (272).]

From extreme *pain (douleur)* to extreme *pleasure (douceur):* within the difference *(écart)* of a paronomasia[21], such is the range of the experience of pain *(mal)* and disease *(maladie).* And Montaigne has experienced illness itself in its opposition (which is at the same time its link) with health and pleasure *(volupté).* The body's experience, which makes us feel "l'estroitte alliance de la douleur et de la volupté" ["the close alliance between pain and pleasure,"] conditions us to accept the idea of another alliance that is equally close: that of the soul and the body. One thus sees, one after another, the antitheses being accepted, the entities *coupled,* and the affirmation of their mandatory coexistence or of their necessary union. In unforgettable terms, the conclusive pages of *Of experience* will stress the "mutuels

---

*A literal translation would read: ". . . I try to lull and beguile (and/or "entertain," from "amuser") the *disease of my imagination* (underlined by Starobinski).—Trans.

20. On this feeling of "douceur" ["pleasure"] see the remarks of Michaël Baraz, "L'intégrité de l'homme selon Montaigne" in *O un Amy. Essays on Montaigne in honor of Donald M. Frame,* ed. R. C. La Charité (Lexington, Kentucky: French Forum 1977), pp. 20–21.

21. See the study by François Rigolot, "Le langage des 'Essais,' référentiel ou mimologique?," in *Cahiers de l'Association internationale des études françaises,* 33, mai 1981, pp. 19–34.

offices" ["reciprocal links"] of the soul and the body, and the necessity of their simultaneous "culture" ["cultivation."]

If, in its *theme* (or in its statement, *énoncé*), the essay ends in the alliance of opposites, it is important to note that, in its formal aspects (and more particuarly in its mode of enunciation), the essay offers us a striking example of contradiction overcome. A homology appears between the thought content, in its essential intricacies, and the elocution invented by Montaigne. He makes the experience of an entire life result in the discreetly lyrical praise of the mutual aid that body and soul must lend each other. He formulates it within a discourse in which spontaneity, refering to bodily life, necessarily allies itself (be it under protest (*à son corps défendant*), with the artifices employed by learned reason.

For whomever reads the essay *Of experience*, nothing seems more clearcut than the distinction between the discursive systems elaborated, by reason, in the arts and sciences (legislation, theology, philosophy, medicine, in which nothing escapes the "conflict des interprétations" ["conflict of interpretations"]) and the truth which lets itself be known in us, and especially within our body, through feeling, through direct experience in all that makes this truth more individual, different, and, by this very fact, more apt to become universalized. Taken seriously, this theoretical distinction should be of some consequence in the mode of its enunciation: it should engage the essayist in the repudiation of the language of the arts and sciences at the very moment he attempts, in opposition to these, to communicate his experience, to express himself according to the conformity with nature to which he claims the greatest obedience. Yet, just as custom and usage interfuse with nature to the point where they produce a second nature, just as the mind's assistance is called upon to comfort the suffering body, Montaigne, in spite of the *ordo neglectus* to which he abandons himself, does not succeed in exposing his "forme de vie" ["way of life"] except through the categories established by the medical arts. The very notion of "forme de vie" grew out of medical thought: it is the field defined, from the time of Greek medicine, by the concepts of diet and hygiene, and divided, according to Galenic tradition, among the six categories of non-naturals. The medical classification of the *faculties* of the soul (internal senses on the one hand, i.e. reason, imagination, and memory; on the other, external senses); the humoral conception of the *complexion*; the diffcrent physiological functions recognized by medicine all constitute the guiding thread, or the mandatory passage-way, of a discourse that claims to be antimedical and which has the ambition of expressing the natural body in its irreducible individuality.

Forced to proceed within the codified language of an art (medicine) in order to say what he would have wished to reveal directly, without art, Montaigne ornaments his remarks, covers his tracks: he comments, makes digressions and exhortations, goes from the particular to the universal, mentions examples, coins maxims: Montaigne could not be accused of abandoning his uneven and "extravagant" tone even when he is, so to speak, filling in the questionnaire of medicine. He has not expelled the language of medicine but broken its systematic unity and coherence in order to scatter its *disjecta membra* in a "marquetterie" in which all languages are welcomed. It is here an instance of an art which denies art. What is more, the most remarkable of his detours *(écarts)*—the long apostrophe of his "mind" to his "imagination"—only distances Montaigne from the language of medicine through even more art: this enemy of oratory *(éloquence)* writes a great piece of eloquent rhetoric. Is there not reason for being surprised when, in order to speak the body in respect to what wounds it most deeply, Montaigne pretends to yield the right to speak to an independent speaker, a third party? And in this eloquent apostrophe to himself, does not rhetoric have to call upon the primary mechanism of classical tragedy: "La crainte et la pitié que le peuple a de ce mal te sert de matiere de gloire" (1091) ["The fear and pity that people feel for this illness is a subject of vainglory for you" (836).] *Phoibos kai eleinos!* The artifice becomes even more marked—we are at the theatre. We are made to hear the spectators' admiring exclamations: "Voylà bien de la force, voylà bien de la patience" (1091). ["There indeed is strength, there indeed is fortitude!" (836).] Thus the body, in its most painful sufferings, is shown to us from the outside, as it is *seen* by all, an actor in "l'acte à un seul personnage" (979) ["an act for one single character" (748)] "on te *voit* suer d'ahan, pallir, rougir, trembler" (1091) ["They *see* you sweat in agony, turn pale, turn red, tremble" (836).] At the culminating point of his suffering, Montaigne, as if any language that issued directly from the body were impossible, enumerates *from the outside*, and through the detour of represented memory, the *signs* that are seen by the group of relatives and friends in the ceremony that surrounds the one they think is dying but who, under the circumstances, admirably holds up "[sa] partie en un discours tendu" (1091)[22]; ["(his) end in a sustained discussion" (837).] Everything is dramatized and made dialectical: "the mind" summoning "the imagination" of Montaigne brings to mind the scene of the sickbed where Montaigne, in order that existence remain a dialogue up to the very end, converses with "les assistans" ["company"],

22. The prosopopeia of "the mind" should be compared with the prosopopeia of Nature in the essay I:20 "That to philosophize is to learn to die," 92–96; 64–68).

clowns with his "gens" ["servants" . . .] We are here at the height of art. The actual experience, in what is literally poignant about it, is communicated to us as a scene of pathos—a successful playing out of the *ars moriendi*, according to "la vraie philosophie" ["true philosophy"]—inserted within a consolatory discourse which is itself inserted within the exposition of the *usage* and the practices *(facons)* to which Montaigne has submitted his bodily life—an exposition which he intends for the reader/table-companion.

Could the body then only be spoken indirectly, through the eyes *(regard)* of the allegorized "mind" which, in its turn, evokes the martyr scene as seen by the spectators? At the very least, let us recognize that the call for the internal truth makes the intervention of looking from the outside gaze inevitable. In order to be spoken, the body's experience demands an "estroitte alliance" ["close alliance"] with the language of art, even when one wishes to surrender one's arms to nature. At that very point where the individual suffers in his inmost flesh, there is no meaning *(sens)* which can be enunciated except through contact with the other: sweating, turning pale, blushing, trembling—for us readers—are *events* which we live by simultaneously identifying ourselves with the man torn by his stone and with the spectators that his text, after the event, represents as on a stage, around him, and who *see* him suffer. It is because he has thus offered himself to us from the outside, that we have the feeling of participating in what he experiences within . . .

Translated by John A. Gallucci

Contributors

JULES BRODY, professor of French at Harvard University, has written extensively on seventeenth-century French literature. His book-length studies include *Boileau and Longinus* (1958), *Du Style à la pensée: Trois études sur Les Caractères de La Bruyère* (1980), *Approches textuelles des "Mémoires de Saint-Simon"* (1980), and *Lectures de Montaigne* (1982).

ANTOINE COMPAGNON teaches French at the University of Rouen. He is the author of two books. *La Seconde main ou le travail de la citation* (1979) and *Nous, Michel de Montaigne* (1981), both published by Les Editions du Seuil.

GÉRARD DEFAUX is professor of French at Johns Hopkins University. His writings include *Pantagruel et les Sophistes* (1973), *Molière ou les Métamorphoses du comique* (1980), and *Le Curieux, le glorieux et la sagesse du monde dans la première moitié du XVIᵉ siècle: l'exemple de Panurge* (1982). He is currently working on Montaigne and Clément Marot.

CATHERINE DEMURE is Maître-Assistante at the University of Aix-Marseille, where she teaches philosophy. She is the author of several articles on Montaigne.

EDWIN M. DUVAL is associate professor of French at the University of California, Santa Barbara. He has written on Scève, Montaigne, and Rabelais and has recently published a book entitled *Poesis and Poetic Tradition in the Early Works of Saint-Amant: Four Essays in Contextual Reading*.

CARLA FRECCERO is a graduate student in Renaissance studies at Yale University and is working on a thesis on Rabelais. "The Other and the Same, the Image of the Hermaphrodite in Rabelais," a paper delivered at the Conference on Renaissance Woman/Renaissance Man held at Yale in the spring of 1982, is being considered for publication.

JOHN GALLUCI, a student in French at Yale University, has been on the staff of *Yale French Studies* for the last two years and on the editorial board for one.

THOMAS M. GREENE is professor of English and comparative literature and chairman of the Renaissance Studies Program at Yale. His most recent book is *The Light in Troy: Imitation and Discovery in Renaissance Poetry.*

MARCEL GUTWIRTH, professor of French at Haverford College, is the author of numerous articles, books, and essays on French literature, including *Molière ou l'invention comique* (1966), *Racine: un itineraire poétique* (1970), and *Montaigne ou le pari d'exemplarité* (1977). He is now completing a book-length study of La Fontaine.

MARIANNE S. MEIJER is associate professor of French at the University of Maryland. She has published on François de Billon, Thomas More, Marguerite de Navarre, and Montaigne. She is currently working on a monograph on the ordering of Montaigne's *Essays.*

FRANÇOIS RIGOLOT, professor of French at Princeton University, is the author of *Les Langages de Rabelais* (Geneva: Droz, 1972) and *Poétique et Onomastique* (Geneva: Droz, 1977). His forthcoming book is entitled *Le Texte de la Renaissance.*

PIERRE SAINT-AMAND, assistant professor in the Department of French and Italian at Stanford University, has just completed a book: *Le Labyrinthe de la relation. Figures de complexité dans l'oeuvre de Diderot.*

DIANNE SEARS is a graduate student in French at Yale University.

MATTHEW SENIOR, a graduate student in French at Yale University, is working on a thesis on seventeenth-century theater.

JOSHUA SCODEL is a student in comparative literature at Yale University.

JEAN STAROBINSKI, writer and critic of international reputation, is professor of French at the University of Geneva. He is the author of *Jean-Jacques Rousseau: La transparence et l'obstacle, L'oeil vivant, L'Invention de la liberté,* and *La Relation critique.* His forthcoming book (Paris: Gallimard, 1983) is devoted to a study of Montaigne's *Essays.*

TZVETAN TODOROV is a fellow of the CNRS, the editor of *Poétique,* and the author of many works on modern critical theory. His latest works include *Théories du symbole* (Paris: éditions du Seuil, 1977), *Mikhaïl Bakhtine: le principe dialogique* (Paris: éditions du Seuil, 1981), and *La conquete de l'Amérique: La question de l'autre,* which has just been published by Seuil (1982).

ANDRÉ TOURNON is professor of French at the University of Aix-Marseille. He has written on Rabelais and Montaigne. His Sorbonne thesis, *Montaigne: de la glose à l'essai,* will be published soon.

The following issue is available through Yale University Press, Customer Service Department, 92 A Yale Station, New Haven, Conn. 06520.

63 The Pedagogical Imperative: Teaching as a Literary Genre $9.95

The following issues are still available through the Yale French Studies Office, 315 William L. Harkness Hall, Yale University, New Haven, Conn. 06520.

19/20	Contemporary Art	$2.50	50	Intoxication and	
23	Humor	$2.50		Literature	$2.50
32	Paris in Literature	$2.50	52	Graphesis: Perspectives in	
33	Shakespeare	$2.50		Literature &	
35	Sade	$2.50		Philosophy	$3.50
38	The Classical Line	$2.50	53	African Literature	$2.50
39	Literature and Revolution	$3.50	54	Mallarmé	$3.00
40	Literature and Society:		57	Locus: Space, Landscape,	
	18th Century	$2.50		Decor	$5.00
41	Game, Play, Literature	$2.50	58	In Memory of Jacques	
42	Zola	$2.50		Ehrmann	$5.00
43	The Child's Part	$2.50	59	Rethinking History	$5.00
44	Paul Valéry	$2.50	60	Cinema/Sound	$5.00
45	Language as Action	$2.50	61	Toward a Theory of	
46	From Stage to Street	$2.50		Description	$5.00
47	Image & Symbol in the		62	Feminist Readings:	
	Renaissance	$2.50		French Texts/	
49	Science, Language, & the			American Contexts	$5.00
	Perspective Mind	$2.50			

Add for postage & handling

United States	$ .75	Foreign countries		
Each additional issue	$ .50	(including Canada)	$1.00	
		Each additional issue	$ .75	

The following issues are now available through Kraus Reprint Company, Route 100, Millwood, N.Y. 10546.

1	Critical Bibliography of Existentialism	16	Foray through Existentialism
2	Modern Poets	17	The Art of the Cinema
3	Criticism & Creation	18	Passion & the Intellect, or Malraux
4	Literature & Ideas	21	Poetry Since the Liberation
5	The Modern Theatre	22	French Education
6	France and World Literature	24	Midnight Novelists
7	André Gide	25	Albert Camus
8	What's Novel in the Novel	26	The Myth of Napoleon
9	Symbolism	27	Women Writers
10	French-American Literature	28	Rousseau
	Relationships	29	The New Dramatists
11	Eros, Variations . . .	30	Sartre
12	God & the Writer	31	Surrealism
13	Romanticism Revisited	34	Proust
14	Motley: Today's French Theater	48	French Freud
15	Social & Political France	51	Approaches to Medieval Romance

---

36/37 Structuralism has been reprinted by Doubleday as an Anchor Book.
55/56 Literature and Psychoanalysis has been reprinted by Johns Hopkins University Press.

YALE FRENCH STUDIES is also available through: Xerox University Microfilms, 300 North Zeeb Road, Ann Arbor, MI 48106.

Flaubert and Kafka
Studies in Psychopoetic Structure
Charles Bernheimer

"An original and exciting book that challenges contemporary rhetorical analysis. Examining the function of writing for Flaubert and Kafka, he discovers an exemplary involvement between literary texts and the 'texts' of psychoanalytical experience. Textual structure becomes a dramatic struggle between deconstructive and erotic interpretive strategies."
—Stanley Corngold

"Distinguished both by its theoretical sophistication and its marvelously subtle and original readings of Flaubert and Kafka."—Leo Bersani $22.95

Inventions
Writing, Textuality, and Understanding in Literary History
Gerald L. Bruns

A topical history of writing and of what it means to understand written texts, ranging from the Scriptures to *Ulysses*.

"Gerald Bruns's wide learning and deep reflection have produced a work of true wisdom....Making a capital distinction between the openness of the text in a manuscript culture and the closure of the text in a print culture, he works incisively and sensitively through significant authors from antiquity to the present, providing fresh and telling critiques of their thought....I have seldom read a book that rings so true."—Walter J. Ong $18.95

The Light in Troy
Imitation and Discovery in Renaissance Poetry
Thomas M. Greene

This articulate book deals with the uses of imitation in literature during the Renaissance period in Italy, France, and England. It is the first thorough study of *imitatio* covering theory and practice in a full range of Renaissance poets, including Ronsard and Du Bellay. More than this, however, it is a book that addresses the perennial problems of literary change, of historical understanding, and of the authority of the past, problems that are of concern to every student of literature.

"An exciting and exemplary combination of modern critical theory and solid learning, this is an achievement that confirms its author as the outstanding scholar of his generation in this field."
—James V. Mirollo $27.50

Yale University Press   New Haven and London